Nonofficial
Asset

William Sewell

DEDICATION

To my wife who inspired me to tell my stories

ACKNOWLEDGMENTS

Just as it takes a village to raise a child, it takes a lot of dedicated people to write a book. Bentley Morriss at Holloway House Publishing (now Knight Publishing) encouraged me to finish this story. His advice, guidance, and introduction to the complexities of the publishing business made this journey not only possible but often times quite fun. The fact that he liked the story and my writing style inspired me to get it done.

My writing partner, who will be known only as "Langley Meade", worked tirelessly to make the telling of the story as interesting as the story itself. Of course, she did all of this in between getting married, a coast-to-coast move, and sharing recipes with me for all kinds of insane desserts.

The cover art was done by Chris Kneller, a master of graphic arts for film and television (and now books). Additional cover concepts were developed by Adrienne Burton. The author photo on the back cover is by Cheryl Ogden of Ogden Photography in Hermosa Beach, CA

Of course, there were countless readers, commenters, advisors, and folks who kindly donated time, effort, good wishes and encouragement.

Finally, my lovely wife and wonderful family who not only sat back and let me do this but also pitched in at just the right times to look over material, discuss ideas, travel to out-of-the-way places to "get the feel" of a location and most importantly add the independent point of view that allowed me to learn and grow.

My most heartfelt thanks to one and all.

.

Prologue

Islamabad, Pakistan

"WHAT INSANITY IS THIS?" HAZIZ AL-JAWAL whispered. He reached into his coat pocket, withdrew the letter, and looked at it again. His expression darkened and his shoulders hunched forward. Deep lines formed between his eyebrows. "This is surely treason," he murmured.

The letter from his brother-in-law had arrived in a diplomatic pouch from Tehran less than an hour ago. When Haziz removed the missive, he was annoyed. Likely another plea for help, yet another of Kuchecki's half-baked political schemes to advance himself. *More likely*, he thought, *to cover up yet another indiscretion.* This could wait until he had nothing better to do. Then he saw the words in bold block letters, "Urgent – Eyes Only." Aware of the driver, he casually opened the envelope. After a quick scan, he folded the two sheets and took a long slow breath as he placed them in his pocket.

The car came to a sudden stop and Haziz exhaled. Up front, the driver complained as a group of people argued in the narrow street. A small crowd had gathered near the open market and completely blocked the route. Haziz stared at the white awning above the whitewashed merchant stalls and drew on the deepest reserves of his diplomatic demeanor to hide the feelings that boiled inside him.

In the street, the crowd dissipated, bored with the dispute. The car moved forward once again. He retrieved the letter from his pocket and re-read it. *Insanity*. The word resounded in his thoughts as they drove. He didn't notice that the car had stopped until the driver opened the limousine door.

Haziz entered the Ambassador's residence by a side door and walked quietly to a large room which served as both his private sanctuary and office. He crossed the thick hand-knotted Heriz Serapi rug that had taken five women more than two years to make. He had often searched but never found the deliberate flaw in the pattern, a reminder that only Allah is perfect. Slowly and deliberately, he read the letter a third time and digested every phrase. A chill emanated from his core as his eyes reached the bottom of the second page. He sank back into his large leather chair, fatigued.

"We have dinner and prayer with the Imam at the mosque this evening. Hurry, my love! We need to be there in an hour." Haziz inhaled quickly when he heard his wife's voice call from the bedroom. He let the tension drain from his chest, down his arms. Then he took a deep breath, held it a beat, and slowly exhaled before he stood. One sheet of paper - one mad declaration - had reordered his world. He looked around his study and shook his head. Every evening he returned here, to this sanctuary. Now his refuge had been violated by this threat. As Noor swept into the room, he decided that this had to be dealt with quickly.

"You're still standing there," she said. A single raised eyebrow conveyed her full intent. But the slight curve of her mouth hinted of love that had deepened with time. Her head covered with a chiffon georgette hijab, she wore the traditional embroidered *abaya* required of all women who entered the mosque. He

4

noticed the large gold stitching on the hem and smiled slightly. *Christian Dior.* She crossed the room and lightly brushed his lips with her finger. They stood quietly for a brief moment.

"If we are late, I will not be pleased." Before he could respond, she raised her face to his and kissed him lightly on his mouth. He marveled how, with a tilt of her head and her soft voice, she could draw him out of his darkness. He cradled the back of her head with his right hand and ran the fingers of his left hand lightly down her spine to the curve below her waist. Noor inhaled quickly then pushed away with a sigh. "Ah, my love, we must go now, but when we return . . ." She smiled provocatively, turned and left as quickly as she had entered. The promise of unspoken words and the soft scent of her perfume trailed behind her.

Haziz smiled as the banter and intimacy washed over him. One glance at his desk, though, brought him back to the present, to the awful implications of the insane declaration. He returned to his desk and picked up the letter. *After so much controversy, after all the lies, accusations, and denials over our nuclear program, we finally stopped the madness. We have a credible stance with the world. And now this.* Another quick glance at his brother-in-law's words before he placed the folded signature page – a reminder of the traitor in their midst - into his pocket. He then lifted the corner of an antique Qālicheh Persian rug and traced his fingers along the grout until he found the loose section of the ornate mosaic floor. He pressed against it and triggered a lift. Once he had removed the tile segment, he opened a small safe and placed the other page inside. After he had lowered the safe and replaced the mosaic tile, he stood and flipped the folded rug with his foot.

He crossed to his dressing room and quickly

changed his clothing. His thoughts tripped over each other as they clawed their way toward an answer. He knew this would have to be addressed as soon as he returned from the mosque, but Noor mustn't know. Her brother's words would devastate her. Obviously, the Foreign Minister had to be informed. Or should he first try to dissuade his idiot brother-in-law from this madness? Perhaps an hour or two of conversation later this evening with Noor's brother might persuade him to amend his insane course of action.

A movement caught his eye and he looked across the room. Noor paused at the door, a well-scrubbed child on either side. Her beauty and grace stirred him even after all these years. He walked over and kissed his daughter who wrapped her arms around his neck. Then he reached toward his son's head but thought better of messing the boy's neatly combed hair. He smiled and said, "Ready. I had to review some papers. I'll deal with the details later. Let's go and enjoy our evening." He could not know how wrong that decision would prove to be.

"LISTEN UP, EVERYBODY, WE'RE A GO." THE TEAM leader stepped quickly to the front of the group assembled in the small, sparsely furnished living room at the center of the safe house attic. Poor ventilation, body odors, and tension coalesced to create an oppressive atmosphere as they huddled together to finalize plans. Rachel Kleinmann carried her mission make-up kit into the next room. There she gathered her belongings and packed everything into a single gym bag, ready for the evening's quick exit.

Earlier in the day, Rachel and two of the team had rolled down the Murree Highway into Islamabad from their insertion point in the hills. At the Sarena Hotel, the driver turned right on Ataturk Avenue and proceeded to Sector G-6/3, Plot 102, the unwieldy address of a large white house. Once inside the garage, the agents quickly exited the van as soon as the roll-up door closed.

The driver walked toward a stack of motor oil cases and moved them to one side. He pressed on the wall and then quickly stepped backward. The partition swung outward to reveal a narrow stairway that led up to a series of low-ceilinged rooms tucked just under the roofline. Invisible from the street below, accessible only by the hidden stairway, these rooms provided the team an operations base devoid of interference, with little chance of discovery.

When they arrived upstairs, five other agents and a local resident were waiting for them. The latter was a Pakistani cable TV technician known only by his code name, Eli. The five agents had arrived two days earlier and checked into local hotels. They posed as Saudi tourists, strolled through the markets, took photographs, and sampled the local cuisine. Each evening, they downloaded and printed the pictures so that all would have visual references in order to confirm and finalize the carefully planned operation.

The team listened intently as the team lead ran over the schedule one more time. "We have no more than fifteen minutes between roving patrols to get in and back out. The entire staff is out for two hours as of this minute. Let's go!"

Down in the garage, the agents, attired in black shirts, pants, and balaclavas, climbed into their van now disguised as a cable TV repair truck. The team held on as they pulled out onto the street.

The van turned off Ishtar Road into the diplomatic enclave. The agents readied themselves mentally and physically for their assignment: obtain codes and classified information from the Iranian embassy. They donned surgical gloves and sheepskin moccasins so that no evidence could tie this operation to anyone. With nuclear program talks at a conclusion, all knew that this could be the last chance to acquire vital information before treaties were signed.

Eli drove past the Embassy and turned left near the British High Council compound. When he reached a turn in the road bordered by the Embassy wall, he slowed only slightly. "Go!"

The loud whisper echoed through the silent van. Rachel and one other agent slipped out the side door of the van and disappeared into the trees. Invisible from the street, the pair quickly scaled the wall and dropped silently into the Iranian compound directly behind the Ambassador's residence.

At the front gate, Eli informed the Pakistani guard that he was here to check the cable. He held out a roll of bills as promised earlier in the day and watched the guard's eyes grow wide. The Embassy guard snatched the wad of bills and walked quickly out of the gate.

An agent grabbed keys from the now-abandoned gatehouse and the team entered the Embassy through the front door. They stopped at a desk next to a wooden door and one of the agents pressed a button under the desk. The door opened and the team entered a vestibule outside a vault. The team leader checked his watch: four minutes, three seconds had passed. "Alright, bring me the PLASMA device for the vault door," he said.

The lock experts placed the muzzle of a pistol-like device against the door and fired a .22 caliber shaped charge. The explosive went off inside the door with a thump. Two more perfectly placed shots disabled the deadbolts in the vault door. The team was inside.

Another time check. "Seven minutes, twenty

seconds." They quickly photographed all codebooks and files identified in the mission-briefing checklist. Four and a half minutes after the agents first entered the room, they packed up everything and headed back to the van.

Inside the Ambassador's residence, Rachel and her partner began a quick search for the inevitable hidden safe. They looked behind artwork and wall mirrors but turned up nothing. Rachel next entered a woman's closet and checked the items stacked on the floor. She noticed a pair of Manolo Blahnik sandals next to Jimmy Choo heels and mused that the shelves were filled with more Western-style shoes than any good Muslim woman should own. *Time, Rachel! Get on with it!* She continued the search.

Rachel crossed the hall and entered the Ambassador's dressing room. She felt behind the racks of clothing, looked carefully at the ceiling and left. Across the hall she saw what appeared to be an office. She walked around the perimeter of the room. Behind a large desk, the upturned corner of a small rug caught her eye. *That's odd.* All of the other rugs were meticulously placed. She shoved the rug aside and tapped the mosaic floor until she heard it, a hollow sound. Her fingers traced the grout as her eyes followed a tiny, almost imperceptible crack that ran around a section of the floor.

Rachel placed both hands on the tile segment and pressed. Her weight triggered the release and she quickly removed the flooring. "I've found it," she called out as she stared down at the sunken safe.

Her partner ran into the room. He examined the safe. "It's a thirty-minute lock." Rachel looked at him. He continued, "An average locksmith would need at least a half hour to break into a safe of this sort.

"We have four minutes." Rachel replied.

"And I'm not average."

Ninety seconds later, with the final click in the electronically amplified stethoscope, he opened the safe door. Rachel removed a packet and some loose papers.

"That's it. Let's get out."

In less than a minute, they were over the wall. A pair of headlights turned towards them. They saw the pre-arranged signal. A flashlight blinked dimly from inside the windshield. The duo sprinted from the trees and piled headlong into the open side door of the van as it slowly rounded the corner.

"All accounted for," the team lead said. "Are you two ok?"

"Not a glitch," said Rachel.

The door slid closed and the team lead checked his watch. Fourteen minutes, eleven seconds. As the van rounded the corner, Eli waved and smiled at the passing Embassy patrol.

ACROSS TOWN, THE BIG BLACK MERCEDES PULLED away from the Faisal Mosque and crossed Gomal Street. The car headed down Faisal Boulevard toward the newly-opened Centaurus Complex, a large, upscale retail and condominium development built to attract foreign investment into Pakistan. The Iranian Ambassador looked across the car's large rear compartment at his wife who sat on the rear-facing bench seat. Noor cradled the heads of their children in her lap. He thought how beautiful she looked as she smiled down at them. Their eight-year-old son and six-year-old daughter were fast asleep, worn out from the strain of good behavior throughout the long dinner.

Haziz studied his wife, conscious of his good fortune. Thoughtful, warm, and kind with an inner strength and an honest manner, she was the polar opposite of her fanatical brother. A military man, Noor's brother was unyielding in his own beliefs. He was rabidly determined to force his views and behaviors on others.

Ambassador Haziz-al-Jawal's wife had taken the veil when she was younger. As she matured, Noor decided that her personal devotion was sufficient, so she went about with her face uncovered. This decision had created a deep rift between brother and sister, one that appeared to heal only when the Ambassador's influence inadvertently allowed the zealot to further his extremist agendas.

Haziz recalled the letter from his brother-in-law. He wished that he had called the Foreign Minister and reported it earlier, then shrugged off his irritation. Three hours wouldn't make a difference but he knew that he had to deal with this insanity before the long-negotiated peace with the West was derailed.

Lulled by the motion of the car, he gazed absently out the window, as sleepy as his children. He had eaten far too much of the bountiful food at the Mosque: breads with zatar – a traditional Arab topping of thyme, sesame seeds, salt and sugar – lamb, salads, humus, beef, vegetables. A remarkably disciplined man, the Ambassador had succumbed to temptation and sampled it all.

Haziz loved going to the Faisal Mosque, one of the largest in the world. The spiritual experience of worship was deeply satisfying as was his appreciation of the structure's aesthetics. With its modern lines and engineering complexities, the mosque broke with tradition: the building had no dome but was shaped, instead, like a Bedouin tent with four pencil-thin minarets of Turkish style. The beauty soothed him and the place underscored his sense of heritage and, personal identity.

Overcome by sleep, his head fell forward onto his chest but the limousine's motion awakened him. He sat up and again looked out the window. Another black Mercedes with diplomatic license plates pulled past, then crossed over into the lane in front of them. The Ambassador's Mercedes pulled behind the other limo at the stop light at Qayban-e-Quaid-e-Azam. His eyelids closed and then fluttered open. He only had to stay awake for another ten minutes. Then he could go to bed in his own residence.

A large truck rumbled by and the squeal of worn brake pads brought him back to full consciousness. "Someone ought to do something about these noisy trucks. A nuisance, possibly dangerous," he added. The driver nodded in agreement. Both saw a bright orange light emanate from the center of the truck. Haziz watched the limousine in front rock up on two wheels as it was pushed to the side. Just as quickly flames engulfed the entire car.

Scraps of paper and dust pushed outward by the blast wave pelted his car, followed by bits of pavement. A piece of macadam the size of a soccer ball hit the windshield and transformed the thick glass into a web-like mosaic. Then the Ambassador heard two bounces on the roof of the armored limo. As the front of the car started to rise up into the air, the glow became fire. Tongues of flame burst through the windshield, pushing the already-shattered safety glass into the front seat. The driver's clothes ignited as he stared straight ahead in surprise. In the next instant, he was encased in the fireball.

Haziz faced his wife and children, their backs to the chaos. Both children had been awakened by the noise. The Ambassador caught only a brief glimpse of their quizzical expressions as the front of the car moved upward. Noor looked at him, confused but oblivious to the death that hurtled toward them at the speed of sound. The fireball swept through the rear compartment of the car. In that ineffable moment between life and death, when time is suspended, an unnatural peace engulfed the Ambassador. Haziz smiled at his wife and drank in her beauty. Then it was gone.

Chapter 1

Shanghai, PRC (China)

FOUR MINUTES EARLIER PEYTON STONE'S LIFE HAD changed forever. For the second time in as many years and this time was no better than the last.

He stared down at the chubby Chinese policeman. In his peripheral vision he could see the yellow crime scene tape that blocked the fire door at the far end of the hotel hallway. Anger, sadness, helplessness, loss - the four horsemen of his neuroses - thundered through his brain on hooves of rage. He fought to maintain rational thought. *Get a grip, Peyton.*

"Breathe," he could hear his shrink's voice. *"Go to the mountaintop. Breathe in the fresh, cold, clear air. Feel it surge through your body. Push out the mental pollution with each breath."*

The rookie cop's eyes simply blinked back at him. Stone's hands balled into fists. As the pressure inside of him grew, he knew he had to hit something. *Not the cop!* He mentally flogged his fists until they opened, took a deep breath and held it. Then he counted to three and slowly, loudly released it. The cop was between him and the hotel room door.

"Murdered?" The pressure in his head muffled his voice. His question seemed a dull echo from down the hall. He slammed his hand hard against a red lacquered table top. The legs creaked under the blow.

The cop backed up a step and unsnapped the flap on his holster. In the rookie's eyes, Stone saw fear, not purpose, and knew that the officer had never shot anyone. That made him more dangerous, not less.

Breathe! He read the name on the cop's name tag: Han.

Stone turned and stared out the third story window of the Embassy Hotel. Emotions swirled as he tried to push them into mental compartments. Cerebral pigeon holes, his friend, Harry called them. He longed to close the door on them as he'd been trained to do many years ago but the door jammed again. Just like the last time.

Stone was completely unprepared for this. He had stopped by the hotel this morning to meet his partner and prepare for today's project meeting just as he'd done every day for two weeks. Today he arrived to a chaotic scene, the place filled with police. He had questioned Han, who told him abruptly that his partner was dead, apparently murdered in his sleep.

A sudden flash of red drew his attention to a group of women across the street, their slow, synchronous Tai Chi movements punctuated by the snapping of red fans. Flow...snap, flow...snap, flow...snap. As he swayed slightly with the rhythm, he felt the tension dissipate slightly.

Conditioned by years in the field, he studied the scene in the Shanghai library plaza. *Take in the whole scene and look for aberrations – things that don't belong. Then look at groups of people and evaluate their behavior, their mood. Then look at individuals. Who are the threats?* He went through the entire process in just under half a second. Such observation was second nature and constant.

Nearby, a man sat on a bench beneath a large tree and read a newspaper. He looked up as though he sensed a watcher, then returned to his paper. A young boy kicked a ball while his mother watched. Peyton chafed at the normalcy of the scene but felt his emotions settle as focus returned.

He turned slowly toward the policeman and

repeated the question with more force than intended. "What do you mean, murdered?" He leaned back against the table so the cop could see his hands. *Breathe in. Breathe out.*

The eyes blinked faster. The policeman shifted his weight backward slightly and moved his hand from the holster flap. The short, rotund cop stared up at Peyton, who stood a good half-foot taller, and shrugged. He sighed and started over, "I'm sorry, sir, but when Mr. Xu not answer his wake up call, the desk clerk came to see. He was found in bed. Not sleeping. Dead." A buzzing sound, "Zjjoo", slid through the policeman's front teeth, the Chinese pronunciation of Xu's name.

"That's impossible. I have to see for myself." Stone said. His voice quivered in his disbelief. "I have to see," he repeated and stepped forward. The cop's hand rested once more on the holster flap. Peyton couldn't tell what kind of sidearm the man had under the flap but he suspected a nine millimeter revolver. Slow muzzle velocity but at this range, deadly.

"I'm very sorry," the policeman replied, "but the body has been taken away and we have begun our investigation. The crime scene is closed. I must get back to my work. You must leave now."

"Who's investigating?" The pressure eased as he tried to impose some control. *Breathe in. Breathe out.* He felt the mental compartment door move slightly on rusty hinges.

"A detective inspector is in the room now. A Crime Scene Team is due here any minute. Looks like a simple robbery gone bad. His wallet was stolen. We will get to the bottom of this. But you must go now and let us work."

Peyton stared down at the policeman for a moment. He struggled to accept the murder of his long-time friend and business partner. While yet a stranger, Xu, had once saved his life. He recalled the cryptic message left on his cell phone last night but decided to keep that to himself.

Now he was left only with the awful truth. The one person he could turn to for help and advice, the friend who had stood by him through the insanity that followed Stephanie's death, gone. The muted cell phone haunted him. What if he'd picked up Xu's call last night? Would his friend still be alive? He felt as if Xu's blood were on his hands as well.

As his rage subsided, sadness filled the void. He saw a man's head lean out of the hotel room door. Two silver diamonds shone on his shoulder boards.   An exchange of verbal machine gun fire between the two police officers ensued.   Too fast for Stone, whose Chinese language skills were limited. Then the inspector stepped into the hallway and faced Stone.

"I am Police Inspector Cho," the man said in almost perfect English. "You are a friend of Mr. Xu?"

"Yes. And his business partner. What happened to him?"

"In what kind of business were you and Mr. Xu involved?"

"Security.   We are...*were* working on the new terminal at Pudong Airport. We designed the systems for the Chinese Aviation Authority. What happened to Xu?"

The Inspector said nothing as he wrote something in a small notebook.

Peyton pressed. "Please tell me what happened."

"It appears that Mr. Xu was murdered. His neck was broken by the hands of a person or persons unknown."

Stone's mouth opened and closed but he said

nothing.

"Where were you last evening, Mr....?"

"Stone. Peyton Stone. And I was in my hotel room. I turned off my phone early and went to sleep. We had been up early that morning for a pre-construction meeting."

"You were alone?"

"Of course, alone."

"Did anyone see you in your room?"

"No and no one saw whether I was there all night, either. But I was." As Stone's voice began to rise, the rookie cop moved a step closer. His holster flap remained unsnapped.

The Inspector tilted his head back and looked down his nose at Stone, "You should be more careful with your temper, Mr. Stone. I am an officer of the People's Republic." The corners of his mouth moved slightly upward. His eyes remained locked on Stone's.

Peyton took a quick breath. "Look, I came over to meet Xu. I find he's been murdered and now you imply that I might have had something to do with it."

"Did you?"

"No."

"I see. And what will you do with the rest of your day?" His pen was poised over the notebook.

Stone looked at the Inspector. His brow furrowed in irritation with the man's callous detachment. "I want to find out what happened."

"And so do I," the Inspector said. "The difference is that this is my job and not yours. So I must ask where I may find you today."

Stone felt heat rise up his neck. He took another deep breath, exhaled slowly and handed the Inspector his business card. "My mobile number is here and I'll be close. Call any time."

The policeman took the card with both hands, simulated a bow with a nod of his head, and then riffed the edge of the card along the fingers of his left hand. "You may count on it, Mr. Stone. Now Constable Han will show you out."

The rookie cop took one step forward, gave a quick nod and snapped his hand to the right. Pointed down the hallway toward the stairs. Peyton looked down at him again and walked quickly to the stairwell. He could hear quick steps behind him as shorter legs tried to keep up.

At the lobby level he barely paused before the automatic door slid open and he walked out into the warm damp air. Another day of oppressive heat and humidity. Han followed him out.

The door swished closed and he looked back over his shoulder. He sensed movement behind him but saw only his reflection in the glass. His hair, once dark brown, was now liberally streaked with gray. Two years earlier he'd been thirty pounds overweight, but his current physique bore testimony to daily workouts. Along with the weight, he had shed the destructive impulses that sent him into a downward spiral after his wife's death. At six feet three inches and two hundred pounds, he wasn't going to win any triathlons but he felt pretty good for fifty.

Peyton carefully reviewed the events from his arrival at the hotel last night until now. He had been exhausted from a long day and had silenced his mobile phone. After the morning hotel wake-up call, he had reached for his cell phone and saw a voice message notification. The timestamp read 11 p.m. the night before, two hours after he'd fallen asleep.

"Peyton, call me as soon as you get this." Xu's message sounded urgent. He had sat up in bed and immediately dialed the number. But the call went straight to voice mail. The self-recrimination began again. *If only I'd picked up when Xu called last night.*

"You know, 'if only' is not a strategy," the Agency shrink had said. *My shrink is a condescending idiot.*

He glanced across the street and watched as the women finished their Tai Chi. The boy with the ball held his mother's hand as they walked toward the corner. The bench in front of the library was now empty. The man with the newspaper had gone about his business. *Lucky bastard.*

Stone pushed again on the mental door. He had learned as a sniper in the Army to suppress his feelings, to disassociate himself from the job. To think of the human on the other end of the shot as nothing more than a target. There were many soldiers who could spray bullets in the general direction of the enemy, often without even looking as they fired. But only a few could wait for hours, sometimes days, to place the crosshairs over the head of another human and squeeze the trigger, watch through the scope as the target fell dead before the sound of the rifle shot even reached its ears. He had perfected his ability to push feelings into a mental compartment and lock the door on them...a talent that had started him down a long road to the shrink's couch.

Later, while under contract to the CIA, he was once again forced to kill. He honed his talent to a fine art. As the years passed, he all too often conveniently locked away all feelings. Stephanie had recognized this tendency early in their marriage. *Stephanie.* A searing pain ripped through him and he struggled to quell the emotion. *Breathe.* That compartment was finally sealed, never to be opened. Even as the thought raced through his mind, though, he recognized the futility of that declaration. *Perhaps one day, but not today.*

At the corner, he looked to his right down Go'An

21

Street and saw Humanity Hospital. An ambulance with its engine running and green lights flashing - just like the one that had pulled away from the Embassy Club only minutes before - was parked by the hospital's emergency entrance. The close proximity of the hospital to the hotel meant that, in all likelihood, Xu was here.

A surge of energy coursed through him as he headed rapidly toward the hospital. He had to see his friend's body, to say a final goodbye. To believe that he was in control of something, anything.

When he reached the door, he hesitated. Alerted by a slight movement at the edge of his peripheral vision, he turned quickly and stared across the street at the small park. It was empty. Perhaps he'd seen a bird or a scrap of paper spiraling in the hot morning breeze. He took another couple of steps and looked back at the park. Nothing there. An automatic door opened and he stepped inside the hospital.

ACROSS THE STREET IN THE PARK, A MAN PEERED carefully from behind a tree only marginally thicker than he and watched as his quarry entered the hospital. He knew that this man was somehow connected to Xu, a business partner perhaps. He'd first observed Stone from a park bench in front of the library where he read the morning newspaper. He saw the American look down from a window that was outside Xu's room, then realized he was staring back and chastised himself as he continued to feign interest in the paper. What had Xu told the American? Did he know where Xu was last night? Was he part of the scheme or an innocent bystander? Curiosity was irrelevant. He knew that this breach justified extreme action.

As he watched the American enter the hospital, he thumbed the safety on the silenced .32 caliber Walther

PPK in the holster under his suit coat and walked calmly toward the emergency entrance. His quarry could not leave Humanity Hospital alive.

Chapter 2

Humanity Hospital
Shanghai

"HOW CAN YOU SAY THAT I CAN'T SEE HIM? I'M family." Stone lied as he struggled to maintain his composure. The orderly confirmed that Xu's body had been brought to the hospital but would not allow Stone access to the morgue.

Quietly but firmly, he persisted. "I just want to say good-bye. Please." The orderly shook his head and turned away. "Wait. Look at this." Stone reached inside his jacket and retrieved a leather wallet from the inner pocket. He removed a photo of Xu and his American wife, Joni, standing next to Peyton and his wife, Stephanie, at a New Year's party. Joni bore a strong resemblance to Stone. After a glance, he handed the photograph to the orderly and hoped that this would gain him entry.

The orderly looked at the photo, then returned it. He shook his head from side to side. "It is a police matter," insisted the orderly. "I cannot let you in. There may be evidence."

Stone countered. "But arrangements need to be made to return his body to his wife. This man is an American citizen!" Again, he lied. Xu had full-time resident status in the United States but legally remained a Chinese national. Since he and Joni were now parents of two American-born children, Xu had recently considered American citizenship.

The orderly remained unfazed. "Sir, you are welcome to take it up with the US Consulate or the

Chinese diplomatic agencies but I have no power to change the policy."

Stone finally accepted the futility of further pleas. He noted the signage behind the desk, turned and exited through the swinging doors. Just outside he stopped, then walked quietly and slowly back toward the large emergency entrance doors. They bore countless scars from gurneys rammed through by paramedics who raced to Triage night and day. A gap between the side jamb and the door allowed each of them to swing open with greater ease. He stood to one side so that shadows below the door wouldn't betray his presence and peered through the gap at the orderly who wrote notes on a clipboard.

At last, the orderly finished his chart notations and walked around the desk. He glanced over his shoulder, walked down the long hallway and disappeared to the right.

Stone slowly pushed open the door and walked past chairs filled with people who waited to be seen. He headed nonchalantly toward the empty hall on the other side. In the stairwell adjacent to the orderly's station, he paused for a moment, then took the stairs two at a time down toward the morgue. At the bottom of the stairs, he glanced down the long hallway that stretched in front of him, saw no one and walked quickly ahead. He stopped when he got to the morgue entrance and peered through the long window on the left side. From this vantage point he could see four autopsy tables and the refrigerated lockers beyond. Just inside the locked door, he spotted a gurney with a body covered in a sheet. The foot of the gurney faced the window. He read the toe tag that bore the same Chinese characters that Xu had taught Peyton to write, the full name of his friend and partner, Guoping Xu.

While Stone had dealt death on many occasions, only once before did he have to deal with it. From the back end of a rifle, he was in control. The power of life and death was his. His skill allowed him to operate through the crosshairs of a riflescope, hundreds of yards away from impact. He interacted with a target, not a person. Any survivors left behind were forgotten. Or more accurately, never considered. Today, as he stared through the glass at the covered body of the man who had once saved his life, sorrow settled over him. Xu's murder made him feel powerless and angry...again. Both friend and business partner, Xu had remained steadfast through Stone's dark journey into alcohol-induced oblivion after Stephanie's death. Xu, alone, knew the depth of Stone's pain. Memories washed over him as he said a silent good-bye and struggled to suppress a surge of emotion that would block rational thought. He felt himself start to spin out of control again. *Don't go there. Breathe, breathe.* Peyton shifted his thoughts to the task ahead but his heart desperately needed to even the score.

The sound of approaching footsteps pulled him back. He looked to his right and saw a security guard. The man walked rapidly toward him, his muscular arms poised for action. The guard stopped directly in front of him and demanded, "What are you doing here? Do you have a pass to be here? Let me see it."

Stone looked at him briefly, refocused and smiled. "I'm afraid I don't know where I am. Made a wrong turn somewhere and can't find an exit."

The guard eyed him for a moment, then seemed to relax slightly.

"Come with me. I'll show you out. This way, please." He extended his arm, an indication that he wanted Peyton to go first.

"Excuse me, sir. One moment, please." Stone looked backwards and searched through his pockets as if he had dropped something. He caught a last glimpse of his friend's body. Then he turned around, shrugged, and walked ahead of the guard down the hallway.

Peyton thanked him as he pushed through a basement door and climbed concrete steps to the street above. The harsh glare stoked an inferno of rage: anger toward his friend's killer, toward himself for the muted cell phone, toward the system that left him powerless to control the situation. Raw with emotion, he thought of the awful moment when he would carry the sad news home and crush the dreams and hopes of those he loved most in the world. He stood for a moment as the magnitude of the loss registered. In an effort to refocus, he walked briskly toward the hotel. When he reached Hengshan Road, he hesitated, then turned toward the American Consulate. Useless alone, he needed help with this. He needed to talk to Harry.

THE MAN FELL INTO STEP BEHIND THE AMERICAN AT a discreet distance. He had lost him at the hospital entrance but saw him re-emerge from a basement stairwell in the middle of the block. He followed him toward the hotel for half a block but suddenly the American stopped, turned and walked straight toward him. Perplexed, he dropped his guard momentarily when the American stopped to look in a store window. A glance out the corner of his eye revealed that the American was watching him in the reflection from the storefront glass. He had no choice but to walk ahead. *An amateurish mistake on my part*, he thought angrily. He walked a block ahead, turned into the doorway of an apartment building and disappeared into the shadows cast by the morning sun. The American passed the doorway. He waited a full minute, then peered carefully around the wall. His prey now a block ahead of him, he stepped from the shadows.

PEYTON STARED AT THE ANGLED GLASS ENTRY WALL of a small neighborhood grocery. The man who had walked past him a few blocks earlier was once more behind him. When the Chinese man had passed him three blocks back, he noted nothing overtly unusual about him. The man, though large for an Asian, was otherwise unremarkable. His eyes, however, caught Stone's attention. They cut to the side as he passed, lingered just a second too long in Stone's direction, then looked quickly away. Endless training and years in the field had taught him to rely on instinct, to look for connections where others might see coincidence.

He filed the face away in his mind and continued walking down the street. Somehow the face was familiar. Half a block from the Consulate, Stone came to a blind alley where a fish-eye mirror was set up so that drivers and pedestrians could see each other. Before he crossed the alley, he slowed slightly to check the mirror for a car that might be coming toward him. He tensed when he saw the same man draw closer. In the reflection, the man appeared to hold a cigar in his right hand but something was wrong. The man's hand was positioned at an odd angle. Then Stone realized that the fisheye mirror had distorted the image and he recognized a sound suppressor attached to a pistol. In the same moment, the man raised his arm and pointed the pistol in Peyton's direction.

Peyton immediately sidestepped into the alley. The cough of the silenced pistol was followed by the splat of a bullet hitting the brick wall opposite him. Unlike in the movies, there was no whistling ricochet. Seconds later, the large man stepped around the corner of the building. Stone brought his closed fist down on the man's wrist and the gun skittered across the sidewalk. The man lunged after it. Stone kicked out and caught the gun with the toe of his shoe. It disappeared beneath a car parked at the curb. He started after the gun but the man reached out with one beefy hand, grabbed him around the throat, and pressed him upright against the side of the building. With one push of his powerful legs, the man lifted Stone off the ground and squeezed, shutting off the air to his lungs. He tried to gasp. Nothing. He felt panic rise. Like a swimmer trapped under water, he needed to breathe but was unable to get to take in fresh air. His lungs were on fire, ready to collapse. His mind headed down a narrow tunnel. Only a few seconds remained until his struggle would be over. Unable to break the vise-like grip of this Chinese stranger, Stone brought his hands up between the stranger's arms. His fingers curled into claws and he gouged at the large man's eyes. The attacker jerked his head to one side and loosened his grip briefly. Long enough for Stone to get a single, quick gulp of air.

Blackout was imminent. Pinpricks of light swirled in eyes as his world spun madly, sickeningly. His scalp tingled from a lack of oxygen and the tunnel narrowed. Then he heard shouts that drew closer fast, just as his sight dimmed. The big man dropped him and started to run down the alley only to be tackled by two US Marine guards from the Consulate. Stone collapsed on the pavement and gasped for breath, then sat up slowly, propped his back against the brick wall and rested his head on his knees. As the dizziness cleared, an overwhelming nausea swept over him. Losing his breakfast was the least of his concerns.

"Are you ok?" a third Marine asked. "We saw you

disappear into the alley along with the guy with the gun and came to check things out. We got him, sir."

"Who is he?" Stone's voice rasped, his vocal chords not yet recovered from the crushing pressure.

"Unfortunately, sir, he's a little out of our jurisdiction. We have to report this and turn him over to the Chinese police. You're lucky that we saw you. What's your name?"

"Peyton Stone. My passport's in my pocket." His vocal chords cleared and he spoke more loudly than he meant to. He reached back, withdrew a diplomatic passport booklet and handed it to the Marine. "But I'll be damned if you're going to let him go. Get him inside. I have some questions for him."

"WHAT THE HELL DO YOU THINK YOU'RE DOING?" The CIA Chief of Station literally shook with anger as he shouted in the soundproof room at the center of the American Consulate in Shanghai. The large Chinese man, handcuffed to an overturned chair, lay on his back in the center of the room. Blood ran from the man's nose as well as from a cut above his left eye. Stone straddled his chest with his fist raised, elbow cocked next to his ear. He was about to resume his interrogation. The big man had said nothing since he had been brought into the Consulate.

"This guy tried to kill me and I want to know why," Stone shouted back. "I was simply walking down the street and he came out of nowhere."

"You're an American. He's a mugger. End of story. He should have been turned over to the police. Since you dragged him in here and kicked the shit out of him, we can't do that now. We'll be lucky to fill out only thirty or forty thousand forms before this is over. Are you insane? Cut him loose."

"What? Just let him go?" Stone jumped up, his face inches from CIA man. "He tried to kill me. Besides, he's dressed pretty well for a mugger."

"So he's a yuppie mugger. The point is this was a Chinese problem until you made it an international incident. We can only hope he keeps his mouth shut. Now let him go, or I swear I'll arrest you and turn you over to the Chinese."

Stone's thoughts raced as he considered what to do next. He stood, calmed himself, and looked at the station chief. Digby was a real bureaucrat prick. On the other hand, in the cold light of day, Stone knew he was right. If he went over the man's head, he would open a new can of worms.

Peyton Stone was a nonofficial asset, the title given to a CIA contractor engaged when the American government needs deniability. His cover was his day job, that of a legitimate and successful security consultant. Stone had frequently used the gray area between Government agent and private citizen to create trouble for a number of bureaucrats, but his pile of blue chips back at Langley had dwindled. He needed to decide quickly whether to press the issue or relent. "Alright, you win," he said, and walked quickly to the door, "but I'm not done with this."

The bureaucrat replied as quickly. "You are most definitely done with this, Mr. Stone. Let's hope that we can get you out of China before the police pick you up and we have to do more paper work. If you had done the right thing at first, we could have pressed this. But you had to take things into your own hands. Now, we're too far outside diplomatic channels. Our only option is to set this guy on the street and deal with the fallout. Hopefully, he doesn't want police involvement any more than we do."

The two men stared at each other in disgust. Stone turned and walked out of the room and headed down the stairs to the PCC - Post Communications Center - located in the basement. He had to call Langley and talk to Harry but first he needed to speak to the Marine sergeant who served as the current watch commander in the security center.

Stone's company had designed the very CCTV systems that tracked activity around the Consulate. He entered the center and addressed the sergeant. "I'm Peyton Stone with Clandestine Operations and I need a photo from the surveillance cameras in the alley. Camera 3 should have video of a fight that took place about a half hour ago."

The Marine clicked his mouse and the alley behind the Consulate appeared on a large flat screen in the center of several smaller monitors. "That's the alley, sir?"

"Yeah," Stone replied. "Wind the DVR back thirty minutes, please."

More clicks and the picture reversed. At the far end of the alley, people moved quickly backward. Then two men in uniform backed into the picture, put a big Asian man on the ground and appeared to remove handcuffs from him. "Stop!" Stone nearly shouted. "Ok, go forward slowly"

The Marines in the picture cuffed on the man on the ground, then helped him to his feet. As they walked him down the alley, the big man looked up at the camera. "Right there," Stone said. "Freeze that facial image and print it for me."

"Yes, sir." The printer whirred in the background and Stone grabbed the image.

"Thanks." Stone turned toward the door.

"Sir, Mr. Digby will have to approve the release of

that picture."

"I'll be sure to ask him before I leave," Stone said, as he folded the picture and put it in his pocket, then headed once again downstairs to the PCC. His sarcasm wasn't lost on the Marine who was satisfied that he had at least followed orders.

THE CHINESE MAN, A BAND-AID OVER HIS EYE, LEFT the consulate quickly. A Marine closed the gate behind him. "You are right. We're not finished, Mr. Peyton Stone," he spoke softly to himself. He brushed his coat, straightened his shirt and walked quickly toward his office.

Chapter 3

CIA Headquarters
Langley, VA

HARRY MORRISON DUMPED THE STYROFOAM container in the trash and placed the tray on top of the countertop. He took a half-step back as he maneuvered his stomach around the trash can and then shifted his weight toward his office. As he turned, he hitched up his belt and tried in vain to tuck his wrinkled shirt. With a snort, he gave up and walked away.

Located in a glass-walled building in the courtyard between the Old Headquarters and the New Headquarters in Langley, Virginia, the CIA food court was reminiscent of a large suburban mall. In addition to saving time, the gathering place was a great spot to catch up on the latest gossip. This low-tech data link provided access to information from across the large, clandestine organization.

The President of the United States appeared on the flat-screen television mounted above the seating area. Harry slowed a little and watched the image as he walked by. Close-caption text scrolled below the picture: "…and our nation will cement this commitment to peace with the new government of Iran. In just over a week from now our two nations will sign a landmark treaty at Camp David. This agreement will begin a new era in the peace and stability of…" The announcement faded in the distance as Harry moved down the hall.

Those who worked in this complex traded not only in rumor and gossip but also in speculation based on observation. Most people thought the first indication

34

that the US would definitely invade Iraq was the early build-up of troops in Camp Doha, Kuwait three months before the invasion. Langley employees, however, knew something serious was in the works months before the troops were deployed. Amidst tough talk from the White House and the UN, the Langley Starbucks posted announcements that, beginning the Tuesday after Labor Day 2002, they would be open 24 hours, seven days a week. This harbinger of long hours of intelligence gathering and assessment was tantamount to an announcement that military action was imminent. Six months later the U.S. rolled into Baghdad.

Harry strode through the food court with his hands stuffed into his pockets. Strains of Mozart drifted through his head. He turned automatically into Mrs. Field's, bought his usual post-lunch chocolate chip cookies, and nibbled as he continued down the hallway toward his office, Room 2T32. The windowless twelve foot square blue cinderblock room contained a standard Government-issue gun metal gray desk, a matching three-shelf bookcase and rows of file cabinets with cipher-locked drawers. He walked behind the desk, picked up the Geospatial Intelligence, or GEOINT, photo that he had studied before lunch and resumed his analysis.

He squinted, then donned his glasses and studied the photo at a more relaxed distance. The wizards from the National Geospatial Intelligence Agency – NGA, for short – using MASINT, the familiar name for Measurement and Signatures Intelligence, had carefully processed this particular image. MASINT was so powerful and secret that the members of the Intelligence Community referred to it as "Magic And Sorcery" Intelligence.

Harry's mind operated at full throttle and often

outpaced his speech. Biased by his linguistic habits and personal appearance, those unacquainted with the man's work frequently dismissed him. But once exposed to his uncanny ability to synthesize information from numerous sensor sources and draw incredibly accurate conclusions, the most cynical quickly became believers.

He compared the current imagery with that of previous days. This allowed him to track the movement of objects and note any images that had disappeared from view as well as those that now appeared in the recent photographs. The green outline of the North Korean freighter on the five-day old photo meant that it had left its port in North Korea. An identical red outline off the Chinese coast near Shanghai indicated the ship's arrival there. *Green is gone, red is returned*, he thought. Harry studied the freighter's latest movements in a series of photos taken over the last two days. The ship had dropped anchor off the Chinese coast. Later, a pleasure craft had tied up alongside in the middle of the night but left before dawn. The infrared imagery indicated that the yacht returned to Shanghai and the freighter steamed off toward Hanoi. Why? This question confounded him.

"Call for you Harry. Red phone," said the voice from the intercom on his desk.

"Got it," Harry muttered as he picked up the secure phone. Each desk had two phones, one gray, the other white. The white one was called the "red phone", a holdover from early days when secure phones actually were red. Accordingly, the gray phone was called "black", the only other color choice in the past. Today's handset colors bore no relationship to the designations.

"This is Harry," he said.

"Hi, Harry. Peyton Stone."

"Peyton!! Egad, man! I haven't talked to you since you disappeared after Cairo. That was what...two, three, years ago? Where are you now?" And how, he thought, do you have access to a red phone?

The two men had met while in the military. Upon discharge from the Army, Harry had capitalized on friendships he'd made in SpecOps and joined the CIA. Stone, ever the loner, chose to go a solo route in business. But the bond between these two markedly disparate characters remained intact. Friendship was the basis of their current on-again/off-again working relationship as they collaborated on projects under contract to the CIA when needed.

Stone had a special talent, born one day in a tractor shed in Ellabell, Georgia when, at age five, his dad gave him the opportunity to shoot a pistol. Over the next fifteen years he had become arguably the best rifle shot in the world, a distinction that Harry believed he held yet, more than twenty years later. The fact that he didn't compete and therefore was unknown was tremendously attractive to the CIA. Trained first by the Army and later by the CIA at Camp Peary, also known as "The Farm" near Williamsburg, Virginia, he excelled in marksmanship, hand-to-hand combat, survival, escape and evasion, and CIA tradecraft. Harry was his contact at the CIA when he served as a nonofficial asset

"I'm in the PCC at the US Consulate in Shanghai." The Post Communications Center, a secure room in the heart of every embassy and many consulates, was a place where coded messages and encrypted telephone communications were sent to Washington through the secure satellite ground link near Beltsville in suburban Maryland.

"It's great to hear from you after all this time. What's up? Nothing serious, I hope," Harry said.

"Very serious," Stone replied. "It's Xu. He and I have been on-site for a project at Pudong Airport here in

Shanghai. When I went to meet him this morning, I found he had been murdered. Then someone tried to get to me as well."

"Murdered? No!" Harry was shocked. "Oh, my God!!" He remembered the day, now more than two decades ago, when they first met Xu. Harry, then a much younger and slimmer rookie field agent, was teamed with Peyton who was on his first contract assignment. In a mission gone horribly wrong, drug dealers had pinned down the pair in the jungles of northern Burma. Their cover blown, senior team members dead, the two made one last desperate attempt to escape. Nearly out of ammunition and options, Harry felt a hand grab his ankle. He turned to fire but the face near his feet smiled. The stranger's hand motioned him to follow so he tapped Stone on the shoulder and the two of them crawled behind the stranger into a hidden tunnel.

Stone had to be coaxed into the small dark space. As a child, he had been trapped in a storm sewer, a bad choice of playgrounds for a seven year old. The county street department worked for four hours to extract him. Decades had passed since that long afternoon but the panic of entrapment returned quickly when he crawled into the tunnel.

Once inside, the three had moved quickly and quietly as they first passed directly beneath the drug dealers, then outside into the undergrowth. Once out of danger, they rested. The stranger offered his hand and said, "You are safe now. I am Xu. Say like 'shoe' like on you foots." Thus began a long friendship among the three men. Xu soon left his job with the Chinese Ministry of Security, joined Peyton's security company as a partner and immigrated to the United States.

Harry snapped back to the present when Peyton

spoke. "He left a message late last night that he had stumbled onto something and needed to talk right away." He rubbed his face with both hands, then continued. "But I have no idea what he meant. When I got to his hotel this morning, a cop outside his room told me Xu had been murdered." He took a deep breath. "I need your help, Harry, to find the killer. On the way to the Embassy, some big Chinese guy followed me and took a shot at me. A pretty strange coincidence if he's not the same guy who took Xu out, wouldn't you agree?"

"Jeez, Louise, are you alright?"

"I'm ok. The Marines from the Consulate came to the rescue. I tried to get some answers out of the shooter but that prick Digby happened by the room, stuck his nose in, and made me release him. Not in our jurisdiction. I got a printout of a face off the surveillance camera in the alley. Digby doesn't know and I'm in no mood to ask before I take it with me. I need you to run it through the OTA computers to see if we can get a match on this guy." OTA, the Office of Terrorism Analysis, was a branch of the CIA's Counterterrorism Center, known as the CTC, located just down the hall and two floors below Harry's office. One of OTA's many responsibilities was to track terrorist state and non-state actors.

"Can do. How will you get it to me?"

"I've decided to turn my airport project over to the design team, then head back to the States. I should land tomorrow morning your time. Want to get together for lunch? I'd like to see what information you have in your databases that might help me find this guy."

"Sure," Harry replied. "We can figure something out. Call me when you get in. By the way, did you notify the local cops? They may have something on this guy."

"Nah, Digby was afraid he might start an international incident. Doesn't want to fill out a bunch of forms and risk a paper cut. The guy's a real ass."

"Well, remember that you'll come home today but he has to live with the mess. He's probably right to be protective."

"Yeah, I guess. Ok, see you tomorrow."

Harry hung up and quickly called OTA to request that an analyst be assigned to process the transmitted image upon receipt. He hung up and reflected on all the times he had worked with Peyton Stone. His eyebrows formed a furrow as he thought of the changes wrought by Stephanie's death and hoped that Stone's newly developed penchant for reckless behavior wouldn't come with fatal consequences.

Chapter 4

Dulles Airport
Washington, DC

THE BLACK '69 CHEVELLE SS EASED ONTO THE Dulles access road. Peyton's plane had landed 30 minutes earlier. By the time her boss retrieved his bag, Clare would be in front of the door. Relieved that he was back, she braced herself for the encounter. Peyton would be in a funk after all that happened in Shanghai. And she felt raw. Xu was her friend, too.

Clare was, in most ways, Peyton's right hand at Stone & Associates. Fifteen years ago she had been an unemployed technical editor about to be evicted from her apartment when she met Peyton Stone at a job fair. Impressed by her forthright manner and skill, he had given her a chance and hired her as a specification reviewer. She quickly caught on to the security construction business. Talented, passionate and enthusiastic, she just as quickly won the respect of co-workers and clients alike. Whatever the situation, Audra Clare Elliott was unflappable.

Except when called by her first name, a perpetually sore subject. Her mother chose the name Audra as part of her own fantasy. The woman lived in a TV inspired and alcohol fueled imaginary universe to escape the poverty of the rural coal town where Clare's father toiled in the mine. When she was born, The Big Valley was her mother's favorite. Clare, much to her chagrin, bore the same name as Audra, the beautiful but helpless daughter of the show's matriarch. Unlike - or perhaps because of - her mother Clare dealt in reality. An older friend and mentor once pointed out, to no avail, that the name had motivated her to make better choices. For many years after leaving her mother and her first name behind, Clare simply immersed herself in work and kept the door to her past firmly closed. This changed when she accepted that the pattern had to break...or she would.

Almost from the start Stone called her "Ace". But he was the only person allowed to use her initials as her name. Others tried but were promptly set straight, sometimes at full volume, in the Stone & Associates warehouse staging area. Over the years she'd assumed greater responsibility as she tackled new and more difficult assignments. Now she was the most trusted and capable Senior Project Manager in the company. When the jobs were tough and the clients were high profile, Ace was almost always involved. And she was the only person Peyton allowed to drive the Chevelle, a true measure of her boss' esteem.

She slowed to the 10 mile per hour speed limit as she approached the terminal. The deep vibration of the 500-plus horsepower tricked-up LS7 crate motor under the hood came through the acoustically-tuned straight pipe exhaust...and always attracted attention. Especially police attention.

She saw Peyton by the curb next to his suitcase. He stared at his phone as he checked email but glanced up as she approached. "Ace! How's my car?"

"Foot on the gas, lift the clutch, go fast. You gotta love it. Oh, and I'm fine, too, thanks for asking."

He quickly glanced in her direction, saw her smile and smiled back. Stone's love of fast cars went back to his childhood when Uncle Artie, his father's older brother, took him to the Speedway at the Georgia State Fairgrounds. Peyton, then six years old, sat in Uncle

Artie's lap and steered his uncle's 1959 Ford stock car around the one mile dirt track again and again. Peyton spent many of his childhood weekends at "Artie's Garage" helping his uncle repair and restore cars. Motorcycle racing first satisfied his need for speed before he moved on to Formula Atlantic. He was good but not great so he decided to concentrate on building his company. Shortly after quitting the racing circuit he put his Artie's Garage experience to a serious test when he found the '69 Chevelle parked in a chicken coop in Bluemont, Virginia and spent the next year bringing it back to life.

He put his suitcase in the back, climbed in the passenger's side next to Clare and immediately pressed buttons on his phone. "Hi, Harry, it's Peyton. Got time for coffee? After two 'red eyes' in a row, a ride on the mobile lounge and an hour wait for my luggage, I could use some." She couldn't hear Harry tell him to go home but Peyton's impatience was palpable as he listened.

"No time," argued Stone. "We have to move on this now. I'll meet you at the Starbucks on Old Dominion Drive near Dolly Madison Boulevard. You know it, right?" A moment of silence followed as Harry objected once again.

"Ace just pulled up. I'll have her drive me over there. Let's say 45 minutes?" Peyton pressed the end button and glanced across the bench seat. His gun-metal blue eyes were sunken and rimmed in red. He looked awful, beyond tired. Not the best time to dive into painful subjects but she knew what dominated his mind.

Clare eased the Chevelle into traffic, then studied his face briefly. Peyton was upset but she hadn't detected any of the danger signals that followed Stephanie's death. So far, at least. After a moment, she spoke. "Any word about Xu and what happened?"

Stone frowned and took a deep breath. "No. The room was clean: no prints, hairs, fibers, nothing." He frowned and added, "As if a ghost floated through the window, killed Xu and disappeared. I hope to get an update from the investigations team today but I don't know what kind of priority they'll assign it."

"The cops have to look into it, right? Surely we'll hear something as the investigation unfolds, won't we?"

"Yeah, but China's a long way away. I can't stay on top of the cops long distance. If I were there, I couldn't do much better. My Chinese is marginal at best. I need..." Stone paused, then continued. "I was going to say what I need now is Xu. He understood the nuances, the culture." Fatigue, grief, and frustration seemed to converge in him. Clare knew he was wired for solutions, not inaction, and she could see him fight to keep emotions in check. When he spoke again, he said simply, "I owe him."

Clare looked at him and said, "Go back, Peyton. You have the airport project there as well. At least you'd be closer and might be able to help in some way."

He glanced at her. The corners of his mouth turned slightly upward. "It's not quite that easy." He told her what happened with the big Chinese man.

"Yuppie mugger? Digby actually said 'yuppie mugger'?"

"He's obviously been an asshole since the 80's. I hope Harry can help us out with this." He realized that he hadn't mentioned the meeting to Ace. "He's meeting us at the Starbucks on Old Dominion Drive. Get in the left lane and take the Beltway to route 123."

The pair drove in silence for several minutes. *At least he wants coffee*, she thought with some relief as she recalled a rocky time in their relationship. When Stone's famous discipline failed after the death of his wife and

44

he spiraled into drink, Clare withdrew in silence. Peyton couldn't understand her distance at the lowest point of his life. Finally, one morning after a particularly lengthy binge, Peyton appeared at the office and apologized. She listened as he slumped over his desk and, without any self-justification, asked for her forgiveness. After a long pause, she walked over to a window and stood silently with her back to him. Finally, when she spoke, she recounted her childhood as the daughter of an alcoholic. The smells and unkind slurs, drunken hugs from her dad, irrational anger that erupted unexpectedly and filled her with shame in front of her friends, special moments ruined by yet another binge. *Never again*, she had told herself, *never again. And now this. Why?* She hated the pity she heard in her own question. When she looked at Peyton - her mentor, her friend, her rock - disheveled and so lost that morning, she saw only the past. And it frightened her.

Peyton was stunned. He never dreamed that this paragon of efficiency and good-humor had dealt with such horror. Yes, his life had tanked but he had given no thought to the hurt he had heaped on everyone around him. His revulsion was complete and mortifying but he chose at that moment not to wallow in it or any other woes going forward. He had a reason to get up and put one foot in front of another. Many reasons, actually, starting with his sons - *Oh, God, my boys* - and his close friends, whether he felt like it or not.

The conversation that began that awful morning morphed into an ongoing, if somewhat fragmented, dialog between two very private people. A catharsis for both, each regained balance and the relationship grew more solid than ever. Clare recognized that walls remained but her fear had abated. While she ached for her friend - all was indeed forgiven if not forgotten - she was grateful that she had finally taken a long look at herself. No one could be another's rock. What a heavy burden to place on another human. She didn't have to take abuse from anyone but she accepted that her emotional health was her responsibility. Now, as she turned into the parking lot, she looked once more at Peyton. And hoped.

"I want the biggest cup of coffee they make." Peyton's voice brought her back to the present.

"Then, let's go inside. I'm holding out for the usual." She stared at him, her left eyebrow in an upright and locked position.

"Well, you're going to have to order because I can't remember the whole thing." The two laughed as they recalled his tortured attempts to order her beloved "grande coffee light frappuccino with two Splendas".

They stood in line, then Clare ordered. Stone had just paid the pleasant young woman at the register when Harry entered.

"Ladies first," he pronounced. "Clare, you're a sight for sore eyes."

"Hello, Harry." Relief swept over her as the big man gave her a quick hug. A quirky genius with "walking around" sense, he was the voice of reason for their troubled friend.

She spoke up. "I hate to interrupt this love fest but one of us has a company to run. Harry, can you give this man a ride?" He nodded as Peyton sighed and dropped the Chevelle keys back into her outstretched palm. She smiled at him and said, "I'll grab my coffee, boss. Thanks." As she approached the counter, she turned and added, "Glad you're home."

Harry found a table, then watched as Peyton waited impatiently at the counter for another cup of coffee. A young man whose backpack had swept the first Triple-

Shot Americano off the counter offered copious apologies. Twice Peyton glanced over the abject fellow's shoulder and shrugged as Harry shook his head and smiled.

Three years had passed since Harry and Peyton had foiled an Islamic Brotherhood terror plot that could have destroyed the peace between Egypt and Israel and ignited the entire region. Harry's intel had identified and located the radical Jihad Group based in Cairo. The terrorists planned to detonate a massive explosion in downtown Cairo that would be attributed to the Israelis. Peyton watched from a distance as the team assembled explosives in a large open flat area in the Egyptian desert. His work finished, the bomb maker walked toward a truck guarded by two men. Peyton made two shots from eighteen hundred yards away. Squeeze the trigger, adjust, squeeze. Both bullets in the air simultaneously.

The bomb maker and one of the guards fell to the ground, dead before either heard the sound of the first shot. A CIA-sponsored Egyptian assault team moved in quickly, secured the truck, and then destroyed it. The second guard was allowed to escape, to carry the message back to the terrorists. The terrorists' plot failed, war didn't start and the media never discovered the story. If normal classifications stayed intact, they never would. But the jihadists knew that a phantom sniper had taken two of their people and vanished without a trace.

Peyton shook his head once more and walked toward Harry. The kid bumped into him again when he headed to the table. He breathed a sigh of relief as he sat the cup on the table.

Harry smiled as he stood up. "Man, you must really want coffee." He placed an arm around Peyton's shoulders, then the two shook hands. "It's been ages but you look just the same."

"Flattery will get you everywhere, fella. I've been living on airplanes for the last 28 hours so I know you're full of crap."

Peyton appraised his friend as they sat down and grinned as he added, "You look the same, too."

"Is that good or bad?" Harry asked. He glanced down at the twenty extra pounds he had added to the two hundred forty he'd carried when Peyton last saw him.

"Depends on your point of view, I guess." Stone smiled genuinely. Two years had passed but he felt as if they had been out for beers last weekend.

Stone picked up his cup and said, "No coffee? You sure?"

"Nah, I've gotta quit. Doc says it's one more thing that will kill me. He has a vested interest in my health. If I die, he doesn't get my insurance checks."

Peyton smiled. "Man, I'm really glad to see you. What trouble have you gotten into since I haven't been here to watch your back?"

"Same old stuff," Harry leaned back in his chair, "After you left, I took on the Middle East Branch, my reward for the Egypt thing. They made me a branch chief, GS-14." Harry paused, then said, "I would have told you but you'd already taken off."

Stone looked down at the table. He studied the packet of sweetener for a few seconds. "Yeah, I had a lot of ends to tie up. Then we won a huge project with the Port Authority in New York to clean up some system integrator's mess. After that we landed the Shanghai job. I've been pretty heads down for a while. But the company has done well, fifty full-time employees now. Shanghai will have a dozen subcontractors."

"That's great!! But how have you been?" Harry leaned forward again. He rested his forearms on the small table and interlaced his fingers.

"I'm ok," Stone replied tersely. He didn't miss the implicit meaning. The late nights after Stephanie's funeral had turned into missing days. A DUI nearly cost him his clearance and did cost him his driver's license. Finally, violent behavior in a bar landed him in the Fairfax County jail for a weekend. All the while, Harry was a constant friend. He had stuck his neck out when Peyton's clearance came up for review and then convinced the County Attorney to drop assault charges against him. In private, though, the two friends had exchanged heated words about the reckless behavior. Peyton had repaid Harry's kindness and honesty by accepting a contract in New York, then leaving with barely a 'thank you'.

Harry waited for more. When nothing came, he dropped it. "So how are the kids?"

Stone relaxed. "Doing great. Both have finished school and work for the Navy now. Ron is stationed at US Navy San Diego. He's in SEAL training on San Clemente Island. Bryan won the Unmanned Underwater Vehicle competition his senior year at Virginia Tech. He was hired on the spot to do research on some remote-controlled submarine program."

"So you're in touch with them?"

The tension returned and Stone struggled to maintain his composure. When he answered, his words were measured. "Yeah, of course. Why wouldn't I be?" As soon as he spoke, he thought with remorse, *Yeah, trust leaves fast and comes home slow but I was the one who pulled the trigger.*

Harry shrugged. "No reason." He moved on. "What happened in Shanghai?"

Stone exhaled. "The whole thing is damned weird. Xu didn't have any enemies that I know of and he wasn't

49

the kind of person to invite robbery. Mugged in a hotel room in the middle of the night? I don't think so. And I can't think of any motive to take him out." He frowned and added, "Then there's the guy who shot at me." He reached into his pocket and handed over the printed CCTV image of the gunman. As he laid it on the table, he swore as a memory returned. "Son of a bitch, this is the guy with the newspaper on the park bench in front of the library." He looked at Harry. "I saw him right across the street from where Xu was murdered. I knew he was familiar."

"Are you sure?"

"Positive. This is the same guy. You wouldn't happen to have any Imagery Intelligence from that area around the time of the murder and the morning after would you?"

Harry shifted his weight. "Unless a bird was tasked to be in that specific area to take pictures, it's not likely. Even if we had the capability to produce IMINT of the detail that you need – and, of course, I'm not saying we do – it would be classified and compartmented. I couldn't show it to you."

"Ok." Stone gave him a weary but cynical smile. "But could you look around for whatever information you may or may not be able to produce to see whether you may or may not have it and then tell me what I may or may not need to know?"

"Sure," Harry grinned, "I may or may not be able to do that."

Peyton gave him a light punch on his arm and grinned, "Thanks, buddy, I may or may not owe you one. At any rate, you can run that photo through the system and see what it hits."

"Let's get out of here. I'll drop you off at your office so you can get your car. Then we'll both head to my office and take a look at what I may or may not find." As they stood up, Harry added, "Glad we're in my car. With no caffeine in my system, no way I could handle you behind the wheel."

Peyton spotted Harry's thirteen-year-old Ford Taurus as soon as they walked outside. Once bronze, the car had faded to the color of watery beef stock. "Geez, Harry, you ever wash the thing?"

"Sure. Park her outside every time we get a hard rain."

"Figures." He opened the door and added, "You need to open the doors next time the wind blows." He shoved a pile of papers into the back seat and climbed in. "I couldn't ride in this heap without caffeine. Get me to my car fast." But he smiled when Harry reached into the glove compartment and pulled out a CD. The car might be a rolling trash bin but Pavarotti's rich tenor poured from an incredible custom sound system. Peyton lay back against the wobbly headrest and listened as Harry sang along.

TWO TABLES AWAY FROM THE SPOT THEY HAD JUST left, a nondescript Asian man made notes on a pad inside a leather folio. When the two Americans started toward the parking lot exit, he went to his car and dialed his cell phone. "I've made contact. What do you want me to do?"

"Take him out," came the reply and the connection clicked off.

The assassin started his car and followed Harry's Taurus down Dolly Madison Highway. With a .45 caliber Sig Sauer Model 220 under his coat, the Asian watched for an opportunity to take a clean shot. He followed the Taurus first to a low rise office building where the tall American got into another car. A delivery truck pulled into the unloading lane and blocked his shot. He followed the two through heavy traffic and several turns, until the final one, a left into the CIA campus. The would-be assassin reached for his cell phone and dialed. "We have a bigger problem than we thought." He explained where he was.

"Just get it done. The more agents you can take out in the process, the better. We only need a few days of confusion and it won't matter how many people know. By that time, it will be too late to make a difference." The Asian man pressed the end button on his cell phone, made a u-turn, then parked on a residential street across from Langley's main gate and waited.

THE BOARD ROOM IN THE LOS ANGELES headquarters of Intra-Coastal Oil was silent except for the light rustle of the white fabric screen that rose and fell slightly with the airflow from the air conditioning vent. Glen Garrison, Assistant to the CFO, stood frozen after his presentation of the newest sales and project profit projection figures. When the bottom of the screen tapped the tray full of dry markers, he jumped slightly and stared at the conference table. His high forehead bore a shadowy tattoo of numbers that continued to shine from the huge ceiling projector. Glenn took a deep breath and looked up. He clasped his hands in front of his belt buckle, shifted his weight to his left foot and bent his right knee slightly. The facts had been presented. What they did about the situation was, thankfully, beyond his pay grade.

The senior management of ICO sat on either side of the long table. Some stared at Garrison and magnified his discomfort while others looked down at the table, deep in thought. Finally, the manager of global operations spoke. "So you're telling us, after we spent billions on consolidation of market share to buy up almost every US oil refinery, that this new treaty will freeze oil prices at forty dollars a barrel? This will kill us!"

"Yes, sir," Garrison replied, "my charts clearly show that it will indeed kill us." He backed off a bit. "Well, it *could* kill us. In the 1960s the price was consistently below thirty-five dollars for an extended time and wasn't a problem. Recently, however, our performance measures have been tied to a fluctuating global market with a price in the seventy to ninety dollar range. Major restructuring would have to occur in order to be viable at forty dollars but it could be done. The downside is that the restructuring would cost nearly double our profits in the first four years. And this assumes that the Iranians will live up to their end of the treaty for a long time. The other option is to sell off the refineries we bought. With the oil prices frozen, we'd have to sell at a loss, if we could find a buyer at all."

"So this really is a no-win situation if this treaty gets signed. Is that what you're saying?"

Garrison ducked his chin and puffed his cheeks as he swallowed the acid that bubbled past his stomach ulcer. Anger fueled his thoughts. *Were you listening? Of course that's what I said. You are such a gutless wonder. Can't drive the nail home yourself, can you?* He raised his head and answered benignly, "Yes, sir."

Dennis Carlson, the peripatetic CEO of Intra-Coastal leaned forward. He propped his elbows on the board room table, steepled his fingers and tapped his thumbs on his lips. Then he interlaced his fingers and slid his elbows to the side until his palms were flat on the table. "We have to come up with a strategy. Garrison, what's the payback time if we decide to restructure?"

"Seven to ten years to break even. Probabilities are closer to ten than seven."

"And if the treaty doesn't get signed?"

"Then we are only dependent on the oil market reaction, which will probably spike the price higher and increase our short term profits. At the very least, we would have some influence on the supply side since we can cut production to move the price point upward. We don't have to worry about payback because we're already positioned."

Carlson sat back in his massive chair at the head of the table and rubbed his temple. "Alright, gentlemen, I need to digest this. Thank you for coming."

The assembled executives gathered their pads, pens, and coffee cups, and left Carlson alone in the room. He sat strangely motionless for several minutes, deep in thought. Then his eyes narrowed as his fingers began to tap against the burl walnut tabletop. He arrived at a decision, uncoiled his body and reached for the phone. Without hesitation, he dialed the private number from memory. When the male voice answered Carlson said brusquely, "It's Dennis. We need to talk."

Chapter 5

Tehran, Iran

RANDALL PERKINS SAT AT A BACK CORNER TABLE, one of six in the miniscule café. The ceiling fan's decrepit blades barely disturbed the heat as he slowly sipped a small cup of strong bitter Arab coffee. He ignored the fly on the small sugar bowl and, instead, savored the smell of freshly fried lamb sausages and the deep rich aroma of the coffee. The soft rays of the early morning sun filtered through the dusty front window. Soon the light would brighten and Randall could read the paper that remained folded by his plate. When he first arrived in the Middle East, he missed his morning cup of Starbucks. Now, however, after three years in the oil fields, he had come to love his four-times-daily cup at the coffee shop here in Tehran.

The bitter brew was a Bedouin tradition, a metaphor for the harsh, bitter nomadic life of the tribes. Bedouin hospitality was legendary. When a traveler came to a tent, the nomads were obligated to provide shelter. Every day the man of the house would make the bitter Arab coffee for himself and his guest. The guest knew that he had overstayed his welcome when no cup of coffee awaited him in the morning.

Randall finished his breakfast. The sun now shone brightly through the window so he reached for the newspaper. As he scanned the front page, he sensed a presence close to his table. He looked up and saw the man with whom he met twice weekly to discuss oil production licenses and the benefits of trading oil futures. Thanks to Perkins who also passed along insider information on oil futures, the man was now financially comfortable, if not wealthy by Iranian standards. In return, Mohammed Reza sometimes concluded his discussions of governmental oil regulations with forays into other areas of keen interest to the American, more specifically, the internal workings of the Iranian government.

Perkins greeted his associate in near-perfect Farsi. "Mohammed, how are you this fine day?" Mohammed Reza pulled out the rickety, old wooden chair and joined him at the small table. The two had met years ago at an oil industry trade show. Reza was introduced at one of the technical sessions as a visiting legislator from the Iranian Parliament, the Majlis. Perkins, who hoped to gain a CIA conduit into the Majlis, struck up a conversation on the intricacies of financing new oil exploration. The Iranian, now code-named PHILOSOPHER, had instantly taken the bait. The pair had become good friends through their regular meetings. Perkins often thought that his next assignment would be neither as easy nor as pleasant as his current one.

After Reza ordered a cup of coffee, he clasped his hands together on the table and leaned forward. "Mr. Randy, I am very troubled and I don't know what to do about it." His face mirrored the stress of his dilemma. After a few moments, he sat back and dropped his hands to his lap. "I'm not sure you should know of this."

"We have been friends for a long time, Mohammed," said Perkins. "I'll help you if I can. What's the problem?"

"Well, as you know, my government and yours are working toward a peace arrangement that is quite complicated. This is very sensitive information because our governments are keeping the real terms secret from the rest of the world. Some in our government vehemently oppose the treaty. We, or rather, *they*, believe that such an agreement would ally us too closely to the most powerful non-Muslim countries. In other words, this is seen as a sell-out. Disagreements are to be expected. But I have heard of an organized plot to overthrow the government. There is talk of *jihad*. I even heard the mention of a nuclear weapon. I have no problem with opposition, but this is madness."

Perkins tried and failed to control his reaction and sat back quickly. He noticed the slip of the tongue. *We, or rather, they...* He let it slide for the moment. "Are you positive about this?" He leaned forward, regained his composure, aware that discretion in this public place was essential.

"No, I only hear that this is in the works. I cannot confirm anything."

We, or rather, they...

"Mohammed, we've known each other for what, a couple of years, right? In that time I have given you investment advice based on privileged information from my company. You have made a good bit of money as a result."

"That's true," Mohammed said, looking curiously at Perkins.

"I need you to tell me all that you can about this as a personal favor to me. How are nukes involved? Who is behind this? I need to know for certain. There are others who may need to know about this." Perkins stretched and casually looked around the room. Two other tables were filled with people engaged in conversation.

Mohammed looked at Perkins for a long time and searched his face for clues. "I'm told some Chinese are aware of the plan. Surely you must know that this involves highly placed people in my government. Eyes and ears are everywhere. If this conversation is discovered, my death is a certainty. And yours, too, if you are who I think you are."

With a quick intake of breath, Perkins responded candidly. "Look, my friend, I am just a simple oil man. That's all you need to know." The statement obviously confirmed a suspicion. He saw Reza's eyes narrow slightly as the man tried to suppress a reaction. "We need to be honest here. I need you to tell me what highly-placed people you're talking about."

Perkins smiled at no one in particular as he noted the faces at other tables. Nothing looked amiss or out of place but a strange feeling persisted. The subject of the conversation had unsettled him but he couldn't give even the slightest hint. Perkins, a careful man, believed the old saw: there are old operatives; there are bold operatives; but there are no old, bold operatives. On the way over he had walked in and out of small shops, checked for a tail and found none. With no evidence at hand, he continued. "Just keep your voice low and I think we are okay."

"I have heard that there will be some kind of event soon that will mark the beginning of a global jihad and result in the destruction of a major city." Reza looked around nervously. "It frightens me because of what can happen in the end if the radical faction of our Government prevails. They use the religion of Islam to further purely political goals. Islam is a religion of peace. The disagreements between Shi'a and Sunni within our faith or between Muslims, Christians, or Jews should be settled by debate. This, of course, assumes that they can be settled, even that they should be settled. Perhaps tolerance would allow everyone to live in peace and find God in a personal way – if desired. This obsession with jihad against the West is lunacy."

"Have you verified this information?" Perkins asked. "A jihad that would be more successful than the last hundred or so attempts would require lot of organization and resources and coordination. It's pretty much impossible."

"I have a cousin who works in the reactor complex in Bushehr. He told me of some kind of weapon that is rumored to be at Bushehr. Or perhaps in transit to Bushehr. He's not sure which. But preparations are in progress."

"And they plan to attack a major city with this weapon?" Randall asked.

"That's what I hear but I don't have any details or know for certain that it's true."

"Let me ask this. If you needed to know what is going on down in Bushehr, could you get your cousin to find out more?"

Reza replied, "That would be extremely difficult because the reactor is very tightly controlled. Lately there has been added security. Besides, my cousin will not want to be involved. If he knew that I had even mentioned him, he likely would not speak to me for a long time. Obviously, he wouldn't report me to authorities since he is the source of my information. But too much attention is a bad thing in this country." Reza shifted back and forth in his seat. Perkins watched him carefully.

We, or rather, they...

PERKINS RETURNED TO HIS OFFICE ABOVE THE OLD clothing store on the northern edge of Tehran. He unlocked the center desk drawer and retrieved an encoding device that looked like a new style e-reader. With a stylus, he quickly scratched a message on the screen, grateful that Walid, his office manager, was out.

He would be able to get this information back to Langley immediately. He tapped a series of short sentences that outlined his earlier conversation. "PHILOSOPHER reports rumor of Govt overthrow plot. Possible nuclear weapon Bushehr. Possible Chinese link. Still checking. Please advise." Message complete, he pressed the "encrypt" button that turned the text into a 1024 bit NSA-encrypted message burst.

He grabbed a backpack from a nearby file cabinet drawer and took the stairs two at a time up to the roof. Once in place, he opened the backpack and pulled out the collapsible satellite dish hidden in a compartment. The dish opened like an umbrella. Usually he had to play with it to get a lock on the signal but this time the green light appeared almost instantly. Before he stood, he pressed the "send" button which transmitted the burst of electronic energy to Orion, the clandestine communications satellite that orbited 22,000 miles above the earth. This satellite in turn relayed the message to the huge dish at the ground station in Beltsville, MD, then on to CIA Headquarters in Langley, Virginia.

He straightened up and waited for a delivery confirmation to appear. Perkins saw the screen only briefly before the bullet entered his left temple and exploded into several fragments. The right side of his head blown away, Perkins fell lifeless to the rooftop. The device tumbled from his hand into a spray of blood and brain tissue. The acknowledgement light flashed green for less than a second, confirming Langley's receipt of his message, before the handheld hit the roof and shattered on contact with the concrete.

Slightly less than a half mile away, the IRGC sniper looked through the scope of his Dragunov SVD-137 rifle and watched Perkins drop behind the low wall to the roof deck. Certain that he had made the shot before the

American could adjust the antenna and communicate with his government, he packed the rifle in a custom foam-lined case and walked quickly down the stairs.

Chapter 6

CIA Headquarters
Langley, Virginia

KENNETH WASHINGTON HURRIED DOWN THE hallway toward the Middle East Division. He knocked on the second door on the right, swiped his badge in the card reader, punched in his PIN, and entered. "Hey, Harry, I have a message from PHILOSOPHER in Tehran that I think you need to see."

Harry looked up. "Well, well, if it isn't the big man from Harvard," he said with a grin. Harry had taken an instant liking to his co-worker when they met on Ken's first day at the Entry on Duty ceremony. A Yale grad, Harry managed to rib Ken as much as time would allow. "You actually found your way here without a map again? This is getting to be a regular thing. Didn't have much hope for you after the EOD." Harry guffawed as usual and pointed to the other man in the room, "Meet Peyton Stone. He's a Green Badge, here to go over some photos with me." Green Badge designation gave Peyton top clearance with 'No Escort Required' rights and allowed him to roam the halls at will. Harry folded his arms and asked, "OK, Mr. Hahvahd, whatcha got?"

Typically Ken was ready with a retort but today he was all business. "Something's going on but we don't know what exactly. The message mentioned government overthrow and nuclear weapons so I thought you'd want to know."

"Well, you got that right," Harry said, suddenly serious. "What's the deal here?"

"The message was vague so I assume more detailed

62

info is coming. Something suspicious at Bushehr, some kind of overthrow plot. We have no other specifics." Ken handed the message to Harry and began to pace in front of his desk, a habit which irritated Harry to no end.

"OK, stand still a minute and let's think about this." Harry drummed the pencil eraser on the edge of his coffee cup. Ken wanted to grab Harry's hand and stop the infernal tapping. But Harry had twenty years' seniority so Ken yielded.

"Do we have any HUMINT on the ground there?" Ken asked.

"The message came from our case officer in a local branch of Intra-Coastal Oil working as an oil specialist. He runs PHILOSOPHER who is tied pretty closely to the Iranian government. He's our only asset there and the rest of the people in the office are simply ICO employees."

The phone on Harry's desk came to life with a distinctive ring tone. "I hate that ring. Makes me feel like I'm on *24* or something. Did you ever watch that show on TV?" Ken shook his head as both Harry and the phone continued. "I expect Jack Bauer to be on the other end every time I answer." Harry reached for the receiver and added, "Or worse, Chloe with a request to move a satellite or something." He scowled as he answered. "Morrison here." Harry sat bolt upright in his chair before he replied, "I'll be right up."

He tossed the phone onto the cradle. "There's some news out of Iran that has the seventh floor's attention. I'm headed up to see the Director of Intelligence. Peyton, come along. We might need your insight since you've spent time over there. Ken, find out what you can from our guy in Teheran."

PEYTON AND HARRY STEPPED OFF THE ELEVATOR

into the massive seventh floor suite, the haven for the Director of Central Intelligence Agency, known as the DCIA, and his many deputies, among them the Director of Intelligence, or DI, and the Director of the National Clandestine Service, formerly called the Deputy Director for Operations.

"Go on in, Mr. Morrison, he's expecting you." A pleasant, professional-looking woman, she sat at one of six desks that lined the outer office. The intimidation factor began as soon as a visitor exited the elevator. All middle-aged women, immaculately dressed in expertly tailored suits or dresses with stylish but appropriate hair, makeup and accessories. Each projected a polished, courteous but somewhat daunting demeanor. As a former Cabinet level advisor to presidents since Truman, the DCIA was entitled to an expansive suite of offices and a large staff. Michael Kopanski, the current DCIA, still had the President's ear and often found himself at the White House for personal briefings even though the cabinet position now belonged to the Director of National Intelligence, or DNI for short. After 9/11, the Office of the DNI was created to better coordinate intelligence activities among the sixteen agencies and countless lesser organizations that collected information in, from and about foreign governments.

Harry rapped on the doorjamb and walked into the inner office.

"Hi, Harry." The DI, George Bettenhause, motioned to a group of wing back chairs near his desk. "Come in and have a seat." One of the chairs was already occupied.

"Harry Morrison, meet Rachael Kleinmann from SCEPTER," A striking woman dressed in a dark brown business suit rose from her chair. Her nearly shoulder length red hair and green eyes hinted of a Celtic heritage, perhaps Irish or Scots.

"SCEPTER?" Harry raised an eyebrow. "That's a new one on me. What exactly is that?"

"Special Combat Equipped Personnel, Tactics, Evaluation and Reconnaissance," Bettenhause explained. "It's a small group that reports directly to the DNI. Teams are made up of CIA, NSA, DIA, FBI, NRO, and NGA." Bettenhause recited the alphabet soup that designated the six primary members of the US Intelligence Community. "Since they report to the DNI, they can draw on Departmental IC agencies: State, Energy, Treasury, Homeland Security and the like and, when they need it, they can get support from the Service agencies over at the Pentagon."

Harry nodded. "And I suppose that the inclusion of all of those domestic agencies gets us around EO 12333. Very handy." An Executive Order from the President of the United States, EO 12333 defines exactly what intelligence agencies can and can't do and prohibits the CIA from conducting operations inside US borders. However, the CIA and the NSA can assist the FBI or Homeland Security both of which have free reign inside the US. Soon after 9/11 President George W. Bush gave the NSA eavesdropping privileges on calls made to America in support of Homeland Security.

Bettenhause ignored the jab and turned to Peyton. "It's been a while since I last saw you. I think it was at the ceremony here right after you and Harry got back from Egypt. Good to see you're doing better."

Peyton smiled thinly and nodded, his reply a perfunctory, "Thanks."

"Oh, excuse me," Harry broke in and turned to Rachel, "this is Peyton Stone. We were working on something together when the call came so I brought him along. Peyton has a bit of time in the Gulf."

They shook hands. Peyton noticed that Rachel's grip was overly firm. Anxious perhaps to be accepted seriously. As she shook his hand, though, she smiled and revealed perfect white teeth. Her brilliant green eyes mirrored a hint of mischief. Rachel Kleinmann was a very sultry package.

"SCEPTER has uncovered some interesting but troubling news," Bettenhause began, "that involves a possible plot to overthrow the government of Iran." The DI stopped and stared at Harry who maintained protracted eye contact with him, unable to breathe.

Harry let the air in his lungs burst forth, finally, as he countered, "That's interesting. We received a similar message from an asset in Teheran just before your call. What is your source?"

Rachel's right eye narrowed slightly for a second as she looked at Harry. She answered, "A very reliable one. We have irrefutable evidence that some within the government of the Islamic Republic of Iran will attempt to overthrow the government and possibly use the event to threaten neighboring countries in the Gulf."

Harry turned to Rachel. "Tell me about this 'irrefutable evidence'." Harry crooked his fingers into air quotation marks and then placed his hands on his hips. "What is it and how did you come by it?"

"We have a document obtained directly from the Iranians that references the operation. As to how we came by it," one corner of her mouth turned up, "well, you know better than to ask that. Sources and methods."

"Wait a minute. Aren't we on the same side?" Harry looked at Bettenhause who sat quietly.

"Do you have a second source confirmation?" Harry continued.

"We're working that," Rachel replied, "but wouldn't your asset be confirmation? I think it's enough to confirm that the threat is credible."

"I suppose that makes sense." Harry said.

Rachel replied firmly, "If this didn't look serious, I wouldn't have come here and put myself on the line. The fact that you've gotten similar info at the same time is no coincidence."

Harry sat back in his chair. He rubbed his chin impatiently and stared at the floor. "Ok, sorry. Old habits. I appreciate, we appreciate, your heads-up."

Rachel looked at him, her lips pursed into a thin line that slowly turned into a tight smile. She sighed a bit too loudly acutely aware that she was the only woman in the room.

Harry went on. "In the grand scheme of things this makes no sense. We're steps away from signing a peace accord with Iran. Why would they work so hard on a treaty and let this happen? Is there any evidence of official involvement?" Harry paused for a moment. "Or if this is a subversive operation. Shouldn't we take it to the Iranian government?"

"We can't take it to the Iranians," Rachel said, "because they'd want to know how we acquired the information. We can't tell them. On top of that, we don't know who in the government might be involved so we don't know who not to tell."

"Yeah, our asset is part of a business and runs a source in the legislature. If we go to the government we'd burn both of them. After all it could be a government action. We don't really know."

Bettenhause steepled his fingers and bounced his index fingers together while he thought. "It doesn't make a lot of sense. The US and Iran have worked for over two years to negotiate the minute details of export agreements, lift embargoes, and phase in trade with other countries. This has been a rough row to hoe. What could they hope to get out of it?"

"Yeah," Harry agreed, "maybe they want to hit Israel."

Bettenhause shifted in his chair. "If they did, we'd respond. And more than the treaty would be at risk at that point. We could easily lay waste to their country. Why would they risk that?"

"There is another possibility." All heads turned toward Rachel who paused for several seconds as she turned something over in her mind. She chose her words slowly, carefully while she tested her idea. "Perhaps this plan isn't a government action but an individual or group acting outside the box?"

"But if it's a rogue individual, how would they get nuclear assets?" Bettenhause held up one hand, then pressed a button on his desk phone. Before his finger left the button a voice said, "Yes, sir?"

"Get me whoever the duty officer at NSTIC is right now. Tell him it's urgent." The National Strategic Threat Information Center, or "en-stick" at Kirtland Air Force Base tracks every one of the thousands of nuclear weapons and weapon component parts in the US inventory and coordinates similar information with foreign governments.

Bettenhause, his hands folded on his desk, looked at Peyton and started to speak when the phone beeped and the 'yes-sir' voice said, "The NSTIC commander is holding, sir."

He pressed the speaker phone button and said, "Thanks for the quick response, Colonel. I have you on speaker with three colleagues from the IC."

"It's not every day I get a call from a Director of the CIA. What can I do for you?"

Bettenhause ignored the mistaken promotion. "We got some intel that a weapon may be on the loose.

Possibly in the Middle East. Anything you can tell me?"

A short silence, then the colonel replied, "Nope. If it were ours, I'd know immediately. We haven't had any reports from OCONUS but that doesn't necessarily mean anything." Reports from OCONUS, or Outside the CONtinental US, were often withheld or delayed to prevent embarrassment over bureaucratic mistakes by other governments when nothing was actually wrong. Much as a security monitoring company calls a homeowner to determine that an alarm is real before contacting the police. No point getting everyone stirred up over a false alarm.

"Well, if anything does come in, put me on the reporting list."

"You got it, sir."

"Thanks, Colonel. Have a good one." By the time the colonel said, "You, too," Bettenhause had already hung up.

Harry spoke. "Just before you called me, Director, I received word that an asset in Iran sent a message about some activity at Bushehr, connected somehow to this government overthrow activity. His source mentioned a nuclear weapon and possible Chinese involvement. I don't believe in coincidence. I'd wager that this is connected to what Rachel has."

"The Chinese? First I've heard of that, what else do we know?" the Director asked bluntly.

Harry frequently forgot that not everyone knew the information stored in his head. "One of our agents who has been in Iran for a number of years has befriended, or at least become a tea-drinking buddy, with a member of the Iranian Majlis, code name PHILOSOPHER. The two have talked for some time now about nothing much in particular. Suddenly PHILOSOPHER came to him with the news of a weapon at Bushehr and a plot to overthrow the government."

"Harry," Bettenhause said, "I want you to look into this further. If there's something to it, I need to brief the White House."

"Yes, sir." Harry replied, "We have to find out what is going on at Bushehr. I'll get our guy in Tehran to push PHILOSOPHER to talk more. He's fairly certain though that PHILOSOPHER doesn't have the information we need."

"Should we bring in someone from the outside?" the Director wondered out loud.

"As you know, Peyton here is one of our nonofficial assets. He works under contract to the Special Activities Division." Harry replied. "I can get with SAD and get him under contract. He can, at the very least, help us think it through."

Bettenhause hesitated. "Are you sure you're up to it, Peyton? When you left after the last mission, we had to do a lot of damage control."

Peyton crossed his arms and looked at the floor. "Look, I lost my wife while I was away on a contract for you guys. I may have been a little distraught," he struggled to tamp down the sarcasm, "but that was two years ago."

"Anyway, you've assumed a lot. I haven't said that I'm even remotely interested in contract work. My best friend was murdered in Shanghai yesterday and I need to get to the bottom of that."

"I'm sorry to hear that," Bettenhause said. "Anything we can do?"

Peyton considered rolling over on Digby while he had the ear of the man four levels above the field bureaucrat. But he quickly decided that this tack would be both futile and petty. Besides, it may cut off some much needed help down the road. He answered, "Not at the moment but I really appreciate your offer. I need to stay on it so I'm going to have to pass on this right now."

"That's for you two to work out." Bettenhause nodded toward Harry.

Bettenhause shifted his attention to Harry. "Let's get on this. If you need this guy and can talk him into it, get him on board. We'll need to activate his contract so prepare a notice to proceed over my signature. I'll notify SAD. You guys figure out the details." He turned toward Peyton. "If you come back on board, Stone, I don't want to have to follow you around with paperwork to cover up your behavior. I'll cut you loose in a heartbeat and I don't care where you are at the time."

Peyton's response was cut off by a soft knock at the door and one of the women entered slowly. "I've just received some news from NCS next door. It's not good." The four stared at her. "We've lost an asset in Tehran."

"Lost an asset? What do you mean?" Bettenhause took off his glasses and laid them on his desk.

"Randall Perkins was shot on the roof of the office. He died instantly."

"Oh, my God!" Bettenhause spoke in a quiet intense voice. "Do we know who did it?"

"The Chief of Station went over from the embassy but the body had already been removed by the police. They've turned it over but the ME in Teheran did nothing and we can't do a thorough exam until the body gets back here. The ME cleaned up the body which removed the evidence but the COS said it looked like a high powered rifle shot."

"Has NCS notified his family?"

"They are making the notification through the cover company. His death will be positioned as a hunting accident."

"Geez!" Harry said, half under his breath. "Peyton, Randy and I worked on half a dozen projects together. We saved each other's butts more than once. How did it happen? Who would do this?"

"He was sending a message from the roof of his office. All indications point to a sniper. High power, large caliber. "

The irony that this perfectly dressed and coiffed woman who delivered a matter of fact report on the shooting death of an agent was not lost on Stone. She could just as easily have been seated next to him at Thanksgiving dinner. *How had this all become so easy?*

"There's more," she added. "The satellite gear was set up and a message had just been transmitted. The antenna was still there but we don't know what happened to the rest of gear. Assumption is the police have it but they deny it. More likely MOIS has it." MOIS is the Iranian Ministry of Intelligence and Security. This organization not only is the keeper of state secrets but also the chief spy agency and exporter of terrorism.

"Crap. This has our fingerprints all over it. Any official reaction yet?"

"Nothing yet," she said. "I'll let you know the instant I hear anything, sir." The woman backed out and closed the door.

Harry jerked his head up. "Shit! Randy ran PHILOSOPHER. If he's been burned, then who else? We need to get assets out of there. I feel sorry for whoever PHILOSOPHER is because he's likely next."

Bettenhause turned to Harry, "Nothing we can do for him. We'll have to wait for an official Iranian reaction to all of this but I'd better get the DNI briefed so he can tell the White House." His voice rose.

"Meanwhile get Stone's paperwork done immediately. And get to the bottom of this mess. The PHILOSOPHER communication confirms Rachel's intel. This is no coincidence."

The DI picked up some papers and began to straighten his desk. Stone spoke up. "I believe I mentioned that I'm not interested in contract work at the moment. I have a murder to investigate."

Harry grabbed his elbow and started toward the door. "We'll work it out. Let's get to it, Peyton. We'll keep you in the loop, George." Harry rushed Stone toward the hall.

"Harry," Bettenhause called, "stay a moment longer. I have a different subject to run by you."

Harry stopped in mid-stride, reached out and caught himself with his right hand on the door jamb. "I'll be down in a minute, guys."

Harry watched as Stone and Rachel continued through the outer office and down the hall to the elevator. He turned and faced Bettenhause. "You're worried about Peyton?"

"Close the door."

"Come on, George. We've been through this. He's fine now."

"Harry, I asked you to come up here and you brought him with you. That was a bit presumptuous. I'm not confident he can keep his head on straight."

"Ok, I should have asked before I brought him up. My bad. Sorry. But he's level even after the death of his business partner..." Harry stopped himself too late and watched Bettenhause's right eyebrow shoot up. "George, we need him."

"You may think you need him but this is a really delicate situation here. I don't deny that he has been valuable over the years but he hasn't been tested since he went a bit berserk after the last mission. This situation seems bad enough already. I don't need some contract asset going off the deep end and winding up on the front page of the *Washington Post*. Especially if this is not as bad as we think it is."

Harry's shoulders drooped for a moment and then he straightened and took a step toward the desk. "George, I can keep him focused. Time has passed. The first thing to do is to get him to agree to work with us. I only hope we can get that done."

Bettenhause breathed out heavily through his nose. "Ok. But you just keep him close. I'm holding you accountable and I don't care that you're one of the best. I want this operation to be invisible."

Harry nodded and took two steps backward before turning to leave. "No worries, George. I'll keep a leash on him."

"It's your ass, Harry." Bettenhause said without looking up from the memo he had just started to read.

HARRY DIDN'T SLOW AS HE WALKED AROUND HIS desk and sat down. "I'll finish your Notice to Proceed post-haste and get you read in. And I'll set up a meeting this evening with Rachel so we can get started. Your paperwork will be ready in a couple of hours. I'll get it to your Contracts Officer for signature on the formal NTP. This will be a sit-on-his-desk-until-he-signs-it situation so it should be completed by COB today. Get some clothes together and be ready to move."

"Wait, wait, wait. Hold on there partner." Stone waved his hands at Harry. "I've just gotten back from project meetings in China and I can't take off again. I need to spend a little time at home to get some things done, not the least of which is to find the Chinese guy who took a shot at me and probably killed Xu."

74

"I appreciate that, Peyton, but this is huge. You heard the intel dump up there. There is a strong possibility that the Iranians plan to launch a nuclear attack. They've killed Randy and have his satcom gear. All of this a couple of weeks before our two countries are going to sign a major treaty." Harry shook his head. "This is world-shaking. We have to get to the bottom and we have what, a week at most, and almost no information?"

"Harry, I've got to find out what happened to Xu. I need to go back to Shanghai and stay on top of the cops. This is a matter of priorities. You got hundreds of people who can do this. For Xu, it's just me."

Harry stood and stretched to his full height. "This is top priority and it's classified TS/SCI/HALO ARC. Besides, Digby has already done his over-reaction thing with the Embassy in Beijing. The Ambassador has declared you PNG, Persona Non-Grata. You won't get a visa to get back into China. They'll stop you at immigration and send you back. By then you'll have wasted three days which is half the time we have to sort out this Iranian thing. You'll be lucky to keep your contract with the airport," Harry took a breath and finished, "but I doubt they'll go that far."

Stone's jaw muscles tightened as his world turned upside down once again.

"So are you in? We really need you. Your country needs you. We need to figure this out for Randy."

Stone let out a compressed breath that whistled through his tight lips. "Hell, Harry. Randy saved us both in Lebanon and again in Somalia. But we never would have lived long enough for that if it hadn't been for Xu. I can't just drop this. I owe Xu first. Besides Digby is on my list."

"Forget Digby. I'm searching for your shooter

through OTA. We'll figure that one out ourselves. Go home and do what you need to do. I'll call you for the read-in and we'll connect with the team later today."

Peyton relented. "Ok, I could really use a shower. But I won't sign up for this Iranian thing until I know what's going on in China."

STONE EXITED THE GREENWAY AT BELMONT RIDGE Road. A black Chrysler 300 followed. The same car had tailed him since he left Langley. Peyton wound through the new housing developments toward his home in River Creek, a gated community on the outskirts of Leesburg, Virginia. When he bought the place on the golf course, he was one of a handful of people who had moved into the Leesburg area. Now the area was flooded with new families and traffic had become unbearable. Even Belmont Ridge Road, once a lovely track that wound through the forest, had become a four-lane parkway as each vinyl-sided beige tract development added a wide entry for the throngs of Federal workers and contractors who had migrated into the region.

Stone's mind wandered back to a time two years ago when he had taken this same exit, driven to his house, and found a police cruiser parked in the driveway. His thoughts then turned to Xu, who now lay in a morgue half a world away. The distant past merged with the present as the worst memory of his life surfaced. He shook it off. Nothing could be done to change the past. He focused on the sense of duty born early in life, taught to him by his father. He knew that his special skills were innate, not the result of practice or desire. When called upon, Peyton felt obligated to respond. Today, more than ever, Peyton understood that he had no choice. He – and Harry – owed Randy and Xu. Both of these current crises were personal. The question now was to whom did he owe more?

As Peyton approached the stone quarry on his left, he checked his rear-view mirror. The Chrysler was still there. Not unlikely on this two-lane section where the road wound around the eastern edge of the quarry. The car gained on him too quickly. He saw the Chrysler pull into the oncoming traffic lane to pass him. As the car pulled alongside, an Asian man leveled a pistol at him. Hitting the brakes hard, Peyton felt the car lurch and saw the muzzle flash. The shot went wide across the front of the car and was lost in the houses on the right side of the road.

He knew he couldn't get trapped behind the assailant's car so he instinctively stepped on the accelerator. The other car accelerated next to him. Another shot. *Where did it go?* No matter. The man was behind him now. The black car drew closer. Peyton felt the Chevelle skid as the man steered into his left rear panel in an attempt to start a PIT maneuver. The back end of the car slid to the right. Stone steered into the skid and expertly applied just enough throttle. The weight shifted to the back. No wheel spin. The oversteer corrected itself. He accelerated enough to pull away from the killer momentarily. Then he thought about the damage to the left rear of his Chevelle.

Stone tapped the brakes as he entered a sharp right hand curve. He felt the body roll shift the weight to the front left tire and accelerated enough to counteract it. When he hit the apex of the turn and glanced at the speedometer, he downshifted and whipped the 500 horses one more time. Ninety miles per hour and still the Chrysler was gaining. The Asian man darted into the oncoming lane. Peyton saw his eyes staring at the Chevelle's rear fender. A left curve in the road coming up. Peyton let the car drift to the right. He put half a wheel on the white edge stripe. Ready to turn left. Right heel on the brake, right toe on the gas. Left foot, clutch NOW! Down shift. Go left. Keep the left front outside the double yellow. Accelerate. Once they were through the next two curves, the road straightened out. Then Peyton's Chevelle would simply outrun him. He checked the side mirror. Still there, focused on Stone's rear fender. Closer, ever closer. Peyton braced himself for what was about to happen. Suddenly he saw a flash of red to his left. The rear of the car stayed straight. He looked in his rearview mirror again. The Chrysler was gone. A cloud of dust spread across the road where a big red gravel hauler had just pulled out of the driveway to the quarry. The truck had jack-knifed across the pavement. A black car was wedged firmly under the trailer just behind the cab. Stone saw the driver of the truck crawl down from the cab. Adrenaline surged through as he rounded another curve, gunned the powerful engine and headed for home.

STONE PULLED INTO HIS GARAGE AND HIT THE CLOSE button seconds before he turned the engine off, a habit acquired when he designed security systems in US Embassies abroad. As the door made contact with the garage floor, a surge of relief exorcised the anxiety of exposure. His first rule of survival: minimize the time that the target is vulnerable, especially when you're the target.

Peyton sat for a minute and took a couple of deep breaths to calm himself. He got out of his car and looked at the rear of his Chevelle. Scratches and bent metal. *What the hell is going on? Should I call the police? No, they'll investigate the truck accident but I wasn't part of that. I can figure this out.*

He opened the mudroom door and heard paws click impatiently against wood, the sound of his golden retriever, Bandito, racing down the stairs. Long hair flew sideways when the dog rounded the corner of the kitchen island at full speed. He slid to a stop in front of Stone who knelt down and buried his face in the dog's soft, warm fur. After a hug and a few pats, he stood up. "Bandito! How you doin', boy? Was Mrs. B good to you while I was gone?"

Mrs. Beeton lived two doors down. She checked on Bandito, let him out for runs in the fenced back yard, brought in the mail and did a little light housework when Stone traveled. In exchange, he did odd jobs for "Mrs. B" who lived alone. They teased each other about moving in together to save rent. Peyton would wink and say to Mrs. B, who was seventy, "I don't know if I could handle you." She'd smile and reply, "Well, if you die, you die." The irony of the joke was not wasted on either.

Bandito, on the other hand, was a perfect roommate: boundless unconditional love on four legs. The retriever bounced up and down the stairs as Stone carried his bag up to his bedroom. "You want to go out?" The large dog was off like a rocket. Stone heard him slide across the kitchen, then stop abruptly as his rear hit the back door with a gentle thump. Almost instantly Peyton heard a familiar clickety-clickety-click as Bandito struggled to get traction on the porcelain tile. The dog reversed direction and backtracked to check on his master. The two met at the bottom of the stairs and crossed the foyer and kitchen together. Bandito turned in frantic circles while Peyton unlocked the back door. As soon as a crack appeared, the dog wiggled through and raced down the back steps, then headed to the side yard, sniffing as he ran.

Peyton went upstairs and turned on the shower. He let the water heat up while he stripped. After nearly 35 hours, the warm water felt incredibly good. He rinsed, then turned the temperature higher still. The hot water cascaded down his aching shoulders and back. Finally refreshed, he reached for a towel. He could hear whines and scratches at the back door. Bandito was ready to rejoin his master.

Peyton threw on a robe and took the steps two at a time. "Coming, big guy. Calm down." As he walked across the kitchen, his cell phone rang.

Harry's voice announced, "We're set for dinner at Galileo's in DC. Six o'clock. Don't be late." He hung up before Stone could respond.

Peyton pressed the end button, set the phone on the island and let Bandito in. He noticed the flashing red light on the wall phone so he checked his messages. The first of three was from his son Bryan in San Diego. He recalled an earlier conversation with his son and thought of their relationship. Something always got in the way.

The second message was a click and a hang-up. Peyton checked the time-stamp: just before he got home. No caller ID was recorded. *Must've been a wrong number.* The third call came while he was in the shower, same as the second one. Two wrong number hang-ups in a row? Nah, probably a telemarketer. He dismissed it from his mind when he saw the time.

He dressed quickly, patted Bandito on the head and vigorously ruffled the thick fur under his neck. The retriever immediately started to romp around the room. "I'll be back in a few hours, fella. You just chill out and we'll go for a run later." The phone rang. He picked it up and heard the click of the receiver hang-up on the other end. *Okay, that's three wrong numbers in a row. What's going on?*

He looked down at the big dog that now spun in circles like a puppy. "Be back sooner this time, Bandito, I promise." Peyton bent over, scratched the Retriever's neck once more, and received the usual lick across the mouth. The dog cocked his head to one side as he watched his master enter the garage, then listened for the door to open. This was his sign: he raced to the window and rested his front paws on the sill as he watched the car back out of the driveway. His tail wagged with such force that his head turned from side to side. Peyton smiled and waved, then turned toward River Creek Parkway. Just past the Leesburg town limit, he exited onto the bypass to head back to the Greenway. Much to his surprise, he realized that he looked forward to a business dinner.

Chapter 7

Galileo's Restaurant
Washington, DC

PEYTON LOVED THIS RESTAURANT AND VISITED AS
often as possible. Once or twice a year the owner, who
was also the head chef, put on an excellent show at a
winery near Barboursville, Virginia, an hour and a half
south of Leesburg. He prepared a seven-course meal,
and the winery's vintner personally selected wine to
complement each dish. Peyton had been twice and
thoroughly enjoyed the entire experience. Once, he
entered the winery's grape-stomping contest.
Competitive as ever, he got carried away and slipped.
When his feet shot out from under him and he landed
hard, waist-deep in a vat of half-smashed grapes,
Stephanie's laughter echoed across the room. The
memory from the dim, distant past lingered as he parked
the car.

Harry and Rachel were already seated. Stone shook
hands with Harry and turned to Rachel. As he took her
hand to shake it, she smiled. For a fleeting moment, he
was aware of a stirring that had been long-absent. "Nice
to see you again," he said in a polite but formal tone that
belied his feelings.

"Good evening," Rachel replied. He shook her
hand a little too long as he noticed how green her eyes
were. Her nose, straight and narrow, suggested
Mediterranean, perhaps Roman, influence in her
ancestry. She had the slightest overbite which gave her
face an interesting shape. Brilliant red hair hung in a
sophisticated straight bob that fell almost to her

shoulders. The highlights complemented her smooth, tanned skin, unusual for a redhead. He watched as she picked up her menu and tried to ignore his stare. *Far too beautiful,* he thought, *to be in this business. She won't last five minutes if the going gets tough.*

Stone opened his menu and looked around the table. "All the dishes here are excellent. Chef Roberto is a genius. He combines flavors in ways you can't imagine. One evening, he prepared a risotto with squid ink. Everyone who tried it was amazed."

Rachel's eyes glanced at Stone over the top of her menu, "So you are not a steak and potato guy?" She smiled as she spoke. His interest already aroused, he felt his face grow warm. He lifted the menu slightly higher until only his eyebrows were visible. He laughed and replied, "No, I'm adventurous." Rachel noticed his eyebrows rise slightly and she smiled.

"Speaking of adventures," Harry said, "I have a contract for you."

Peyton closed his menu and put it carefully on the table. "I'm happy to charge you for tonight's brainstorming session but I don't plan to sign up for anything beyond that."

At that moment the waiter arrived and took their order. When he left, Peyton turned to Rachel. "How did you get into the business?"

Rachel looked around the restaurant at the other diners for a minute. She rested one forearm on the table and leaned forward as she turned toward Peyton. "I have a special talent with firearms." She smiled.

Peyton stared for a second as her words registered. With a graceful arc of her hand, she swept a strand of hair behind her ear. Rachel Kleinmann was a study in contradictions: a sharpshooter in emerald silk and pearls.

"I read your dossier and noticed that you also have a

talent. Yours, however, is with long guns while mine is with hand guns. I was national pistol champion two years in a row." She leaned back in her chair and sipped her water, then added, "Before my current job, I worked in Secret Service."

Peyton made a quick head nod. "Impressive. Have you ever used your weapon in the line of duty?"

"Have I ever shot anyone, you mean? No, but I've run the MOUT at Ft. Benning and at Twenty-Nine Palms over a dozen times each with perfect scores." The MOUT, or Military Operations in Urban Terrain, is a training area similar to a small town. Constructed almost like a theme park, the realistic simulation creates an environment where trainees are subjected to situations that they would likely face in the real world. Live actors portray bad guys, terrorists, families and business people. Trainees shoot laser weapons that look, sound and feel like the real thing. Actors fitted with movie blood effects make a hit look real. The exercise gives a trainee the closest thing possible to a real live battle environment.

Rachel continued. "I've also done six night MOUTs because fighting in the dark is exponentially more difficult."

Peyton looked at her for a moment and tried to picture this beautiful creature in battle dress and face paint. "It's different when the person is live and you put your sights on him," he looked into her eyes, then said, "and watch him go down."

"Not any different than training with simmunition." Her head was up now, her back straight, her hands folded on the table.

"I didn't mean anything by that," Peyton said quickly. "It's just different than, what was it? simmunition?"

"Yeah, simmunition. Plastic 9mm bullets that hurt like hell and when you're hit with them you go down whether you want to or not."

"Got it." Peyton let the subject drop. Rachel was now defensive and he had no desire to discuss killing. Especially not in a restaurant. In Washington, DC, he never knew who was listening but he knew that the list usually included everyone.

Satiated, the group returned to Langley where they met inside a conference room and finally got down to business. Harry pushed a folder across the table to Stone who slowly read the statement of work, his contract for this task. Basically the same as always, the directive outlined the scope of responsibility: on-call consultant to assist and support the Director with ongoing studies and contractor to provide services at the discretion of the Director. Harry pointed to the paper below the contract. "Need your signature in the usual spot on the SF Form 33 and then I'll send it to the Contracts Officer over in SAD."

Stone didn't look at the form. He pushed the folder back to Harry. "Remember I told you about that guy who tried to kill me in Shanghai?"

"Yeah."

"Well, a guy tried to put a bullet in me on the way home today. Right on Belmont Ridge Road. I got lucky. He tangled with a gravel truck and the truck won."

Harry's head jerked up. "Why didn't you tell me sooner?"

Peyton spread his palms. "You hung up too fast when you called me and I didn't want to get into it in the restaurant."

"Any idea who it was?"

"Nope, but I managed to get a plate number when

we tangled. Can you have someone run it?" Stone handed a scrap of paper to Harry who picked up the phone, pushed five digits, relayed the number, and waited.

After a moment, he replaced the receiver. "It's a rental registered to Avis. Our guy is looking into who rented it but we're treading on thin ice here. Domestic collection has to be done by FBI. I won't be able to go much farther."

"I've got a contact there if I need the Feebies. Meanwhile I'll keep my gun close."

"Good idea." Harry opened another folder that he'd brought with him. "I got an ID on the shooter in Shanghai. He's one Guong Fang, a construction business owner." Peyton blinked when he heard the name. Harry looked at him and said, "More interestingly, he has a hobby. He deals arms on the international market and has warrants in a half dozen countries. He's seldom seen outside China or central Asia so we haven't been able to touch him. I don't know how that idiot Digby let him slip right out of the Consulate." Peyton, grateful for the information, decided not to mention his friend's earlier defense of the officious prick. Harry closed the folder. "Anyway, our gun-running assassin hasn't been back to his office since he left the Consulate. We don't know why but we have some folks keeping an eye out."

"I've never seen Fang before but, as part of our design-build approach, Xu pitched our project to him and several other contractors." Stone thought for a minute. "Do you think there's a connection?"

Harry's brow furrowed. "This doesn't make sense. Xu is murdered. Fang tries to shoot you. People possibly tied to Fang have now tried to kill you here at home. How does all of that tie together exactly? Did Xu get dirt on Fang? If he did, was it arms or construction?"

"What tie would Xu have to arms? Unless he saw or heard something when he was there."

Harry shuffled the papers in his folder.

Stone sat up straight. "Wait a minute. The voice mail from Xu. That was only a couple of hours after Xu met with Fang. I wonder what he needed to tell me."

"Beats me, Peyton. That's one thing we'll probably never know. Right now let's set that aside for a moment and put our heads together on this Iranian thing, okay? Then we'll see what help I can give you on Xu's murder. Hopefully we can make the pieces fall into place."

Peyton looked down at the table, then up at Harry. He spoke with a resigned air. "Agreed."

Harry turned back to the table. "Rachel, can you give us an overview of what you know? Before you start, I think we need to declare the classification level of this meeting at TS/SCI/HALO ARC so that we can discuss information that might be connected to sources and methods. We need to get everything out in the open so we can come up with the best approach. This is too important for any of us to hold back." The two men turned toward Rachel.

She gave them a short version of the events at the Iranian Embassy in Pakistan which included facts about the explosion that killed the Iranian Ambassador.

"Alright," Harry replied, "my turn." He looked at Rachel and Peyton in turn and leaned over, his palms flat on the table in front of him. "You heard earlier that we've developed a source, code-named PHILOSOPHER. He is an Iranian citizen, a member of the Majlis. You also heard the news about Randy Perkins being killed." Harry went on to explain how Perkins and Reza had gotten together and what types of information had been exchanged between the two men over the course of a year.

Rachel sat forward in her chair. "What PHILOSOPHER told Perkins in their last meeting could be related to what we found in the Ambassador's bedroom safe."

Stone did a slight double take. "You didn't say it was in his bedroom. What were you doing in the Ambassador's bedroom?" His tone made him cringe inside. Get a grip. This is business. He sat up straighter and picked up a pen as a distraction.

Rachel looked at him with a coy smile and answered, "Is that important or even relevant?"

Stone went red from the neck up. "Well, of course not. I was just curious."

"My team and I broke into the Ambassador's residence and cleaned out his safe. Except for jewelry and personal valuables. That would be robbery, not intelligence gathering." She smiled and her green eyes sparkled. "In the safe, we found a letter that referred to a possible overthrow of the Iranian government."

"There were no details of the plot?" Peyton asked. "This scenario could unfold in any number of ways."

"Well, that's the unfortunate part. We retrieved what appears to be the cover page of a longer letter. It refers to the overthrow of the government of Iran but doesn't give any details. This was in the Ambassador's personal safe. The implication is that the Ambassador didn't trust his own SCIF. Maybe he had reason to suspect prying eyes or perhaps he was just paranoid. Unfortunately that trail died when the ambassador and his family were killed in a truck bomb attack."

"Yeah, it's unfortunate that we don't have a way to find out more. What else do we know?" Harry asked.

Rachel continued, "The fact that the US and Iran have nearly concluded a peace treaty is significant. The long process is in the final stages and should be signed in the next several weeks. Iran will get sanctions lifted with US support in the United Nations. They will also get financial support. In exchange, they'll provide complete visibility into their nuclear program and officially denounce terrorism. Specifically they will aggressively prosecute suspected terrorists within their borders and stop supporting terrorism abroad. Iran will have to disband the IRGC, which we've designated as a terrorist organization. This is a bit of a lopsided deal since the IRGC consists of approximately a hundred thousand troops. But they'll probably go to the regular military, and so will the problems that the rest of the world has had with them."

Stone went to an electronic white board in the corner and began to write.

"We think, or at least suspect, that a weapon of some sort is at Bushehr, or will be." He wrote *nuclear weapon* on the board.

"Second, we know that an Iranian person or persons may be planning a nuclear attack of some kind. Third, we know that PHILOSOPHER, a member of the Iranian legislature, has mixed feelings about this. He might want to work with us. But his contact, Randy Perkins, was killed. Coincidence? Probably not. What else?"

Rachel spoke up. "The Iranian Ambassador was killed. Could be connected."

Peyton added it to the list. "But is it connected in some way to Randy's death?"

"Then we have the attempts on your life," Harry added. "How does that tie into this?"

Stone wrote this on the board. "That has crossed my mind more than once since we found out that the Chinese are involved and Fang is also an arms dealer. What else?"

"Precious little else at the moment," Rachel observed. "We need to look for threads to put this together."

"Ok," Stone said, "Here's one scenario. Fang sells a nuke to the Iranians...maybe to the government, maybe to some splinter group in the military. Let's assume that it's the government. What motivation does the government have for doing this, given that we're close to a peace deal that recognizes Palestine, lifts sanctions, and garners global respect for Iran. I can't see any benefit in the government derailing the plan at this point, no matter how untrustworthy they are."

"Well, we have an ambassador involved so it looks like a government-sponsored operation. But what if it's not? Could these two guys have been plotting this outside of official channels?"

"The Ambassador may have been solicited but we don't know that he was involved." Rachel said. "There's the reference to 'right-minded people' in the letter which points to a splinter group. The size of the group depends on how they plan to execute the attack and the scope of their expectations. The fact that it's pointed out to the Ambassador implies that he didn't know about it before he got the letter.

"What if a group disagrees with the peace process and wants to derail it?" Rachel went on. "Wouldn't that be a more likely scenario? I think that's the most probable premise and should be our working thesis." Harry and Peyton nodded in agreement.

"We need a plan." Harry switched to results mode. "And we need to get it to the Director in the morning for approval. We don't have a lot of time, so let's get to it."

Stone checked the white board's list of bulleted discussion points. Then he spoke. "We need to know more about what is going on at Bushehr. We need an asset on the ground there to look for evidence of a device or other suspicious activity. Agreed?" Heads nodded and Stone added another bullet point.

"That will take care of what and where but I think equally important is who and why," Harry said.

"I have a feeling that the why will become clearer once we figure out who. We have the now-deceased ambassador and someone who knew him well enough to solicit his involvement," Rachel said. "Unless he was already involved and this was just a routine correspondence." She considered this possibility briefly, then added, "Personally, I don't think so. My gut says that the wording indicates that the ambassador had just found out about the plot."

"So the mystery is who's on the other end of the letter," Harry thought out loud. "You're on target that the writer knew the Ambassador well enough to risk this confidence. I also agree that the tone of the letter implies the sender is announcing the scheme to the ambassador. So what else can we surmise about who?"

"An associate of the ambassador?"

Rachel suddenly sat straight and flattened both hands on the table as she asked, "What about a relative? What do we know about the ambassador's family?"

"Good point." Harry added, "I'll get Ken on it when he gets here in the morning."

"Ok," Rachel continued, "we can infer from the document's language that the writer needs logistical help from Pakistan. This indicates that the weapon will either originate in Pakistan or transit Pakistan, a supposition that favors an outside, rather than inside, source of the device."

"Excellent point," Harry said, impressed, "We need to consider collaboration with another country."

"Or a collaboration between two rogues, such as the

writer of the letter and someone like Kahn," Rachel added. Abdul Qadeer Kahn headed the Pakistani nuclear program until 2004, when he was caught selling nuclear secrets, and possibly nuclear technology, to Iran, Libya, North Korea and an, as yet unnamed, fourth country. He was placed under house arrest in his villa on Hillside Road between Islamabad and the Margalla Hills.

"Let's not forget Fang." Stone added the name to the growing list. With no space to continue writing, he pressed a button at the bottom of the board and a printout of the information appeared in a tray below the white board. Peyton erased the now-documented notes and waited for the discussion to continue.

"Any more ideas?" Rachel asked.

"I think the next thing to do is get in there and look around,"

Harry said. "I have an idea about how we do that."

Heads turned as one toward Stone. "Hold on," he said, "I'm not signed up for any of this. I've agreed only to help you think this through. On," he paused for emphasis, "I might add, my own time." He turned and wrote a new bullet on the clean board: *Infiltration*.

FATIGUE SETTLED LIKE A POTOMAC FOG OVER Peyton as he drove home. The days since Xu's murder were a blur. As he entered the gate to River Creek and turned down his street, the scene seemed surreal. He needed rest. Thank God he was almost home. Several seconds passed before the street's unnatural darkness fully registered. The streetlight was out as were the carriage lights on several of the houses. A red and white Suburban that belonged to the Loudoun County Fire Marshall was parked at his corner behind a fire truck. He strained to see his house in the thick gloom. Slender wraith-like shapes rose irregularly from the ground. As he grew closer, these morphed into the charred remnants of timbers that had once framed his house. He sped up, then braked to a stop at the curb and bolted from the car. His mouth agape, his breathing ragged, he crossed his lawn to the smoldering ruins. A man in uniform walked quickly over to him. "Excuse me, you shouldn't be here. Can I help you?" He moved between Stone and the rubble and stood with his feet apart, hands propped on his hips.

Peyton stopped but continued to stare at the scorched remains of what had been his home. "I'm Peyton Stone. This is my house." He added after a moment's hesitation, "At least, this was my house. What happened?" He shook his head in disbelief his voice louder. "How did this happen?"

The man dropped his hands to his side and looked at Stone with sad eyes that were all too accustomed to delivering bad news.

"You got some ID?" Peyton reached for his wallet and handed the Fire Marshall his driver's license.

He glanced at the photo and said. "Some neighbors said they heard an explosion, then the house was engulfed in flames. At first, we suspected a gas leak, but Virginia Gas says their monitoring equipment shows no fluctuations to indicate a leak. We've found traces of an accelerant on the back side of the house." He looked at Peyton and added, "We suspect arson now."

"Arson?" Peyton was stunned.

"Do you know anyone who has a grudge or an axe to grind with you?"

Stone thought about the Asian man and the two attempts on his life in the last two days but decided to let the CIA follow those threads. Perhaps the fire investigators would discover clues independently. "No, I have no idea who might do this but I'll certainly cooperate."

He held onto his mouth with his right hand as though it were the only way he could keep his jaw closed. Then it hit him. Bandito. "I have a dog. Any sign of him? I mean, did you find ...?" He stopped in mid-question.

The marshal glanced quickly at the ground, which told Stone everything. "I'm sorry but we did find animal remains, probably a large dog like a retriever or shepherd. I'm really sorry."

Stone stood for a second staring at the Fire Marshal, then turned to look at the black pile of smoldering, wet charcoal. He tried to speak but couldn't. The pit of his stomach whirled as his arms tensed at his sides. His hands balled into fists. His chest felt as if it were in a vise. The fury that he struggled to control grew into a maelstrom of rage as he envisioned the people responsible: Guong Fang, an Iranian jihadist, an Asian arms dealer. All had to be tied together somehow. But how? And why this? Tears filled his eyes and spilled onto his face as he stared at the ruins and recalled Bandito at the window.

Now it had gotten personal. He lowered his head and rubbed the back of his neck. In the thick of the foul, acrid smoke, he was numb to all but one certainty: he would go to the ends of the earth to find the bastards who did this. And when he did, they would pay dearly. He looked up abruptly, his lips hardened into a thin straight line. The decision was made.

He handed the marshal a business card. "This has my cell phone on it. If you need anything, please call. I need to get myself organized and find a place to sleep. I'll be with friends."

The Fire Marshal took the card and looked into Stone's haunted eyes, raw with anguish and fury. He stepped back and said, "Mr. Stone, we'll probably need to talk with you in a day or so. Go get some rest and we'll be in touch. I'm really sorry about your house and your dog."

As Peyton turned to leave, the marshal called out to him. "An older lady came by earlier. She's about . . ."

Peyton interrupted, "...seventy. Her name is Mrs. Beeton. I know how to reach her. Thanks."

"She wanted me to give you a message. Had to go to her sister's but couldn't get through to you on your cell phone. Wants you to call her as soon as you have time. Said to tell you she's heartbroken."

He reached into his pocket and thought, Dammit, I left my cell phone on the kitchen counter. If she had gotten through . . . No, he reasoned, I couldn't have made a difference. He turned to the fire marshal and retrieved his business card. "My cell phone was in the house." He scribbled Harry's public number on the back and returned the card to the marshal. "If you need to reach me, call this number and I'll get your message. For now, could I borrow your phone? I need to make some arrangements."

"Sure." He handed Peyton his phone. As he walked over to the arson investigator, he called over his shoulder, "Take as long as you need."

Peyton dialed and shifted from one foot to the other while he waited for an answer. The phone clicked once but Harry only got half a breath out before Peyton started through clenched teeth. "Harry, the fuckers killed my dog. I'm headed to Langley to put together an infiltration plan overnight so we can get started in the morning. I also want to dig up everything we can to connect the dots on Fang and this Iranian plot."

"Man, you should get some sleep. Stay home and let's work it in the morning."

"Well, that's the thing, Harry. They torched my house with Bandito inside."

"No, oh, God, no, Peyton. I'm so sorry. Who did this?" Peyton heard Harry slam his hand down on a hard surface.

"Fang and his guys most likely. Like I said, I'm headed to Langley. I'll check into the dorm at the Scattergood Conference Center. It's the only place I have to stay but I need you to call and authorize it. I guess I'll have to stop and get some clothes and essentials at a Wal-Mart. My cell phone was lost in the fire." Exhausted, he fought to keep his emotions in check. He took a deep breath and said, "I'll see you in the morning, Harry, and we'll figure out how to pound these assholes to dust. Bring my contract with you."

Chapter 8

Beyik, China
Near the Afghanistan Border

THE BIG VEHICLE SHOOK AS THE FRONT WHEELS LEFT the pavement and dropped six inches to the mixture of sand and rocks. Guong Fang squinted through the windshield into the sunset and tried to make out the faint ruts that defined the track between the hills. The rapidly fading light made the drive even more difficult. Since he was on the west side of the valley headed toward the peaks, darkness would fall suddenly when the sun dipped behind the crest of the mountain ahead, already tinted deep purple. The track had no vegetation, no tire prints from previous vehicles. Fang wasn't certain that these particular ruts would carry him to his destination up the incline.

This area was officially in China but the borders between China, Pakistan, Turkmenistan and Afghanistan are fuzzy at best. Each country claims parts of the others' territories. Fang knew that the confusion makes the area a fairly safe place as long as a traveler knows the basics: stay close enough to the local tribesmen for protection and far enough from the fluid Afghani border to escape American spy satellites. The satellites looked at this spot but typically saw only a mountain a few miles from tiny villages in China. These were separated from American meddling by a nearly insurmountable Great Wall, one not of stone and mortar but diplomatic red tape.

The rugged beauty of the terrain coupled with a clandestine meeting would have once been an adventure for Fang. Now accustomed to comfort and routine, he sent others to the middle of nowhere. This meeting, however, promised him a payout of hundreds of millions of Chinese Yuan - more than twelve million U.S. Dollars - and therefore demanded his presence. The fewer people who knew about this the better. To his knowledge, only three people were aware of this scheme: Fang, Kuchecki, and the Arab who lived at the end of this desolate valley. Undoubtedly, more people would be brought in to accomplish different tasks but only the top three would remain alive long enough to make a difference. Fang stipulated this condition and was prepared to eliminate any unnecessary people himself. Just like that annoying Xu who happened upon some private papers that Fang had stupidly left on his desk.

He continued up the vague track as the light faded. When he spotted a dark area at the base of the rock face, Fang pulled his Land Rover into the opening as far as possible so that no overhead satellite could get a clear picture. Of course, an infrared sensor would see the heat from the engine, possibly. *Did they have IR satellites? Probably,* he thought. But such a possibility was no longer a significant factor. Only one trip remained. Tonight he would give the final instructions. After this meeting, this end of the plan would operate on autopilot.

Fang got out of the Rover and walked about thirty yards into the cave. The front wall of a small hut spanned the width of the cave like a stopper in the mouth of a bottle. The five thousand foot elevation left him a little light-headed, even after a short walk. He took a couple of deep breaths to recover, then knocked twice on the battered wooden door set into the stone and mud windowless wall. A perfect hideout: the door was barely visible in the dim light. In the unlikely event that someone stumbled into this place, he would never guess what lay behind the wall. The exterior provided no clues.

Fang heard a scrabbling sound near the door. He didn't investigate but pressed the latch and walked inside where an old Arab man sat at an ancient scarred wooden table. Besides the table, the room contained only a bed, two chairs, a cupboard and a small stove: Spartan quarters, indeed, for a man who, a decade ago, had been one of the richest men on earth. A rusted lantern rested on the table and a dim light passed through what must be a chimney above the stove. A bucket of coal sat nearby. Fang wondered to himself where the old man got his supplies since there was no other evidence of human life in this remote place.

The first thing he noticed was the chill. The outside temperature was hot, even at this elevation, but inside, the atmosphere was as chilly as the dour old Arab who sat in the chair that faced the door. He was tall, even seated, with an all-too-slender look about him with an angular nose that jutted out from his face. His large salt and pepper mustache and grayish beard that curved outward reminded Fang of the cartoon caliphs of Ali Baba. But it was the heavily lidded, deep-set eyes that defined the man. Fang would never forget the first time he had looked into those eyes or, more accurately, when they looked into him. The daunting, coal-black orbs pieced his very soul and the fire tamped deep behind them spoke of horrors too terrible to imagine. *Beware*, they admonished ominously, *danger lurks here*.

"What news from Tehran?" the Arab man asked as if Fang had been in the room for an hour.

Fang smiled slightly. "The peace talks are essentially complete and the treaty is scheduled to be signed in just over a week. Our friend Kuchecki is busy with his plans as well his staff."

"I've always thought that ownership of a project motivates people to do a good job. I'm glad that he believes in what we're about here even if his are the wrong reasons." The Arab waved his hands as he talked, driving home the import of his words. "You and I both know the reason for this so-called *jihad*. America owes me well over a billion dollars in stolen bank accounts and I will extract it one way or another."

"Yes." *It's always about the money*, Fang thought.

The Arab nodded and appeared to brush a fly from in front of his face. "And what of the weapon? Is the delivery still moving as expected?"

"As I said," Fang replied, his eyes narrowed slightly with mild irritation, "we are still on plan." He was a man who meant what he said when it came to business. When he stated that things were where they should be, he expected no further questions.

"And what of security?" the Arab man asked. "No leaks, no suspicions, nothing that might compromise the plan?"

"Security is tight," Fang offered. He neglected to mention the break-in at his office since he had personally taken care of those loose ends. Xu was dead and Stone was merely a moving target.

"I hope we can be sure of that. We are too far down the road to turn back now. We must stay on course."

Fang inclined his head to the side. "Of course we must. Don't forget that you have Zawahiri to keep a close eye on things. I trust he reports back to you regularly. Or is his loyalty only to himself since Bin Laden is dead?"

The Arab's eye narrowed and he spat on the floor. "Don't toy with Allegiances. I worked hard to make sure that the Russians were defeated in Afghanistan during the 1980's. Osama Bin Laden led the people, worked with them, organized them and financed the training of the *mujahedeen*. But I financed Bin Laden and Zawahiri knows that well. Bin Laden was wealthy in his own right but winning the war cost ten times his fortune, not counting American weapons and CIA funding." The Arab raised his fist and shook it with each phrase to emphasize the pent-up emotion behind his tirade.

"I became richer than Bill Gates, had billions in supposedly safe, secret bank accounts, made the right investments. Over twenty years ago, I organized Afghanistan's poppy trade with Thailand through Burma and used contacts in Europe to organize the heroin trade so that we got a better profit. I was even able to save a little of the American handouts as they passed through our organization during the war with the Russians. But, after a time, the US aid was such a small percentage that I didn't even bother any more.

"Even after that cursed Taliban tried to take over my poppy trade and shut it down, I was able to hold on to the distribution channel through Thailand. I leveraged the Thai relationships, paid the right people, fought off American attempts to disrupt the flow through Burma, and refused to accept any Taliban product until we had worked out the details."

Fang nodded idly and shifted his weight. He'd heard all of this before but the old Arab was lost in the bitter memories that fueled his desire for vengeance.

"After 9/11, the Americans looked into every bank account in the world, even the so-called safe ones in Switzerland and especially in Cayman where law enforcement barely needs a warrant. They stole almost all of my money. All I have left is less than a few million of hidden cash that affords me to make immediate payments when I need to." When the old Arab finished the recitation his achievements and his downfall, he slapped the table with his open palm. Cups rose in the air, then landed sideways. His dark eyes blazed as he shouted, "We must make them pay!"

"We will," Fang replied. "America owes us much and we will most assuredly settle the debt, with interest."

"Settle it we will, Mr. Fang," the Arab agreed.

"I've set up the accounts in Martinique and have the numbers for you." Fang handed the Arab a sheet of paper that bore the engraved crest of the South Island Bank of Martinique in the letterhead. On this, several series of numbers were listed. "As agreed, you will deposit fifty percent of my fee immediately and the remainder when I deliver the weapon."

The Arab got up and walked to the cupboard. He opened the upper cabinet and retrieved a slip of paper, then walked back to the table and handed it to Fang. "Go into Beyik and find a pay phone in the market. Call this number and say these words, 'Allah is great and my father sends his regards across the hills.' You must say them exactly. Check your account in twenty-four hours. The money will be there." He smiled across the table as they shook hands. "You have made an arduous journey to meet here. Thank you."

Fang tried to hide his disdain for the constant religious references that accompanied every transaction with this man. "Thank you for your hospitality," he replied tightly. Although he stood only five feet six inches, he had to duck as he walked through the five-foot high door. The Arab who had to stoop more than a foot to pass through watched as the Chinese man walked away.

Once outside, Fang climbed into the Land Rover for the twelve-hour drive back to the edge of civilization.

He thought of the mud hovel and the Arab who was one of the richest people in the world, or would be had the United States not frozen most of his assets. Still, a few millions were more cash than Fang had at the moment. But that would change soon. At the end of the day, the money wasn't bad for less than a week's work.

Chapter 9

Persian Gulf
Near Bushehr, Iran

STONE ADJUSTED HIS MASK AND BIT DOWN ON THE mouthpiece of his rebreather. He climbed down the stairs that led from the deck of the Kuwaiti fishing dhow to the diving platform at the water line. First he checked the equipment on the platform and then slid into the warm water of the Gulf for a standard infiltration from offshore. Since a rebreather had limited capacity, he would travel the first hour on the surface with an electric water sled. He would then submerge and go the last mile along the bottom at 35 feet with the rebreather to avoid telltale scuba bubbles. Advance intel indicated that the Iranians had not installed a net or underwater fence around the pier. This would allow him to tie the sled to a piling near the bottom. A waterproof backpack inside the sled's cargo compartment held his dry clothes and papers. He'd change into dry clothes underneath the pier, then get to work. At least this was the plan.

Stone looked at his Omega dive watch which registered 11 P.M. He would need about 90 minutes to get to the pier. He hoped that he would not encounter any other watercraft while on the surface.

The first forty-five minutes were easy, even a bit boring. The high salt content of the water made him more buoyant than he remembered from childhood summers when he swam daily in the Atlantic off Tybee Island. At four miles per hour, he created little wake. The sound of the water moving past was the only sound in the pitch-black night. He kept the sled's compass

104

needle centered and fought the urge to sleep.

How ironic, he thought. *I'm sneaking into a hostile country in the middle of the night to investigate illegal nuclear weapons as well as a possible attack and I'm half asleep. I must be getting too old for this.*

Just over two miles out, he heard the chugging of a motor and stopped to look around. Off to his right side, he saw a spotlight beam sweep the water. He quickly submerged to avoid detection.

Stone pointed the sled down and headed for the bottom. When he leveled out, he checked his depth gauge: 37 feet. He looked off to his right and saw the spotlight beam slice through the water, not as bright but still visible. The water was so clear at this relatively shallow depth that the strong light from the patrol boat could penetrate almost to the bottom. *Time to move*, he thought.

He pointed the sled toward the point where the pier was supposed to be, checked his compass, and headed toward the dock. To his right, he could see the spotlight beam cut wide arcs across the bottom as the patrol boat came nearer and nearer. His only hope was the laws of physics. If he put enough distance between himself and the patrol boat's path, the diffraction would take the beam away from him.

Peyton knew that when the boat's light shone straight down or at a slight angle, the light could penetrate nearly to the bottom. But when the light entered at an angle, part of the beam was reflected off the surface and less light energy pierced the water. Simultaneously, the laws of refraction bent the light beam and further reduced penetration. Stone's plan was to move perpendicular to the patrol boat's path and get as far away as possible. Fortunately, he noted that the patrol boat moved parallel to the shore, not in a zigzag security pattern. Stone's best path was one that would move him toward his goal the fastest. He pushed the speed switch to full and hoped that the battery would last.

A few minutes later he saw the sweep of the light beam draw closer, dim but headed in his direction nonetheless. He cut power and stopped. If he continued, his movement would give him a way. He hoped for reflections, refraction, human error, anything that would conceal his whereabouts.

The light beam swept across him, so dim he thought it useless. Then he heard the engines of the patrol boat rev up and set its course toward him. The beam stopped its sweep and moved closer, closer. He thought about the clarity of the water and wondered how easily he could be spotted from nearly forty feet above. *Should I run?* He was still trying to decide when the light went out. The boat passed directly over him but didn't stop. He relaxed briefly, then almost immediately heard the sound of a second boat. *What the...,* he thought, as he looked for rocks, debris, anything, that offered concealment or might break up his profile. In the blackness, he could see nothing at all. What were they up to? The most likely explanation was that he had been spotted. They were getting in position to close on him and cut off his escape. Suddenly a light came on behind him and began a new sweep. Relief coursed through his body as the sounds of engines faded and the light dimmed.

Stone maintained perfect stillness as he checked his dive watch. *Midnight shift change*, he thought. *You guys really know how to scare a person.* Once again he moved slowly along the bottom until he saw the bottom change from a natural ripple to an unnatural surface. Sand swirled in the shallow water. *I must be inside the breakwater*, he thought, *not much farther now*. A few minutes later, he saw the dim outline of pilings in the gloom. He wound through them and came to a stop in the middle of the pier. Quickly, Stone tied the sled to the piling with a piece of cable and a D-ring clip. He then opened the small cargo compartment, retrieved the backpack, and swam slowly to the surface. A silent breach of the surface was tricky. Water could drip from hair, ears, face and chin and make distinctive splashing sounds that could alert a nearby guard.

Stone had often played 'Capture the Flag' as a Boy Scout at Camp Benjamin Hawkins in central Georgia. Given a choice in this cowboy and Indian game, he usually chose to join the Creek Indian tribe. He practiced Indian lore religiously in the woods surrounding the family home. The young make-believe Creek scout learned to move without noise through the woods and swim silently in the Ogeechee River. Most impressively, he could enter Lake Hawkins, swim around the cowboy fort, climb out of the lake and steal the flag so quietly that no one noticed until he dove head first into the lake to make the triumphant swim back to the Creek camp.

His head slipped through the surface of the water down to his nose. Then he stopped. His eyes swept the area under the pier. He saw only darkness, a good indicator that he was some distance from the edge of the pier. Then he slowly rotated his head to look over his shoulder. *Still dark. Good,* he thought, *stay still for a minute and then let your ears surface and listen.* A bit trickier now than when a boy. Middle-age body fat, coupled with the salinity of the Arabian Gulf, increased his buoyancy and caused him to rise faster than planned. He treaded water in reverse in an attempt to control his ascent.

Stone's thoughts turned to recent events while he

waited in the salty water. Fang, a Chinese arms dealer and killer, probably killed Xu and now trailed him. Two assassination attempts had failed, but his home was destroyed and Bandito killed. Randy Perkins had sent a brief, encrypted message about nuclear *jihad*, seconds before a sniper killed him on a rooftop in Tehran. A plot to overthrow the Iranian government on the eve of a significant peace agreement had surfaced. The timing of these events was far from coincidental. Stone knew that all were somehow connected. The question was how? Hopefully after tonight he'd know more.

His thoughts wandered to his sons. He desperately needed to get out to San Diego and see them. He was proud of their work on automated boats for the Navy. He didn't know the details of their assignments or what they had accomplished, only that sea trials had been good. His project schedule for the last six months had been a killer but offered no real excuse. He felt guilty that he had not made time to see them, to share in their successes. More than anything, he wanted their presence. He longed to see their smiles, to breathe the same air. He'd missed much of their transition to adulthood. They remained his boys but he longed to know better the men they had become.

He suddenly snapped back to the present. *Focus, Peyton*, he thought, *stay with the mission brief and, for God's sake, stay alert. Deal with personal stuff later. You won't see anyone if you die. And if you fail, many others will be killed.*

He slowly let his ears break the surface. As they drained, he heard the water lap, first against the pilings and then, in the distance, against the shore. Good, he thought. The natural sound of moving water would help mask the sound of his presence.

Peyton carefully removed the rebreather and put it

in his pocket. Then he slipped his arms through the backpack straps and slowly made his way under the pier. He moved from piling to piling as he looked for a service ladder that led down from the pier to the water. Finally he brushed against something metal. The ladder was right where it was supposed to be. The tide was higher than expected or the pier lower. Either way, he had little room underneath to change clothes. He would have to climb the ladder to the top of the pier.

His ascent was now trickier and slower. He raised himself up rung by rung and let the water trapped in his swim trunks drain before he lifted himself out of the water. *If only a Speed-O had sufficient pockets.* He smiled at the thought. *And I'd look absolutely ridiculous.*

He topped the ladder and looked over the edge of the concrete pier. The only life he could make out was a guard at the far end, approximately seventy-five feet away. The man stood under a light and smoked a cigarette. Stone figured the guard could probably see no more than fifteen feet into the dark with his eyes adjusted to the light. Idiots really make my life easier, he thought.

Stone first grabbed the wooden edge-stop. Bolted to the concrete pier deck, it marked the edge and kept anything round from splashing into the water. Then he rolled onto the pier deck. A pile of crates were stacked on the pier about six feet away. He crab-walked until the crates stood between him and the guard. He stopped to listen. After a moment he sat up and looked around. The guard remained under the light and puffed away on the cigarette. The questions now were how long will the guard remain under the light and which way will he go when he moves? Stone saw only one way off the pier. He was directly between the guard and the spot where the pier connected to the land. *Perhaps*, he thought, this might be the guard's post, in which case he won't leave. He shook his head and looked down. *Get a grip, Peyton. Wishful thinking is an invitation to death.* Then he saw the wet footprints that led from the ladder to his hiding place. Damn! He could only hope that, should the guard walk in this direction, he'd pass on the other side of the stack of crates.

Good a time as any, Peyton thought. He opened the backpack and gently lifted out the still-dry contents: blue overalls, utility boots, socks, under shorts, ID badge and papers compliments of CIA Technical Services Division, makeup kit, metal spike, flashlight, hand-held GPS receiver, AN/PRC-152C handheld radio, and his Glock Model 17 nine millimeter automatic pistol complete with four extra clips and a paddle holster.

He quickly stripped off his trunks and stuffed them in the pack. Then he loaded the Glock and the clips into the holster and strapped them in the middle of his back. Pulling on the overalls and boots, he then went back down the ladder and squeezed between the pier and the water.

In an out-of-the-way spot behind a wooden beam, he pushed the spike into a crack in the wood, then hung the pack. He transformed himself into an ordinary Arab worker with the make-up, climbed back up the ladder and looked toward the end of the deck. The guard was gone. Stone looked around as best he could in the small circle of light but the guard was nowhere to be found.

As he rolled onto the surface of the pier, he again noticed the wet footprints he had left. They were nearly dry now, a combination of absorption into the pier and evaporation into the night desert air. *Which way did the guard go? Did he see the tell-tale signs? Nothing to do now except to get on with it,* he thought.

He moved slowly and quietly along the pier toward land. Even a legitimate Arab plant worker, Stone knew, would have no business on the pier. He didn't want to have to explain his presence to security. Other than two rusty maintenance barges, a dredge, and a couple of boats tied to the pier, the area was empty. When he reached the shore end, he found himself on an unpaved security patrol road. He crossed the road and prepared to climb or cut a security fence but none was to be found on this part of the perimeter.

Odd that they wouldn't have a fence, he thought. At that moment, he tripped lightly over rusty chain link lying on the ground. Apparently struck by a vehicle some time ago, the fence repair was probably low on the to-do list when the budget was allocated.

Stone smiled that this high security plant could be so easily penetrated. He kicked up dust as he walked the two hundred yards across the dirt and pebble path to the reactor building and shops. At the first shop, he opened the door and casually stepped inside. His modus operandi - *look like you know what you're doing and people will believe that you do* – was brilliant in its simplicity. He knew that nothing draws attention like tentative behavior. Uncertainty would telegraph the message that he wasn't quite sure if he belonged. Others would inevitably assume that he didn't.

The outer office was empty but he could hear activity in the larger work area beyond. The test was to walk into the shop and be accepted as one of the staff. Stone mentally reviewed his story. He was a day-shift worker from Reactor One who had swapped shifts with his cousin who was home ill. *Here's hoping they buy it*, Peyton thought.

Stone adjusted the Glock at his back through the pocket cutouts and walked into the shop area where two men welded a machine part. The electric arc lent an acrid odor to the hazy air. The cool light from industrial fluorescent fixtures filtered through a thin smoky haze onto racks of piping and sheet metal scraps. Pipe fittings were scattered among tools and machinery. In stark contrast to the gray concrete floor, black and yellow non-skid safety tape outlined the area around each machine. As he walked up to the pair, the one who held the welding rod pushed his visor up and looked at Stone expectantly.

"Salām aleikom," Stone said in perfectly accented Farsi. Peace be upon you.

The welder nodded, "Aleikom Salām." And upon you.

Stone smiled. "I've been assigned to the night shift because an illness in my family requires me to be home during the day. Since my normal duties in the reactor building have enough people assigned in the evening, I came here to look for something to do so the supervisor doesn't send me home. I need the pay." Hopefully, neither worker would ask him to do something that required specialized knowledge.

The welder first looked suspicious, then glanced at Stone's employee badge, and shrugged. "We're repairing a pump. Other than that, there's nothing here."

"What do all of these silver tubes do?" Stone pointed to a number of racks attached to the wall holding aluminum tubing.

"They came on a ship from North Korea several days ago," the welder replied. "Once the spinner bearings arrive, they'll be used in the centrifuge. These have been on back order for nearly a year. The Americans have stopped shipments of centrifuge parts to us from every manufacturer in Europe so we have to find other sources for bearings."

112

"I see," said Stone who shrugged his shoulders as if uninterested in further discussion. Frustrated, wanting to press further, he knew he had to avoid suspicion. "Well, if I can't help here, I should head back to the Reactor One shop before I get into trouble. Khodāfez." The welder nodded in his direction and watched him go.

Stone stepped back through the door to the outer office area and then exited the building. *That's odd*, he thought, *they're waiting for a critical part for their centrifuge, which indicates that they don't have a way to enrich the spent fuel to make weapons. If that's true, then what's the "breakthrough" that we've heard about? Maybe these guys just aren't in the loop.* He checked the time. 1:30 A.M. A few hours remained before dawn and the swim back to the pickup point. He walked over to the Number One reactor building and entered the shop. The shop area was empty but he could hear talking, loud talking, in an adjacent room at the far end.

He walked nonchalantly across the shop and stopped just short of the slightly ajar door. The narrow opening revealed what appeared to be a break room with an ancient, dirty refrigerator and a small stove with a teapot on top. The door blocked his view of the rest of the room. The spirited conversation continued as one speaker berated a bad call by an official in a recent soccer match between Esteghlal and Persepolis. Although a member of his favored team had swept the feet out from under an opposing player for the third time in a single match, the worker saw no reason for a red card. The fan of the other team saw it quite differently.

As Stone grasped the doorknob, he heard a door open on the opposite side of the break room. The soccer debate suddenly stopped as an authoritative voice boomed. "Have you seen anyone who doesn't belong here?" A different speaker continued, "We have reason to believe that a foreigner has entered the complex and may be in the area."

Shit, shit, shit. Peyton listened as the two shop workers mumbled unintelligible responses to the men he could only assume were policemen or soldiers. He backed away from the door as quietly as possible and hurried to the other end of the shop where he had entered.

Once outside, he quietly pulled the door toward him. A voice from inside the shop called out, "You! Stop!" He took off in a dead run beside the building toward the front where the policemen had entered. *Good*, he thought, when he heard them run in the opposite direction through the building. *This bought a little time.*

He heard the door crash open. One policeman ordered another to circle the building in the opposite direction. Ok, at least two, Stone thought to himself as he rounded the corner at the front. He glanced left and right to confirm that no one else was out front. *It's a patrol officer and his partner*, he thought. He could hear the crackle of a radio just around the corner of the building. *Great, reinforcements will be here soon.*

Then he saw it. The Special Security Police cruiser was parked in front of the shop with the engine still running. Obviously the policemen were treating the search as high-priority. But how did they know? Or was it someone or something else? Peyton had to assume that he was their quarry. The guard on the pier had probably seen the water trail he had left. *That was stupid, Peyton.* Nothing could be done about it now. Luckily, he had been under the pier when the guard came by; otherwise, he would have been captured on the spot.

Stone jumped in the car and threw the shifter into

reverse as the two policemen bolted around opposite corners of the building. He floored the gas and the car shot backwards. His arms crossed, he placed his hands on opposite sides of the steering wheel and accelerated backwards at about thirty miles an hour. Peyton slammed the brakes and uncrossed his arms. The steering wheel spun against the locks and the car executed a perfect J-turn. When he hit the gas again, he had already accelerated in the opposite direction. Bill Scott's driving instructors at BSR Racing had taught him that move and made him practice it on the skid pad until he could do it in his sleep. Stone made a mental note to send a bottle of Edradour, his favorite Scotch whisky, to these men who had taught him much about evasive driving techniques

"OK, Peyton, focus," he said out loud. "Those guys on the walkie-talkies will converge here and things will get dicey pretty quick." He headed toward the pier. As he slowed and turned down the patrol road that ran along the enclosed harbor, his headlights swung past the pier. He could see a small group of people who stood and talked as a patrol boat idled nearby. His sled was on the pier and, as he drove past, he saw a diver climb up the ladder with his pack. He handed it to the guard Peyton had first seen when he came ashore.

"Dammit," Stone swore softly. As the group looked up at the approaching police car, he reached down and turned on the flashing lights. He turned and sped away, as if he were another officer who responded to the current emergency. A glance in the mirror indicated that the group had taken the bait.

I have to get out of here, he thought. *The front gate isn't an option and there is a block wall around most of the compound...except near the water, where the fence is chain link with a large section down. Bingo,* he thought, and turned right toward the corner of the compound.

He was approaching the fence when he saw a dozen flashing lights headed down the perimeter patrol road just inside the fence. The dust from the front cars dimmed the headlights of the cars following behind. He reached down and turned his roof flashers off as he reached the fence and drove slowly over it. When his front wheels rolled across the chain link fabric, he heard the fencing scrape on the underside of the car. *Please don't let me get hung up on this,* he thought. *Just a little farther.* In the rearview mirror, the flashing lights were getting closer.

His rear wheels rolled up on the fencing and Stone immediately swerved left and ran over the fence pole that lay on the ground. The slight bend that the weight of the car put into the pole caused the fence fabric behind the car to lift two or three feet off the ground on the side that faced the pursuit vehicles. Not much of a delta barrier, he thought as he sped away from the compound, but it might slow them down a little.

Just over a minute later, the first pursuit car hit the spot where Stone had crossed the fence. The small gap under the fence fabric caused the chain link to slide up over the hood of the car. The force pushed the fence up enough for the car to nose under it. This action entangled the car and pushed the fence so that it now stood upright. In the side mirror, he could see a cloud of dust rise as other cars skidded to a stop and then spun around to find another way out. Doors opened as police and army got out and pulled at the fence. Weakened by rust and the pile-up, the obstacle finally fell again. The delay, however, bought Stone enough time to slip into the nearby fishing village of Bandar-Gah. Now, at least, he was out of the open.

Peyton was consumed by one burning question:

What now? Bandar-Gah is a small village of two or three hundred houses next to the reactor complex. Beyond the village, open desert stretched endlessly. Not a creosote and scrub brush-covered desert but one of sand, millions of acres of sand, encircled by hills that would stop even the toughest four-wheel drive vehicle. The closest civilization was the city of Bushehr but his only access was the single road that cut through the tract housing and local village built for the workers in the reactor complex. The army would certainly have roadblocks in place while the police searched the town. The only other escape was the Gulf, which now crawled with patrol boats. After dawn, a swimmer could easily be spotted. Without his underwater sled and breathing gear, he had no chance of covering the six to ten miles of sea to the pick-up point. He couldn't swim that far when he was eighteen.

He had only a little over two hours before he would lose the cover of darkness. *Stay focused*, he thought. *First things first.* The car was of little use and stood out like a sore thumb. Stone knew that he had to ditch it quickly. He turned down a street and drove toward a lot surrounded by a fence of corrugated tin. Inside the open gate he saw a number of dilapidated buildings and junked cars. He pulled into the enclosure and parked close to the tin fence behind the gate. After he checked the area for any movement or noise, he slipped quietly out to the street. He turned and looked at the entrance to assure himself that a patrol would not be able to see the car from the street.

On foot, he projected a smaller profile and had greater agility. He was, however, alone on a street in a small village long before sunrise. In his Bushehr overalls he was unsure if he looked out of place but thought not. Some workers probably lived in the village.

Should curfews be enforced, however, his presence might be hard to explain. He stood still and listened. In America he would hear at least one dog bark. No dogs here. He saw a police car roll slowly along, one street away. As he stepped back into a doorway, the car crossed a street that led away from him. When the car was out of sight, Stone quickly moved out of the shadows and headed to the street where he had seen the car pass. If he could stay close behind them he had a better chance of remaining undetected.

To his right, three large brown ceramic urns stood next to a doorway. Stone moved the middle urn out from the wall, climbed behind it and sat down. Wedged between the urns adjacent to the small front entry step, he would not be easily spotted. Peyton knew that he had to collect his thoughts. He needed an escape plan. The night was not getting any younger. He crouched even lower as another patrol car passed and kept going.

He remained huddled on the ground for a while and gazed between the urns at the street. The adrenaline from the chase wore off and he realized how tired he was. Fatigue dulled his mental acuity and increased the risk of mistakes. Suddenly Xu flitted into his mind. *Oh, my God,* he thought, *I still haven't talked to Joni about what happened.* A malaise settled over him as he struggled to keep his dry, heavy eyelids open.

After what seemed mere seconds, Stone jerked awake. The sky was a little lighter now. Peyton looked at his watch and realized that he had been asleep in that position for almost two hours. *Five o'clock, in the morning,* he thought. *Now what?* The question was quickly answered by the sound of footsteps on the side street. Peyton looked through the space between the urns and saw a single policeman turn the corner. He paused briefly then turned toward Stone.

His muscles knotted and stiff, Peyton struggled to position himself quietly. He squatted behind the large urn with his feet beneath him and his head tucked. Now directly in front of Stone's hiding place, the policeman stooped a bit to peer over the pottery that jutted out into the sidewalk. Stone's cramped, aching leg muscles miraculously propelled him upward as his right hand struck rapidly and forcefully. He caught the policeman in the larynx with the middle knuckle and silenced the foot patrol. The policeman's head snapped back. Stone cradled the back of the skull with his left hand. Then he placed the heel of his right hand against the policeman's jaw and pushed with all his strength until he heard the snap of the neck breaking. He quickly pulled the body of the policeman up and over the urns and placed the dead patrol close to the building. The street empty, he stepped out and hurriedly tugged at the heavy urns until no gap was visible. He looked up and appeared to study the sky as his eyes swept the area before he walked slowly down the street. As he reached the corner, a door across the street opened and a man stepped out.

Chapter 10

The White House
Washington, DC

ADMIRAL MCKINLEY, THE DIRECTOR OF NATIONAL Intelligence, walked into the Oval Office and sat down on the pale blue couch. He placed the folder across his lap with his yellow legal pad on top and looked across the coffee table at a matching sofa. The President and the country's top advisors would soon join him soon to be briefed on current world situations. To serve at the pleasure the President of the United States, in close proximity to the world's greatest power, had long been a goal, but he had grown to dread these encounters. He and the president rarely connected.

To his left beyond the Great Seal of the United States, intricately woven into the sapphire blue carpet, was the seat of power: the oversized, hand-carved Resolute desk. Built from the timbers of the HMS Resolute, the desk was presented to President Rutherford B. Hayes by Queen Victoria in 1879. McKinley looked over the end table at the fireplace where two chairs had stood since the tenure of President Franklin Roosevelt. From here he had brought the presidency live into American homes for the first time with his fireside chats. A tradition was born during FDR's day: the President sat on the left and visiting dignitaries sat on the right. During internal meetings, the right seat belonged to the Vice President.

The Admiral had been appointed DNI by the previous President shortly before McKinley retired from the Navy. The two men had gone to the Naval Academy together and had remained friends for the last 30 years. As often happens in Washington, back room deals were made. McKinley was promoted to Vice Admiral and then retired at that rank in exchange for his promise to serve as DNI for four years. That meant the final two years of his friend's term and the first two years of the next president's.

Now, three years into his commitment with a year yet to go, he could not abide this president. The big bone of contention at the moment was the treaty about to be signed with Iran. Iran, a significant part of George W. Bush's Axis of Evil. And now we were about to sign a treaty that would control oil prices and give the money to the enemy. This was insane. Yes, a bloody coup had ousted the Supreme Leader and the Council of Guardians and replaced them with a more Western style secular government. This action alone, however significant, did not portend widespread reform.

But every successful bureaucrat knows the rules. Within a debate, disagreement encouraged discovery whereas rigid opposition silenced dialogue. He carefully managed the perception of the relationship between himself and the president. A team player, he answered every question carefully and thoughtfully. And carried out the President's initiatives with the skill and care that had won him promotion to three-star ahead of the rest of his class. He not only knew the game. He was a master player.

McKinley quickly stood as the door opened and President Margaret Harkins, first woman to serve as leader of the nation, entered the Oval Office through the hidden side door.

"Madam President," he said with his carefully cultivated Texas-style drawl. An Arizonan by birth, he thought the accent added to his appeal but many who knew him disagreed. Admiral McKinley had objected when women had shown up on his ship in the second Gulf War. As commander of the entire battle group, he was able to shuffle them off into jobs that ensured he didn't have to see them. He thought the idea of women in battle was simply preposterous. But now a woman served as the Commander-in-Chief and she certainly needed his help. The fact that she wanted to bring Iran into the United States' circle of friends was difficult to swallow. He had repeatedly argued against the proposed accord to no avail. Now, he shivered imperceptibly, took a deep breath, and held it for a beat. Only his mouth smiled.

President Harkins was, at age 62, sharper than most of the folks she encountered in her job as leader of the most powerful nation on earth. Tall and slim, she would never have been described as pretty but she was a strikingly attractive woman, in large part due to her engaging nature. She wore a dark blue business suit, skirt rather than pants, with a white blouse and a blue and gold scarf. Her silver hair was pulled back into a loose chignon, her signature style.

Growing up, her role model had been Margaret Thatcher and she was proud to share the same first name. Her policies were her own but, like Thatcher, she was smart, well read and did not wish to be BS'd by anyone, friend or foe. To filter the political banter, she asked questions, hard questions and lots of them. Experience had taught her that, when people brought ideas or sought her support, the better her questions, the better the information provided. She was particularly careful in her dealings with the Admiral because she considered him a player. She needed to know where he stood. As DNI he controlled all information that came from overseas. This made him either one of her most valuable allies or an exceedingly dangerous enemy. She worked hard to keep him in the former camp.

"Good morning, Daniel." The President made a point of being overly gracious because she knew it irritated him a little. "I hope you are quite well today. I absolutely love that tie. Naval Academy, right?"

"Yes, Ma'am." McKinley tried his best to keep his military bearing intact. "Madam President," he went on, "I need to inform you about a situation. Some of our people have acquired information that indicates possible offensive action by Iran. The intelligence suggests that nuclear weapons or nuclear materials may be involved. An attack may be in the planning stages. The timing is unknown but all indications point to soon."

"An attack by Iran?"

"Yes, Ma'am."

"Against whom?"

McKinley opened the folder and then closed it.

"We don't know yet but our information seems to indicate a US interest. Possibly Israel but there are no hard facts to indicate the target beyond a doubt."

"Am I the first to know about this?" the President asked.

"Other than a few at CIA, yes, Ma'am." McKinley replied.

"And this is reliable information?"

"Yes, Ma'am."

"Ok, tell me what you know," the President said.

Admiral McKinley forged ahead. "We found a letter between two Iranian officials that described a jihad and implied an attack of some kind. Another highly placed source in the government, code-name PHILOSOPHER, also reported possible nuclear weapons activity at Bushehr that would make this jihad possible."

"That's it?"

"Yes, Ma'am."

"When you say 'highly placed sources' what do you mean? Official Iran?"

McKinley shifted on the couch, staring at the coffee table, "We don't know exactly but it could be. Those sneaky bastards could plan something while they keep us distracted with this treaty." He stopped and looked up, aware of his slip. He seemed to come back from another mental place.

"Thanks for the analysis." The President's lips pursed slightly before she took a quick breath. "This seems pretty thin, Dan. We're on the verge of signing a peace treaty with Iran that gives them a lot of benefit. They will be guaranteed oil sales. Their assets in the US will be unfrozen and decades of interest on money we've held will be paid off. This deal is too sweet for them to sabotage the treaty now. We've worked long and hard to get where we are, often with little support from our allies. But it's come together with the most powerful countries behind it. We even gotten Israel to give up some long-held positions." She then added with emphasis, "I do not want to take even a half-step backwards."

McKinley sat back. He could feel the pulse in his carotid as heat crept up his face. He hoped that his face was not bright red but the president's reaction left no doubt that he had lost the battle to his anger. *How*, he thought, *could anyone pander to the very towel-heads who attacked my ships, killed my sailors and desecrated lower Manhattan on 9/11? Now these same terrorists threaten action on a global scale and she doesn't want to hurt their feelings? Give me a break.* He took a deep breath, held it for three seconds and then slowly exhaled deliberately through his nose. He could feel the color in his face return to normal. "Yes, Ma'am," he said. "On the other hand, we don't want to get blindsided."

"I agree with that but the negotiations have been honest and straightforward from all accounts. It seems that the government in Iran has turned its back on extremism. The move toward a position of tolerance and peace seems, to all who have participated in this process, truly genuine. We have to support that. A nuclear attack is completely out of character for them today."

The President pressed a button on her desk and spoke into the intercom. "Frank, get the SECDEF and State and have them either come over here or get on a secure video to the Situation Room immediately." She turned to the Admiral and said, "Come with me."

They started for the side door of the Oval Office but the President stopped short, went back to her desk and spoke into the intercom. "Frank, include the DCI as well."

"Madam President, I have received a thorough briefing from the Director of Central Intelligence and I have it right here." McKinley held up the folder.

"We can't have enough heads on this Dan," the President replied, "Let's get down to The Tank."

THE SITUATION ROOM IN THE LOWER LEVEL OF THE White House was sometimes referred to as The Tank because just as a tank is designed to hold liquids without leaking, this room was designed not to leak conversations, sounds, electronic emissions. Nothing escaped its walls. It was a Secure Compartmented Information Facility or SCIF in Government parlance.

The room was added in the basement of the West Wing in 1962 by President Kennedy after the Bay of Pigs debacle. He hoped that a command center would prevent kinds of miscommunications that were a vital part of the failed US invasion of Cuba. The room was designed so that sounds and conversations did not travel through the HVAC ducts. Bars and motion sensors were placed in the ductwork to detect people crawling in them. Power was filtered so that electronic information could not be intercepted by anyone connected to the power lines. Even with the extraordinary security measures, the Situation Room appeared to be nothing more than a well-appointed conference room. Unless one paid close attention, the four-inch thick steel vault door finished in fine wood on both sides might even be overlooked. Well-balanced, the door moved with ease. Only the rubber and copper seals that stopped both sound and electronic waves when the door was closed were noticeable. The walls, covered in a thick, carpet-like beige fabric on the inside of the room to deaden sound, were designed to look like a high-end commercial wall finish.

Admiral McKinley, the President, and two of her aides sat at the long mahogany conference table. McKinley put his legal pad in front of him and drew a line from top to bottom to divide the page into two columns, one for each side of the debate. McKinley lived in a black and white world, one in which any debate could be neatly divided into two sides. He had applauded former President George Bush, the second one, when Bush made his war on terror speech and said, "Either you are with us or you are our enemy." As he now waited on the group to assemble, he drew another line across the top of the page to create a header. Again, he noted, he was the first person to get organized. He was prepared to take names. As for sides, he had already chosen.

In a few minutes the screens on the long wall of the room flickered and displayed the presidential seal.

Frank Adams, the President's long-time friend and current Chief of Staff, came in and spoke as he took his seat. "The DCI is in town and should be here momentarily. The Secretaries of Defense and State are in transit to their secure video conference rooms. We should be ready to go in a few minutes."

Minutes later the Director of Central Intelligence, Michael Kopanski entered the room. He closed the door and turned the handle that sealed the room. "Good morning, Madam President. I'm glad I was close when you called. Good morning, Admiral."

"Hello, Mike. Thanks for coming by on short notice," the President said. "I hope this is not as serious as it seems."

Admiral McKinley nodded and looked down at the table. At that moment one of the screens came to life. An impeccably dressed, slightly overweight woman in her mid-fifties, unaware that the transmission had begun, fiddled with a microphone. When she looked up and saw the red light on the camera, she sat up quickly and smiled. "Good morning, Madam President." A man walked self-consciously into the picture. He adjusted the microphone then quickly stepped out of the frame.

"Good morning, Lisa," the President replied, "thanks for joining us. We're waiting on Defense to show up. Should only be a minute. I have Mike from CIA and Admiral McKinley with me. I trust things are calm at State for the moment?" The President smiled at the camera.

"For the moment," Lisa Cunningham, the Secretary of State, replied, "but you don't usually call me on the secure video to chat so we'll know better how things are in a few minutes, I suppose."

The other screen in the Tank lit up. A distinguished looking man with silver-white hair, a deep tan and pale blue eyes sat with his hands folded on a desk. "Good morning, Tony," the President said, "glad you could join us."

"Good morning, Madam President. "I hope that I'm not late." Tony Capetti, former Senator from New York and now Secretary of Defense replied. Urbane and experienced, he was the consummate political player.

"We're just starting so let's dive right in. Admiral McKinley has informed me that we may have a situation in Iran. The intel is still unconfirmed but the scenario is potentially serious enough that I thought we should come together this morning to review the details. Admiral McKinley?"

McKinley spent the next twenty minutes recapping the information from both his agents and the CIA sources: a letter referenced a plot to overthrow the Iranian government; rumored activity with nuclear overtones at Bushehr; talk of a global jihad by a source close to the Iranian legislature.

"This sounds serious on the surface," the President said, "but what do we really have in the way of hard facts? Do we have any idea what exactly is going on in Bushehr?"

McKinley started to speak again but the DCI cut him off. "We currently have an undercover asset in Bushehr for this purpose. He is tasked to systematically search the nuclear reactor compound for evidence of weapons activity there."

"This was done without my authorization. Is this a detail I want to know?" she asked.

"No, Ma'am. I authorized it based on a detailed finding." Kopanski answered. "I have a copy for you if you want it." He held up an official looking document.

"Then let's leave it at that," the President replied. *The last thing I need*, she thought, *is for this to go south and then to have some senator asking what I knew and when I knew it.*

McKinley leaned his forearms on the table. His eyebrows came together as he slowly rolled his pen between his thumbs and forefingers. He took a deep breath and thought carefully about the speed at which he was letting it out through his nose. He leaned back and looked at the President as she spoke.

"Do the Iranians have a weapon and delivery system we don't know about?" the president asked. "Mike, isn't there an Estimate on this?"

"Yes, Ma'am, we have an Estimate in draft form and it's in review by the NFIB." The Intelligence community often put its collective heads together on a particular issue such as whether a foreign country such as Iran has certain kinds of weapons, what they are likely to do with them and what things were being developed in those countries along with likely timeframes. The products of these efforts were referred to as Estimates which is shorthand for National Intelligence Estimate, or NIE. Because of the complexity of the issues being studied and their potential impact on US policy, NIEs are sent to a National Foreign Intelligence Board, or NFIB, where members of the different intelligence agencies review, debate and qualify the contents of the Estimate before it is published.

"Do you have the Key Judgments developed?"

McKinley shifted in his chair. "The document is still in review…" he began.

"So the answer is no?" she cut him off.

Kopanski came to the rescue, "We have the Key Judgments done and they are in review as the Admiral started to say. We are, of course, still reviewing the accuracy of the information but I could share a couple of the draft judgments with you."

"First, we believe that the Iranian government is a couple of years away from the successful development and test of a viable nuclear device. That doesn't preclude them from getting one from a supplier nation such as North Korea, China, Pakistan or India. We also believe that they stopped their nuclear weapons program in 2003 but recently started it back up. Shutting it down is one of the key points of the treaty, as you know, Ma'am."

"Second, the Iranian Navy has upgraded at least two of its Kilo class submarines to the Club-S1A missile system which can launch nuclear capable cruise missiles with a range of over two hundred fifty miles."

"If they could get a submarine undetected close enough to shore, it's possible that they could launch against nearly any major city in the world including ours. Possible, but the probability is still open for a lot of debate."

"I don't know that we have time for debate," the President said. "We need to know more and assess just how real this is. For now, we keep it close. I'd hate to have this leak out, find it's not true and be left with egg on our faces right before we sign a treaty. In the unlikely event that it *is* true, I don't want the public speculating about whether a nuclear attack is coming. That's all our economy needs right now. We're just about to get out of this recession, housing prices are on the rise again and unemployment is on the way down. We just don't need to go backwards."

Everyone around the table nodded. For the last two years, the country had struggled back from a recession caused by record oil prices, a credit crisis and uncertainty in the country's ability to deal with the fragile relationships among oil suppliers. One of the drivers behind the Iranian peace deal was to at least give the appearance of stability between the US and Middle Eastern oil producers.

"More than that, I don't want the Iranians finding out that we're running an intelligence operation in their country because we don't trust them to do what they say they are going to do."

"So, actions from this meeting," Frank was always the process oriented Chief of Staff, "CIA will run its asset in Bushehr and get back to us. By when?"

"First thing tomorrow morning'" Kopanski replied.

"CIA will status us on the NIE. By when?"

"I'll try to get that wrapped this afternoon"

"State will assess diplomatic contingencies?"

"Of course," replied Secretary Cunningham. "we're on it as soon as the meeting here ends."

"Ok," Frank continued, "and we'll follow up at 8 A.M. tomorrow morning with updates?"

"Sounds good," the President said to the group, "Let's get to it."

AS THE DCI AND DNI WALKED TO THE DOOR OF THE West Wing, McKinley turned to Kopanski. "Mike, you should have cleared an incursion into Iran through me and up through the chain. The President should have signed off on it, for Christ sake. From now on, I want all information on this channeled through me. This is too important to go sideways because of some cowboy action."

Kopanski stopped, recognizing the opening move of the familiar political chess game about to begin. In Washington, knowledge is power and sometimes, often times, the quest for power overtook the quest to get the right thing done. "Of course, I'll keep you in the loop on anything we develop."

"I think you misunderstand me, Mike." McKinley

countered. "I don't want to be in the loop on this. I am the loop. I don't need to remind you that the entire intelligence community works for me, not you. That old reporting chain went out right after 9/11. You should not have committed an asset without approval. I'm assigning an action officer from my office to ride herd on this and all information and decisions will come from me to him to the rest of you. I'll personally keep the White House informed. The President needs to be completely on top of this. Clear?"

"Clear." Kopanski relented as he thought through how to keep things moving around this bottle neck without appearing to thwart the DNI's authority. Kopanski knew that the professionals would have no choice but to take a back seat to McKinley. Shortly after 9/11, investigations exposed how poorly intelligence agencies shared information outside their own stovepipes. A previous DNI had produced a vision and plan that did away with the "need to know" mentality and replaced it with a "responsibility to provide" way of thinking. This was aimed at making sure that intelligence information was shared and shared freely. Information from different agencies was accessed in "fusion centers" and pieced together in different ways to shine the light on terrorist activities. McKinley had, in one statement, implemented the old Washington policy and undone a decade of culture shift.

The DNI turned and got into the back of his limousine. As Kopanski stared after him, McKinley picked up his secure phone and, starting with the Director of NSA, called each of the agency heads to direct them to channel the information flow through him, effectively shutting down Kopanski's ability to run the agency that was entrusted to his stewardship.

Chapter 11

Bushehr, Iran

PEYTON WALKED CASUALLY TOWARD THE CORNER and watched the man across the street first lock his door, then turn toward the harbor. Stone crossed the street in slow pursuit. At first he stepped from doorway to doorway so that, should the Arab turn around, he would not see Stone in the otherwise empty street. With greater distance between them, he moved onto the street.

The man was shorter than he, stocky, maybe sixty years old, dressed in work slacks and a long sleeve white work shirt. His sandals shuffled as he walked slowly with his head down, the hallmarks of an all-too-familiar trek. Stone stuffed his hands into his pockets and occasionally glanced around nonchalantly. He followed the man down to the harbor where a dozen fishing dhows were tied up inside a stone and gravel breakwater. A gravel roadway stretched along the breakwater's flat top to the end where boats passed in and out of the harbor. At the edge of the harbor, the man stopped in front of a small, corrugated metal shed by the shore, opened the padlocked door and went inside. The shed sat on a six-by-six foot concrete slab. A coat of ancient green paint hid beneath a liberal coat of rust. Stone moved behind the small building and stood close to the corrugated metal. He could hear loud, rattling sounds of the man at work inside.

A minute or two later the Arab came out with a large tool box and locked the door. He stepped around the side toward the water, then pulled up short and dropped the toolbox as he collided with Stone. He obviously didn't expect anyone in the vicinity. Stone could see white all the way around the man's black pupils as his eyes widened in surprise.

"Peace, brother," Stone said in Farsi, "I didn't mean to startle you. I was out for a walk and heard noise over here so I came to see if everything was alright."

The man sat down on the toolbox to catch his breath. "You nearly gave me a heart attack. Yes, everything's all right. I have to get down to the boat so I can get ready to go out."

The man struggled to breathe again. As Stone looked closer, he recalculated the Arab's age, probably middle to late sixties. The man's weathered face bore witness to years at sea. He pulled in his daily catch and ferried people and cargo on his boat to make a living as best he could in this little village next to the reactor site. "Let me carry the toolbox for you. It's the least I can do after giving you such a start."

"That's alright. I can manage," the man said as he stood up.

Stone reached around him, grabbed the handle and picked up the box. "I insist. I have two hours before I have to be at work. Now where's your boat?" He hoped that the man wouldn't realize that Stone was a stranger. In such a small village, the man was likely to know everyone.

The man shrugged in response to Peyton's repeated offer and pointed toward the harbor. Stone followed him down the dirt road that topped the breakwater. Midway, the man stopped, pointed to a fishing dhow and said with a hint of pride, "That's mine."

Stone stepped aboard the boat and turned around. "Where do you want this?"

The man waved his arm and said, "Just put it down anywhere. Thank you for your help."

"No trouble. I'm the reason you dropped it." Stone laughed as he stepped under the white canvas awning and placed the box on the deck. He looked quickly around at the boat. It was a typical wood fishing and cargo dhow known as an Al Boum, about forty feet long. A single mast for a lateen sail rose from the deck. A canvas awning covered the aft third of the boat and another, the forward section. Like many dhows, this one not only had a large sail but had also been converted to diesel. This modification allowed the sailor to maneuver with greater ease in and out of the harbor and, more importantly, to return to shore when the wind died.

Stone walked back to the tiller and noted that the fuel tank held about fifty gallons and the float gauge read full. *Good man, skipper*, Stone thought as he ducked from beneath the awning. The Arab stepped across the gunwale into the boat and blinked in the dim light cast by a single streetlight on shore and wondered what, if anything, Stone was up to.

Over the man's shoulder, Stone could see police cars slowly cruise up and down the streets of the town as they searched for him. Their search pattern was not random. They had started at the east side of the town and searched every street in an attempt to drive him toward the water.

"I need to go out to Karg Island," Stone said suddenly. "Can you take me?"

The man continued to stare. Then he blinked twice, suddenly animated, and answered, "No, no, it's impossible. I must fish today to make my delivery quota. If I go to Karg, that's a whole day wasted."

Stone reached into the back of his overalls for the Glock, which he pointed at the man's nose. "Are you sure?"

The man grabbed at his chest and sank down on one
135

knee. "Please, I have a family. I'll take you wherever you need to go. Please don't hurt me."

"All right, get up. Let's get this thing under way." The man remained motionless for a moment then skittered backwards on his hands and feet as Stone stepped toward him. "Get on the tiller. I'm about to cast off. No big hurry. We're just two fishermen."

The man moved slowly to the tiller as Stone untied the line at the stern. He stepped over the lines and stood next to the Arab, then pressed the starter button on the engine panel. The battery spun the diesel for what seemed an eternity. The engine caught, sputtered, died and caught again before the motor settled down to the familiar pocka-pocka-pocka rhythm. The small boat moved slowly on the tide toward the harbor entrance, then slipped out into the Gulf..

When they were some five hundred yards past the breakwater, Stone noticed a police car drive out the gravel road. At the same time, another patrol turned onto the breakwater on the other side of the harbor. Both cars drove to the end of the road and the drivers got out. Stone waved a friendly salute to the policemen who stood and watched the boat. He hoped they would think that he was just a fisherman out for the day's catch. Then he saw one of the officers hold a walkie-talkie to his mouth and speak into it.

Crap, Stone thought. *That probably means patrol boats will be showing up pretty soon. There's no way this dhow can outrun them. Well, we'll deal with that when it happens.*

He turned around and sat next to the Arab who was visibly shaking. "Relax, it's going to be ok. Unless you do something really stupid, you'll be home tonight for dinner with your family." The man seemed to comprehend Peyton's words but his shaking didn't abate much.

"What's your name?"

"Hamadi," the man said, rubbing his right hand across his mouth. He quickly brought his hand down and leaned forward.

"Why do you take my boat at gunpoint? What have I done to you?"

"You've done nothing. You are just along for the ride."

Hamadi's hands moved forward, palms up as he pleaded with Stone for information. "But who are you really? I knew that I didn't recognize you but I thought you must be from the reactor plant."

"I'm simply someone from the Bushehr plant who needs to go to Karg. It's important that I not be delayed," Stone explained. "On the other hand, perhaps Karg is not where I need to go."

Stone pulled the GPS receiver from his pocket and turned it on. The small handheld looked like a Blackberry cell phone. The screen lit up and a color display came on with a map that showed only water and an arrow. "Turn to port about ten degrees. See the arrow here on the screen?" Stone held the GPS receiver in front of Hamadi. "We have to keep that arrow pointed at the dot at the top of the screen. At this speed we will be where we need to be in an hour or so. Then you can get on with your life."

Hamadi looked at the screen, "And where is it that you need to be? There is nothing out there but water."

"Don't worry about that. Just think about tonight at home with your family."

Hamadi smiled thinly, unsure that everything would work out as the stranger said.

The two men rode in silence. The sky behind them lightened until the GPS display screen was no longer the brightest spot in the boat. As the minutes passed, Hamadi seemed to resign himself to the situation. He propped against the portable stadium seat that appeared to have been next to the tiller for many years. Nylon stuffing popped out of the worn padded back in at least four places.

"Ok," Stone said, "come right about 10 degrees. We should see a ship pretty soon."

"A ship? We're going to a ship? I thought you wanted to go to Karg. What kind of ship? There are very strict rules about cruise ships. We are not permitted to interfere or visit with foreigners. Do you plan to leave the country illegally?"

"You might say that." Stone tried not to smile. "You really need to calm down." He could hear the distant rumble of a boat but none was visible. As the sound grew louder, Stone's eyes swept across the horizon for evidence of a ship. Still nothing.

A movement in his peripheral vision caused him to jerk his head around. The sound was from behind them. An IRIN patrol boat bore down on them from about three or four miles away. He guessed their speed through the water to be approximately ten knots. The patrol boat was easily capable of twenty-five knots. Peyton knew they didn't have much time before this trip would be over.

"Open the throttle," Stone shouted at Hamadi, "Move as fast as she'll go. He stared into the Arab's eyes. "Stay on the current course and," and, for emphasis, he repeated, "make this boat go as fast as possible." There was a dull thud from behind, then, a few seconds later, a splash of water in front of them as a shell from the patrol boat's deck-mounted gun sailed over their heads.

This plan is headed to hell in short order, Stone

thought. He reached into his pocket and pulled out the PRC-152C radio. The radio, referred to by soldiers as the "Prick 152", was developed as a state-of-the-art battlefield walkie-talkie. This sophisticated radio, whose features included embedded GPS and data link capability with NSA-approved encryption, was basically a secure phone with email capability. He screwed the antenna onto the bayonet connector and switched on the radio.

After fifteen seconds the GPS synchronization lock-light illuminated. Stone held the radio near his mouth and spoke in English, "X-ray tango five requesting emergency extraction. I have hostiles less than three miles away and closing fast."

"X-ray tango five, Bluetail 3, radar contact. We have two targets, your radio and a surface vessel two and a half miles to your east. What's your situation?" On board the E-2C Hawkeye thirty thousand feet over the Straights of Hormuz, the US Navy radar operator tagged Stone's coded data transmission as a target of interest.

Stone fell to his knees as the boat suddenly jerked to the right and he spun around to face a wide-eyed Hamadi, "You speak English!!" Hamadi nearly screamed, "You are not from Bushehr. Who are you? You are American. You are a spy..."

Stone nearly tripped over a pile of fishnets in the bottom of the boat as it swayed, then quickly regained his balance. He reached out and grabbed the end of the tiller with one hand and pushed Hamadi backwards over the gunwale with his foot. The Iranian fisherman hit the water behind the boat and spluttered as he came up. He shook his fist and yelled when Stone quickly put the dhow back on course away from the patrol boat.

They'll pick him up eventually, he thought. *Just keep running.* He slipped the loop of rope around the tiller to keep it steady and felt around in the pile of netting for his radio.

"Bluetail 3, I have an Iranian patrol boat making twenty-five knots right up my ass and I'm on a local dhow doing about ten to fifteen. It won't be long before I'll have to explain a lot to people who won't be in a mood to listen."

"Roger that, X-ray Tango 5. Keep your head down. The cavalry's coming."

"Well, they damn well better hurry!" Stone heard a noise that was hard to describe but unmistakable to anyone who had heard it before: a convergence of hums, whistles, and hisses. The sound grew louder, lasted about three seconds and was followed by a loud "slosh" as a thirty-foot high fountain of water erupted just ahead of the dhow.

The Iranians slowed almost to a stop as two deckhands hurriedly dropped a zodiac inflatable launch over the side. Two sailors got in, started the outboard and headed over to the spot where Hamadi was treading water. They pulled him into the zodiac and, as Hamadi shook his fist in Stone's direction, they opened the throttle and closed on the dhow.

"Bluetail3, they're about 200 yards out, you got anything for me?"

"Negative, X-ray Tango 5. Your ride is still about 10 minutes away."

"Alright, I'm going to turn on the locator on the Prick radio. Keep an eye on me." Stone heard the pitch of the throttle on the Zodiac decrease the sound fade as the Iranians pulled alongside and cut power.

"Good luck, man." Stone's radio crackled as the barbed tips of the Iranian M-26 Military Taser embedded themselves in his back and sent 200,000 volts of electricity through his body. A scrap of a thought passed through his mind before he lost consciousness and fell to the deck.

IN THE SECURITY COMMAND CENTER, THE NEW Director of Training for the Second Naval District of the IRIN, Admiral Kuchecki, looked at the image frozen on the screen as he hit the "print" button. The voice had called him several hours ago to let him know that an American was about to show up in Bushehr. The Admiral picked up the phone and quickly dialed the home number of the Iranian Revolutionary Guard Corps Commander from memory. When the commander answered, Kuchecki said, "We got him. Get to the security command center as fast as you can." He put the phone down, picked up the printout and walked slowly back to his office.

Kuchecki unrolled his prayer rug and knelt in observance of Zuhr, the noon prayer that was one of two obligatory daily prayers. A devout Muslim, he didn't choose the minimum observance but prayed each time he heard the Mullah's call.

When he had completed the ritual, he rolled up his prayer rug and placed it in a handsome bespoke cover.

He looked at the framed handwritten inscription in his office, the *Shahâdah*: *none has the right to be worshipped but Allâh and Muhammad is the Messenger of Allâh.* This was the required confession that every true Muslim made as a first fundamental belief of the faith. The words helped him focus his thoughts and ensured that his prayers were offered in the strictest observance of Muslim law and tradition. In accordance with that tradition, devout Muslims prayed five times each day facing the *Ka'bah* in Mecca. The confession that hung on the western wall was his own *al Qiblah*, a locator of the holy site. The *Ka'bah*, a large square stone building, was believed to have been built first by angels and then rebuilt by Adam, Abraham and others. Surrounded now by the Great Mosque at Mecca, the *Ka'bah* remained the center of the Muslim universe: the holiest shrine in Islam. He picked up his well-worn, much-loved copy of the Holy Quran and placed it on his desk – his much smaller desk.

Kuchecki, relegated to a small concrete building perched on the edge of the desert, missed his plush office in Tehran. Bushehr was not a small town. With one hundred-seventy thousand people, a large Air Base, a navy base and a city center dating from the 1500's, the city was a vital, historic locale. But it was not – nor would it ever be - Tehran. The former Admiral of the Navy knew that he was now on the edge of power. Whatever his official rank, though, Kuchecki retained enough influence to turn the tables. The admiral knew how to play the hand he had been dealt.

Adazi, who now served as Commander of the Islamic Republic of Iran Navy, Kuchecki's former position, had won almost all of the political battles of the last six months. Not only had he kowtowed to the Defense Minister, he had also spread vicious lies about Kuchecki's involvement with the wife of another high-ranking naval officer under his command. Kuchecki, in a rare moment of personal honesty, accepted that he had slipped. How the indiscretion was discovered, though, was a matter of pure conjecture. That asshole Adazi had betrayed a trust between officers, a vicious, inexcusable act of self-promotion. Adazi was not even a good Muslim, a fact that made Kuchecki's blood boil. The man paid lip service to the religion. Kuchecki knew that while Adazi attended the Mosque on Fridays and Saturdays, he was one of the moderates who sought change and reform that would dilute the true way of The Word and the Tradition – the Sunnah. Kuchecki had grown up with a cleric father who had forced his son to memorize much of the Quran. As a child, he attended the Mosque several times a week to hear his father preach, then listened as he preached again at home during meals, before bed, anytime there was a captive audience. The same father had beaten him mercilessly when he recited the words improperly and locked him in a closet when he failed to pray at the proper times. He had learned the consequences that resulted from a lack of devotion and vowed never to suffer a greater fate from the infinitely powerful hands of Allâh.

The admiral's devotion to the faith, noticed by many at the top of the previous Iranian government, had helped propel him up through the ranks his one slip with that woman – a harlot who had seduced him, tested his will, made a mockery of his resolve when she caused him to cave to temptations of the flesh - had been his downfall as he knew it should have been. Kuchecki, however, conveniently "found" classified documents in her possession and had her arrested and jailed. If he had his way, she would be executed as a traitor.

He was startled back to reality when one of his three desk phones rang. Who knew his new phone extension? Perhaps the call was for the old Training Director. He lifted the receiver and answered, "Kuchecki."

A smooth, hypnotic voice responded, "The Chinese Military Attaché's office informs me that the training they requested from your organization has been completed. The certificates have been received and they wish to apply now for advanced courses. We hope that you will approve their application for course fifteen point five."

Kuchecki's five-foot-nine, one hundred seventy pound frame tensed as he sat up straight, now fully alert. He had waited a week for this coded message from the mysterious voice. "I believe that you have the wrong course number. You likely meant course ten." The voice was, by the description of the course numbers, trying to raise the price from ten million to fifteen and a half. Kuchecki needed to keep as much of the fifty million set aside from his operations budget intact in the event of unexpected problems. In any case, succeed or fail, any funds still in his account would be transferred to Switzerland into a numbered account that only he could access.

The voice replied, "We have already completed that basic course but you are correct about the advanced course. We would like to apply for the intermediate course number twelve."

"Very well." Kuchecki conceded to the twelve million dollar figure. "Send me the paperwork and I will approve your application."

"Thank you. The application will be sent to you and we will begin our training immediately."

The line went dead and Kuchecki hung up the phone. He sat very still and stared at the wall in front of his desk. This was a big step and he had to be certain that he was ready to proceed. Conceptually, the plan was simple: buy a nuclear device, then launch an attack to create a smoke screen for the overthrow of the West-leaning Iranian government and the start of a world-wide Islamic revolution. In actuality, however, the scheme was extraordinarily complex and involved a multitude of variables that must be managed in order to achieve victory. The secret coordination of dozens of revolutionary leaders throughout the Middle East and Asia was vital to the plan. He would also have to manage blowback from moderate Islamic countries and, most importantly, keep the United States confused so that they stayed out of the fray until he had consolidated his power across the Islamic world.

The old Arab in the Afghanistan wilderness, Ali, was Kuchecki's only contact to the weapon he was acquiring. The US Government had frozen a significant portion of the old man's assets in response to alleged funding of terrorist activities. Now he sought revenge.

The soothing voice on the other end of the call had contacted Kuchecki months earlier. The anonymous caller promised justice and it knew things: knew that Kuchecki wanted revenge for Adazi's betrayal, knew about clandestine dealings in Tehran. The voice had important connections.

At first Kuchecki thought the caller who wanted him to serve as "an instrument of change" might be SAVAK, the secret police. But the voice shared secrets. SAVAK would never do that. As the plan unfolded, the voice stated one caveat - Ali was to be the intermediary in the weapon transaction - and then cemented the deal. Kuchecki knew Ali's story and knew he could be trusted. Ali would maintain distance between the principal players and shield each of them from discovery should the plan sour on either end. Since the old Arab was a folk hero of sorts in the outlying northern provinces of Iran and Pakistan, he could travel with relative ease and calm the various factions.

Kuchecki had been surprised to learn that Ali had been part of Bin Laden's Al-Qaeda organization, the moneyman, the CFO. The voice revealed that Ali set up the money channels through various shell corporations and charities.

Ali's access to the Al-Qaeda communication channels expedited Kuchecki's critical task: to marshal an uprising of Islamic fundamentalists worldwide once the attack was launched. Again, more moving parts had to be overseen and coordinated, but at least some organization was already in place. An operation of this magnitude required both extensive planning and cooperation. One person could not manage the complexity and scope of such an implementation. At the same time, the plan required absolute secrecy: the fewer who knew, the better. For this reason, Kuchecki wanted to work within his own small circle of intensely loyal supporters.

The Admiral stared at the phone as though it might ring once again, this time with a new message: forget the last conversation and abandon the plan. He knew, though, that the coded conversation had set things in motion. Turning back was no longer an option. Negotiations to purchase the device had now begun. The transportation channel was established: an Iranian submarine crew, maintenance people at Suez, IRGC assets in eastern Iran, Al Qaeda operatives in a dozen countries. Money would soon change hands.

Kuchecki took in a deep breath and puffed his cheeks as he blew it out. He rubbed his eyes hard with both hands and stood up. *Ok*, he told himself, *the game is afoot,* as Sherlock Holmes would say. *I have to focus, think through the steps, get organized and keep the schedule intact.* The insiders would gather this afternoon. Internal squabbles over leadership would stop now that he held the trump card. All would get behind him as he led the nation, and then the world, into a new era of devotion and peace. He stared at the writing on the wall. *Father will be so proud.*

Chapter 12

Kolovostok, Kazakhstan

DMITRI ROLLED OVER AND UNTANGLED HIS FEET from the covers. He blinked in the light that streamed in around the curtains, then suddenly sat up and threw the covers back. Oh, no, it's late! His feet hit the cold floor with a double thud. He took three steps across the room and banged on the wall with his fist. "Greggor, it's light outside. Get up!"

He heard a low moan from the other side of the wall followed by, "Shut up! I'm still asleep!"

Dmitri walked quickly into his brother's room. "Get your ass up now!" He tugged at the covers and Greggor landed in a heap on the floor. "Today is the day. We have a lot to do so move it."

Twenty minutes later the brothers were headed to the nuclear storage facility south of Semipalatinsk, the vast nuclear test facility some two hundred miles north of Lake Balkhash. During the cold war, surveillance - first U-2 aircraft, then satellites - monitored activity at the sprawling complex.

The Soviet Union tested the first nuclear bomb at Semipalatinsk in 1949. The residual fallout blanketed nearby cities and towns the Soviets never bothered to evacuate. Dmitri and Greggor's father was one of many who succumbed to cancer caused by the fallout. In 1965, the Chagan test blew a crater 1,338 feet across and 328 feet deep in the Chagan River and created a new radioactive lake. The downstream flow to farms was diverted for more than six months as the crater filled.

Semipalatinsk Test Site closed in 1991 and all

remaining nuclear weapons were moved to storage bunkers where the Russian and US representatives oversaw the destruction of the entire arsenal. The storage facilities finally emptied and all weapons accounted for, the Soviets sealed the bunkers with brick and concrete and abandoned the site. The assumption that nothing remained endured. Unfortunately, record-keeping was not a Soviet strong suit.

Dmitri, a former chief accountant at the test site, drove a grey military-style truck slowly up the access road behind his brother, Greggor, who bounced up and down inside the cab of a backhoe. Responsible for oversight of the Kolovostok storage facility, Dmitri had seen the writing on the wall after the collapse of the USSR: give all of the nukes to Russia and Russia will have all of the nukes. Not a good thing, in his view. On the other hand, a single nuclear weapon would bring an unimaginable sum of money on the black market. Now that the deal was done, Dmitri now had to deal with a different problem: the attention that sudden wealth attracts.

Today, the two brothers looked like a typical repair party headed out to do maintenance on the complex. The guards at the gate barely looked at the work order that Dmitri presented. He had issued the order himself on an official form that he had taken home from work. Dimitri held the clipboard out the window of the truck. The guard simply waved him by and returned to his card game. The other three guards, who were supposed to be out on patrol around the complex, checked the cards they had been dealt while they waited, then complained about the interruption. After all weapons had been moved to supervised sites, patrols became increasingly lax, card games grew longer, and on-the-job vodka consumption increased from excessive to ludicrous. Through the closed window, Dmitri could hear the blast of rock music from a boom box in the tiny security office.

The brothers turned onto the road that Dmitri had driven dozens of times during weapons inspections and made their way a mile and a half to Bunker No. 1A01. From the exterior, the bunker appeared at first glance nothing more than a small grass-covered mound. But a long, flat sliding door was set into one side, fronted by a concrete driveway where trucks had once loaded and unloaded weapons. Greggor moved the backhoe into position in front of the concrete-encased door. He set the hydraulic hammer at the spot where the door's front apron met the vertical concrete wall, then climbed down from the cab. "Are we ready?" he asked.

"How much time will this take, Greggor? We need to be as quick as possible. Even though the patrols do a half-hearted job, I'd hate to have to explain this."

Greggor looked at his brother. "You worry more than an old woman. I have told you countless times. We break the concrete along the seam, place the charges, blow the door. We're in and out in two hours tops. Those guards will be playing cards and drinking in the gate building for at least four hours."

"And you don't worry enough, Greggor."

"A-a-h!" Greggor swatted the air in Dmitri's direction, climbed back into the cab and turned to the backhoe's controls. As he had done countless times in his job with the Road Department of the Ministry of Civil Works, he lowered the hammer and engaged the lever that triggered the hammer's rapid up and down pounding. Within minutes, large cracks appeared in the paved apron and chunks of pavement buckled and broke loose. The concrete, strong in compression, was weak in tension. After the initial breakthrough, he moved the backhoe every few minutes, then pressed the edge of the trench as he moved it along the front of the door.

Thirty minutes later Greggor stopped the machine and climbed down to examine the trench. "This is good enough, Dmitri. Let's get the explosives from the truck and get the next stage done."

Dmitri and Greggor walked quickly to the truck and retrieved a wooden crate filled with dynamite, blasting caps and a detonator box. Using the trench, they packed dynamite under the concrete that sealed the door, attached the blasting caps, and unrolled the detonator wires. The pair then dragged the wire spool around the side of the storage bunker. Greggor quickly connected the wires and set the box down next to the bunker.

"Dmitri, move the truck behind the bunker and come stand next to me. I don't want to blow your bureaucratic ass into the sky."

Dmitri feigned a hurt look, then smiled at Greggor. "How you treat me, brother, when I am about to make you a wealthy man." The two had squabbled incessantly since they were children, mostly nothing more than good-natured bluster. Family ties strong, either would have laid down his life for the other.

"We'll see. Now cover your ears and look toward the back of the bunker."

Dmitri stuck a forefinger in each ear and pressed hard as Greggor turned the charging handle on the detonator box. A loud rolling boom resounded when the dynamite went off in sequence down the trench. The brothers walked around the side of the bunker to the exposed metal door surrounded by concrete rubble strewn over the apron of the bunker.

Dmitri slapped Greggor on the back, "Nice job, brother. Now let's get to it." Greggor smiled, climbed up on the backhoe and drove around to the front of the bunker. He used the scoop shovel to clear rubble from the doorway, then Dmitri reached into his pocket and pulled out a set of keys. He approached the metal door and turned the lock. "Ha, we're most of the way there." After a few more runs across the apron, Greggor had cleared a wide-enough path to open the door and drive the backhoe into the bunker. Dmitri looked around nervously. "I just hope this noise doesn't bring the security force here."

"Well, then, let's be finished and gone."

Greggor drove inside the semicircular tube that supported the hill and Dmitri followed him. He found the breaker box and turned on the lights. Sealed for nearly twenty years, the place stank of mold and stale air. Dmitri directed Greggor past a dozen rows of shelves that contained nothing more than trash, broken electronics kits, and empty boxes. When they reached the last row of shelves, Dmitri pointed right and Greggor drove past him into the aisle. There Dmitri slid two large steel cables with eyelets on either end under a wooden crate and attached the eyelets to a bolt on the backhoe's hydraulic arm. "Ok, Greggor, lift slowly." The crate moved slightly and the cables slipped a little under the weight. "Easy! Easy! Don't you know what's in there?"

"Of course I do," Greggor replied. "It's our future," he paused for effect, then added, "or the end of it."

The crate rose off the floor. Greggor drove slowly to the open door as the crate swung precariously from the backhoe's arm. "Go get the truck, Dmitri, and let's get out of here."

He pulled forward as Dmitri backed the truck up to the front of the storage bunker and maneuvered the crate over the back of the truck's cargo bed, then stopped. Dmitri continued to back up slowly until the rear of the truck hit the backhoe. The crate swung back and forth from the cables.

"Idiot!" Greggor screamed. He jumped down from the backhoe cab, ran to the front of the truck and pulled open the driver's door. "You just backed into me. Are you crazy? You'll get us killed!"

"Well, we're still alive so go back to the tractor and get the crate on the truck."

"It's a backhoe, not a tractor!" Greggor growled. "There's a difference."

Dmitri rolled his eyes and wondered out loud whether he and Greggor shared the same parents. Greggor walked to the back of the truck and inspected the crease in the bumper covered with yellow paint from his backhoe, then climbed into the machine's cab and gently set the crate on the truck bed. After he disconnected the cables, he once more drove the backhoe inside into the bunker to the back wall. He then reversed the backhoe and, as he backed out, toppled shelves along the middle aisle with the scoop. The rubble would be a formidable barrier, he reasoned, to block the guards' access. They would not be overly eager to determine what had happened and reveal their laxity.

As the brothers drove back down the access road, Dmitri thought through the next steps. They would return to the equipment shed and leave the backhoe there to avert suspicion as long as possible. *With the work ethic on site,* he thought, *and any luck at all, forever.* Next, they would then make their way southeast to the border-crossing town of Druzhba. Dmitri much preferred the Kazakh name, Dostyk, to the harsher Russian version. The brothers would wait at a designated warehouse where the Chinese contactor sent by Mr. Fang would contact them. He would take the crate with the two warheads, then drive to the Alashankou station just across the border and authorize a wire transfer into the brothers' accounts already set up in Hong Kong. The large payment would be divided into smaller sums that could be transferred all over the globe until consolidated in the Caymans.

The truck's front tire dropped into a pothole in the poorly maintained road and Dmitri felt a shock move through his stomach, then dissipate. *Focus, you fool.* These warheads had been around for some time. While he knew that more than a simple jolt was needed to trigger a detonation, Dmitri felt fear as he drove the equivalent of a hundred and fifty thousand pounds of TNT along the deeply rutted roads.

FANG'S VOICE ANSWERED ON THE OTHER END OF THE call. "Mr. Xin," he said cheerily, "how nice to hear from you. I trust our produce has arrived at the market?"

Xin smiled to himself and looked around the large warehouse next to the rail yard in Dostyk, "Everything has arrived. The freshest I have seen in a long time."

"Excellent," Fang replied. "And I assume that our farmer partners are satisfied?"

"All taken care of," Xin said as he nudged Dmitri's dust-covered dead body with his toe. Xin stood on one foot and wiped the toe of his shoe on the back of his pant leg.

"Very well," Fang said, "I will meet you at the office," then abruptly hung up.

Xin climbed into the grey truck and drove out through the overhead door. He then got out and pushed the button to close the door. Highly unlikely that someone would come to the warehouse to deliver cargo, a couple of days would pass before the smell of decay led anyone to the two bodies. By then, he'd be long gone.

Chapter 13

Bushehr, Iran

PEYTON ROLLED OVER ONTO HIS SIDE AND SQUINTED through one eye. No movement, no sunlight. He opened his eye wider and listened to the sounds of a city that sifted through the walls: cars, conversations, the shrieks and calls of children...the same sounds heard every day around the world. He turned his head slowly but the view seemed to lag as though his conscious was slightly out of sync with the real world.

He realized that he was lying on the floor in a room furnished only with a bed and a small table. A dusty light bulb suspended on a bare wire hung from a pull box in the ceiling.

When he tried to sit up, he felt groggy and disconnected. *Have I been drugged?* He tried again to sit up. As he tried to move his arm to support his weight, he lost his balance and fell back on his side. His hands were bound behind him, his feet secured with plastic zip-ties. But he had enough wriggle room to roll on the floor and then swing up to his knees.

He slowly got up to his knees and looked around. Light passed between the louvers of a small window. Dust danced in the bright slivers that shone upon the uneven floor and undulated like gentle swells on a sunlit sea. Definitely drugs, he thought. No telling how long I've been out or where I am.

He slowly made his way on his knees to the shuttered window and struggled to stay upright. Drugged, yes, but the trash and dust along the wall in front of him confirmed that the floor sloped downward. Now balanced against the sill, he jerked his head around when the door opened. A man with a Heckler & Koch G3 rifle, dressed in a white *dishdasha* and a black and white hound's-tooth *kaffiya*, entered and looked toward the far corner of the room where he had left the prisoner. His brow wrinkled with confusion until he saw his captive by the window. He walked over and clubbed Stone with the butt of the rifle until he fell over onto his side and lay defenseless, trussed, on the dirty floor. The guard then kicked him repeatedly and spat the words, "American spy!" as Peyton's head hit the floor.

Stone rolled over on his back and groaned. "Sorry, pal," he said in Arabic, "I'm not a spy."

"Stop your lies!" The man screamed and hit him in the stomach with the butt of the rifle.

Stone huffed as air rushed from his lungs. *This is going nowhere,* he thought as he rolled onto his side, pulled his knees up to his chest and lay still. He focused on his training which taught him that, unlike fictional heroes that spat defiantly in their captor's faces, the best approach was to remain neutral, neither friendly nor confrontational.

"What do you want from me? I don't understand why I'm here." Stone, his voice even, addressed the man in the same manner that he would ask directions from a stranger.

The toe of a shoe hit his back as the captor answered quickly, "Shut up! Answer my questions, nothing more."

The door opened again and a man dressed in a white Iranian Naval officer's uniform walked into the room. Black shoulder boards bore the Iranian national symbol inside a laurel wreath, crossed scimitars and the three stars of a Daryabod, an Admiral. Peyton sized him up:

medium height, stocky build with dark hair, black eyes, thick Saddam-style moustache, and dark skin of his Arab heritage. The guard stiffened and stepped back as the admiral walked straight to Stone, stood fists on hips, and looked down at him. "Who are you?"

Stone thought for a moment as he looked for a name tag on the officer's uniform. He saw none. "My name is Peyton Stone. Why am I here?"

"That's exactly what I want to know. Who are you?" The admiral grabbed Stone's hair and pulled him into a sitting position as he asked the question.

"I'm just a regular person. I was fishing and your patrol boat picked me up illegally. I want to be sent to the American Embassy in Kuwait."

A flash of lightning erupted behind Stone's eyes as the admiral's fist connected with his cheek. Blood and saliva flew across the wall next to Peyton's head as he went down hard but he was determined not to show how much it hurt. He shook his head slightly. With every beat of his heart, he felt a corresponding throb. When he sensed that the pain had peaked, he closed his eyes, rolled on his side and sat up.

The admiral screamed. "Don't lie to me!"

"I don't understand what you want from me." Stone fought to clear the cobwebs that lingered in his brain. "How can I help you if I don't know what you want?"

"I want to know who you are and why you were in my facility." The admiral replied, his voice raspy from the strain. He bent down, put his nose inches from the captive's face and stared into his eyes. The strong smell garlic and olive oil washed over Stone but he didn't move, merely blinked and waited.

The admiral stood up and ran the fingers of his right hand through his hair, then took a deep breath and walked to the table. Stone's Glock minus the clip and his PRC-152 radio were on the table. The admiral picked up the radio, turned it over in his hands and smashed it on the tabletop. The back of the radio flew off and the admiral pulled the battery out and set both back on the table. "In case you get any ideas."

He squatted down on his haunches and rested his arms on his thighs, fingers interlaced in front of him. Now eye-level, he stared at Stone for a minute and then continued slowly and deliberately, "Look, you are an American caught in Iran without a passport, ID card or visa. That alone makes you a spy. But you were caught in a Government facility. That is far worse. You pulled a gun on an Iranian citizen and commandeered his boat. I could have my government arrest you and put you to death."

Stone maintained eye contact as he digested that sentence. "Aren't I already under arrest by your Government? After all, you already have me here."

The admiral cocked his head to the side and stared at Stone while he formulated an answer. He put both hands on his knees, pushed himself up, and spoke to the guard. "I don't have time for this. We can't keep him here. Send him to Kazim." The officer walked to the door, turned, looked back for a second, and left.

CYNDI PARIS SAT AT ONE OF THE ONE HUNDRED twenty-eight consoles located on the operations floor of the National Action Center. The NAC, located on the edge of a Government campus in Northern Virginia, was housed in a nondescript beige concrete box with a flat roof that concealed one of the most advanced real-time intelligence facilities in the world. Satellite and live reconnaissance feeds streamed in from all over the globe, available for view at the touch of a button on a sixteen-foot screen. A curved wall at the end of the room, known as "the race track", gave a God's-eye view of the earth and could be zoomed in to any hot spot anywhere, anytime.

Each analyst in the NAC was assigned surveillance of a different part of the world. Cyndi's sector displayed western Iran and the Arabian Gulf on three computer screens. The right-hand screen displayed the City of Bushehr using GeoReach, an image fusion tool that could overlay maps, drawings, satellite images and a number of other sources to produce a highly detailed picture that reached down to underground utilities and plumbing. She watched the center screen which broadcast a live video feed from a specially outfitted RQ-9 Predator Unmanned Aerial Vehicle, known simply as a UAV. The Predator was equipped with daylight and infrared television cameras that could zoom in to have a close look at events on the ground. To her left, a screen contained a suite of MASINT tools for detailed analysis of the data shown on the other two screens.

Ken Washington pulled a chair up to her console, sat down next to her and laid a sheaf of papers on the desk. "We have a beacon transmission that puts Stone about here." He pointed to a map of Bushehr. "We don't know if he's actually there or if the bad guys took his radio with the beacon. In any event, the beacon transmission stopped a few minutes ago. Do you have a way to look at this spot?" He pointed to a building that looked like a house covered by a red dot on the GeoReach image.

"The Predator is over the Navy base. I could have it moved to catch a look at this house but I'd need authorization."

"You have it." Ken said.

"Well, I'd need the Director of Missions to say it's

ok."

Ken gave her an exasperated look as he stood up. With a sigh, he headed toward the elevated office known as "The Bridge" at the back of the room which overlooked the ops floor. He climbed the three steps into the small room. "Where's the DOM?" he asked to no one in particular. The Director of Missions, a woman in an Air Force Captain's flight suit, raised her hand and he walked over to show her his CIA credential. "I need to retask a Predator over Bushehr."

"And I need a Porsche and a date with George Clooney but that ain't happening either." the woman replied.

The woman, short and slender with dark brown hair pulled back in a knot, turned her brown eyes to Ken with a half smirk. He reached in front of her, picked up the secure phone and dialed five digits. When a voice answered on the other end, Ken spoke. "Harry, I need some help." He explained the situation and then listened for a minute. "Thanks." He half tossed the phone back in the cradle, crossed his arms and glared at the woman.

"What?" she said, gesturing with upturned palms.

Ken continued to stare for about thirty seconds when the phone rang. "NAC Bridge, Sweeny". Irritation was evident in her rehearsed response. After a minute she sighed, "Yes, Sir," and hung up the phone.

Sweeny punched a button on the COM panel and spoke into her headset, "Paris, I'm sending this Agency goofball back to your station. Get on the hot line to the Air Force and put the Predator wherever he wants it." She turned and glared at Ken, "Up your ass is where I want it."

Ken smirked and bowed slightly, "Thank you kindly, Ma'am. Tell Clooney I said 'Hey!' and I hope your date likes your Porsche."

Sweeney made a rotating motion with her right hand as though she were winching up the middle finger of her left hand. Ken laughed as he turned to leave. "Oh, yeah", she said to his back," tell the DCI to be sure to wipe the lipstick off his ass after you've kissed it." His back to the DOM, Ken lowered his head, raised his hand, index and middle finger extended in a "V" and waved.

Sweeny entered the re-tasking order with Kenneth Washington as the requester into her console and pushed "send". Within minutes, the re-tasking was confirmed by both the Air Force and the NRO, then, in turn, was sent to the CIA and the Office of the DNI at Bolling Air Force Base.

IMMEDIATELY AFTER THE IRANIAN ADMIRAL LEFT, the door opened again and Peyton watched as three men entered.

"Get up," one of the men commanded.

"I am up," Peyton replied, "I can't stand with my hands behind me and my feet tied together."

Two of the men walked quickly over, grabbed him under his arms and dragged him to his feet. One of them pulled a large folding knife from his pocket. As he opened it, Stone felt a tingling in his groin that moved up to his stomach. He tensed, not knowing what to expect. The man reached down and cut the plastic ties at Peyton's ankles. Together, they pulled him forward and he stumbled slightly.

"Where are we going?" he asked.

"Cover his head."

One of the men pulled a black cloth bag from his pocket, slipped it over Stone's head, then pulled the drawstring tight and tied it to keep the bag from slipping off. Stone's thoughts returned to the cramped, dark storm sewer of his childhood but he fought hard to squelch the memories as the men grabbed him under each armpit and marched him out the door.

The first hint that they had reached the top of a flight of stairs was a change in the grip on his arms and slight downward pressure as the two men stepped off the first of the stairs. It caught Stone by surprise and he instinctively pulled slightly backwards to counteract the downward force. His feet went out from under him and he sat down hard on the first step, then slid on his butt down the flight of stairs to the landing.

"Quiet, fool!" one of the men snarled. They hauled him to his feet again and pulled him three steps to the right.

"There are more stairs here," one man said. "Step down." Stone did as he was told and this time he made it all the way down the flight of stairs and through another door. The change in sounds and the cooler air suggested that he was now outside. He could hear a constant hum in the background...not traffic, something lower in frequency. Electrical hum, maybe? Perhaps a power transformer or open high voltage lines was nearby.

He was dragged forward a couple of steps and the sound of a van door sliding open confirmed that they were indeed on the street. He tripped as one of the men pushed him forward through the van door. He fell on his side in the back cargo area and rolled to his back as he heard the door slide shut and lock.

Both front doors opened and closed when the two captors climbed aboard. The driver turned the ignition and the engine started after a couple of splutters. Once the van started to move, Stone tried to sit up but when they accelerated around a corner, he fell back and hit his head on a wheel well.

Stone's mind began to wander over the possibilities of what might follow. *Get a grip, Peyton,* he thought. The sensory deprivation of that locked room was bad enough but now with the bag over his head, he felt panic rise in his throat.

As always, when in a small space, dark sepulchral images returned. The mind games began: he imagined himself under ground where he fought against the weight of earth that pressed down on him and wouldn't allow his chest to expand. As the seconds ticked, his body began to tingle with sheer terror.

Stop it! Peyton fought to reclaim reality as he reached back into his training to get a handle on his mental state. He put his head back, opened his mouth wide and took a deep, almost yawning, breath and recalled up events and ordered them into a timeline. His mind calmed and, with this, a sense that he had control of his knowledge, if not the events, settled over him. His mind turned from the nightmarish future vision and anchored in the present.

Kuchecki's desk phone rang. When he answered, the ever-secretive Fang said, "Admiral, this is Mr. Po."

Kuchecki sighed. "I know who you are, Fang. Can we dispense with the game?"

"Security is important. We mustn't leave any room for error."

Kuchecki said nothing and waited for Fang to continue.

"There is an American who has information that could damage us. I hope to eliminate this threat but you should be aware and tighten security. You need to make certain that no information leaks."

"Who is this American?"

"From everything I can tell, he is CIA. I ran into him in Shanghai and tried to take care of the problem but U.S. military intervened. I was held for a time but they released me. Since then, I have gotten close twice but each time he managed to escape."

"And does this American have a name? Where is he now?"

"I've lost him temporarily but my resources are searching for him. His name is Peyton Stone."

Kuchecki stiffened. His stomach tingled for a moment. He took a deep breath and smiled broadly. Fang was not so mysterious and intimidating after all. "This is no longer a problem," he smiled as he emphasized the name, "Mr. *Po*."

"What do you mean?"

Kuchecki paused for dramatic effect. Elated, he was in control of the situation now. "I have him in custody."

"What? Where?"

"The American is on his way to see a friend of mine named Kazim. He'll stay there for safekeeping. But, if I know Kazim, he has about twelve hours to live. Now, don't call me again unless it's important." Kuchecki dropped the receiver into the cradle and sat back in his chair, his fingers interlaced behind his head. As he savored the moment, he leaned back, propped his feet on his desk, and grinned.

Chapter 14

National Action Center
Ft. Belvoir, VA

KEN PACED WHILE CYNDI PARIS LOOKED AT THE printed GeoReach images and compared them to the time sequenced satellite photos on her screen. She noted a location and circled the same area on each photo with grease pencil, then looked up at Ken. "It looks like a van was parked outside the building you indicated. "Here." She pointed at the next picture in the sequence. "Some people entered the van. In the third and fourth pictures, the van drives away."

Ken followed her finger as she traced the sequence on her screen. "Can you zoom in on the people? I need to know if it's Stone."

"I can try." Cyndi clicked several icons and dragged the mouse pointer across the images of the people near the van. "This is the best I can get. This guy," she pointed at the screen, "appears to have something unusual on his head. The other two are dragging him to the van."

"That's good enough for me. Is there any way to follow the van's route?"

"The satellite takes a series of images as it passes overhead. I can pull up everything I have until the bird passes the target."

Ken thought for a minute. "Is there any way to correlate recorded Predator video with the still images?"

"Sure. I can pin a location in the video to the same location on the still and GeoReach will do the overlay."

"Do it."

After what seemed an eternity to Ken, the analyst turned to him. "OK, the van headed south, the only way off the peninsula and out of the city. The Predator picked them up as they turned onto the main street south and tracked them past the Navy base, Motahery Square, and on to Azadi Square. They turned left up Highway 55 about two hours ago; then we lost them. I'm flying the Predator straight across to intercept Highway 55 about 250 clicks up the road. We should see them in about twenty minutes."

Ken walked down the hall to the cafeteria, got a cup of coffee and returned. "Anything?"

"Nope. Wait…there. That's the van. I see the same huge rust spot on the back corner of the roof. They're headed north toward Ganaveh. That's a port city. We'll just have to watch until they do something."

"Ok, I'm headed back to Langley." He handed her a small note. "Here's my cell phone number and one for an alternate contact, Harry Morrison. Call me if you see anything or, if you can't reach me, call Harry."

Ken headed to the NAC entrance where he retrieved his cell phone from the locker in the vestibule, then walked to his car. Three minutes later, he passed through the high security gate and waved at the guard who reached down and picked up the secure phone. "Washington has just left the NAC," he said when the duty officer answered.

THE VAN THAT CARRIED PEYTON AND HIS TWO captors away from Bushehr began to bounce violently as it left the pavement and the driver headed across country. After an hour or so, the ride smoothed out again when it turned onto another paved road. Now Stone could hear other cars, an indication that they were on a main road.

"Hey!" he banged his feet on the floor of the van. "I have to use the toilet! Hey!" He yelled at the top of his lungs. The van stopped and the side door slid open. Stone, caught off-guard by a sudden crushing blow to the solar plexus, fought to recover. The spasm that followed the gut punch pushed all of the air from his lungs. He couldn't draw a breath for a long time. Just before he passed out, Stone regained control of his abdomen and bladder, inhaled deeply with a loud wheeze and filled his lungs with air.

"Shut your mouth," the man whispered through clenched teeth.

"Look, if I don't get to a toilet, I'm going to piss all over the back of your van."

"All right," the man replied, "just sit still and we'll take care of it."

The van pulled into a gas station and the captor crawled into the back of the van. He removed the hood and cut the plastic ties from Stone's hands. "I will walk you to the toilet and you can go inside. If you try anything stupid, I'll kill you. Do you understand?"

Peyton nodded, then sat up and rubbed his wrists to get the circulation back. He crawled to the door of the van and stepped out. The man walked him to the men's room, opened the door, and motioned for Stone to enter. He walked in, closed the door, and latched it, grateful for a locked door between him and the world, however temporary.

The toilet room was brightly lit and the walls were finished in bright white ceramic tile but the floor was filthy, with toilet paper, paper hand towels, and a puddle of what he hoped was plain water. He quickly scanned the walls as he stood in front of the single urinal and read the graffiti scribbled at random intervals. Then he saw a sign next to the sink on the far side of the room that implored patrons to keep the rest room clean. A number to call in the event the restroom needed maintenance was printed in bold followed by a single phrase: "Thank you – The Oil Ministry of Iraq." Stone realized the off-road excursion must have taken them across the border in order to by-pass guards at the checkpoint.

He heard a knock on the door. "You've had plenty of time. Let's go."

Stone took a deep breath and studied his bruised and bloodied face in the cloudy mirror. He lathered his face with the hard soap stuck to the edge of the lavatory and rinsed. Dirt and blood swirled down the sides of the sink into a rusty drain. He then turned, opened the door and stepped out to face his captors. "I still don't know why you are doing this to me."

"Just get in the van." The man said.

CYNDI DIALED KEN'S CELL PHONE. NO ANSWER. She picked up the secure line and called Harry Morrison. "This is Cyndi Paris at the NAC," she said when Harry answered. "I've been working with Ken Washington on locating an asset in Iran." She caught Harry up on everything that had happened before Ken left the NAC.

"The van I've been following just crossed into Iraq. They passed through a breach in the fence near Shalamcheh Mosque, north of Basra and south of Camp Sinbad. The U.S. forces should have access now if you're trying to get your guy back. I can give you a position update."

"Yeah, where are they exactly?" Harry asked.

"They turned west on the highway approximately three miles from Border crossing #7. The van stopped at the first gas station about 10 miles up the highway on the outskirts of Basra. I can zoom in...wait a minute.

Something just happened. My feed went blank. Let me try a couple of things and call you back."

"Ok, I'm going to call CENTCOM and get them moving. Call me when you have something."

STONE SAT IN THE BACK OF THE VAN AS THEY LEFT the Iraqi gas station and tried to focus his mind. Thankful that he no longer wore the hood, he sank back against the wheel well as the rear wheels spun slightly on loose gravel, then caught. The van bumped forward and headed down the highway.

Peyton looked for potential escape routes. He couldn't go forward and overpower the driver. Even if he could get free and was physically able to subdue the passenger, a thick wire mesh safety screen stood between him and the front of the van. The side door was locked from the outside. Stone had seen the padlock hasp as he crawled into the van, heard the lock turn as he waited for the driver to climb aboard. He could only surmise that the back door had the same padlock, typical for a delivery van in this part of the world.

They continued in silence for almost an hour. Peyton ignored his hunger. He tried to sleep but every time he drifted off, the van jerked and awakened him. The metal skin of the vehicle acted as a giant speaker cone that amplified the whine of the rear wheels on the highway.

The two men in the front barely spoke to each other until the driver let out a string of expletives in Farsi. His attention was focused on the left-hand rear-view mirror. He looked up every few seconds to keep the van on the road. Peyton could hear the whine of the tires and the drive shaft increase in pitch, a sign that they were steadily increasing speed. Every thirty seconds or so, the right-front passenger stuck his head out the window and look backward. Peyton was perplexed. Something was going on, but what?

The two men turned their attention to the road in front and the van accelerated until the entire vehicle vibrated. From the back of the van, Peyton could see only the scenery in front, blurred by speed. He no longer rocked gently from side to side. As they dodged slower traffic, Peyton was now thrown from one wheel well to the other. He could have been severely hurt had he not braced himself by flipping his bound hands under his feet so they were in front of him. He rolled onto his side and stretched across the van with his arms extended above his head.

Suddenly a loud bang reverberated and a hole appeared in the rear door. A stream of light laden with airborne particles and dust now shone throughout the interior. The van continued to rock while the driver raced around slower traffic. Another bang and a second hole ripped through the back door. Peyton heard the bullet slam into one of the wire mesh screen that separated him from the front compartment. The passenger yelped and grabbed his shoulder as a piece of hot shrapnel tore through his shirt and entered the soft tissue at the base of his neck. The wild-eyed driver glanced sideways quickly and then looked back at the road. He swerved just in time to miss a slower car in front of them. Then he looked in the rear view mirror and drew in his breath as the entire van shuddered. Peyton was thrown against the back doors. Someone had just hit them in the back end – hard. The van rocked violently and the driver waggled the steering wheel as he regained control.

Peyton skittered forward and braced himself as another large whump sounded and the back doors opened wide, bounced off the sides of the van, then swung shut. In that split second, Peyton saw a U.S. Army Humvee. This up-armored, high mobility, multi-purpose wheeled vehicle weighed 5,200 pounds without 2,000 additional pounds of O'Gara-Hess & Eisenhardt armor. Peyton held on as best he could and braced for the impact. This time the flat nose of the Humvee bent the back doors so they stayed half open. Peyton climbed to the back, stood up, and held his bound wrists high so that the Americans could see him.

The Humvee came at the van again but this time slowed as it got almost to the point of contact, then held its distance a few inches from the back bumper of the fleeing van. Peyton calculated the distance and the likelihood that he could leap onto the hood of the Humvee. He swung his weight back to make a leap. As he jumped, the van driver swerved. Peyton hit the half-open door and held on as he swung precariously over the pavement that flashed past beneath him. Without the floor for resistance, he couldn't jump onto the Humvee nor could he jump back into the van. He hung onto the door, redoubled his efforts, painfully aware of the consequences should he lose his grip.

The wind generated by the speeding van pushed against the door which remained at a right angle to the cargo compartment. Peyton reached as far as he could with the toe of his shoe and hooked the top of the bumper and pulled. Slowly, the door began to close and he moved closer to the van. At that moment the top hinge of the door bent from the strain and he felt his weight shift away from the compartment. He now swung uncomfortably close to the pavement. The Humvee moved to the right. Peyton knew that if he fell he would not be crushed under the tire of the three-ton vehicle but, at high speed, this knowledge provided little comfort.

Peyton reached back with his foot to no avail since the distance was too great. He passed hand over hand across the top of the door and hoped that the battered metal would hold until he could get back inside the van. He slid his right hand closer to the van as much as the plastic ties would allow and shifted his weight. The door bent a little farther outward and he quickly moved his left hand. When the driver swerved to go around a slower car, the door swung inward and Peyton fell backwards into the cargo compartment of the van. At this moment, the lower door hinge snapped and the door flipped backwards, sideways at first, then under the front wheel of the Humvee. The heavy vehicle barely changed course as it crushed the door. The bent metal bounced off the underbelly armor, flipped into the air behind the Humvee and landed with a crash beside the road.

Peyton crawled quickly to the back of the van and positioned himself in the back door. Once again he positioned himself to leap onto the huge hood of the Humvee. If only he could get his hands free. It was then that he saw the jagged metal where the door had broken free and he quickly used the raw steel to cut the ties from his wrists.

The gunner in the Humvee's turret held up his hand for Peyton to stop and then climbed down the windshield. He inched forward on his belly onto the hood of the Humvee and spread his legs until his feet were splayed at the bottom of the windshield. Braced on the truck's brush guard, he reached out to Peyton and motioned him forward.

The vehicle ran over a set of rumble strips on the roadway and he had to reposition. As soon as the American soldier was once more in position, Peyton started to reach out. The van swerved again and he barely hung on. *Ok, let's try again*, Peyton thought. The Humvee moved into position again as the van hit another set of rumble strips.

Stone grabbed the top of the remaining door, pushed off with his foot and the door swung hard from the van. He arced outwards and stretched. He felt as if his shoulder had separated and his arm now floated toward the Humvee. He was still inches too short.

The soldier readjusted his boot's grip on the hood and stretched closer. Closer. Closer. Time slowed and Peyton saw the fingertips inch toward his. Another set of rumble strips and the van slowed slightly, a half-mile an hour. Enough.

Fingers locked. Weight and position shifted. Hands locked. Then eyes.

With a slight nod, the solder pulled as Peyton let go and flew suspended over the speeding pavement. He could hear a loud "Hooyah!" as the soldier expelled his breath. With all of his strength and concentration, he pulled Peyton toward the Humvee. The driver kept the speed constant since braking would shift weight forward against the soldier's pull.

Stone felt no sense of movement but suddenly the front of the Humvee touched his chest. He grabbed the steel tube frame of the brush guard and held on so tightly that he was convinced he would leave permanent fingerprints in the metal. The soldier grabbed the back of Peyton's belt and hauled him onto the hood of the Humvee while the driver began to slow the vehicle.

The soldier pointed urgently over Stone's shoulder. Peyton looked back to see an Apache helicopter lining up on the van. He scrambled forward, pushed his foot into the space behind the brush guard frame and held on as the Humvee quickly pulled to the side of the road and stopped.

Peyton lay on the hood of the Humvee and collected his breath, his thoughts, his sanity. He rolled onto his back and looked at the van. The Apache approached from the side and he watched the M230 cannon blast push the van sideways. The battered vehicle left the road and tumbled into a drainage ditch. The Humvee pulled slowly forward toward the smoking pile of metal and Peyton saw scorched bits of clothing that confirmed the two jihadists had successfully made the transition to martyrdom.

KEN ENTERED THE LANGLEY HEADQUARTERS building and showed his badge to the night shift guard in the lobby. As he made his way to Harry's office, he thought, *Man, you'd better be here.* He had no doubt that he would find Harry at his desk, once again burning the midnight oil. When the man got his teeth into something, he was a bulldog. Ken turned the combination lock on Harry's door and opened it. Sure enough, the lights were on and Harry was hunched over his desk with his brow attached to a 3-D viewer.

"Anything?" Ken asked as he stepped into the room.

Harry jumped with a start and whirled around, an angry look on his face. "You scared the bejeezus out of me, asshole. Don't do that!!"

Ken looked at the floor, suddenly embarrassed. "Sorry. I didn't mean to."

"I got a call from the NAC. They couldn't reach you but they say that the van with Peyton has entered Iraq. NAC lost its feed but not before I got a good location and I called CENTCOM."

"So, did we get Peyton back?" Ken stood in front of Harry's desk.

"Don't know yet. We should get a call from CENTCOM as soon as something happens."

"Man, how long do they think it will take to find him on the ground and get him back?"

Harry looked a little flustered. He loathed not having answers when people asked questions, even if the answers were impossible. "We'll just have to wait and see. Meanwhile we have new images from NGA."

"Right," Ken said, "Let's have a look."

"Ok, Rookie, pull up a chair. These photos just came in from the Dakota Ground Station. The resolution is ten times better than the earlier passes. Take a look and tell me what you see." Harry handed a twenty-four-inch square photo to Ken.

Ken looked at the photo, then placed it on the desk under the viewer. "Still a little hard to read. Put the digital on your screen and let's play with it."

Harry brought the digital images up on his computer screen, turned, magnified and enhanced the images. He pointed to the first scan. "The shadow appears to be mounted under the hull here." Harry opened another photo. Here, the smudge doesn't seem attached at all." Finally, he brought up another photo. "In this view, two unknown shapes are present. I'm stumped."

They sat for the next two hours and tried different magnifications and color and resolution enhancements,. "Look, I'm feeling brain dead." Ken said. "It's two in the morning and I have a nine o'clock stand-up briefing. I'm going to cash it in. Let's work on this tomorrow. Let me rephrase. Later today."

"Ok, go ahead. I'll shut down and be right behind you. I want to try one more thing."

"Harry, you are way too dedicated for a GS-13. You really need to examine your life goals." Ken grinned and added, "You need to get a life."

The big man turned toward him, his left eyebrow raised, and replied, "Excuse me while I calculate how

174

many ways to say 'career-ending conversation'."

Ken laughed nervously, reached out and offered his hand. "See you tomorrow."

"Later today." Harry smiled and turned back to his screen. He put the images side by side on the screen. As he stared at the picture, an idea began to form. He looked at each picture in turn, then looked at each one again, only a little faster this time.

"Ah-ha!" he mumbled. "Do I see what I think I see?"

Harry called up another image processing program and stitched the photo frames together into a motion strip. When he had the last two images matched, he pressed the motion play button and sat back slightly in his chair. His mouth dropped open as he watched the motion loop run over and over. This revealed an image not next to the ship but under it. The smudge moved almost imperceptibly, closer and closer to the ship, until it virtually disappeared.

What in the world? That looks like a submarine positioning itself under the ship. *I need more film*, he said to himself as he wrote a note on his desk pad. Harry smiled at the irony. *We still call images film although all are digital.* The photo chemical processing lab was turned into a fitness center years ago. *I need to put a visit there in my schedule. Yeah, right.* He pulled up the tasking manifest on his screen and sent an urgent request to the duty officer for a photograph.

Harry noted exact coordinates, as well as the number and image types he expected on his desk later that morning. The duty officer would relay the request to the National Reconnaissance Office which would then forward it to a ground station in a remote part of the US. The coordinates would then be uplinked to the satellite that would photograph the specified area. In this case,

Harry requested movie speed: high-resolution HD electro-optical images at twenty frames per second.

Chapter 15

Jerusalem, Israel

THE CIA JET WITH PEYTON STONE ON BOARD touched ground at Ben Gurion airport just over an hour ago. A driver met him and hurried him to an official Government car which was now on its way to Jerusalem. The only international airport in Israel was named in honor David Ben Gurion, the first Prime Minister, whose good friend, Reuven Shiloah, had spurred Ben Gurion to create the Mossad in 1949. At that time, Ben Gurion named Shiloah the Mossad's first Director. The Prime Minister had not forgotten who managed to obtain the Arab League's war plans just before the outbreak of the 1948 Arab-Israeli War, turning the tide for Israel with his counter-planning and execution of the war. Only in 1951, after two years of political infighting, did the Mossad became a functioning organization with Shiloah at the helm. He coordinated intelligence activities between the Army, the domestic service known as Shin Bet, and the foreign intelligence office, leaving in 1952 to work in the Israeli Embassy in Washington. Fatigue didn't diminish Stone's respect for these men who, against all odds, built the foundation of the nation of Israel. Peyton gazed out of the window and knew that he was passing through the very core of history.

Peyton thought of Harry and was grateful that he was able to get the jet but he would rather have gone home than come here. Harry insisted that a contact at Mossad had information that was vital to the case. Rachel landed earlier that morning and would meet him at Mossad headquarters. The black Mercedes sedan traveled southwest from the airport through vast fruit orchards and farmland along Road 6, past the Latrun Interchange, then up Jaffa Road to Jerusalem. As the road snaked up through the pass and into higher country, Stone noticed memorials along the roadside, reminders of the past battles with neighboring Arab states. The ongoing conflict stretched back over three thousand years. Stability following the hard fought victories of the late 1940s and early 1950s did not materialize as hoped. The bloody struggle for a tiny strip of land, holy to millions of people of differing faiths, continued with only brief respites.

The sedan stopped in front of the headquarters building. Stone, wearing a borrowed flight suit in place of his filthy Bushehr coveralls, was ushered into a gray, institutional reception area. Awake for more than forty-eight hours, Stone wanted only to check into a hotel somewhere – anywhere – and sleep. Why did they have to meet in Jerusalem rather than at the American Embassy in Tel Aviv, much closer to the airport? Arms crossed, legs stretched out, crossed at the ankles, Peyton sat waiting, the droning buzz of a fly near the window lulling him to sleep.

As his head dropped onto his chest, a woman entered the reception area through the far door. She was dressed in a bright print dress and wore her hair in a 1940's style, her bright red lipstick reminiscent of the Andrews Sisters. She took two steps into the room, held the door open behind her, and looked straight at Peyton. "Mr. Stone, follow me, please?"

Stone shook his head slightly as he stood and walked to the door. Light-headed, eyelids dry and scratchy, he desperately needed rest. The Danny Glover line from *Lethal Weapon* surfaced. *I'm getting too old for this shit.* Stone smiled tiredly at the woman as they entered a long hallway.

"This way." As she brushed past him, he breathed in her soft, appealing fragrance, one that he didn't recognize. Stone wanted to ask the name but was too tired to speak. She opened a door on the right-hand side of the hall, issuing him into an office.

A man sat behind a desk. Rachel sat across from him in one of two leather chairs.

"You're not with them are you?" Peyton's thought came out of his mouth before his tired mind could stop it.

Rachel sat back and let a short laugh, "No. This is Sylvan Kelman, Director of the Collections Department in the headquarters of the Institute for Intelligence and Special Operations."

"Yes, yes, Mossad. I know where we are. No need to get all formal."

Silvan rose slightly, shook Stone's hand and then motioned to the other chair. Silvan was an internationally renowned intelligence operative but in person he seemed a bit awkward and unpolished to Peyton. Stone collapsed into the chair next to Rachel and looked over at her.

"You look as if you've had better days," she said. He was uncertain whether fatigue or Rachel's presence made his dizziness a little more pronounced. Her red hair fell just above her shoulders and her brilliant green eyes sparkled in the light that streamed through the window. She didn't seem to mind that Stone was simply staring at her. He wondered why he didn't feel guilty, only attracted. He concluded that he must be more tired than he thought.

Finally, Peyton responded. "I have, indeed."

"Well, we're glad you came here today." Silvan quickly snatched Stone's attention from Rachel. "Your government has asked for our help. We thought that, in the interest of time, you should come here instead of returning to the U.S. Your government agreed."

"I certainly appreciate that," Stone said, "but, frankly, I need some rest before I start a detailed debrief."

"Of course, but if you would indulge us for just a short while, I'd be most grateful."

"Sure. I didn't find anything, got captured, and barely got out. Anything else?"

Silvan's tight smile disappeared quickly. "Just a little more detail would be nice. For example, what areas did you see, where did you go, to whom did you speak?"

"Look, I don't want to be difficult but I need sleep." Stone could not keep his eyes open. "I'm not answering any more questions right now."

"All right, Mr. Stone." Silvan turned slightly and slapped the palm of his hand on the desktop as he rose stiffly from his chair. "Ms. Kleinmann will show you out. How much time do you need?"

Stone thought of bygone days when a power nap, a shower and a cup of coffee could revive him. Today a couple of days in a big bed sounded great. He compromised. "How about tomorrow morning?"

"How about three o'clock this afternoon?"

"How about dinner?"

"Fine." Silvan agreed, adding, "You have a room at the King David. We'll see you in the lobby at six."

Stone turned and waved at Silvan over his shoulder as he headed down the hall with Rachel walking closely behind him.

"You shouldn't take him too lightly," she said in low voice that gave her statement a conspiratorial urgency. Rachel had seen Silvan's frown as they left his office. "He's helping us and has significant resources. Please don't piss him off."

"I know, but we can handle this. Who asked for his help anyway? Not me."

"No, the White House asked."

Stone stopped and turned. "Seriously? It's gotten to the White House?"

Rachel stopped a step away. Stone caught a slight whiff of lemons. "Of course it has. This is serious. We have a treaty a week away and either the government of Iran is pulling a fast one or someone is working to derail the process. Either way, it has to be stopped."

"Perhaps so, but I got into this because my friend was murdered and I just happened to be in the building when you showed up. Now I'm getting sucked in deeper and deeper. My feelings wouldn't be hurt if he threw me out." They crossed the reception area and he reached down and opened the front door.

A shadow crossed her face. Peyton took a deep breath. "Look, I'm tired and cranky." He continued. "Let's start over at dinner and I'll bring you both up to speed on what I know, ok?"

She hesitated slightly, smiled and nodded. Looking over his shoulder toward the car waiting outside, she said, "I'll see you tonight then."

Stone turned and walked toward the car. As he opened the passenger door, he looked back but she was already gone. As he settled into the leather seat, thoughts of Stephanie crept into his mind and a sadness washed over him. The past, never far away, surfaced when his guard was down. Now, exhaustion was taking a heavy toll.

"King David Hotel." The driver turned and handed him a check-in packet, then dropped the car into gear.

"Room six twenty-one. You are already checked in,

Mr. Stone." The driver spoke without looking in the rear view mirror as he drove through the courtyard gate and into the street. "Go straight to your room and no one will connect you with us."

Peyton stared sightlessly out the side window, no longer able to focus, as they passed the Damascus Gate to the old city and made the sweeping right turn onto King David Street. The car pulled up to the pink sandstone building and Stone leaned forward, his hand on the door handle. Suddenly he realized that he was still in the flight suit from the jet, hardly appropriate dinner attire.

He got out, leaned into the passenger window and addressed the driver. "Are there any good shops nearby where I could find a change of clothes? The hotel shops are pricey."

"All of your requirements are waiting in your room, Mr. Stone." The driver slowly pulled away as Stone stared at the car.

"Resources," Stone muttered to himself as he entered the lobby. Taking the elevator to the sixth floor, he quickly located his room.

SOMEWHERE IN THE DISTANCE, AN ANNOYING ringing sound increased in volume. In Stone's dream, Xu was riding a bicycle, ringing the bell on the handle bar as he approached Stone at breakneck speed. Xu continued to ring the bell frantically, reaching out to Stone with his other hand, a terrified look on his face. Behind Xu, a Russian-built car with Fang at the wheel quickly closed the gap between the front bumper and the bicycle. Peyton reached to help Xu, knocked over a bottle of single malt scotch whiskey and found he couldn't stand up to help his friend.

He awoke with a start. His head came up off the

pillow so fast his neck muscles cramped slightly. As the fog of sleep cleared, he realized that the telephone on the nightstand next to the bed was ringing. He picked it up as his head fall back onto the pillow.

"Good evening, sir." A detached but cheerful voice said, "This is your 5 p.m. wake up call."

"Where am I?"

"Excuse me, sir?"

"Never mind, thanks."

"Would you like a follow-up call in ten minutes, sir?"

"Probably a good idea."

Stone clumsily aimed the receiver at the cradle as the voice continued, "Certainly, sir. Thank you for staying at the King David Hotel."

Peyton forced himself into a sitting position. Six hours had passed since he had fallen across the bed into a deep sleep. Light leaking around the edges of the room-darkening draperies revealed the shadowy outlines of furnishings. He drifted back to consciousness in the semi-darkness then turned on the bedside lamp. Peyton slowly stood up, stretched, and walked toward a shopping bag on a nearby table.

He opened the curtains slightly and looked in the bag. There were three sets of Jockey briefs, three pairs of socks, and a bathroom kit. In the closet he found three shirts, three pairs of slacks, a blazer, belt and a pair of shoes. As Peyton started toward the bathroom, he thought, *Here's hoping they know my sizes as well as they know Hasan Nazrallahs's.* Mossad scrutinized every aspect of Nazrallah, Hezbollah's rabid, long-time leader, who held an intense, abiding hatred of Jews. They knew everything about him, "right down to his shoe size" as the saying goes.

The phone rang loudly. Stone's whole body tensed

as he turned toward the bedside table. He took a quick breath and picked up the receiver. A cheery voice announced, "This is your follow-up wake up call, sir."

"Thanks."

"Certainly, sir. Thank you for sta..." Stone had already hung up the phone, picked up the bag and headed for the bathroom before the desk clerk could finish.

Freshly showered, dressed in his new clothes, Stone headed across the lobby of the hotel to meet Silvan, trying not to limp. All of the clothes were a perfect fit, except for the shoes, which were a bit tight.

Peyton assumed - hoped - that Rachel would be there as well. The feelings she engendered continued to intrigue him. He still couldn't figure out what they meant.

The large, high-ceilinged lobby was reminiscent of the nineteen twenties and thirties. The hotel, just shy of its one hundred year anniversary, had hosted renowned guests from Europe, Africa, Asia and the Americas. This eclectic group included celebrities such as Cary Grant and famous exiles, among them Spain's ousted King Alfonso XIII and Ethiopia's *Haile Selassie*. The King David turned a blind eye to the region's feuding, welcoming King Abdulla I of Jordan, Henry Kissinger, and countless Israeli dignitaries.

Stone approached a group of wing chairs and heard a cheery, "Well, you're looking better." Rachel stood next to a large column, gave him a half wave when he turned toward her.

Peyton thought, *You're not so bad yourself.* Responding politely, he smiled and said, "Thanks, I feel better after a little rest. Where's Silvan?"

"He had an emergency meeting but will be here as soon as possible, perhaps an hour or two." Peyton felt relief when Rachel quickly added, "We won't wait for him. You must be starving. While we eat, you can tell me what you found and we'll go from there." She smiled and said, "There's a nice restaurant right here in the hotel."

"Sounds good to me."

Rachel turned toward Peyton as they crossed the lobby. "I'll call Silvan if he's not here in an hour and see how things are going."

The pair walked up the grand staircase to the restaurant. A maitre d' with a pencil-thin moustache perched above equally thin lips led them to a private corner of the restaurant to a table set for three. In the dimly lit room, the fine crystal and silver settings shone with the warm glow of candlelight. The menu was extensive but each decided quickly. Peyton ordered drinks, a glass of wine for Rachel, a Diet Coke for himself, and their entrées as well.

As the waiter left, Rachel spoke first. "I'd love to hear about your visit to the beach. I'm ready for a vacation myself. And feel free to make hotel and restaurant recommendations." Laughing, she held up her purse size notepad. "I came prepared." Careful to avoid words that might draw the attention of others seated nearby, she leaned toward Peyton.

Peyton smiled, speaking in a quiet voice. "Pretty uneventful for the most part. I left some pretty expensive gear behind, spent time as a guest of a Navy Admiral, and made a quick exit; but, otherwise, I didn't find much."

"Is the gear traceable?"

"I hope not. The sled and rebreather are definitely our manufacture but we put Egyptian property tags on them. The Iranians won't believe for a minute that Egypt is spying on them but, then again, they might.

They can't trace the equipment directly to us." Rachel cut her eyes left and right to check for reaction from other tables, giving Stone a subtle 'be careful' look.

Peyton leaned toward her and lowered his voice more, almost to a whisper. "I talked to a couple of shop workers who said they were waiting on production parts and couldn't get them. I know that the EU is not interested in selling parts in that country and the UN has tried to lock down as much of the supply channel as possible. North Korea is struggling with its own issues. This leaves Russia and the Chinese. We've been watching both carefully and the only thing remotely resembling reactor equipment is a picture of a North Korean freighter tied up at Bushehr but that would seem to be nothing if you can believe the workers I talked to. They said it only brought piping for centrifuges."

Rachel sipped her wine. "Did you get to check the reactor building?"

"I only got as far as the shop when the drama started. I had to get out fast. Reactor #1 is up and running and reactor #2 is close. When I got there, I could see that the cooling spillways are nearly finished but, otherwise, nothing out of the ordinary."

"I got a boat and headed out for the pick up when the bad guys caught up with me and brought me to some building in Bushehr. An Admiral came in and questioned me but when I wouldn't tell him anything, he sent me to 'Kazim,' whoever that is. The Army pulled me out on the way there and now I'm here."

Rachel looked around again, ostensibly searching for the waiter. The sudden cessation of conversation at the next table concerned her. The two men were eating ravenously but, in the past, her suspicions had served her well. As Rachel smiled at Peyton, she ran her fingers through her hair and tossed her head slightly toward the two men, furrowing her brows to signal Stone.

At that moment the waiter arrived and placed their appetizers on the table with way too much flourish and swished away.

"So, are you married?" Peyton asked with a smile.

"No. You?"

"No." Peyton pushed a piece of calamari across his plate before continuing. "Not now."

Rachel looked at him quizzically but asked no questions. She noticed a change in his demeanor as soon as he answered her. His eyebrows moved downward. When he spoke, his lips had lost their animation.

"I was married for many years." Peyton added continuing to slowly move the piece of fried squid from one side of his plate to the other. "My wife was killed."

Rachel, unsure how to respond, said nothing but her face asked the question.

Peyton slowly answered, "I was away working on a project for Harry. We were successful and stopped some really bad guys in the desert not all that far from here. I guess they wanted to even the score and rigged my car right in my driveway. I missed my connection in Frankfurt and had to stay over to catch the a flight the next day." He spread his hands to speak the unspeakable conclusion.

Rachel looked into his red-rimmed eyes and shared his sadness for a moment.

He put his fork down and abruptly changed the subject. "I have two boys. One is a professional diver and the other is an engineer. They work together on a military program involving robots or something. I'm embarrassed that I don't know more about their work. The cycle repeats: I'm busy, they're busy, life seems to move by too fast." He looked at Rachel, a rare note of nostalgia creeping into his voice. "I keep thinking about that old Harry Chapin song, *Cat's in the Cradle.*" He sat quietly, the lyrics running through his mind. *"And as I hung up the phone, it occurred to me he'd grown up just like me. My boy was just like me ...".* The last line of the final chorus haunted him. *"When you coming home, son? I don't know when, but we'll get together then. We're gonna have a good time then."* Peyton had already realized he had to change his priorities before the damage was irrevocable. *Too many broken promises, too many,* he thought.

He looked up, embarrassed, as if Rachel could read his thoughts. "Well, I'm a real party this evening. Sorry about that."

Rachel looked at him for a moment, her eyes meeting his. She smiled. "I understand. I was married once." A cloud settled over her face and she looked down at the table, moving her thumb and forefinger up and down the stem of the wine glass. "We didn't have children."

"We were both in the IC. I was at Langley and he was at Ft. Meade. He drew an assignment to go to Australia for a couple of months to work on some new systems at the ground station there. He went to Bali for a weekend, as many of them do, and a bomb at the hotel brought down the whole wing where he was staying."

"Geez, I'm so sorry." He reached across the table and placed his hand lightly on top of hers, then pulled away. She looked into his eyes again, searching. Slow to trust and deeply private, both Rachel and Peyton felt awkward.

Rachel spoke again, in part to relieve the tension of the moment. "I grieved for him. Went through emotional hell. We were that perfect couple. At least everyone thought so. Then I got my hands on a copy of the CIA investigation report. Turns out his body was found still in the burned bed but there was another body with him." Her lips disappeared and her eyes turned slightly red for a moment.

She took a deep breath. "Still, the bombing took so many innocent lives. Along with the not so innocent. When SCEPTER was formed, I put in a request to transfer and was the first woman to join. Since then, my life's mission has been to get as many terrorist bastards as I can before I'm too old to hunt them anymore." All previous emotion gone, she continued. "I've had more successes than disappointments. For nearly five years, this has been my life. I have had little time for anything else."

Stone looked at Rachel who was staring into the candlelight, a brief antidote to the darkness that haunted her. She looked up rather abruptly, her rigid discipline over-ruling the pain. "I'm really sorry," Peyton repeated. The two sat in silence for a few moments.

She ran her fingers through her hair. "Me, too." She smiled and said, "Tell me about more about yourself."

"Oh, not a lot more to tell. After my wife died, I went through a dark time." He stopped and look at her wondering why he was telling her this. Not even realizing he was telling her until it was already out. *What is it about her?*

"Things got a little touchy and I sort of checked out. Still went to work, still ran my business. Well, sort of. If it hadn't been for Ace, my senior manager, I probably wouldn't have a business. She saw me through some really tough times."

Rachel stared for a moment as an unexpected feeling passed, saw an opportunity to liven the conversation. "What exactly *is* your business?"

"After I got out of the military, I started a security

consulting company, taking care of high profile people: executives, sports figures, celebrities. The clientele list grew, as did the scope of our work. We moved from small home systems to more sophisticated, comprehensive security strategies for business and government. I took on a partner and we went international. A few days ago, my partner was murdered in Shanghai. I was at the agency looking for information when you showed up." Rachel brushed her lips lightly with her index finger. Her expression reminded Stone to lower his voice.

"Along the way, I've done 'odd jobs' for the Government. Sometimes a civilian is needed to take care of matters that would otherwise implicate a member of government. Occasionally I get a call because a department is short on resources or because my past ventures were successful and they know they can count on me. That's how I ended up here today."

Rachel continued to look into his eyes. A desire passed between them and just as quickly faded. "Well, I'm glad you're here. This is a tough one to figure out."

"I'll do what I can. I have to admit that I've been at this for a while. I'm beginning to notice a creaking noise in my left knee that wasn't there before."

Rachel laughed loudly. "Welcome to the club, old timer. But, I must say, you look fit." She blushed slightly. "I notice the same creaks but I can still do a mile in just under five and a half minutes. Not bad for, well, for my age."

Stone smiled. Small talk had never been easy for him but, with Rachel, he felt relaxed. Caught up in the conversation, Peyton was surprised when he glanced at his watch. He and Rachel had been talking for almost an hour but he felt as if they had just sat down.

They were daring each other to order dessert when Silvan walked toward the table. As the two men from the adjacent table rose and walked toward the door, he stepped aside to let them pass. Silvan watched them discreetly for a second, then continued walking toward the table where Peyton and Rachel sat. He couldn't shake the feeling that he had seen the two men before. Perhaps in a photo or on a watch list, he couldn't be sure. But an uneasy feeling persisted. The association had negative overtones.

"Sorry I'm late. We had a small crisis that had to be addressed before I could leave. I see you've eaten. Good." Silvan caught a waiter's attention and signaled him over. "I'd like the large salad plate, please. Also, I have a wine locker here. Please bring the 2001 Galil Cabernet Sauvignon and three glasses." The waiter nodded and moved away. "So," Silvan began, looking at Peyton and Rachel, "have you solved this mystery yet?"

"Not a lot of data," Stone answered. "I was spotted in Bushehr four hours after arriving last night. The plan to spend a couple of days there died on the vine. I did get a look in one of the shops and was told that the centrifuge bearings are back ordered. The rank and file seems to have little hope that anything will happen soon. I made it to the number one reactor when all hell broke loose and I had to run. With the coerced cooperation of Hamadi, a fisherman, I made it out to sea and nearly got away but was intercepted by a patrol boat. I was questioned briefly by an Iranian Naval officer who sent me to Iraq where the US Army pulled me out. What doesn't make any sense is the Iranian Admiral. I would think, in that situation, that police or military security would hold me. But I seemed to be in a house or some other kind of building. The Admiral was the only military type I saw. They took me to Iraq in a standard

191

delivery van. It didn't seem kosher to me." Peyton smiled slightly at his choice of phrase but Sylvan ignored it.

"So what is your assessment of the likelihood of a nuclear device?"

"Who knows? I don't think they are building one nor did I see anything that indicates they will any time soon. This doesn't preclude the possibility that they could have gotten a device elsewhere, perhaps from a hidden plant elsewhere in Iran. Of course, we can't rule out an outside source either. Pictures of the North Korean freighter that docked in Bushehr didn't really show evidence that a weapon was smuggled via the ship. Even with today's technology, however, we can't watch every move. So it's possible that the freighter could have delivered the goods."

The waiter appeared, displayed the wine bottle for Silvan's approval. When the Mossad director nodded, the waiter poured a small amount of wine into a glass. Silvan raised the glass and swirled the contents, sniffing. Then he took a sip of the dark, berry-colored kosher Cabernet. He rolled the wine around in his mouth first, and then swallowed. A second small sip drained the glass. Silvan pursed his lips and pulled in a stream of air noisily. He motioned to the waiter with a nod of his head. The waiter presented the cork to Silvan, poured three glasses, placed the bottle on the table, and left.

Rachel sipped the wine and asked, "So what's next?"

"Well, we can't go back to Bushehr. They're on high alert now," Silvan replied. "We could ask the US to task some satellite sensors to see what else they can find." Looking directly at Peyton, Silvan commented, "I hear a new hybrid sensor that combines radar and optoelectronics allows photos to be taken through concrete walls up to four inches thick. Can that be true?" Silvan, holding the stem of the wine glass, twirled it slightly, as he awaited Stone's response.

Stone, leaning back in his chair, looked at him, held his hands up with his palms outward in a noncommittal gesture and smiled. "Don't look at me. I'm just a contractor."

Silvan looked around, appearing to admire the décor. He checked out each table in the restaurant. Leaning forward, he put both forearms flat on the table and spoke in a low voice. "I have some information but we should go where it's quieter. Let's take my car and go for a drive."

Peyton and Rachel looked at each other and then back at Silvan, "What about the wine?" Rachel asked.

Rising from his chair, Silvan replied, "Bring it."

HARRY SCANNED A MOUNTAIN OF DATA WHILE HE rocked in his large, well-worn leather chair. The soft squeaks mixed with Pavarotti's powerful voice in the Klipsch THX speakers signaled that Harry was lost in process as he made connections, evaluated the information, then discarded or filed it in the labyrinth of his mind. New photos from the electro-optical imagery lab at the NGA New Campus East building on Ft. Belvoir covered the desk top.

The National Geospatial Intelligence Agency's building, sometime called simply the NCE, is one million plus square feet of office space, housing over 8,000 people dedicated to a single mission: to provide decision makers, intelligence agencies, and war fighters in the field with some of the most amazing pictures, charts, maps and graphs imaginable. Much of the work done at the campus is classified so that the other nations and groups can't know the full extent of the NGA's capabilities.

Harry concentrated on the Iranian coastline in the new images taken by U.S. satellites over the Arabian Gulf. He noticed a green track in the first photo, a notation by the NGA analyst. This indicated that a North Korean freighter previously identified at the reactor in Bushehr had put to sea yesterday and was now approaching the Strait of Hormuz between Iran and Oman. This by itself wasn't unusual. North Korean ships came and went regularly from Iranian ports but Harry made a mental note to track the ship's bearing. The most likely scenario would be a return voyage to North Korea with a stop or two along the African coast anywhere from Ethiopia to Somalia or Tanzania.

As he put the photo aside, he noticed a strange smudge on the image. At first glance, the paper appeared to have jammed temporarily during printing. When he checked other photos from the same pass, however, the smudge was still there.

He placed a call to Ft. Belvoir on the secure phone and explained what he had noticed. After he gave the photo specialist the image numbers, he requested a copy of the digital image. A few moments later, Harry glanced at his inbox. "They just showed up. Let me get them on the screen." Harry clicked the file attachment and a color photograph filled the screen. He manipulated the viewer and watched the smudge get bigger until the resolution of the picture pixelated. "Ok, I got 'em." Without taking his eyes off the screen, he put the phone down with a terse "Thanks" at the same instant the handset hit the cradle.

Harry backed down the resolution with his mouse and studied the defined margin around the smudge. *A shadow, perhaps?* He squinted and quickly concluded that this was no smudge. Admittedly what he viewed could be anything, from a weapon or sensor system installed on a freighter to a whale. His mind raced as he stared at the image. *Whale? Not likely in this water.* Still, he couldn't identify the grey blobs. He ordered better resolution on the next pass coming up in six hours and filled out the requisite task request to get the order in the queue.

A glance at the clock revealed that dinner time was close at hand. He decided to get a bite and come back in six hours to review the next set of photos. Just as soon as *Nessun Dorma* from Puccini's Turandot was finished.

Chapter 16

Jerusalem, Israel

THEY WALKED THROUGH THE RESTAURANT AND Silvan motioned to the maître d', pointed to himself and kept walking toward the door. The older tuxedoed gentleman smiled, nodded and bowed at the waist, a discreet confirmation that the check would be forwarded to Mossad. Must be nice, Stone thought, as the maitre d' picked up the house phone and spoke quickly into it.

When they reached the front door of the hotel, the Mercedes was waiting. Silvan waved to the valet and they climbed into the car, Rachel in the front passenger seat, Peyton behind her in the back. Silvan turned left out of the driveway, then spoke. "We received a SIGINT report from the U.S. a few hours ago. The NSA recorded a phone conversation between an Iranian Navy Admiral and an unknown second person calling himself 'Mr. Po.' The admiral responded, I know who you are, Fang.'

Peyton's whole body stiffened and his eyes narrowed. "The same Fang?"

"Very probably. Your name came up in the conversation and triggered Cyclops to pass the conversation to an analyst. They know who you are."

"Well, I met an Admiral recently," Peyton said, "He had no name tag so I don't know who he was. But he certainly wasn't friendly nor did he seem to be working within official channels." Peyton absently rubbed his bruised cheek. "As I said, he wasn't at all congenial."

Silvan continued. "This is the same one. In fact, at the time of the conversation, he believed you were still in custody and he said so to Fang. If there's any communication between the Admiral and this Kazim, then he'll know you never made it. Depends on how meticulous this admiral is."

Stone slowly sucked in his breath, then whistled softly. "So do you think this Admiral is getting a nuke from Fang?"

"That crossed my mind. Fang is a known arms dealer after all."

"Then perhaps there is no nuclear capability in Bushehr," Stone said, "and our hypothesis that a device is being smuggled into Iran is on target. Who is the seller? China? Russia?"

"Well, this Fang character," Rachel said, "implicates China, unless, of course, he's brokering a deal through Russia or even Pakistan or India. They're all nuclear."

"This is the dilemma," Silvan replied. "A number of possibilities exist, so how do we narrow them down? How do we know it's not a private deal?"

"The intel doesn't add up," Rachel said. A frown creased her brow. "We have alleged 'activity' that PHILOSOPHER reported at Bushehr and a weapon that is somehow tied to a jihad. How do those things relate to each other? And where was this admiral when he discussed the package?"

"That one is easy," Silvan jumped in. "Satellite triangulation on the signal put it in Navy District headquarters in Bushehr. The satellites were tasked to look for conversations so we got a good fix. The other end was elsewhere so we don't know the location of the other caller or his identity."

"Ok," Rachel continued, "then what is the tie between the weapon and the reactor? Could it be used to make weapons grade material?"

"Could be," Stone said, "but wouldn't that take an awfully long time? There seems to be a lot of current activity so a day or a week or even a month would pale in comparison to the time required to enrich uranium."

"Unless…," Rachel began, "unless it's not about the reactor. What else is in Bushehr?"

"Cement plant, Air Force Base, and Second Navy District Headquarters. Perhaps we have a clandestine military operation here."

They rode in silence for several minutes as each tried in vain to fit the pieces together but the intel had too many gaps. Finally, Silvan broke the silence. "We do have enough information, albeit incomplete, to warrant bringing other brains to bear on the question. It's still afternoon in the U.S. Let's go to our office, see if we can get Harry on a secure conference and lay all of this out."

He made a left at the next corner, then another, and headed back toward the office. When they pulled up to the garage door, Silvan pushed a button under the dashboard. The door rose, exposing what appeared to be a single car garage with a keypad on the wall to close the door. Silvan punched in a code and the door began to close behind them. Stone realized that the walls were too close to open the car doors and he felt a claustrophobic prickle at the back of his neck. As soon as the garage door closed completely, bright floodlights illuminated the narrow space and retractable cameras fell from the ceiling and scanned the interior of the car. Silvan retrieved the ID from his pocket and held it next to his face in front of the nearest camera. Immediately the cameras retracted into the ceiling and the front wall of the garage opened into a closed, covered courtyard large enough to hold six or seven cars.

"Pretty slick," Stone remarked, obviously

impressed.

"From the street this looks like a garage next to an office building," Silvan explained. "An aerial view reveals the roof of a single large building. The fewer sightseers, the better."

SEATED AT HIS DESK IN ROOM 2T32 AT LANGLEY, Harry listened to the final strains, "All'alba vincerò! vincerò, vincerò!" He quickly reached for the phone to stem the annoying four-tone ring that competed poorly with Pavarotti's powerful voice. He wanted to get up and walk away when he saw the caller ID. The "DIN 0" indicated that the secure call was coming from outside the Joint Worldwide Intelligence Communications System community made up of the CIA; Defense Intelligence Agency; and the Office of the Director of National Intelligence. Instead he answered simply, "Harry here."

"Don't you ever sleep, you old fart?"

"Peyton! What are you doing calling so early? I came in to get some peace and quiet." Harry forgot the headache he had woken up with this morning when he heard Stone's voice.

"Actually it's late here in Jerusalem."

"So you made it. Glad to hear you're alive. Of course, you could have called before now." He smiled and asked, "What's up?"

"I'm here with our two friends. We need your help. Here's what we know so far." Stone gave him a rundown of the events at Bushehr. "We don't - well, at least I don't - think a weapons manufacturing facility is located there. I didn't get to see a lot but, frankly, not a lot is there. Of course, they could be building or buying this device somewhere else. However, both the message and the intel say Bushehr."

Harry sounded perplexed. "So we really don't have much more than we did before. Nothing really points us anywhere."

"Do you know about the SIGINT intercept from the Iranian admiral?" Stone asked.

"No, what's that about?"

Stone recapped the U.S. intelligence report that Silvan had revealed. "You might find it on the Intellipedia or Intelink if you're on line on the classified network." Intellipedia , much like Wikipedia on the Internet, provided a forum for intelligence agencies to share information with each other. Unlike Wikipedia, the intelligence version could only be accessed on the secure classified network, known by the agencies simply as "the high side." Since all connections were dedicated, no one could hack into the network. No physical connection existed between the secure network and the Internet.

They waited as Harry investigated. Suddenly he said, "I've found something. It's the NSA intercept just as you described it." He let out a low whistle. I'm going to do a search on Bushehr, admiral, and *jihad* and see what comes back. Hang on." Peyton looked at Silvan and Rachel and raised a finger to signal that he was on hold.

In a couple of minutes, Harry came back on the line. "There's not a lot here. I found one old file saying that an Admiral Adazi replaced a long time submariner admiral named Kuchecki. Lots of discussion about the new guy is available but the old guy seems to have disappeared. 'Reassigned to a headquarters staff position' the message says. Sounds like he pissed somebody off."

Peyton waited for more.

"Hold on," Harry said. He muttered into the phone

as he read the information under his breath. "This guy Kuchecki was reassigned to the training staff position at the Second Division Headquarters."

"Yeah?" Peyton said as he made a hurry-up motion with his free hand.

Harry answered slowly as he re-read the intelligence. "Second Division Headquarters is in Bushehr."

Peyton sat up. "Holy crap. The Admiral I ran into had submariner insignia on his uniform. Harry, take a look at the your data bases and see what you can put together. We'll call you in the morning our time, your end-of-business in D.C."

"Will do," Harry replied, "The clock is ticking on the treaty signing so the President wants actionable intelligence that we simply don't have. This link may be a key piece of the puzzle. I'll get Ken on it."

Stone spoke quickly before Harry left the call. One more thing. Have you talked to Joni about Xu's murder?"

"Yeah, I went over there yesterday afternoon and broke the news. I expected tears but she just sat on the sofa, never spoke. Guess she's in shock. I stayed with her until her sister from Olney arrived. The kids were out with friends so I don't know how they took it."

"Dammit, I need to be there. Check on her, ok? Let her know that I'll help in any way that I can when I get back." Stone knew better than most the trauma of a spouse's sudden death.

"Sure, Peyton. They're family to both of us."

"Ok, Harry. Thanks. Talk to you tomorrow. Well, this afternoon for you."

Stone hung up the secure phone and turned to Silvan. "Intel indicates that the Admiral is named Kuchecki and is assigned to Bushehr. Harry's going to search the database to find out what he can about this Admiral and we'll get back together tomorrow morning your time. Does this work for you?"

"Since I have to be in Tel Aviv for an eight o'clock meeting, I'll have to leave home by six a.m. to get there. Rachel, can you be here in the morning?"

"Certainly." She turned to Peyton and said, "I'll pick you up; otherwise you won't be able to get in." Peyton nodded.

"Good." Silvan sat back, rubbed his palms together twice, and pushed himself up out of the chair. "Well, if I have to be up early, I should be getting home. Stone, I'll drop you at the hotel. Rachel, where's your car?"

"Parked at the hotel so you can drop me off at the same time if it's ok."

"Let's go, then."

PEYTON AND RACHEL GOT OUT OF THE CAR AND walked toward the valet desk as Silvan drove away. "You know, I just got up and it's still early. Would you like a drink or something?" Peyton's feigned nonchalance did not conceal the obvious. He wanted her to stay, a fact not lost on Rachel.

"I don't know. It's after ten and we have to be in the office early to call Harry."

"Yeah, but I know Harry. He stays late so we don't have to head in all that early. Harry never leaves before six in the evening eastern U.S. time. That's nine in the morning here." Peyton looked into Rachel's eyes in anticipation that she would change her mind.

"Ok," she smiled, "but just one drink and then I have to get some sleep." She smiled and Stone felt his right knee weaken slightly.

"Good, let's go." He reached out and took her elbow and steered her up the front steps of the old hotel.

"Did you know that there's a garden behind the hotel? It was built in the 1930's to attract movie stars and wealthy tourists." Rachel pointed to a large set of French doors as they walked toward the lobby bar. Peyton could see lighted trees just outside. "The hotel has maintained the original design as closely as possible. A high wall surrounds the garden so that it's hidden from the street."

"This is a wonderful evening to sit outside. What say we grab a drink and take a walk? Or as they say in England, 'Take a turn 'round the garden'?" He made a stab at an upper crust English accent.

Rachel laughed. Her look assured him they were of like mind and she responded in kind. "How very charming, sir."

Drinks in hand, the pair strolled around the beautiful garden. "I'm glad you suggested this," Rachel said. "When I was ten years old, my father once brought me here while he searched for our family's roots. We walked and talked and laughed. My memories are as warm and beautiful as the garden."

"The conflicts here have been really hard on the locals."

"Yes, but that's one more reason that I do what I do. My roots are here."

Peyton stared into the darkness. World conflicts had been hard on his family as well. He blamed his frequent absences for Stephanie's death and for the distance that now existed between himself and his sons. Now the family home had been burned and Bandito killed. Dark thoughts had tormented him for the last three years. He knew, though, that he could not allow himself to focus on the pain or a long decline into alcohol, pity and self-destruction would follow. Xu had rescued him from the darkness more than a few times but now he was dead as well. Peyton was on his own.

He was suddenly aware that Rachel seemed uneasy. While he had been lost in thought, two men had entered the garden and now looked casually around the landscape. Training and experience, however, told Peyton and Rachel that the pair were not casual sightseers. The scan had purpose.

The men looked at Peyton and Rachel and their gaze lingered for several seconds, before the closer of the two turned his back and appeared to confer with his colleague. The other man reached inside his pocket and pulled out a folded picture. The two men studied the picture for a moment and then looked back at Stone. The man nearest Stone pulled an automatic pistol from his waistband. He brought it up level with Peyton who instinctively knelt to retrieve the Glock from his ankle holster but the gun wasn't there. No! He had lost it when he was captured in Bushehr.

Two quick shots rang out. He saw Rachel flinch in his peripheral vision. Shit!! He'd left her exposed. How bad? He'd seen her flinch twice. She must have taken both bullets. He rolled to the side, certain that he would be next. Escape was impossible. Her body would fall to the ground as he was hit. He looked up in anticipation of the horror.

But Rachel stood straight with her right arm extended, the dark grey .41 caliber Jericho 941 in her hand. A light wisp of smoke swirled up from the muzzle. She released her breath, dropped her arm and looked down at Peyton. "You ok, partner?"

"Uh, yeah," Peyton strained to readjust his mindset from imminent death to outright admiration for this woman who had now saved his life. "What the hell just happened?"

"I suppose we should ask them." Rachel nodded

toward the two men on the ground. She flipped up the bottom of her jacket and put the Jericho back in the holster in the small of her back. Some hotel guests had begun to drift toward the doors. Unlike other countries, people in Israel knew not to let curiosity get them killed. No rush of curious onlookers to see what had happened, only faces that appeared one by one at the hotel windows.

"Where did you get a gun?" Peyton asked.

"Compliments of Mossad. I'm SCEPTRE, remember?"

Rachel flashed her credentials as hotel security ran to the two men. She calmly but firmly gave orders. "Keep the people back. Close the curtains if you can. Then notify the police and medical." A security officer nodded and moved quickly toward the hotel. "And give us some privacy with these two until the police arrive."

The officer gave a small wave and entered the hotel door.

Stone reach down and placed his finger on the first man's carotid artery. "This one's dead." Stone said. Rachel's first shot had hit him squarely in the middle of his forehead.

Rachel was on one knee next to the other man who moaned softly as he began to stir. Blood spread from the hole in his chest. He wheezed when he breathed in and then he coughed. The cough sent a stream of blood from his punctured lung through the bullet hole. Rachel looked up at Peyton. "He's not going to last much longer."

Peyton moved closer and looked at the man's face. His dark Mediterranean features were twisted with pain and his breathing became more labored, each breath louder than the last. "You got a name, pal?" Peyton asked first in English, then Arabic. Rachel asked the same question in Hebrew.

The man shook his head.

Peyton searched his pockets and found a wallet that contained three hundred Israeli shekels, about seventy-five American dollars, hardly enough for a professional hit. An Israeli identity card, the *Teudat Zehut*, required of everyone living in Israel, was in his other trouser pocket. Peyton handed it to Rachel.

She opened the plastic cover. "It's blue," she said, "so this guy is Israeli. It also has a Hebrew birth date so he's Jewish, not Arabic." She pulled a slip of paper, the identity appendix, from the cover. "According to the card, he's an Israeli citizen."

"So why are they after us? Who sent them?"

Rachel held the card closer to her face and studied it carefully. "Wait a minute. Look at this." She held the card a little closer to Peyton. "The menorah stamp over the picture is off. The part of the stamp on the picture doesn't line up with the card."

"It's barely off but you're right."

She worked her thumbnail between the two pieces of laminate. The picture fell out to reveal the true cardholder's face. "It's a fake."

"So, who is he?"

"Let's ask him again."

Rachel again knelt next to the man as Stone went down on one knee on the opposite side. "Your *Teudat Zehut* is a fake," she said, "It's been doctored. Why is that? Who are you?"

The man shook his head from side to side.

Stone repeated Rachel's words in Arabic as he leaned with the heel of his hand on the man's chest. The man tried to get a breath but, with Stone's weight on him and the hole in his lung, he managed only a wheeze.

"I asked you a question." Stone said, pushed harder

for a moment and then released the pressure.

The man screamed as loudly as he could and then lay still. As Stone put his hand back on the man's chest, the assassin tried to roll away but convulsed with spasms of pain instead. "Please," the man whispered, "this is not my doing. I was sent here."

"Sent by whom?" Stone asked and applied more pressure to the man's chest.

"A man named Amin," the man said.

"And where do I find this Amin?"

"I don't know."

When Stone pressed again, he rose up on his knees so that his full weight rested on the man's chest. The man screamed loudly this time and lay gasping for air. "Manger Square, Bethlehem, behind the Mosque of Omar. He lives upstairs. This I know but I don't know which house. I swear it!"

"But why did you come after us?"

"Because you stand in the way." The man's respiration grew more labored. His words rode small puffs of air as he pushed them from his body.

"In the way of what?"

The man convulsed and rocked back and forth in a futile attempt to get air into his lungs now filled with blood. "Israel." The word gurgled from deep in his throat. He pressed his lips together several times and tried to form the next word. As his face began to turn blue from oxygen deprivation, he was finally able to push one last word out. "Martyrdom!"

Chapter 17

CIA Headquarters
Langley, VA

HARRY SAT IN THE SMALL SCIF, THE DOOR TO THE hallway sealed shut. Annoyed by the debriefer's monotonous voice broadcasting from the red speakerphone, he listened distractedly as his analytical mind processed the information that Peyton had just shared with the team. Harry looked at Ken Washington, then at the phone, and said, "If there's nothing more for me, I'm out of here. I need to get back to work."

"Thanks, Harry," the debriefer said.

Peyton's familiar voice followed. "I'll call you later."

Harry pushed the speaker button to hang up. He sat back and draped his left arm over the back of the adjacent chair. "So, what do we know here? Kuchecki gets fired from his job and relocates to Bushehr. Suddenly he's interested in an American sent to investigate a nuclear plot at the facility there. What are the odds?"

"Getting slimmer by the minute, Harry."

"So, if Kuchecki is indeed behind this and has plans to buy a weapon, what do we conclude?"

Ken thought a minute before he responded. "He has a connection in China?"

"Well, of course. That would be Fang. But what's the source? Could be Russia, China, Pakistan, India, probably in that order of likelihood."

"Logical."

Both men sat back, crossed their arms and stared at

the table. Harry leaned forward quickly and put his elbows on the table, his fingers steepled against his brow. "Ken, if our conclusion is correct and Kuchecki is buying a weapon, then we've overlooked an important factor."

Ken looked at Harry, one eyebrow raised.

Harry quietly continued. "A lot of money has just changed hands."

Ken leaned back in his chair and raised his hands. "Of course. We follow the money," he replied.

"Let's get the Financial Intelligence Operations people on this. They need to look for sums out of Iran to numbered accounts as well as similar amounts between numbered accounts in the last week." The FIO tracked money in and out of bank accounts to identify possible terrorist funding sources. Although a closely guarded secret, not even numbered accounts in the Caribbean or Switzerland were safe from scrutiny by the FIO.

"I'm on it." Ken pushed the chair back and headed quickly to the door.

As the door clicked shut behind him Harry leaned way back in the chair, put his feet up, and interlaced his fingers behind his head. He closed his eyes and began to hum Wagner's Flight of the Valkyries while he mentally sorted though the scraps of information for each and every possible connection. Each thread by itself led to a dead end but taken together they began to form a picture. Now, at least, he had catalogued the possibilities.

PEYTON TOOK A TAXI DOWN HIGHWAY 60 THROUGH the checkpoint and into the West Bank. He looked at a mural on the high concrete wall that said "Peace be with you" and shook his head. How ironic that a mural which exhorted harmony was situated next to the round guard tower, a symbol of force and violence. He showed his

Teudat Zehut to the border guard. Mossad had given him a fresh Palestinian ID card that loosely matched the Arab make-up that transformed him into a common laborer headed home.

On this side of the wall, the Palestinian flag with its red triangle and green, white and black stripes hung from nearly every streetlight. The driver turned left onto Manger Street and they continued past open shops that offered hardware, breads, even whole skinned and dressed lambs which hung from hooks over the sidewalk. Men stood in front of the shops, chatted and laughed while they caught up on each other's news, views and gossip.

The taxi wound around the base of a hill and into Manger Square. Peyton considered how he would locate Amin. His contact near the square was a paid informant of the Israeli military who supposedly knew the Hamas and old PLO network. Considered a deep informant to the military, his identity was well-protected. Only the potential gravity of this situation allowed Peyton to make contact.

He paid the cabbie and made his way across the square past the Bethlehem Peace Center to the street that led to the neighborhood behind the Omar Mosque. The houses were a dense tangle of limestone and concrete structures connected by alleyways and stairs. The design, if there was one, appeared random, as if the next family who needed shelter simply found an open spot and built.

Peyton climbed the stone stairs to a second, then a third level, and knocked on the pale green door. A short man with several days' stubble on his face, dressed in a white t-shirt and utility slacks, opened the door and squinted from the gloom at Peyton. "I need a house painter. I was recommended to Ibrahim." Peyton said.

"Where is your house?"

"Not far but you'll have to cross the wall"

"I don't go there. I have no helpers there."

"Perhaps my cousin can help." Peyton finished the authenticating exchange.

"In that case, come in," the man said and stepped to the side. Peyton entered the small apartment and the man stuck his head out the door, looked both ways, and quickly shut the door.

"Please, sit. Would you like coffee or tea?" the man asked.

"Tea would be fine."

Ibrahim scurried off to the kitchen. Peyton first heard the clang of the tea pot, then water from the faucet as the man prepared the tea. He looked around the room which contained a small couch, two chairs, a coffee table, and a bookshelf filled with pictures of family. A rug hung across an arched doorway that led to the bedroom. Another larger arch separated the kitchen from the living room. The third-floor apartment's only window looked down upon a small alley and provided a view of the Wall and the Jewish settlement Har Homa in the distance.

The man came back with two cups of tea. "Now what can I do for you?" He smiled graciously as he placed the tea cup on the table in front of Peyton.

"I need to see Amin."

The tea cup rattled in Ibrahim's hand and his smile evaporated for a second. His lips curled up again but his eyes had narrowed slightly at the mention of the name. "Amin? There are many named Amin. Why would I know this particular man?"

Stone pulled out a folded sheet of paper and laid it on the coffee table. A picture, sent by secure fax from Harry to Mossad, showed a man in his late twenties or early thirties. "This is Amin," Stone tapped his finger on the photo, "and you've been seen in his company. Now, where is he?"

"You must be mistaken. I don't know this man. He doesn't look familiar at all."

"Look, I don't really have time for this. You get paid because you know people like him. He could be behind a plot to destroy not only the people who pay you but you as well."

"Still," Ibrahim spread his hands, palms outward, "he doesn't look familiar to me."

Stone stared at the Palestinian for a moment and let his right eye narrow. "Then perhaps I'll have to ask on the street. Tell people that, although Mossad pays you for information, you're no help."

Ibrahim sat for a full minute and stared back at Stone. He tightened his jaw muscles, then finally spoke. "He comes to the mosque here in the square a couple of times a week, usually in the mornings." He looked at his watch and added, "About this time, as a matter of fact. I don't know if he will come today, tomorrow, or the next day. He avoids patterns but he will come. This I know."

"And how do you know this?" Stone tilted his head to one side and weighed his suspicions against the little man's obvious fear of discovery.

Peyton watched carefully for any evidence that he was lying. "And what do you talk about?"

"Normal things. The weather, family, what the incompetent government will do to screw up the lives of our people. Nothing more than this, I swear. He does not see me as his confidant. I have other sources for worthwhile information."

Stone put his teacup on the coffee table. "Then I guess we're done." He stood and moved toward the door. He almost added that he'd wait at the mosque but thought better of it. A phone call could be placed as soon as he left.

"Wait!" Ibrahim jumped to his feet and held out his hand to stop Peyton. The little man opened the door and again put his head out and looked both ways before he turned back to Stone. "Quickly." His hand made a circular motion meant to hurry him toward the door. When Stone hesitated at the door and turned toward the informant, Ibrahim moved his hand more urgently. "He will not be alone. Now, go!"

The green door closed quietly behind him and Peyton headed down the stone steps and into the square as the Imam's voice wailed from the loudspeaker high in the Omar Mosque's minaret. He took up a position across the street from the two palm trees in front of the mosque and waited.

HARRY JUMPED WITH A START WHEN THE RED PHONE rang and swung his feet off the table, surprised to find that he had no feeling below his ankles. Needles prickled his feet as blood began to flow again. Ken's voice brought him into focus. "Better come down here, Harry."

"You found something already?"

"Yep, only took a couple of hours but there's something you should see."

"I'll be right there." Harry looked at his watch. Holy crap, he thought, I must have dozed off. "Where are you?"

"FIO. I found some money trails that confirm part of what we suspected and others that go off in some very interesting directions. Come on down. I'll show you."

Harry stood gingerly, held on to the edge of the table and waited for the circulation in his feet to return completely. He spun the vault lock to let himself out of the SCIF and walked as quickly as he could downstairs to the FIO.

When he arrived, he found Ken beside a printer that spat out sheets of paper with columns of numbers on them. Ken turned when the door opened and motioned for Harry to sit at a worktable close to the printer. He then spread the papers on the table in front of Harry.

"Look at this," Ken said. He pointed to a couple of highlighted entries. "Here's a payment of just over five million dollars two days ago. What triggered me to look at this is that the account is on the watch list."

"Really," Harry's eyebrows rose. He pushed his glasses up on his nose and bent over the document. "And why would that be?"

"The account belongs to Ali al-Muzzafar, Osama's CFO."

"So he's turned up again. I thought we had him run to ground."

"He disappeared a couple of years ago so we designated him 'inactive' but he's still in the database."

"Ok, so to whom did he pay five million dollars?"

"That's the interesting part. The payment went from a Cayman account to one in Martinique – the South Island Bank. That account, it turns out, is owned by one Guong Fang."

Harry turned his head toward Ken. The corners of his mouth slowly moved upward. "Now, that is interesting indeed."

"There's more," Ken said, "Look at this one, a payment of ten million from a Swiss account to the Cayman account. We don't have the owner of this account in the database so I've submitted a formal request for the ownership information from the Swiss. They're cooperative but slow. Sometimes the process takes a day or so."

"Can I get a copy of this?" Harry smiled broadly, his mental wheels shifting to sixth gear. Connections, possibilities, scenarios played out simultaneously as his mind processed what he'd just heard.

"Take that one," Ken said. "I'll print another for my files."

"Thanks." Harry stood and gathered up the papers. "I'm headed back to my office to think through this. Call me when you get the ID on the Swiss account." He turned for the door so quickly that he barely opened the door wide enough to squeeze through.

He stopped just outside the door and turned again. "Oh, by the way, Ken…"

Washington looked up.

"Not bad for a Harvard puke."

Ken smiled and went back to work.

PEYTON SAT AT A TABLE IN A SMALL CAFÉ ON THE square across from the Mosque of Omar in Bethlehem's West Bank. He unfolded the picture of Amin and studied it carefully, committing the man's face to memory. When Amin showed up, Stone needed to be certain that he had the right man. He'd get only one chance. A movement and shadow over his left shoulder caught his attention as the waiter arrived with a refill of his tea cup. He folded the picture and quickly put it away. The man filled his cup and went back inside.

Built in 1860, the Mosque of Omar was named after Omar ibn al-Khattab, a Muslim Caliph who traveled to Bethlehem in 637 to issue a law that guaranteed respect for the Christian Shrine of the Nativity and ensured the safety of Christian clergy. All across the square people from the al-Fawaghreh quarter of Bethlehem, the only Muslim quarter in the old city, were answering the Imam's call, heading toward the mosque for prayers.

Peyton watched an old Toyota with three men inside pull up next to the stone bollards along the square and stop. One man with wraparound sun glasses got out and scanned the square before opening the back door for another man. The man in the back seat followed. Even though he had on a black and white checked *kaffiya*, Peyton recognized Amin.

Stone put ten shekels on the table and left. He walked toward the mosque, just one more of the faithful. Amin headed toward the building. The driver, a large, burly man, certainly a bodyguard, answered his cell phone as he opened the car door. He turned and looked at the café Stone had just left, then closed the car door and walked quickly after Amin.

Inside the Imam led the faithful through the prayer ritual: four Raka'ah, sets of bending, kneeling, prostrating and sitting while reciting the appropriate prayers and verses from the Qur'an. After the last Raka'ah along with the ritual greetings for the Prophet Mohammed and the Prophet Abraham, each person turned first to the right and then to the left and said, "Peace be with you." Stone had positioned himself on Amin's left side. When Amin turned to the left, Peyton said, "I have a message from Ibrahim. We must talk."

The men began to file out of the mosque. Amin stood and stared at Stone. "Who are you?" Amin asked.

"I'm a friend of Ibrahim. He has news from Iran for you and sent me to bring you to him."

"And why do you think I'm interested in news from Iran? Who do you think I am?"

"I know from Ibrahim that you're Amin. As to why you are interested in Iran, that's between you and Ibrahim. I'm only a messenger. He told me that he has news for you that you must know immediately or all is lost. I don't know more than that."

Amin grabbed Stone's arm and pulled him close. "'No more than that' is still too much." His words were hushed but the malice was palpable, like sand paper on balsa wood. "You are coming, too."

"Of course. I'll show you the way." *As if you didn't already know it.*

Stone walked past the bodyguard without eye contact and turned right when he passed through the door of the mosque. He looked back to make sure that Amin was still behind him and headed up the alleyway to Ibrahim's house.

This time he didn't knock and go through the identification ritual. He turned the doorknob and walked right. Ibrahim jumped up from his chair at the sound of the intrusion. "What is this? How dare…?" He stopped short when he recognized Amin who followed Stone through the door and turned quickly to Stone who closed the door behind the bodyguard.

Ibrahim looked at the bodyguard, then Amin, then Stone. "You brought him here? Are you crazy?"

Amin looked at Ibrahim, his brow furrowed. "He said you had news for me. That you told him to bring me here. What's going on?"

Ibrahim's mouth dropped open then snapped shut. He shifted his weight to his right foot and moved his hands from his sides, palms outward. "I don't know…I called…" He stopped himself when Peyton's head snapped around. The man's steely blue eyes bore into him. "I meant to say…"

The sound of a muffled pistol shot stopped him in mid-sentence. Stone stood with his arm extended, a Jericho automatic barely inches from the bodyguard's head as the big man dropped to the floor. A dark red spot between his dull lifeless eyes began to ooze blood across the powder burns.

Stone swung the Jericho slightly left and pointed it at Amin. "Sit."

Amin crossed his arms. Shifted his weight backward. Did not sit. "What the hell is this?"

"You sent people to kill me at the King David. I want to know why." Amin dropped his arms and leaned forward closer to Stone, searching his face. His head snapped back slightly and his eyes grew wide as he recognized who was standing in front of him.

"You're Peyton Stone. But you're supposed to be..."

"Yeah, dead. But your two goons were a bit less than competent. They got themselves killed by a woman. Not much chance of martyrdom in that, is there?"

Amin's eyes narrowed again and his lip curled upward on one side pushing wrinkles across one nostril. "You infidel dog. Why have you brought me here?"

"I need details. Your man mentioned Israel and martyrdom."

"What of it?"

"I want to know what he meant. What's the connection?"

Amin tilted his head back and looked at Stone from the bottom of his eyes. "And why would I know that?"

Stone took a step forward and pushed Ibrahim down onto the couch. He stood in front of Amin just inches out of arm's length. "I don't have time to screw around here. So tell me now. What's the connection between martyrdom and Israel and Iran and Kuchecki?"

The color drained from Amin's face before he could muster control, then, as quickly, flushed deep red. "Who the fuck do you think you are, asking me these questions?" The muscles in Amin's neck moved back and forth like taut cords as he screamed at Peyton.

Amin stepped forward.

Peyton dropped his arm and pulled the trigger.

Amin's knee exploded in a shower of blood, ligaments and bone fragments.

Ibrahim screeched.

As Amin fell backward onto the couch, Ibrahim recoiled into the corner of a cushion as though gunshots wounds were contagious.

"I'm going to ask you one more time. Then we'll work our way from knees to arms to privates. You'll want to die but you won't."

"Fuck you" Amin screamed.

Peyton blasted his other knee, quickly angling the gun to take off the kneecap but miss the femoral artery.

Amin screamed and Ibrahim hurriedly drew his feet up until he was sitting in a fetal position against the arm of the couch. Then he uncoiled and started to get up. When Peyton looked at him, he fell limply back against the couch.

"Your left elbow is next."

"Alright, alright." Amin said through clenched teeth. "Just get me some help. The pain…"

"Talk first, help later." Peyton grabbed Amin's left arm.

Amin jerked his arm back. "Iran and the US cannot sign the peace treaty. This will mean the end of any chance for an Islamic government. No one in his right mind will let this happen."

"So what is the talk of martyrdom?"

"Kuchecki has the power to unleash the wrath of Allah on Israel. When that happens, the false government in Tehran will fall and the jihad will begin in earnest. The Sunnah will prevail."

"How does Kuchecki have the power to…"

The driver who had been left behind at the mosque

burst through the door, an AK-47 in his hand.

Stone dove past Amin. The driver started to fire but stopped when he saw that even a near miss would hit his boss.

Stone spun and fired as he fell. The shot hit the driver's left shoulder. When Peyton hit the floor, he somersaulted, came up on his feet, and headed for the window.

The driver fired but the slugs went over Peyton's head. Peyton grabbed the windowsill and vaulted outward. His body spun ninety degrees and he hung on to narrow ledge. A second later his toes hit the side of the building.

He heard a loud clicking sound from just inside the room above his head when the driver stuffed another magazine into the rifle and released the bolt. Peyton looked down at the alleyway three floors below.

HARRY ENTERED THE LOBBY OF THE NGA NEW Campus East building and reached for his credential. He quickly waved his ID card over the guard's electronic keypad. When the light turned green and the keypad beeped, Harry entered his PIN and placed his thumb on the print reader. Since the Intelligence Community had implemented the Common Access Card program, egress into the various agencies was simpler, a move that facilitated meetings and information sharing. Security was tight for outsiders but agency employees with a standard card and information - ID, PIN number and biometric information - were in the DNI's master data system. Access to all authorized areas was expedited now that clearance transfers and the usual "lost" paperwork no longer encumbered the process.

Harry walked down the hall to the Middle East Section and entered a conference room where a lone

NGA employee looked up, stood, and stuck out his hand.

"Good morning, I'm Harry from up the river." Harry referred to Langley as though it were a secret even in this secure building.

"Sean, from pretty much down the river." He smiled at Harry. "At least that's how it feels sometimes." They both chuckled and Sean continued. "As I said when you called, I work in the Arabian Gulf Branch, concentrating on Iran and the Saudi peninsula."

"I work in the Middle East section at Langley and specialize in whatever is hot at the moment," Harry said. "I need to get access to imagery from Iran around the Bushehr power plant. It needs to be the latest with as much detail as possible."

Sean thought for a second, "Yeah, I can take a look. We probably have something on the server since it was just yesterday."

"I'd appreciate it. Something is going on over there, possibly nuclear. This situation could become everyone's top priority pretty quick once we get a handle on it."

"Ok. Let's go down the lab and see what we have."

Harry followed Sean down a beige corridor lined with poster-sized imagery of former hotspots around the world. They passed pictures of a Soviet Navy ship being launched, Russian soldiers in Afghanistan, an overhead shot looking down at crowds on either side of the Berlin wall, central Baghdad before and after the US invasion. All of these were a tribute to the marriage of technology and the practiced eye of NGA analysts.

Sean stopped at a grey door that looked more like a safe than an office door and spun the tumblers on the spin lock. Careful to position his body between Harry and the lock, he quickly entered the combination and pulled the handle to horizontal. Inside, the room was a standard government office: grey carpet, white modular furniture, florescent lighting and the constant low murmur of work.

They walked to a cubicle near the back wall and Sean logged into his computer. "Ok, what do you want to see?"

Harry shifted behind Sean and stood as close as his waistline would let him. "I want to look at the Naval base at Bushehr. You saw the images with the smudges? I want to know what those are and where they came from."

Sean shrugged. "I reported that to SysE. It looked like a sensor anomaly. They'll get to it one day." Sean knew that Systems Engineering priorities were outside his job description.

Harry gave a knowing smile. "Well, let's take a look anyway."

Sean loaded an image onto his screen. "Wonders never cease. The smudges are gone."

"Right, now let's walk the cat back and see when they disappeared and what that looked like." Harry's curiosity was borne of continual payback: look at just one more thing; make one more connection; catalogue all of the relationships. In the parlance of the intelligence world, *walking the cat back*. Anyone who has watched a cat wander around a small yard can appreciate the apparent randomness of its path. Walking the cat back means doing the impossible task of tracing each random path to its source and connecting it to the previous random path. Harry was a master of this art.

Sean opened a folder on the computer and said over his shoulder, "Here are the video loops for the last three days. We can run them fast but, if we get too fast, we'll likely miss a lot."

Harry stood up, placed both hands on the small of

his back and stretched. He said to the ceiling, "Ok, get to the point where the spot appears. I have to step to the men's room."

When Harry returned, Sean was eating a piece of a chocolate bar. The other half of the bar lay on his desk. Harry felt a surge of saliva but swallowed and looked at the screen. "Whatcha got?"

Sean pointed, "Ok, day before yesterday this freighter was moored at the pier at the Base all day. No smudge. Overnight we were blind but IR shows nothing."

Harry looked at Sean. "You have infrared, too?"

"Yeah, it's a different bird but the computer resolves both views and can do an overlay. I checked the raw data while you were gone."

Harry was impressed with this kid's thoroughness. "So what happened yesterday?"

"I've just started that loop."

Harry and Sean watched the picture on the screen change first from a night scene to dawn, then to daylight. "Look at that." Sean pointed at the screen. A small grey spot had appeared next to the freighter.

"Can you zoom in?"

Sean pressed a key. The picture zoomed toward the spot and the image became pixilated.

"Can you sharpen the image?"

"A little but this isn't like on TV." Sean clicked his mouse on several on-screen buttons and the image got sharper.

Harry leaned in and adjusted his glasses on his nose. Sean scooted as far as he could to keep from getting crushed between Harry and the desk-top. Harry inclined his head first to one side and then to the other as he considered what he saw. "Hmmm..., huh!" was all he said.

"What do you think it is?" Sean asked.

"Roll fast forward and let's see what it does."

The two watched as smaller boats - fishing and pleasure boats as well as small cargo haulers - arrived and left throughout the day. Cranes swung back and forth over the freighter. Toward midday the cranes stopped and tug boats hurried toward the ship. Minutes later the ship began to move away from the pier and covered the fuzzy grey spot. Harry's head moved slightly closer to the screen. The ship began its journey into the Gulf but when it passed the place where the grey spot should have been, the blurry shadow didn't reappear.

"Now the spot's disappeared," Sean said.

"Or it moved with the ship." Harry stood up and stretched again. "Let's keep going. A little faster and just stay with the ship."

Sean manipulated more on-screen buttons. The ship sped up as it cruised down the Gulf, then the picture began to dim and redden. "It's the end of the day. We're going to lose visual in a second."

"Go to yesterday morning and stay on the ship."

Sean brought up the next video segment and the night turned to day. He skewed the picture to the point where the ship should be. "There it is. Still plodding along."

Harry leaned in and squinted down at the screen through the bottom of his glasses. "Wait! Zoom out slowly."

He hesitated a couple of beats. "Stop!!"

With this, he stabbed a finger at the screen. "Look at that!'

"It's that spot again. But it's trailing the ship. What the hell…?"

Harry stood straight. "It's a submarine. It's fuzzy

because it's at depth. The natural movement of the water and the sub's movement through it causes a discontinuity in the density of the water around the hull. The resulting scintillation blurs the shape but when it's in the open like that there's enough there to tell us it's a sub."

Sean nodded, "Sure, it makes sense but why did a sub shadow a freighter all the way down the gulf?"

Harry rubbed his right index finger up and down behind his ear as he thought. "We'll that's the sixty-four zillion dollar question, isn't it?"

Chapter 18

Mossad HQ
North Tel Aviv

RACHEL AND SILVAN LOOKED AT THE PHOTOS ON one of the secure computer screens. "Those are the two guys. No doubt about it." She sat at a computer in the maze of cubicles connected to the Interior Ministry's identity database. Using face-matching software, certain features had been encoded in the pictures taken at last night's crime scene. The massive photo identification database was then scanned as the software searched for identical strings of ones and zeros. Out of the several million photos in the database, six possible matches were found and presented to Rachel. She had just now made the final selection by examining the six photos. The two dead men in the hotel garden were identified as Palestinian nationals with ties to families in Iran. All corresponding statistical data as well as current addresses were established. The fake identity card had once belonged to an Israeli whose body had been found in a dumpster a couple of hours ago.

"The lead on this has gone to the police. We'll, of course, cooperate with them as we always do," Silvan told her. "I'll email the pictures to the Inspector and let him know background and the urgency here. The words 'Martyrdom' and 'Israel' in the same sentence coming from these guys will put some priority on it. We'll assign a research team to support the police and I'm sure the Army will mobilize. They may want to talk to you as well." Silvan swiveled in his chair, looked away from Rachel momentarily, then turned toward her again.

"These men were sitting next to us at the restaurant last night." He pounded his fist on the table, scowled, then continued. "I don't know who they are but, dammit, I knew that I had seen those faces somewhere before." Silvan took pride in the high level of distrust he typically maintained. He had let this slip by him but vowed that this wouldn't happen again.

Rachel sat silently for a moment and then said, "I'll cooperate with the police."

"So, your colleague?" Silvan's voice took on an almost imperceptible edge that registered deep inside Rachel. "He's not at the hotel this morning. Any idea where he might have gotten to?"

Caught off guard, Rachel answered somewhat defensively. "Not a clue. He didn't check in with me today. I'll see if I can track him down if you'd like, though."

"No need. While the police check out the houses of your would-be assassins, I have something else you might want to look into. A Russian arms dealer in Caesarea was caught selling weapons through Haifa to the Syrians. He has expressed a willingness to work with us in exchange for amnesty. Go talk to him. If weapons are moving in the market, he may know. If the police turn up anything on the shooters, I assure you I'll alert you as soon as possible.

"Certainly," Rachel replied, her face a mask. *So many senseless deaths. I've seen too many.* She glanced at her iPhone, then added, "I'll drive up to Caesarea and track down the Russian. The connection back to us is crucial and disturbing." *The word is 'frightening',* she thought. Always aware of her role in a largely male profession, she had disciplined herself to choose words carefully. This morning, fatigued by violence and personal loss, tired of games, she thought better of her self-edit and added, "The implications are frightful." Rachel looked directly at Silvan as she spoke quietly but with resolve. "I want to take a lead role on this Iranian situation. Working against those who deal in terror keeps me going."

"I know. And you're good. But you don't work for me." Silvan looked at her, one eyebrow slightly raised.

Rachel nodded.

His mouth turned up slightly on one side as he spoke. "So, why are you still here? Go talk to the Russian. We have a puzzle before us and this arms dealer could very well have an important piece."

"Okay. How do I find him?"

"Here's your background packet. The directions are included." Silvan smiled as he handed her a two-inch thick packet that contained every known detail about Ivan Radanovich. "He lives on the golf course just off the sixth green, a short par three. Should be easy to find."

RACHEL DROVE UP THE COAST HIGHWAY FROM TEL Aviv to Caesarea. She took the Caesarea exit and turned right onto the road that led up to the golf club driveway. The club, designed in 1961, had recently undergone extensive renovation. The new Pete Dye course with its country club lifestyle attracted the wealthy, and sometimes shady, to the huge houses that lined the fairways.

She passed through the gates and followed the curved driveway that led up to the Radanovich mansion. A hurried scan of the information in her packet before she left Headquarters revealed that Radanovich was in the small package shipping business when the Soviet Union dissolved. He sold his small trucking business to the Russian Mafia and bought two container ships. In addition to machinery and farm products, his ships also moved drugs, weapons, even Russian slaves, from the Black Sea through the Dardanelles, and into the Mediterranean. He had recently made the mistake of unloading a shipment of automatic weapons and mortars along with ammunition in Haifa with plans to move them through the Golan Heights into Syria. An alert customs agent noticed that, when the container marked "textiles" was loaded on the lorry frame, a tire blew. When he weighed the container, the tonnage far exceeded a reasonable weight. The ensuing detailed inspection revealed a container packed to the rafters with illegal weapons. Ivan was called down to identify the "textile" crate. When he arrived, he was immediately taken into custody and turned over to Mossad.

A police matron answered the bell. Rachel showed her credential and was ushered into an entrance hall larger than her own apartment. *I don't like this guy already*, Rachel thought, as she looked around at the art and statuary in the hallway. In the center of the foyer hung a large gold medallion conspicuously patterned after the United Nations symbol. Suspended by a gold chain from the center of a skylight, the centerpiece hung more than thirty feet above the floor, surrounded by sweeping circular stairs. These led to a landing at the second floor, then continued to a third where a white haired man had stood perfectly still and stared down at her for nearly a minute. Then, as if suddenly recalling his role of gracious host, Ivan gave a subtle wave of his hand and started down the stairs.

Ivan Radanovich appeared to be in his early sixties, a little older than Rachel expected. He was short, around five and a half feet tall with piercing blue eyes. His intense expression and arrogant posture lent an air of intimidation in spite of his diminutive build. Rachel extended her hand, "Rachel Kleinmann, Israeli Customs."

Ivan bent his head forward slightly and looked at her from the top of his eyes as a father would a child caught in a lie. "Customs? You're American. Did Israel turn this inconvenience over to America? That would be even more inconvenient. If we are to talk candidly, we need to trust each other. This is not a good start."

Rachel snatched her hand back as if she had touched a hot grille. "This is an Israeli Customs-led investigation. I'm on loan to them, that's all." Rachel maintained a stoic expression as she cringed inside. *Why*, she thought, *do I feel defensive and how did he take charge of this meeting so easily?*

"A reasonable recovery," Ivan half smiled, "but if we are to be completely honest with each other, neither of us can hold back. You are an agent with the American government, here to see what I know about weapons shipments in Syria because intelligence collection is Mossad's charter, and intelligence about Syria is important to you and your organization." Ivan, who seemed to run out of air at the end of his sentence, stopped and took a deep breath. "So what do you wish to know? I'm sure you want the identity of the 'big guns', if you'll pardon my choice of words, the kingpins as it were." He gestured toward an archway off the right side of the foyer.

They entered a large room with a high vaulted ceiling and slate floors. The sophisticated neutral color palette with an eclectic design paired antique accessories with expensive contemporary furnishings. The room was meant to impress, to intimidate. Rachel eyed a pair of couches upholstered with the skins of rare African animals, her dislike of this man growing by the minute. She turned toward the Russian, her confidence restored, and addressed him. "We know that you deal in all kinds of traditional arms – machine pistols, mortars, RPGs, all that. True?"

"Of course. You know precisely why I am here under house arrest and not collecting the cash from the sale of those containers that you confiscated in Haifa."

Rachel walked over to the exterior glass wall that ran from floor to ceiling and spanned the length of the room. She looked down the sixth fairway of the golf course, across the tee box and beyond, over the old Roman Coliseum and the ruins of the ancient port city of Caesarea. The deep blue of the Mediterranean exploded into bright white foam each time a wave crashed into the dark tan stone of the two-thousand year old seawall built by an earlier group of arms dealers. Rachel smiled briefly at the irony, composed herself, and turned quickly to face Ivan. "What about weapons of mass destruction? Do you deal in chemical and biological agents or nuclear devices?"

Ivan raised his eyebrows. "This is an unexpected turn." He reached down and opened a small silver box sitting on the thick and highly polished imbuia wood table. Lifting a Cuban cigar to his nose, he inhaled deeply. "Do you mind if I smoke?"

"It's your house. At least for now."

"Ah, you wound me." Ivan dramatically placed his hand over his heart and bent slightly to the side. Pointing to a door at the end of the glass wall, he smiled and said, "Let's go out on the veranda so that I don't offend your sensibilities." He casually picked up a lighter fashioned from a small ram's horn and led her out to the stone veranda.

As she walked over to a small wrought-iron patio table, Rachel looked back into the room and noticed for the first time that the opposite wall was also glass. She could see completely through the room, to the hills above the West Bank. Mount Hermon was visible to the northeast. *What a great view*, Rachel thought, *purchased at the expense of innocent lives by proliferating arms around the world.* She sank into the deep cushions of a heavy wrought iron chair and smoothed the skirt of her navy blue business suit. Her face did not reveal the contempt she felt for the man standing nearby.

"I'm terribly sorry," Ivan said as she sat down. "May I offer you something to drink? Vodka perhaps?"

"It's ten in the morning. You can't be serious."

"To a Russian, vodka is a serious business." Ivan smiled. "It's 6 P.M. in Kamchatka and that's part of Russia, so I think I'll have vodka. Are you sure you won't join me?"

Rachel demurred and he pressed a button on a box mounted on the wall next to the door. A voice answered, "What is your wish, sir?"

"Vodka for me and a bottle of water for my guest."

"Right away, sir."

As Ivan walked back to the table and sat down, Rachel watched him carefully. "Do you plan to answer my question?"

"Oh, yes, weapons of mass destruction. Well, despite the conversations that governments have about chemical and biological weapons, the truth is that, in many respects, these are not easily deployed and are reasonably easy to contain. That's not to say they won't do damage but recall the anthrax attacks in the US right after 9/11. A substantial amount of anthrax powder sent through the mail resulted in only three deaths. Had it not been for the hysteria created by the recent World Trade Center and Pentagon attacks, those three anthrax deaths might have received less press than the Tylenol scare in the eighties. More people died from contaminated Tylenol than from the 2001 anthrax attacks."

"Right after Mother Russia was transformed from a communist dictatorship to a land of organized economic chaos, numerous opportunities to obtain biological agents existed. Laboratories that contained entire refrigerators full of anthrax were abandoned. I, myself, had six hundred pounds of the stuff and couldn't unload it. Al Qaeda was, in many ways, in its infancy and most of the minor terrorist organizations were neither sophisticated enough nor financed adequately to seek biological agents. Governments understood the difficulties associated with the storage and deployment of biological agents. In my case, the whole lot went bad before I could make any connections."

A matronly looking woman, who also appeared to be Russian, stepped onto the veranda with an ice cold bottle of vodka, an equally frosty bottle of water, and two shot glasses. She put them down and Ivan filled one glass from the vodka bottle and offered it to Rachel who shook her head and took the bottle of water from the tray.

"As for chemical weapons, they are harder to come by. Russia had a reasonable inventory system for them since they had already been weaponized and weren't in laboratories. The U.S. Defense Threat Reduction Agency and the U.S. Department of Energy worked closely with the Russian government. They were quite diligent about collecting and destroying all of the weapons. That's not to say that more isn't out there. The U.S. has a large inventory but all of it is carefully stored and guarded. Some of the Middle Eastern countries have some – surprisingly, not Iraq – but the chemical weapons aren't as plentiful as the press would have you believe."

"That leaves nuclear," Rachel said. "Do you deal in nuclear weapons?"

"No. Even a diabolical scion of organized crime has limits. I draw the line at nuclear devices."

"Why? Wouldn't they be extremely profitable?"

"Of course, but it's a short-term gain. There's a bigger picture at play here. I make my money selling arms to people who don't have defense departments that would supply them through legitimate channels. If governments get involved, I make no money from them. Just as Coca-Cola shapes its markets through advertising and is very protective of the balance of products in the marketplace, so must I be careful to preserve my markets. I make my money on small, contained conflicts where the two sides meet in the middle, covet each other's weapons, and then use up all of their bullets. This is where I come into the picture. I sell to each side weapons that the other side has plus something new for the other side to covet. I also renew their supply of bullets so that they can repeat the cycle. If you introduce nuclear weapons, the balance is upset. One side unleashes a nuke and then governments get involved. I stand to lose millions and I can't have that. I'm a business man."

"You're a long way from communist socialism," Rachel said, irritation apparent in her voice.

Ivan smiled, "That's dead. Marx was an idiot to think that we could trade one dictator king for a dictator socialist and still be successful. Of course, Marx had nothing to do with our revolution so I guess I have been unkind to Karl and should blame Lenin and Stalin. No matter now, all of that is behind us. I'm a staunch capitalist and a firm believer in enlightened self-interest. You don't think that the West has a corner on Adam Smith, David Hume, or John Locke, do you? They were a hundred years ahead of Marx, after all. Free enterprise is the engine that moves us forward. The fact that my activities are frowned on by governments doesn't refute that they fit a business model and need to be carefully managed."

"Free enterprise? You sell weapons to the Palestinians who then murder innocent Israelis!" Rachel's anger was palpable.

"I sell to the Syrians who sell to the Palestinians."

"Who cares to whom you sell? I can't believe I'm hearing this!" Rachel placed her palms down on the table and started to stand.

"Now hold on, hear me out." Ivan remained seated and motioned for her to sit back down. "As long as I am in control of the flow of weapons, I can keep things small. Look around you. Do you seriously think I want a bunch of scruffy-faced fanatics with tea towels on their heads to overrun this country? I have invested millions in this place and I pay over a million a year in taxes to the Israeli government. If I don't provide these weapons, someone else will and things could get out of hand. Israel must solve the underlying problems of jobs and education for Israeli Arabs and better stabilize the standard of living across ethnic groups. And," he paused to catch his breath, then added, "stop stealing homes and land from one ethnic group and giving them to another one. Then – and only then – will the demand for weapons naturally decrease and I'll be forced to seek new markets. I take comfort in the fact that I will be retired and probably long dead of natural causes by the time that happens."

Rachel sat down. "I'll remind you that selling arms to Syria from Israel is a capital crime so you'll probably be dead sooner rather than later."

Ivan waved his hand as if shooing a fly. "Phah! I'm

not worried about that. Donald Trump wrote a book in the late eighties or early nineties, I forget exactly, called The Art of the Deal. The premise was that, to be successful, really successful, you have to take well thought-out risks: the greater the risk, the greater the reward. Everyone knows that, but the key, according to Trump, is, 'Always protect the down side.' I am a good student of highly successful people."

Rachel shook her head quickly and furrowed her brow. "And what exactly does that mean?"

"I have certain information squirreled away in a private place that only I and few very close associates can access. This information, were it in the government's care, would be classified; but, since I'm a Russian citizen and not an employee of the government, I'm not covered by the Israeli Secrets Act. Therefore, these documents are not classified as long as they are in my possession. The release of unclassified documents does not constitute treason, especially if done by a foreign national. So if I am tried, convicted, and executed by the Israeli government, these documents will be released. Having informed your government of the documents' contents, I find that they are in no hurry to proceed. There's no precedent and the principle has never been tested in court but that doesn't matter since the outcome will be the same regardless of what they do."

"But if you stole this classified information..."

"I never said I stole it. I travel in circles where things are discussed, where pieces of the puzzle are put together. Your CIA calls me 'a well-informed private citizen'. My success depends on my knowing in excruciating detail the political situations in places where I do business. I simply wrote down my thoughts and put them in a safe place. Some of this information

236

has to do with Israel, some with the U.S. Neither wants the particulars out in the open."

"But my government will never bow to your threats. We'd rather have it out in the open and deal with it than be blackmailed." Rachel's agitation was increasing visible.

"Be that as it may, the U.S. government knows what I know. Israel can behave like a petulant puppy and bark and scratch and make a mess on the floor, but when the U.S. rattles the feeding bowl, suddenly the puppy sits up with its front paws high in the air."

Rachel glared at him, speechless.

"The bottom line is this, my dear: I will cooperate with the government and no longer trade arms with the Syrians. The world has many conflicts that need my support, such as it is. In return, the government will turn a blind eye to the rest of my enterprise and their secrets will stay safe with me. On the issue of nuclear arms, we are on the same side. If I can help you stop some craziness out there, I am more than happy to do so. I happen to have better intelligence on that subject than any government."

Rachel sat silent for several minutes and stared at Ivan who downed another shot of vodka and gazed off into the distance at the Mediterranean. She steadied her voice and asked quietly, "So, what do you know about nukes?"

Ivan smiled broadly, aware that he had not quite won her over but satisfied that she now exhibited a degree of tolerance. "I know that most of the old Russian weapons have been accounted for and either locked up or destroyed by the U.S./Russian threat reduction program. I know that the records in some places are not accurate. And I know that there are people in Russia who are also aware of this because they were the ones who kept the records. In most cases, they have come forward. Withholding this information brings serious penalties and the weapons are just too hard to turn into cash. I was approached by someone named Dmitri who worked at Kolovostok, a weapons storage facility near one of Russia's largest test sites. He sought to unload a nuclear device. I tried to keep him on the hook until I could find out more and put him out of business.

"Recently he called to say that he had a buyer. He wanted to know if I could best an eight million dollar bid. I offered ten and he said he'd call back. He never did. I assume one of three things: his story was a hoax and he thought better of it; his buyer made an offer he couldn't refuse; or some tragedy befell him. My gut says number two is the correct answer. Knowing some of the people in my business, a combination of two and three is more likely. Of course, I would gladly go to Kolovostok and check on things myself, but, as you undoubtedly read in your file on me, I have been asked to remain here for a time."

Ivan smiled again as Rachel stood up. She moved toward the door, then turned and glared at Ivan. "Thank you for your hospitality. I'll check out the information you've given me," her tone as frosty as the glass which held Ivan's vodka.

"I am at your service," Ivan replied with a sugary stickiness to his voice. "Let me show you out."

"I can find my own way just fine, thank you," she said, then walked stiffly to the front door. With great restraint, she closed it quietly behind her and got into the car. The detritus of the afternoon's conversation clung to her as she drove along the highway. *I need a shower*, she thought, *a long one as soon as possible.*

PEYTON HUNG BY HIS HANDS FROM THE NARROW window sill with only seconds to decide what to do next. He could hear the rattling sounds from above as Amin's driver moved around the couch toward the window. He looked quickly to his left at a solid stucco wall. No good.

He looked down at a twenty-five foot drop: survivable, but barely. Overhead, a man with an AK-47. To his right, a roof top patio one floor below. He needed cover and he needed it fast. Sizing up his options, he looked toward the patio, a good six feet to his side. Hanging by his hands, he had no way to generate enough momentum to cross the gap.

Hand over hand, he moved as close to the corner of the windowsill as he could and saw a single drain tile protruding from the building. He swung slightly to his right and wedged his left foot above the tile. Above him, the driver was positioning his AK-47. The man hesitated for a moment. Perhaps he had never shot anyone at this range before. Squeezing a shot into another human's face is not as easy as it seems in the movies.

Peyton lunged to his right and pushed off with his left foot. His hips caught the top of the patio wall. The momentum from his heavier upper torso cartwheeled him over onto his back. He heard the driver discharge half of the thirty round clip into the concrete. Large pieces of stucco flew in every direction.

Stone crawled on his belly to the door that led into the house. He took a deep breath and stayed as close to the patio wall as possible, then got into position and lunged at the door. He could hear the splat of 5.56mm slugs that dug into the travertine tiles of the patio deck as he went head first through the door.

A woman screamed. Stone's eyes adjusted slowly

to the light inside the house. As he came up on his feet, he saw a woman and two small children huddled against the wall. *No time to deal with them. Where's the door?*

His vision returned fully as his pupils dilated in the dim light. A thin sliver of light on the floor to his right marked the way outside. He ran toward it.

He found himself in a walkway between the buildings with steps that led upward to his left, downward to his right. Up would take him back toward Ibrahim's house, to certain death. Down was his only choice. He ran toward the steps. The sound of footsteps approached from behind and urged him on. At the landing, he turned the corner of the building as several more shots took off large pieces of stucco and stone.

Now he was in a long straight alleyway with a few randomly spaced doors but no place to hide. He hoped that the driver's hesitation back at the window ledge indicated that he wasn't very skilled with the rifle.

Stone heard the driver round the corner of the building. When the footsteps stopped momentarily, he pressed himself into a doorway. Four more shots went past him and out into the square at the end of the alleyway.

He bolted down the narrow alley. Two more shots careened off the walls. The sound of rapid footsteps resumed behind him and echoed off those same walls. His lungs were on fire, his legs rubbery. As the initial adrenaline surge began to subside, he knew that couldn't continue at this speed much longer.

His breathing was labored by the time he reached the end of the alley. He rounded the corner into the square and saw three policemen racing toward him in a dead run, pistols drawn. Stone stopped and leaned against the wall of the building as he tried to catch his breath. He waved his hands at the cops, "There's a man in the alley with a gun. Be careful."

The policemen stationed themselves on either side of the alley and the closest one said to Peyton, "Stay here. We'll need a statement."

"Just be careful. He shot at several others and me. I don't know why."

The policemen stormed into the alley. When Peyton heard the sound of the now empty AK-47 hit the ground, he turned to his left and headed down the square to the taxi stand.

"Jerusalem. David's Gate." He called out to the first cabdriver in the line. The driver hurried into his cab while Peyton climbed in the back. Once inside, he pulled out the Palestinian identity card and stuffed it into his waistband at the small of his back next to the Jericho. He then took his U.S. passport from its hiding place in his ankle band and placed it in his shirt pocket ready to show the Israeli security forces at the wall. Finally he sat back and watched the scenery move past as his body melted into the seat.

Chapter 19

Stagecoach Saloon
Tel Aviv, Israel

THE STAGECOACH SALOON WAS ONE OF THOSE
establishments found in many cosmopolitan cities
around the world. A mix of odd themes from disparate
cultures. As soon as Peyton walked through the Old
West style swinging doors into the saloon's restaurant,
he noticed the big Texas Lone Star flag that hung over
an authentic Western stagecoach. Wanted posters on the
walls proclaimed rewards for Billy the Kid, Jesse James,
and a number of other famous desperadoes. He stifled a
laugh when he saw the owner, an Irishman named Liam,
replace a missing nail using the butt of a six-shooter for
a hammer. Past a large "Don't Mess with Texas" sign,
the entry to the bar was visible, decorated with flags
from all over the world. Inside, the atmosphere was
reminiscent of an English pub. Just past the bar,
rounding out the cultural cacophony, Peyton could see
the door to the Shalom Hotel lobby, part of the Howard
Johnson's chain.

He spotted Rachel seated at a booth along the wall
and watched as a waiter handed her a martini while she
perused the menu unaware of Peyton's attention. He
smiled as he slid into the banquette opposite her and
said, "Wow, you look great." A bit embarrassed, he
added, "This place would look just like home except
American restaurants are too busy trying to look
European."

She laughed and he noticed how her eyes sparkled

in the candlelight. She brushed her hair behind one ear and said, "I wondered where you were. Did you get checked into a hotel?"

"Yeah, I'm at the Hilton across the street. I'm glad to be out of Jerusalem after all that's happened in the last couple of days." He looked directly into her bright green eyes as he spoke.

Rachel held his stare. "I have a flight at eleven in the morning so I have to leave for the airport early. I'm headed to Russia, Kazakhstan actually, to check out the weapon thread we got from Ivan." She sat back and glanced down at the table, straightening the silverware and cocktail napkin before returning Peyton's gaze. Her fingers slid up and down the stem of the martini glass as she spoke softly. "Any advice for me?"

Peyton saw the sparkle leave her eyes. "Yeah, come back in one piece." Slightly embarrassed that his tone might have betrayed his thoughts, he made a feeble attempt to change the subject. He picked up his menu and asked, "What looks good for dinner?"

Rachel smiled as she answered him. "This is an American restaurant, owned by two Irish brothers, situated in an American hotel with an Israeli name. I imagine you can get just about anything here." She again laughed lightly and looked down when Peyton reached across the table and took her hand in his with a gentle squeeze. When she lifted her head, he once more looked into her eyes and smiled. She glowed in the candlelight. After a moment of silence, he said, "You are an amazing woman."

Her face tingled slightly and she turned toward a large painting, aware that she was blushing. This is so intense, Peyton thought. *How? How have things moved to this point in only a few days? We've had so little time together.* Suddenly Stephanie's face drifted through his mind but the details were blurred. The pain that he usually associated with her memory wasn't there. Perhaps she was giving him her blessing. *Peyton*, he thought, *you're going mad.*

The waiter appeared. Rachel ordered comfort food, a salad and a side macaroni and cheese. Peyton chose the barbecued ribs, an unusual find in Israel, imported from Denmark once a week. He watched until the waiter was out of earshot and said, "I want to see how an Irishman in Israel prepares a classic American pork dish." When the entrée was served, he took a bite and rolled his eyes in pleasure. Rachel smiled, then laughed as he proceeded to review the dish with mock solemnity. "I always compare ribs to the ones I get at the Blue Ridge Grill in Leesburg, Virginia, which rate a ten on my scale." He took another bite, his eyes closed as he chewed, then pronounced, "I give The Stagecoach an eight plus, not bad for a foreign chef."

The conversation turned to the events of the last few days. Peyton filled her in as best he could in a public setting. When they finished dinner, both declined dessert. Not ready for the evening to end, Peyton leaned toward Rachel and said, "I have an idea. There's a park in front of the hotel. Why don't we take a walk? The path leads down to the beach." He took a sip of water. Then, in one last attempt to convince her, he added, "The night is beautiful. It might be our last for a while." He flinched as he heard his own words. *Did I just say that? Hell's bells, that's the standard WWII fighter pilot movie line. You are pathetic.*

"I'd love a stroll," Rachel replied. Her mood was lighter, her features softer. Peyton hoped that his face didn't register the surprise he felt when she accepted his rather lame invitation. He stood and offered her his hand.

They walked out of the saloon to Hayarkon Street.

Peyton guided her, his hand at her waist, as they turned left and walked to the corner. When the light changed, he grabbed her hand and they hurried across the street to the Hilton entrance, laughing. At the end of the driveway, they turned right and strolled slowly up the path to Spiegel Park.

Rachel led Peyton to a solitary large stone inscribed "This park was donated to Tel Aviv by Abraham and Edita Spiegel." Peyton watched her as she told the story of the Spiegel family, originally from the Ukraine. "They were sent to Auschwitz in 1944, along with their two-year old son. The couple survived but their young son died in the gas chambers." Rachel stood for a moment, her eyes brimming with tears, and then continued. "After liberation by the Russian Army, they moved to America." She looked up at Peyton, a sad smile on her face. "They spoke very little English and had even less money. Abraham, though, established himself as a successful land developer and banker.

"The Spiegels were benefactors of the Children's Memorial at Yad Vashem Holocaust Memorial in Jerusalem." A tear broke loose and tumbled down her cheek as she thought of the Spiegel's tiny son, one of the million and a half who perished in the Holocaust. She brushed the tear quickly with the back of her hand, then added, "They also gave generously to the Holocaust Museum in Washington, DC."

Peyton put his arm around her shoulder as they turned and crossed the park in silence. They walked to the edge closest to the beach. The sun now approached the horizon over the Mediterranean. He sat down on the grass, reached up, and took Rachel's hand, then gently pulled her down next to him. They watched the sun tint the sky a soft pink as it sank toward the water. "Watch." Rachel pointed to the horizon. "See how the sun moves ever so slowly toward the water, so slowly you can't detect the movement? Then, once it touches the sea, it slides quickly beneath the surface. I never tire of this." He looked at the wonder on her face. No trace of the earlier tear remained. He followed her gaze as the fiery orb hung for a moment and then, exactly as she had described, slipped in a blink from the ever-changing sky into the depths. He pulled her closer to his chest and she looked up into his eyes. "I'm drawn to you, Peyton. I can't explain it."

"Neither can I." The strong attraction had arrived without warning and consumed him. "Please, let's not fight this."

Rachel leaned into him and put her head on his shoulder. He squeezed her gently and they sat still as the sky morphed into a deep purple. Then he turned to her and said, "Come with me, Rachel. My room has a nice balcony with a lovely view. We could pick up a bottle of wine in the lobby shop. I don't want you to leave yet."

They walked hand in hand into the hotel and turned left past reception toward the elevators, past antique and jewelry boutiques. When Peyton turned toward the hotel wine shop, Rachel pulled back on his hand. "Why don't you forget the wine and let's just go up?"

Peyton squeezed her hand and smiled down at her. "That's fine with me."

When they reached his room on the fourteenth floor, Peyton walked over to the patio door, opened it and walked out onto the balcony, skewed slightly to face the sea. Rachel followed and stood next to him. The lights of the city south of the hotel sparkled gently in the twilight. They looked across Spiegel Park to the marina where the boats bobbed on gentle waves stirred by the evening breeze. Lulled by the masts of the sailboats that swayed in unison, they stared at the water in silence.

Finally Rachel turned toward him and looked up into his eyes. He put both arms around her and she rested her cheek on his chest as her body melted into his. When she looked up again, a trace of a tear was visible on her cheek. "Is something wrong?" Peyton asked.

She shook her head, then buried her face in his chest and sobbed once. "It's all so confusing," she said, a soft catch in her voice.

He stroked the back of her head and held her a little closer. "You can tell me," he said tenderly.

"I feel a bit frightened," she spoke softly, "by this attraction. I know that I wouldn't feel as I do if I didn't trust you. But I've lost everyone I've ever cared for: my brother, my mother, my father, my husband. I haven't wanted to take the risk again. Years have passed without complications, without feelings. Yet here I am with you and I've begun to care." She closed her eyes and shook her head slightly. "Look at who you are...a high risk operative for the American intelligence community! That's exactly where I was when my husband left for Australia. I don't want to throw away something good but this seems impossible." She looked into his eyes and said, "Peyton, I don't know if I have another good-bye in me."

She tried to step back but he pulled her gently toward him. "I understand better than you think. This is hard for me, too. But I don't want to walk away from someone as special as you. None of us have guarantees, Rachel." Peyton knew he could not ignore this chance to return to the land of the living. His feelings for Rachel were powerful, good, worthy of the struggle through his own guilt and grief.

His last words reminded him of the journal that Stephanie had given him on their first anniversary. That year had been filled with moments of love and laughter but Stephanie quickly learned that she had married a complex man, one who kept everything in little compartments. She saw that he could easily remain a stranger even to those who loved him. Years would pass before she understood how the pattern was formed in his early life. But her first instincts were sound. On the inside cover of the journal, she had inscribed a quote from C.S. Lewis: *"To love at all is to be vulnerable. Love anything, and your heart will certainly be wrung and possibly broken. If you want to make sure of keeping it intact, you must give your heart to no one, not even to an animal. Wrap it carefully round with hobbies and little luxuries; avoid all entanglements; lock it up safe in the casket or coffin of your selfishness. But in that casket - safe, dark, motionless, airless - it will change. It will not be broken; it will become unbreakable, impenetrable, irredeemable."* He had lost the journal in the house fire, but the words were burned into his soul. "Rachel, I've been afraid, too. But I am more afraid of not caring." For the first time in a long time, the words rang true and, with this admission, unexpected joy filled him.

Rachel looked up into his face, her eyes wet with tears, and smiled. As she did, the sparkle returned to her green eyes and Peyton leaned down to kiss her. The kiss was intended to be soft, but when his hand slid down, down toward her waist, she responded, her lips parting, tongues touching. They held each other tightly, as if afraid that, should they let go, they might fall. Joined in a kiss that grew in intensity, then lingered until they were spent, they looked deeply into each other's eyes, breathing heavily, searching for assurance that this union was real, meant to be. Peyton pulled back, took her hand and led her inside to the bed. He lowered her head onto the pillow and pulled her close. They kissed again and gave themselves to the night.

PEYTON AWOKE WITH A START TO THE PHONE'S insistent ring. His eyelids felt scratchy after only two hours sleep as he reached for the receiver and listened. "Good morning, shalom, this is your Hilton wake up call. The weather today..." He dropped the phone back onto the cradle. As he stretched, he felt Rachel stir next to him. He lay down again and put his arm around her. She turned over and pressed against him. Underneath her soft exterior were well-developed muscles, hard and strong. He found this combination of strength and softness intoxicating.

She wrapped her leg over his and they tangled together, pressing harder and harder, not wanting to let go. He kissed her neck and ran his hands gently up and down her spine. Her back arched as his lips traced down her throat and beyond. She wound her fingers in his hair and moaned. Before they could stop, they had once more made love again and now lay breathless on the bed.

Rachel got up. "I'll be right back," she said and headed toward the bathroom. Peyton watched her naked body as she crossed the room. *My God, she's the most beautiful woman in the world,* he thought. *Should I take her to the airport or just convince her to stay here for the next couple of years?* He smiled as she called out from the next room, "The shower is quite large. You could join me, if you'd like." He heard her turn on the water.

"Well," Peyton teased, "That's an excellent idea. We shower together and save time. Be right there."

"Ooh, this might take longer," she called out. Peyton laughed and headed for the bathroom. The phone rang. *What now?*

Peyton picked up the phone and said, "Hello."

"Hi, Peyton, it's Clare."

He abruptly shifted gears. "Ace! Good to hear from you. How're things going there?"

"I just talked with Harry and also spoke with Bryan. Thought you'd want to get up to speed on some of the latest developments."

"Sure do. What's up?"

"Harry and Ken are following a money trail. Harry will call you with details so I'll skip that but Bryan is really excited about his project."

Peyton's first reaction was *what project?* but he didn't say that. He forced the excitement that he should have felt naturally had he kept up with his son's accomplishments. "Yes, the Navy one." Peyton depleted all of his knowledge on the subject in three words. "Did he say how that's coming along?"

"Well, of course he did. His remote-controlled submarine will start sea trials in the Med at the end of the week."

"He's coming here? The Med, I mean."

"No, the sub is coming there," Clare continued, "and Bryan is going to test it over a satellite link. He'll be in San Diego and control the boat from there. He built the control system and had the software developed at Systems Command."

"Wow." Proud, gutted, stunned, ashamed...he could summon no other words.

Rachel walked in from the bathroom, naked, water droplets glistening on her smooth skin. "Aren't you going to shower?"

Peyton, already in another mental compartment, held one hand up and turned his back to her as he hunched over the phone. "So," he continued, "when do the tests start?"

There was silence on the other end of the phone. Then Clare spoke briskly, "Day after tomorrow. You should call him. I gotta go."

"I will." He heard a click and the background on the line changed. "Ace?" He stared motionless at the silent handset, then jumped as the bathroom door slammed hard behind him.

CLARE STOOD, HANDS ON HIPS, AND LOOKED DOWN at the phone on her desk. A rational person, she was caught off-guard by the wave of strong emotions that rocked her. She took a deep breath and replayed the call in her mind. *She* was in his room. Something about a shower. They had probably slept together. What else could it be?

Why do you care? she asked herself. *Why?* The answer came quickly to mind. Because of Stephanie. But the internal debate continued. *Stephanie's been gone two years. Peyton has a right to move on.* Try as she might, her feelings were not assuaged by this logic. From within, a caveat. *But not with her.*

She sat with her elbows on the desk, head in her hands, and reasoned that what had, at first, seemed anger was perhaps only disappointment. The wash of emotion, atypical for Clare, left her fatigued, confused, even frightened perhaps. *No,* she thought, *I'm not scared. I'm annoyed. Yes, annoyed. That's it.* She had no romantic feelings for Peyton. She cared about her boss. *This is a protective reaction, pure and simple. Of course.* Wasn't it? She sat up, brushed a loose strand of hair from her eyes and glanced, unseeing, at the detailed project matrix on her computer screen.

Chapter 20

Sary Arka Airport
Karaganda, Kazakhstan

THE ONE-HUNDRED PASSENGER TUPOLEV TU-334 made a sweeping turn across downtown Karaganda and descended for final approach to runway 23 at Sary-Arka airport twelve miles southwest of the city. As late as 1950, German slaves lived in nearby labor camps and continued to mine coal to power the Soviet military industrial complex. The city, situated next to the massive Kazakh coalfields, once had a population of a half-million people, most of German descent. In the years since the fall of the Soviet Union, though, over 150,000 people left to return to the land of their ancestry.

The two thousand mile flight from Moscow was one of the first non-stops scheduled after the 334 re-design added extended range tanks. Rachel stretched after the long flight in a packed plane and walked toward the terminal where she headed to the rental car desk. She spoke enough Russian to get by - certainly enough to find Dmitri - but hoped that she would be given a standard rental agreement because she had no plans to read it. Once at the desk, she glanced at the forms in a bored fashion before signing, then picked up a new Saab. Rachel smiled at the lot attendant. *Maybe this place isn't as backward as some people say.* Now, though, she had to ask for directions. "I am trying to get to Kolovostok." The man stared back. Rachel added, "It's near Karkaralinsk."

"Ah, in the mountains. You cannot go there directly. The best route is south through Spassk," the

252

agent answered as he pulled out a regional map. He spoke rapidly as he pointed and gave specific directions to the edge of the map. "After you reach this location," he continued, "follow the road. If you get lost, ask."

As she settled in for the long drive ahead, Rachel recalled what she knew of Spassk. The Soviet Gulag system once stretched from the Arctic to these bitter, windswept steppes in Kazakhstan. Just outside the tiny village of Spassk, the camps had housed - she grimaced at that word - Soviet dissidents as well as WWII-era foreign prisoners. She'd seen photographs of the cemetery outside Spassk and heard of memorials placed there after the dissolution of the Soviet Union. A deep sadness reached into her soul as she drove along the barren, desolate landscape that stretched as far as the eye could see in every direction. In this brutal place, she mused, escape from the gulag would have been little more than an ineffectual trade, one death for another.

After she'd left the hotel in Tel Aviv, she had operated on auto-pilot as she prepared for this next phase of her assignment. Until now, that is. The map didn't lie. The long hours spent on this stretch of god-forsaken highway offered no distractions from her thoughts, thoughts that took her back to Peyton…to their night together in the hotel and the awful morning that followed.

She hit the steering wheel with the heel of her right hand and said to the universe, "What was I thinking?" A wry snort followed as she continued the one-sided conversation. "That's all I can come up with? The question everyone asks?" She reached for a bottled water and shifted in the seat. The answer was obvious. She hadn't been thinking. Period. The walls she had so carefully tended had collapsed without warning. Well, with hints of a breach, perhaps. *But why?*

As angry as she was, as betrayed as she felt, she couldn't foist the blame onto Peyton. He hadn't misled her. She knew that he had his own wounds, his own walls. Why, then, had both allowed themselves to cross a line each now regretted? *At least, I didn't regret the night I spent with you, Peyton Stone, before I'd even had a chance to brush my teeth.* She seethed as she recalled her humiliation when she had walked into the room and been roundly ignored while he talked to his Ace, or Clare, or whatever. But what if the phone had rung for her? Would she have responded differently? She honestly couldn't answer those questions.

Mile after miserable mile she drove, imprisoned in her own personal gulag. Guilt, anger, and fear - emotions she had struggled to banish - returned with a vengeance. She had shed much more than her clothing that night. *I won't do that again, mark my word. Never again.* In the somber quiet of the lonely drive, that thought penetrated and chilled her. Was this to be her life? Devoid of love, of touch? Had she long ago crossed another line, one that obliterated all hope of partnership, that had rendered her invulnerable? She shook her head, drank the rest of the water and focused on the horizon. There was no escape, only work.

SIX HOURS LATER, AN EXHAUSTED RACHEL SPOTTED the sign: Karkaralinsk 66km. *Good grief, this is a long way from anything.* She rounded the next curve where a sign next to a gravel road pointed the way to the Kolovostok Army Storage Facility. Set in the geographic center of nowhere, the location needed no disguise.

Rachel pulled up to the gate and the large guard looked out at her. Suddenly three more men appeared in the window behind him. Attractive women rarely presented themselves at the gate. "I am looking for someone named Dmitri who works here or perhaps worked here in the past."

"I am Dmitri," the guard said as he pointed to his ample chest. The other guards laughed. A second guard elbowed the first out of the way and, with slurred speech, declared, "No, I am Dmitri. You must come inside now."

Rachel put the car in reverse and stepped on the gas. When she was several hundred yards from the guard booth, she hit the brakes, pulled to the side, and turned around. Now what? She turned north and headed toward Karkaralinsk, where, hopefully, she could find a hotel and information about this Dmitri who lived here. Twenty minutes later she saw a pair of duplexes on her right. She pulled over next to the low cinder block wall that surrounded the houses and got out of the car. If her information was correct, Dmitri lived in one of the duplexes.

The experience at the Army storage facility gate had rattled her. The guards were big young men and she was unarmed. Rachel, whose street fighting skills were respected, knew that four armed, drunken soldiers would have easily overpowered her. She breathed deeply to regain her composure, then walked up to the first house and knocked. No one answered the door. She knocked once more. As she turned to walk away, a voice called out, "They are not at home."

Rachel looked around but saw no one. "Excuse me?" she said in Russian.

"The boys are not at home." The voice came from the house next door but Rachel couldn't locate the speaker. She crossed the small yard and saw an old woman in a faded floral print housedress standing just inside the open doorway. "Dmitri and Greggor, they left this morning and are not at home."

"Any idea where they went? I am looking for a Dmitri who works at the storage facility."

"Those boys never tell a mother where they are going. They said they might be gone for a time because they have to drive down to Dostyk to deliver machinery. Dmitri works at that army place down the road. He makes records of what is there - something to do with the Americans - but he can't say what, or won't. His brother, Greggor, works on the highway. They took Dmitri's truck and went that way," the old woman pointed south, the direction Rachel had just come from. "I haven't seen them since. Maybe you should come back tomorrow or the next day."

"You're Dmitri's mother?"

"Yes, and Greggor's. They are good boys but I worry about them. But then, what mother doesn't?"

"You say they went to Dostyk? What's in Dostyk?"

"It's a small town with only a train station and railroad yard near the border with China," the old woman answered absently as she waved her hand at a fly. "I heard them talk about taking some machinery to Dostyk. I don't know what it's about. They are good boys but sometimes they scheme with each other. Their plans always come to nothing." She shook her head. "Too much vodka."

Rachel spoke. "You wouldn't happen to have a picture of Dmitri, would you?"

The woman looked hurt. "We are poor but not that poor. Of course, I have many pictures of my sons. Their father, too."

"Please forgive me. I didn't mean to be rude. Of course, you have pictures. I meant to ask if you have a picture that you could spare. I must meet Dmitri to discuss an urgent government matter and can't wait until he returns. If I knew what he looked like, I could go to Dostyk and find him."

The old woman eyed her suspiciously. "A government matter? Is there some trouble?"

"Oh, no." Rachel immediately regretted her words. "Just an inventory problem at the army base. Boxes and boxes of cabbages have been shipped to the base. The extras will spoil if I don't solve this quickly. Only Dmitri knows where things go. He's very important and I need to speak to him." Not even Rachel found the explanation reasonable.

The old woman squinted at Rachel and considered the information as she swatted at the fly. "Come in and I'll show you some pictures."

Rachel sat politely while the matriarch of the family recounted a detailed family history that included an aunt's battle with a defective gall bladder. The effort to dispel the woman's suspicions paid off an hour later when Rachel thanked her for her hospitality and left with a picture of Dmitri and Greggor.

Hours later, Rachel pulled into Dostyk just after midnight. The brown and white rail station more closely resembled an apartment building than an international transshipment point. The station was deserted. Only the freight yard showed any signs of life. She drove up and down the unpaved streets and looked for a hotel. *Well, this won't be the first time that I've slept in a car, or worse,* Rachel thought, as she looked for a discreet place to park.

EARLY THE NEXT MORNING RACHEL SET OUT TO FIND the brothers. They would likely be in the warehouse complex, a lofty designation for the row of twelve storage buildings near the rail station. She drove along the gravel track that served as the main street of Dostyk and looked for a truck parked anywhere nearby. All of the buildings were closed, some padlocked. She quickly realized this approach wouldn't work. Even if the truck were here, it could easily be hidden inside a warehouse building.

Rachel parked at the train station and crossed the gravel ruts to the nearest warehouse. A man sat in a wooden chair tipped back against the building. Older with a tanned, weathered face and grey stubble that revealed he hadn't shaved in several days, he listened as she inquired if he had seen the two men in the picture she handed him. "Nyet," he answered and shook his head from side to side. She walked to the next warehouse and circled it, then continued to walk around each in turn but found no unlocked doors or windows. She was about to start around the sixth building when she heard a commotion down the street. A man was yelling something in Russian that she couldn't make out and people were running toward him.

She jogged behind the warehouses and rounded the corner of a building where she saw three people. A man pointed at an open door to the warehouse and screamed, "They're dead; they're dead!" The other two craned their necks but didn't go inside the building.

Rachel ran to the door and saw two bodies face down on the floor in a large pool of blood. Her mind and body on full alert, she took a step inside the door, touched her hip where her gun would have been, then leaned over and picked up a pry bar from the floor near a stack of crates. She gripped the bar with both hands and looked around for any movement that might indicate a hidden assailant in the building. The only sounds were from the growing crowd behind her, which now numbered seven or eight people. After a careful scan of the warehouse, she relaxed slightly.

Rather than touch the bodies, Rachel used the pry bar to turn the body. She pulled the picture that the woman had given her from her pocket and recognized Greggor. Once again she used the pry bar to turn the other body. The old woman's face haunted Rachel as she stared down at Dmitri's lifeless body sprawled next to his brother's. She had reached a dead end, literally.

Voices rose behind her when a Kazakh official from the Customs shed entered. He told everyone to stand back as he took control of the scene. Rachel stood up and backed slowly away. The last thing she needed right now was to be stuck in a murder investigation.

"Who found the bodies?" the official asked.

Rachel pointed in the general direction of the people by the door, then walked toward them. She turned when she reached the group and endeavored to blend into the crowd.

"You!" He pointed at Rachel. "What did you see?"

"Nothing. I heard a disturbance and ran to see what had happened. A man was shouting that someone was dead. I went inside to see. That's all."

"You're certain that's all?" The Customs man, obviously not trained in criminal investigation, made his best effort to get to the bottom of things.

"Yes, that's it," Rachel replied. Two men in the crowd nodded in support of her story.

"We shall see," the man replied and turned his eyes upward to the ceiling.

Rachel followed his gaze upward and then saw it. A CCTV security camera was mounted in the inside corner of the warehouse space. *Of course*, she thought, *this is a Customs warehouse.* The Russians would want to be alerted to any attempt to smuggle goods from China to Kazakhstan. This time the camera had recorded goods going in the opposite direction, along with a double murder. Not that the video would matter at this point. The killer was probably across the border and long gone.

THE SMALL ROOM THAT SERVED AS THE SECURITY monitoring point in the Customs House was stifling. Rachel felt sickened by the fetid, hot air redolent with the odor of cabbage and unwashed bodies. She explained that she was in Dostyk to inquire about the missing sons of a family friend. The alibi was easy enough to check out but hoped the man would not want to create any additional work for himself. After a long, tedious session, the Customs man was satisfied that she was not here in any official capacity, relieved that no government coordination with the attendant forms would be required. Five crisp American one hundred dollar bills were all the paperwork he needed.

The Customs official now turned his attention to the video and toggled past the image of the slain bodies in the center of the frame. He and Rachel watched as a man backed into the frame. The bodies jumped up backwards and faced the stranger, a pistol now visible in his hand. Then the two Russians walked backwards to a hand truck and backed out of the frame. At the same time the man with the handgun pocketed the weapon and backed out of the frame. "Ok, I have it," said the Customs official. Rachel leaned close to the screen to get a better look.

The Customs man pressed the Play button. They watched as an Asian man walked into the picture from the top of the screen. Seconds later two men walked into the picture from the bottom. One pushed a hand truck with a crate on it. The two talked for a few minutes while the Asian man looked around the room. His eyes constantly made slow, deliberate sweeps of the space.

The other two continued to stand and talk throughout the inspection. At one point in the conversation, the two men lowered the hand truck's base flat onto the floor, then pried the top off the crate with a crowbar to reveal a pair of shiny objects inside. Rachel recognized the nuclear warheads from the pictures she had studied in her prep kit. She realized that this confirmed that the nuclear device was real and had traveled through the Kazakh border, probably on its way to Bushehr.

As she watched, the man in the picture pulled an automatic pistol with a silencer from his coat pocket and killed the two Russians. Each had a single shot to the forehead, no waste of ammunition. Rachel saw the backs of each head erupt in a spray of pink as they crumpled to the ground. The Asian man looked at the bodies before he very slowly scanned the room one more time. He didn't stop and look at the camera but, during his slow scan of the space, a clear image of the killer's face was visible on the tape. Definitely Asian, with a long handlebar moustache and a very dangerous look, he stood about five feet seven inches. He took a cell phone from his jacket pocket, dialed, then spoke for a few moments. Then he nudged one of the bodies with his foot, wiped his shoe on a pants leg and hung up the phone.

Rachel turned to the agent and asked, "Can you print a copy of the full face picture?"

"Coming out of the printer now," the Customs man said. A black and white laser print, the detail was good enough for her to recognize the Asian if she came across him again.

The logged time from the security system was printed in the lower right hand corner of the picture: seven thirty this morning. Rachel looked at her watch: current time, nine o'clock. Only an hour and a half had passed. A quick calculation of an approximate time needed to load the crate and then wait in line at the border crossing suggested that he had not gone far.

She thanked the Customs official, put the picture in her pocket and ran toward the Saab. Rachel started the car, dropped it in gear and drove as quickly as she could toward the border crossing seven miles away. Almost as soon as she drove past the edge of town, she came upon the last truck in the inspection queue that stretched all the way to the crossing. This could take hours, she thought. But then the shooter would be detained as well. She pulled over to the left and raced toward the front in the oncoming traffic lane, ignoring the blare of horns and angry shouts from drivers who waited in line to cross. Rachel looked at every driver she passed as she tried to spot the man in the picture. Luckily, the border inspection process modulated the traffic that came toward her. Only one truck approached. She drove onto the left shoulder, slipped between the truck on the roadway and the railroad tracks to her left and kept going.

When she reached the front of the line, she parked on the shoulder, ran to the fence, and peered through. More trucks on the other side were now spread out into the inspection lanes. She craned to see inside each cab and finally spotted him. The long handlebar moustache gave him away. *Now what?* Rachel wondered. She looked at the cell phone in her hand but had no signal. Her training took over and she snapped pictures with the otherwise useless phone.

The Asian walked behind a truck and pushed back the canvas flap while another man, stout but solidly built, climbed up into the back. The other man stood next to the truck and scanned his surroundings. Once he stopped and stared directly at her but she fought the urge to duck.

The stout man stuck his head out of the back of the truck, pushed the canopy aside, and jumped down. *Fang!* Rachel recognized him from the photo Peyton had shown her. The two men shook hands, then Moustache handed Fang a set of keys. Both wore big smiles when they embraced and patted each other on the back. While the killer walked toward the town of Alashancou, a mile inside the Chinese side of the border, Fang got into the truck and drove around the inspection lane and down the road. No one with Chinese Customs even glanced in his direction.

Chapter 21

Beyik, China
Near the Afghanistan Border

FANG TURNED OUT OF THE DIRT TRACK AND ONTO the highway for the last time and headed toward the market in Beyik where he would make the same call as before to the same number. Probably not the smartest thing to do, but, if he only made the call twice, he should be ok. He would repeat the words that the Arab told him to say and, by this time tomorrow, the second installment of his money would be deposited in the Cayman account. In no hurry to return to Beijing now that he was a wealthy man, rich beyond his dreams, he planned to travel at his leisure. He would take the train across the desert to Mongolia, enjoy some of the sensual pleasures of central Russia, and then make his way home where he would decide his next move.

Fang pulled into the market and walked to the phone. He made the call that would make him rich and then placed the other call, one he was obliged to make. "Admiral, this is Mr. Po. We are ready to begin our final training and would like to bring our equipment to the training base."

There was a long silence on the other end. Finally, the response. "We're ready. I will be there tomorrow to personally see to things."

"Thank you," Fang replied and hung up.

My part of this is done, Fang thought, *unless I don't get my money. That would be a fatal mistake.*

THE FOURTEEN-YEAR-OLD BOY RAN ALONG THE

blacktop road out of Beyik, southward toward the turnoff to his uncle's hut in the mountain cave. In a single year he had grown six inches to his present height of five feet, four inches. He had no transportation so he ran or walked everywhere. His preference was to run as fast as possible. On those rare occasions when he was able to go to school, he could beat most of the boys in a foot race. Today his uncle had promised him adventure: a man's job, a man's adventure. His face beamed, his dark eyes shone and his black hair streamed behind him in the wind as he flew to his uncle's hut.

Here in this desolate place, a fourteen-year-old boy was closer to manhood than in almost any other area of the world. He had somehow maintained the wide-eyed innocence of a child even though he had seen atrocities in Afghanistan that most humans could not imagine. An impersonal view of dead bodies on the evening news could not compare to what the boy had experienced. As he ran, he thought of the terrible past. He had watched friends and family gunned down, had seen them suffer painfully slow, agonizing deaths while he watched from a hiding place. There he had cowered and hoped that the enemy – Taliban, Pashtu, Northern Alliance, Americans, whoever the invader de jour – would be too lazy to get out of their vehicles, search, find, and slaughter him.

Today he ran the six kilometers from the spot where the Chinese man had given him the message to his uncle's door in just thirty minutes. Completely winded, he sat by the front door and panted for several minutes. He caught his breath and went inside to deliver the news. "Uncle!" the boy cried out. "I have a message from the Chinaman."

The boy heard a scrabbling sound from the back room of the hut and his uncle walked through the door. "What is it, Samer?" the elderly man asked. "Did you get the destination for our trip?"

"Yes, Uncle, we are to go to Iran." The boy added excitedly, "I've never been to Iran." He had traveled quite a lot compared to others in the region, though. Many grew up in small villages and never saw the nearest settlement thirty kilometers away. Samer had been born in a small village near Kabul. When the Taliban wiped out most of his small town, he traveled alone to the city in search of his uncle. His uncle was a great leader, high up in the Bin Laden organization, and gave the boy a good life. He saw much of the Afghan countryside around Kabul as he accompanied his uncle on journeys to visit tribal chieftains. After the Americans came, the pair moved quickly out of the country and into the cave in China. Over time they built a home in the cave where they now lived, far from prying eyes, deep in the mountains. The boy talked rapidly to his uncle. "The Chinaman has been here twice now in the last few weeks. We should find a safe place, a new home, perhaps a palace in Iran!"

The boy's uncle smiled a fatherly smile, amused by the boy's enthusiasm. "But, first the message. Where exactly in Iran are we to go?"

"To an Army Camp near the big city of Zabol in the eastern part of the country. We'll have to drive all the way across Afghanistan. How will we do that? The Americans will certainly stop us and want to know our business. What will we tell them?"

"You are sure this is what he said?" The old man tried not to look skeptical but, at the same time, this was too important to get wrong.

"Oh, yes, Uncle. I made up a rhyme in my head to help me remember. Do you want to hear it?"

"If you say that it's true, then it's true." The old Arab smiled at the boy. "Now, you leave the details of our journey to me. We have many friends who will help us with the Pakistanis and the Americans. You have only one assignment but it's the most important one. You must drive the truck that the Chinaman left at the bus station. You must bring it back here and fetch me and we will leave together. Can you do that?"

"All the way back to town?" He thought, *I've just run from town and could have driven instead*, but said only, "Of course, Uncle."

"You will find the truck, loaded with hay, parked next to the bus lot. The key will be on top of the left front tire. Drive it back here and I will meet you at the road. Make sure that the tarp is tied down tight across the hay so we don't lose it on our journey. The border at Afghanistan is closed so we are going to take the Karakoram Highway and cross into Pakistan at the Khunjerab Pass. Then we will make our way across Pakistan to another Afghan crossing where we have friends. From there we'll go to Iran, to Zabol. You must speak to no one until you pick me up on the road."

An hour later, the ancient farm truck rolled to a stop on the side of the highway where the old man sat. He smiled when he saw the small head barely visible above the steering wheel. When the truck stopped, the excited boy's face grinned down from the driver's window. "I am here, Uncle. I have driven all the way from Beyik."

"I can see that," replied his Uncle. "You will be an expert by the time we reach Iran. We have to travel as quickly as possible to cover the distance. The terrain will slow our pace and the roads are not fast so we must keep ourselves alert." The boy had driven an old Toyota pickup truck since he was twelve, propped on an old pillow so that he could see through the windshield. While not exactly legal by the strict reading of Afghanistan law, the law under the Taliban was fluid, often molded to fit a given situation. The old Arab knew that legal was best defined as whatever payoff he and the current political expedient could reach.

The old man walked around to the passenger door and climbed up into the cab, then nodded to the boy. What appeared to be an innocent farm truck full of hay rolled down the Karakoram Highway, known simply as the KKH, past goatherds and men on horseback with their yaks and dzu, a cross between a yak and a cow. This was the old Silk Road where the Scythians had traveled to join the Assyrians for the invasion of Egypt four thousand years ago. Now the old Arab and his protégée were headed along the same road toward yet another invasion. This one, however, would not result in archeological sites where university students unearthed arrowheads and bits of charcoal to tell a story. This modern day invasion would start with a pair of weapons: the two nuclear warheads in a lead-lined box hidden under the pile of hay. In the end, little evidence would remain for future academicians to study.

They rolled up to the border between China and Pakistan - the highest paved border crossing in the world, nearly 16,000 feet above sea level. The Arab fidgeted a little in his seat. This would be one of several stressful parts of the journey. Leaving China was not terribly difficult. But at the 'Zero Point,' where Pakistani-controlled Kashmir began, he would need to produce papers in order to cross. He had a fake Pakistani passport and a goods transporter permit issued by the Chinese-Pakistani Joint Commission. Unless, however, his contacts in the Northern Areas government had placed a call, he was subject to scrutiny, which included a search of the hay load. They pulled up to the checkpoint, and the boy handed down a packet of papers. The guard looked at the names, immediately handed the papers back, and waved them onward.

Now the pair faced only two more hurdles, the security checkpoint at Dih and the customs checkpoint in Sust. Once they reached the Khyber, the friendly tribesmen would easily smuggle them into Afghanistan. From that point forward, they would be in familiar territory all the way to Iran. The two would have to avoid American patrols and roadblocks, but the details had long been worked out.

THERE WAS A HIGH MEADOW ACROSS THE RIVER from where the old Arab had waited to be picked up by a boy in a farm truck. A bird watcher packed his binoculars and camera equipment. He carefully unscrewed the 500mm lens and folded the bipod that stabilized the picture from this distance. He had taken a couple of good shots of the old man and the boy: one as they spoke to each other, the other as the old man climbed into the truck. He packed the small one-man nylon tent into the carrying case and moved down the slope to his Land Rover. He made a few notes on a pad in his native Chinese language and plugged the camera and satellite phone into the laptop computer on the passenger seat. Within minutes, he was headed south on the KKH toward Khunjerab.

Once on the highway, he opened the laptop and pressed the start button. Even though powered only by the cigarette lighter, this particular operation would take no more than a few minutes. The battery would be fine. He then opened the camera download application and transferred the pictures from the camera onto his hard drive. Once the import was complete, he opened his email, attached the photos, typed the words "big explosion, massive deaths, kill the Americans" in the subject line. He then keyed up a wireless account on his satellite phone and sent the email to himself at a bogus email address.

IN A CORNER OF THE SECOND BASEMENT LEVEL OF Building Two at Ft. Meade's NSA Headquarters, a computer chime softly alerted the operator to a new message. Echelon's massively parallel processors had identified keyword phrases that indicated potential danger to US interests and sent the message to Diane Fairchild's screen. From the email router information in the header, she could tell that the intercepted message had been sent by someone in China to someone else in China. Although the subject was "big explosion, massive deaths, kill the Americans," the attachments showed a man and a boy getting into what appeared to be a farm truck loaded with hay. The message had been picked up by an NSA Satellite over western China and eastern Afghanistan. The satellite vacuumed up nearly every electronic peep and beep that emanated from the earth's surface within its footprint. As everyone knew, the hard part was to distinguish between a terrorist's message and an innocent phone call between spouses with a "please stop for milk on the way home" petition. The extremely complex, highly classified Echelon computers at NSA had perfected text mining and could detect word patterns and text patterns out of millions of random conversations in almost any language.

Many conversations, whether voice or data, were encrypted so that the computers could not recognize and interpret them. This message, however, was sent with no additional encryption other than the normal Sat phone scrambling.

"What do you make of this?" Diane asked as she walked the few steps to her supervisor's cubicle in the NSA rat maze. "The message came in unencrypted. I'd be tempted to call it a hoax, except the sender hasn't made an effort to create a fake. Other than the subject, only two simple pictures have been attached."

"This is odd," said her supervisor. "Forward it through regular channels and see if any hits come back." Often information was shared with CIA, the NGA, and the Defense Intelligence Agency at DIA's Headquarters on Bolling Air Force Base, in the event that a related issue was under review. Until 9/11 all of the information collected by any agency stayed within that agency's stove pipe and was protected by the old "need to know" test. The DNI prior to McKinley had instituted a new philosophy that changed "need to know" into "responsibility to provide" to facilitate cooperation between agencies.

"Ok, I'll send it out and then I need to get out of here. My nine-year-old daughter is the Wicked Witch of the West in the school play tonight." Diane had worked as a signals analyst at NSA for twelve years. She had a PhD in mathematics and enjoyed her work but struggled to balance the demands of career with her role as a single mother to three girls. Whenever one of them was involved in an after-school activity, she made certain she was there.

Her supervisor smiled. "That sounds like fun. See you tomorrow."

Diane went back to her cubicle, logged on to NSAnet, composed a TOP SECRET//COMINT message and sent the intercept to the usual mailboxes. She then shut down her station and went home to transform her beautiful daughter into an evil hag.

THE IRANIAN NAVY HELICOPTER FLEW OVER THE AIR base southwest of the city of Bushehr and made a sweeping right turn toward the helipad behind the naval headquarters building. Kuchecki noticed two new surface-to-air missile batteries near completion. The same Russian military that had developed and built his Kilo class submarines had also provided the Iranian Air Force with the latest in protection against air attacks. The irony, in Kuchecki's view, was that air attacks were not the biggest threat to the Iranian Government.

He believed Iran faced a greater peril. The imminent U.S./Iran treaty was a disaster in the making. If Iran got too cozy with the U.S., the culture of his country would be endangered and good Muslim values would begin to decay. Since the Government in Tehran was too strongly aligned with the infidels, Kuchecki was prepared to end the alliance himself: he would crush the West and destroy America's decadent lifestyle. He watched the ground sweep past below as he fueled his passion. *I'll wipe the United States' nose in its misfortune just as a master wipes a puppy's nose in excrement to teach a lesson. The West had made mistakes for centuries with no one to hold them accountable. But I will. Before Allah, I vow that I will.*

Chapter 22

CIA Headquarters

KEN WASHINGTON LEANED BACK IN HIS CHAIR, stretched and rubbed his face with both hands. His eyes were red and scratchy after long hours in front of a computer screen filled with endless columns of numbers the previous day. He had probably looked less haggard after a night out with his Omega Men fraternity brothers. A soft chime called his attention back to the large, flat-screen monitor where a pop-up window announced New Transaction In Tagged Account.

Ken sat up and clicked his mouse on the tag. Numbers scrolled upward in a blur and stopped at a highlighted line on his screen. *Son of a ...*

He picked up the red phone and punched in Harry's extension. Come on, come on. Harry picked up. Ken, his breath shallow, said, "Harry, Ali just transferred four and a half million to Fang. I think the weapon is moving. Why else would he do that?" A moment of silence followed. Ken wondered if the connection had been lost. Then he heard Harry's reply.

"Crap, we need a location. I need to think, see what I can come up with."

"Ok, Harry, but there's no physical connection between the account transfers and the origin of the transactions. These guys could be anywhere. Remember, Ali has been on the most wanted list for years and Fang is probably in China somewhere."

"Yeah, but there's always a trail of breadcrumbs. Let me spend some time arranging the pieces. You're sure the money moved between these guys?"

"Well, yeah, I'm looking at it right here. The

273

money went from Ali's account in Cayman to Fang's account in Martinique. The numbers match."

"Alright, I'll work on it," Harry said, and the line clicked in Ken's ear.

HARRY STOOD AT HIS WHITE BOARD, HIS HAND nearly a blur while he quickly translated his thoughts into a list of facts, assumptions and speculation. Christened "the brain dump" by co-workers, Harry wrote whatever came into his mind and then sorted after he had emptied his thoughts.

The squeaks of the Dri-erase marker went unnoticed as the strains of the aria from Verde's Aida heightened his concentration. While Radamès prepared for the Egyptian war with Ethiopia, Harry faced his own war with the ever-growing list of disconnected facts. He hummed while he wrote, erased with the side of his fist and wrote some more.

He sang out, "Ergerti un trono vicino al sol" as he dropped the marker into the tray with a flourish and stood back. To an outsider, the scribbles that filled the entire board seemed little more than random thoughts but Harry could see emergent patterns. A quote from the mathematician, Alfred North Whitehead, ran through his mind: *"Art is the imposing of a pattern on experience, and our aesthetic enjoyment is recognition of the pattern."* He smiled as he sat down. *An artist and opera devotee,* he thought. *Harry Morrison, you are a renaissance man.* He glanced down at the jelly stain on his tie and chuckled, then reached into his desk drawer for a candy bar.

He rested his head against the back of his chair and closed his eyes for a moment. Where would Fang and Ali come together? Or would they? They had to for something as big as this. But where?

The color printer next to his desk suddenly came to life with a click and whirred incessantly as it printed an alert message from the NSA followed by a series of photos. Harry reached over and picked up the stack of images, glanced at them briefly, then turned his attention to the white board once more. The patterns began to come together in his mind. He couldn't afford any distractions now. He stapled the top left corner of the stack and tossed the images onto his chair. After one more glance at the scribbles, he stepped up to the second white board and began a list:

U.S. and Iran agree to a treaty
Sell out accused – source unknown – likely Kuchecki
Kuchecki related to Ambassador to Pakistan – Ambassador killed. Why?
Nuclear something in Bushehr. Kuchecki in Bushehr. What?
Randy killed. Why? – who?
Randy's gear found but not reported. Why?
Xu killed probably by Fang. Why?
Peyton captured & rescued. Not reported - Why?
Money moved from Swiss account to Ali. Who?
Money moved from Ali to Fang – 2 installments equal to 90% of Swiss transaction - connection? Almost certainly.
Israel – martyrdom. What does this mean?
Amin: Kuchecki has the ability to unleash Allah's wrath on Israel. Nuclear strike?
Swiss account Kuchecki? Confirm with Ken.
Where are Kuchecki, Fang and Ali now?

His list complete, at least for the moment, Harry picked up the stack of papers from his chair and ruffled the edges. He sat down to determine if he had missed anything in the first cursory glance. Nothing immediately jumped out at him. He looked with idle curiosity at the NSA message, a routine intercept with photo attachments.

Harry flipped through the photos, his mind focused on the list and possible connections. Suddenly he stopped flipping pages as an image appeared before him: a face, one that Harry had sought for several years, one that had flashed through his mind as he wrote on the white board. Harry's mouth dropped opened and he sucked in a short breath when he recognized the owner of the Cayman bank account, Ali al-Muzzafar.

KEN WASHINGTON LOOKED UP FROM THE COMPUTER when Harry's girth cast a shadow over the screen. A message packet stapled on one corner plopped down on his keyboard. His eyes moved from Harry to the packet and back to Harry.

"Did you see this?" Harry asked. His index finger tapped the packet with such force that Ken thought he'd poke a hole in it. "That's Ali al- Muzzafar getting into a truck. And look at the message in the header."

"Big explosion, massive deaths, kill the Americans." Ken read. He looked up at Harry and frowned. "Weird. Where did this come from?"

Harry picked up the packet with both hands and shook it. His face began to turn red. "From the freakin' NSA. Look at the cover!"

Ken quickly decided not to tell the senior man to calm down. "Right, but I meant where were the photos taken?"

Harry turned the packet around so he could read it right side up and the palpitations around his mid-section subsided somewhat. He took a deep breath and let it out slowly.

"The location isn't noted. The background is just sand and mountains. Did you get it?"

Ken turned back to his computer. "Yeah, here it is." He double-clicked on the message and the screen opened a blank page.

"Strange," Ken said, "there's a header but no message."

Harry looked over his shoulder. "Let's go to my office. Maybe we can zoom in on parts and pick up some geographic cues."

"After you, boss." Ken rose and gestured toward the door.

The two men walked down the long hall to Harry's office. Once inside, Harry opened his desk drawer for antacid. He chewed on the pink tablet as he logged on to the high side network. "Ok, here it is."

He double-clicked on the message and the same blank page appeared. "What the...?" He sat back quickly and Ken looked over his shoulder.

"There must be some server issue," Ken said.

Harry looked at the printout, picked up the secure phone and pounded out an extension on the keypad. The voice on the other end answered, "Diane Fairchild."

"Diane, it's Harry Morrison at CIA and I'm calling about a message you sent titled 'Big explosion, massive deaths, kill the Americans.' Photos were attached but my server has dumped them. Can you resend that to me?"

"Sure. Hang on a second...now that's strange. The photos are gone. No wait, the entire incoming message has been purged."

"You mean someone accidentally deleted it. How can that happen?" Harry's middle was starting to quake again. He turned slightly in his chair and placed his

277

hand on the arm of the chair, elbow outward to stretch his abdomen.

"No, Harry, purged. The message was erased and the whole sector was overwritten with random characters. There's not a scrap of data left."

"Who would do that?" Harry moved his hand from the arm of the chair to his forehead and leaned forward. With his elbow on the desk, he briefly rested his forehead on his open palm. His eyes mirrored exasperated disbelief as he looked up at the screen.

"I don't know," Diane continued. "This usually doesn't happen for at least five days after the archive is generated."

"Who received this message?"

"You, your ops center, your counterpart at NGA, the DNI ops center and DIA. It's the usual distribution for something like this."

"And who can purge the files?"

"IT mostly. They purge when they archive or by special request from management. It has to be a division manager or higher."

"So, can you open the archive?"

"Sure," he heard keyboard clicks through the phone.

"Nope, there's no backup on the archive server."

Harry spun around in his chair. He pursed his lips on one side of his mouth and rolled his eyes to the right, his usual thinking mode. Occasionally his subordinates mimicked the gesture and Harry took no offense but felt flattered that they recognized his cognitive powers. His entire team was in awe of his genius and felt a deep loyalty to him as well. He enjoyed the jokes as much as the perpetrators. Today, though, Harry was in no laughing mood.

"Ok, do me a favor and double check the archives and get IT to help. This represents a possible imminent threat. Call me at this number when you find something." He dropped the phone into the cradle.

Harry turned back to Ken. "Now what?" Ken asked.

"The images have been purged, purposely, if Diane is right. An order had to be given to delete and overwrite the file.

"Really? Who would do that?"

"Now that's the next sixty-four zillion dollar question, isn't it?"

"So what do we do?"

"I'm going to call NGA and ask for some imagery. I have a contact over there who can get the tasking done in pretty short order. We'll see what we get."

Harry picked up the secure phone and dialed the two-digit access code for the NGA segment of the secure telephone system, then dialed the five-digit extension for Hal Baker. "Hello, Mr. Baker's office." A raspy voice that bore witness to thirty years of chain smoking answered. Harry quickly recalled Hal's assistant, Victoria, who always answered with a distinctive British accent. Before Harry met her, he pictured a very proper English woman with hair swept back in a chignon and perfect makeup. To his amazement, Victoria was a short woman with wrinkled, leathery skin from years in the sun and bronze-tinted hair pulled back in a frizzy pony tail. Except for the greeting on the phone, no trace of a British accent existed. The other secretaries claimed that Victoria adopted the accent to exaggerate the prominence of her boss. She evidently felt that such an association would elevate her status. From that point forward, Harry had trouble keeping a straight face whenever he called Hal.

"This is Harry Morrison over at Langley. Is Hal in?"

"I'm sorry, Mr. Morrison, he's not." Her stiff reply implied that she was too important to deal with such matters. "He's on leave for the next several weeks. May I take a message?"

"No, thanks," Harry replied. "This can't wait."

Harry hung up and wracked his brain for any connection that would help him bypass the tasking desk and get the info he needed quickly. He thumbed through his notepad from the recent meeting at NGA. Harry pressed seven digits on the phone.

"Sean Johnson." The flat voice of one who was otherwise preoccupied responded.

"Hi, Sean, this is Harry Morrison over at Langley."

Alert now, Sean asked, "What can I do for you?"

"I have some photos and need to match them to a location. Can you help me?"

"I'll take a look and see what I can do. Send them over. I'm in the IC global email address book."

"Well, that's the thing," Harry said. "I only have hard copies. The files were purged."

"Aw, man! There isn't much I can do with hard copies. I normally match photo sections electronically. Can you get the files restored?"

"I'm looking into that but I don't have a lot of time. Let me work it a little more on this end and I'll call you back." Harry dropped the phone into the cradle and turned to Ken.

"We're screwed without the electronic versions," Harry said to Ken as he placed the phone back in the cradle. "Let's go to the Ops Center and see if they saved the data on their server."

HARRY AND KEN WALKED INTO THE OPERATIONS Center and made their way to the message desk. Harry knew the woman at the desk. "Hi, Dana," Harry said.

Dana Radke looked up. Her eyes crinkled as her round face broke into a wide smile. "Harry! How are you? Have you been to the opera lately?"

Harry put his open hand across his mouth and pulled at the corners with his fingers.

"It's, uh, been a while." He quickly dropped the subject and inclined his head to the right. "I got a message from NSA a bit ago that has now been purged. I'm wondering if you got a copy."

"Let's look." She entered a password for the messaging system. While the screens changed, she turned to Harry. "So, how've you been?"

"Uh, ok." Harry shifted his massive weight to his other foot.

"That's good. You know, I really enjoyed our evening at the opera that one time at the Kennedy Center. Perhaps we can go again sometime soon. I enjoyed it so much that I've bought a few CDs. My appreciation and understanding has grown considerably."

"Uh, sure, that would be nice," Harry lied. Harry wasn't terribly interested in another outing. He had, in fact, never had a worse night at the opera, one worthy of the Marx Brothers. Two years earlier, when he had been given a pair of tickets, he'd asked Dana to go with him to the Kennedy Center for a performance of Turandot. A middle-aged woman, widowed, she had always seemed quite intelligent and very nice. During the opera, however, Harry decided her husband might have succumbed to get some peace and quiet or perhaps she had actually talked him to death.

Dana turned a bit stiffly to her computer, offended by Harry's polite but distant comment. "Here it is," she double-clicked, "but all I have is an empty header. No content."

"That's what I was afraid of." Harry said and turned toward the door.

"Do you know what the message was?" Dana called behind him.

"I only have a hard copy of the photos. I'm trying to get the electronic copies so I can get a location on the images." Harry held up the stack as he continued to edge toward the door.

"Let me see."

Harry took a deep breath, walked back to her desk and handed her the pictures.

"I know exactly where this is," Dana said after she examined the first two.

Harry's head snapped upright. "Where? How?" He stepped closer.

"Look at this road sign. It's close enough in the foreground that you can make out some sort of character that's not a numeral." She pointed and continued, "See? Square like a Chinese character. But more telling is the shape and color of the sign: blue, shaped like a mulberry bush. This is found on the old Silk Road. The Chinese government had a campaign in one area of western China to preserve history and tradition in order to counterbalance the Tibetan uprisings. One of the things they did was emphasize the history of trading along the Silk Road. These signs start at the Pakistan border. The plan was to place them all the way to Hangzhou in the east. Once the uprising petered out, they stopped at Subash to save money."

Harry stared openmouthed. "You're making this up, right? How would you know this?"

"I wasn't always just a pretty face. I worked in the Central Asia section downstairs until my position was 're-organized' out of existence. Anyway, this could be anywhere along a hundred twenty mile stretch of the

Karakorum Highway. The locals call it the KKH. It's the old road used by the ancients who traded silk, spices and animals between eastern China and the Arab world."

Harry turned to Ken, "Get cracking on the KKH and find out where exactly these photos came from."

He turned back to Dana with a smile. "Thanks for your help on this. I'm floored."

"You owe me, Harry Morrison."

"Indeed I do." Harry's smile grew. He considered the score closer to even after that night at the Kennedy. Then again, as long as they stayed away from opera or anything else that required silence, Dana's company might not be so bad.

Chapter 23

NGA Headquarters
Ft. Belvoir, VA

HARRY SHOWED HIS ICAC, INTELLIGENCE COMMON Access Card, at the guard station located inside the lobby of the NGA New Campus East and headed down the hallway to find Sean. He knocked on the vault door of the Middle East IMINT Analysis office. After a moment Sean's voice came through the intercom mounted next to the door. "May I help you?"

"It's Harry Morrison from Langley."

The door lock buzzed and Harry went in.

He looked across the tops of the cubicles and saw Sean standing inside the labyrinth. Harry made his way to Sean's cube. "I figured out where the pictures were taken and I need to see the archives to track down a possible nuke that's gotten loose from the Russians or the Chinese. It may be on its way through Pakistan to Iran." Harry gave him the location of the possible route. "I want imagery along this highway for the last," he paused and looked at the time stamp on the photos, then finished, "...twelve hours. And I don't want raw images. I need some of your MASINT products to determine what has changed during that time. Concentrate on an hour before to an hour after the time stamp. Look particularly at vehicles that pull off of and onto the highway between Subash and the Pakistan border."

"In other words, you want a miracle."

"A miracle would be acceptable. Make it happen."

Sean pulled up a photo taken at the same time as on

284

the photo and spent a few minutes studying it. "I have sixteen cars and nine trucks. This could take a while."

"Forget the cars. We're looking for a farm truck; the one in the picture." Harry handed him the photo.

"Well, that's a bit of useful information." Sean rolled his eyes, let out a breath and turned back to the screen.

"I have two farm trucks with hay. One is leaving Dabu Daer and the other is about forty miles from the Pakistan border."

"Let's start with the one closer to the border. Roll the sequence backward and forward and look at fifteen-minute intervals. Let's see what comes up."

Sean entered some commands on his keyboard and the truck lurched forward four times, representing an hour of travel.

"Looks like he just drove to the border."

"Try backing it up."

Sean typed again. The truck image skipped backward up the highway, then to the side of the road and then back on the pavement.

"Looks like he pulled off the road. Judging from the travel distance over time, he was stopped there for a few minutes. Maybe five minutes, no more." Harry scratched his head. "Ok, can you look at images from a minute before he stopped until he moved on? This time zoom in as close as you can."

Sean and Harry watched the image motion. The subjects in the image jerked as they moved. Noticing Harry's impatience, Sean explained, "These images are taken at a two frames per second rate. That's why they seem jerky. A standard movie runs between twelve and sixteen frames per second, fast enough to fool your eye into thinking the motion is constant."

"What's that?" Harry pointed to a spot moving

across the frame toward the truck.

Sean zoomed in.

"Looks like a person walking toward the truck. Sean pointed to the screen. "Here he's getting into the passenger side." A moment later, "Now the truck is driving away."

"See if you can figure out where he is now. We need to know where he's going and what's in the truck."

"It'll take a few minutes but I'll just tag the image and have the video analysis page plot us a motion loop of his movements." Sean said.

"Great," Harry said. "Once you find him in real time, I'll need IR, look-down radar, some photo analysis and I need it fast. I don't want to end up stuck in the tasking queue while I try to justify the priority on this. I hope you can go around the line and get what I need because lives may depend on it. Can you do that?"

"The radar bird is finishing up a run across Afghanistan. I can get you images of what's inside the hay on the next pass in a couple of hours. The electro-optical bird should be back there any minute so I can find the truck on the old photos and direct the camera from here. Thing is, we'll need to be fast and accurate because the DOM will override our control as soon as someone notices that the camera has wandered off mission."

"But you can do it, right? We really need to find this truck and stop it before it gets to its destination.

"No problem," Sean said. "I'll have a complete report in about two hours, except for the radar which will take a little longer."

"Thanks, man. If we pull this off because of your hard work, you can count on me to tell your management all the way to the top what a great job you did for us. Call me when you get something, ok?" He gave Sean his red phone extension and hurried toward the hallway.

HARRY WALKED ACROSS THE LOBBY AND RETRIEVED his cell phone from the temporary storage locker. As he headed out the door, he dialed Peyton's number. The phone rang once and then switched to the distinctive blurp-blurp ring tone from an overseas exchange.

"Stone," the voice said.

"Peyton," Harry said, "can you go secure?"

A series of clicks followed by a flashing red light on his phone signaled that the 256 bit AES/FIPS-197 encryption was activated. To anyone but Harry and Peyton the conversation would now sound like a series of buzzes.

"I think we've found the weapon."

"Where?"

"Well, we know that it's in a truck somewhere on its way across Pakistan. NGA is working on pinpointing its exact location and then we can track it."

"Any idea where it might be headed?"

"No but the closest point in Iran is Zabol."

"Can you get me in there?"

"Doubtful, but we could get you close. Zabol is near the Pakistan and Afghan borders. Lots of Pashtu there so it's not a really friendly place for Americans."

"Then I'll go in as Arab. It's not like I haven't done that before."

"Let me confirm and I'll call you back. Meanwhile, get yourself staged and ready, as close as you can to the Iranian border. We'll go from there."

"On my way."

SEAN PULLED UP THE IMAGES THAT HARRY NEEDED and sent them to the printer. At this resolution the batch would take about twenty minutes to print. He hit 'send' and then walked over to his co-worker's cubicle. He had asked his partner to run some radar images of the Gulf where he and Harry had seen what they believed to be a submarine.

On the desk he found a folder with the photos which showed the smudges that he and Harry had examined earlier. Beneath this, a second folder was filled with photos shot by a radar bird, code-named Onyx, from a different angle several minutes later. The satellite, which bounced radar energy several hundred feet below the surface, did not pick up surface reflections or glare off the water. And the radar returned energy from hard surfaces. If the smudges on the optical photos were an atmospheric anomaly, they wouldn't show up on these latest images.

Sean picked up the prints and studied them quickly. Onyx had captured a crystal clear image of a submarine located precisely where the blurry spots could be seen on the visual picture.

He decided to send the digital images to Harry but they were on his co-worker's PC. Harry's words - *lives may depend on it* - reverberated as Sean quickly considered his options. He knew the young woman's password, assuming she hadn't changed it. A few days earlier, while away from her cubicle, she needed a file but her computer was locked. She called Sean and gave him her password so that he could get the needed information. This serious security violation occurred frequently between team members. They were both cleared to see the information on each other's computer, so what was the harm?

Lives may depend on it. The decision made, Sean sat down at his teammate's PC and called up the login screen. Her user name, *foxwelma*, appeared in the box. He typed in her password and the Windows background loaded. *Now where did she file the pictures?* Sean scrolled quickly through her My Docs directory until, near the bottom of the list, he saw a folder named 'radar-iran'. He clicked on the icon to see the contents and found several images that she had stitched together into a video from a set of stills. He opened the first one and watched as the submarine sailed on its return path from the ship back to the Base.

He was so focused on the moving image that he didn't hear the footsteps behind him. Suddenly a loud voice rang out. "What the hell do you think you're doing?"

He spun around to face the IT Security Supervisor. "I'm working. What the hell does it look like I'm doing? You scared the bejeebers out of me!" Sean's pulse raced. As his body worked to neutralize the fight or flight response, he realized that he had used Mandy's exact phrase of exasperation.

"That's Mandy Foxwell's PC. She's on the 'out of office' list. I saw her login request come through on the monitor in the IT Ops Center so I came down to check. Did you log in as her?"

He saw no use in lying. The situation would be worse if he did. *Own up to it, Sean, and hope that you get off with a warning.* "Yeah, I needed some files and she had the only copies. We've been working on a project and I'm dead in the water without the files. She's not here so I just went ahead." He immediately realized he was rambling and wished he could climb under a big rock.

"How did you happen to have her password?"

Shit. Now I'm going to get someone a piece of the violation as well. He could say that he had seen it over her shoulder but then he would be guilty of password theft. Might as well confess. "As I said, she and I have been working on a project together. I had an urgent request for some images and she was away. To avoid delays, she gave me the password and said she'd change it when she got back."

"That's why you don't give away your password in the first place. Why do you people think we have these rules? You need to come with me."

"Aw, geez, come on, can't you cut me some slack this one time? She and I work together on projects and we needed to share a file. It's not like I was stealing secrets!"

"And how do I know that? Let's head down to the security office and check it out."

Sean followed the Geek Nazi and watched in shock as the man disabled both Sean and Mandy's passwords, denying them access to the information they needed to do their jobs. Then he sent an explanation of the violation via email to the head of security. Within fifteen minutes an answer came back. Sean was on immediate administrative leave while the particulars of the case were adjudicated, by order of the Office of the Director of National Intelligence. Curiously, the ODNI also asked for all files Sean had been working on. Not just the ones he had accessed on Mandy's computer but the entire lot. This had never happened before. Why was the ODNI interested in his simple password violation?

Sean walked to his car, picked up a piece of gravel from the parking lot and threw it as hard as he could at the trees at the edge of the lot. Then he remembered Harry's request. Aw jeez!! He reached into the console compartment of his car, removed his cell phone and dialed the CIA's unclassified switchboard number.

Harry cringed at the grating sound of his unclassified phone and answered quickly to silence the infernal noise. He wedged the phone between his ear and shoulder while he finished an email. "Hello."

"Harry, Sean at NGA. We've got a bit of a problem."

Harry dropped his shoulder, let the phone slide down into his hand and then held it against his ear. "What kind of problem? Have you found out anything from the imagery yet?"

"Well, that's the problem," Sean replied. "I got the files you asked for and sent them to the printer. Then I went to another computer that belongs to a co-worker. We partner on projects so I know her password. I logged in with her user ID to get video files stored on her hard drive that I thought would be helpful. IT Security caught me. I'm on administrative leave and my access card has been deactivated. I can't even get in the building."

"Kay-ryst!!" Harry moaned as he silently thought, *What an idiot to breach security, especially now.* "We have to get those images. Where are you?"

"In my car in the parking lot. I was about to head home but I thought I'd call you first. I'm really sorry about this."

"Me, too, but right now we have to figure out how to get the images and finish the analysis. Sit tight where you are while I come down there." Harry thought for a second. "No, better yet, give me two hours and then meet me in the lobby at the NGA building. I'll get this straightened out and we can work on this in real time together, ok?"

"Alright, I'll see you in two hours."

Harry put the phone down, picked up the secure line, and dialed a four-digit extension. When the woman on the other end picked up, he said with all of the authority he could muster, "This is Harry Morrison. I need to speak to Mike right now."

"One moment," the Assistant to the Director of Central Intelligence said. Harry heard two clicks as the call was routed.

"This is Mike. What's up Harry?"

HARRY WALKED INTO THE LOBBY OF THE NGA NEW Campus East building and saw Sean slumped in a chair. The young man stood as Harry approached him. Without slowing down, Harry put out his hand to guide him over to the security desk.

"Your badge should be reactivated now. Let's get a move on. We don't have a lot of time."

Sean held his badge over the keypad, punched in his PIN and placed his index finger on the fingerprint reader. A series of green arrows flashed on the top of the security portal to indicate that his information had been accepted and he was cleared to enter the building. "Thanks," Sean said. "I don't know how you did that but I really appreciate it."

"Well, you're not completely out of the woods. The security violation will stay in your record." Harry looked directly at the young analyst. "Let's just say that my stack of blue chips just got shorter because of you." Sean's eyes opened wide and Harry could see the guilt that hung heavy on the young man's shoulders. Good. Harry smiled to himself but revealed nothing to Sean.

They made their way down to the Arabian Gulf Branch and through the secure door that led to Sean's cube. Sean retrieved the printed images and brought them back to his desk only to find that Harry wasn't there. He then heard Harry's voice from Mandy's cube. "This is Harry Morrison. You should have received a priority message from the CIA Director within the last hour concerning data on Mandy Foxwell's computer.

Can you send someone down to log on for me, please?"
There was a moment of silence as Harry listened.
"Thanks. See you in a few." Harry hung up the phone
and popped his head over the top of the cubicle. "Ok, IT
security will be here in a few minutes to help get the
video loops. What do you have there, Sean?"

"These are images from an Iranian training camp
near Zabol taken three hours ago. They don't show
much by themselves but let's do some trickery and see
what we can find out." He went to his own computer,
logged on, and double-clicked his mouse on an analysis
application icon. "This is an application called blink
photometry. I have a digital image from yesterday. I'll
match these latest images to the earlier one by
overlaying them." He pointed to an image. "When the
small cross hairs in each corner of the photos merge to
become one, we have an exact match."

Harry watched over his shoulder. "And so what
does that do?"

"By itself nothing until I activate the program. The
pictures then switch back and forth at an approximate
one second rate. Things that are identical on both
pictures remain static but anything that has changed
from one to the other appears to flash as the pictures go
back and forth. Watch." Sean clicked on the "blink"
icon. Various parts of the picture appeared to flash off
and on.

"There's a helicopter that arrived in the last three
hours and some heavy vehicle tracks. Looks like they're
getting ready for something."

"Can you zoom in on that chopper?" Harry asked.

"Sure. Why don't you pull your chair over? I can
do it better and faster on this screen." Sean manipulated
his mouse as Harry retrieved his chair and got
comfortable. Once the image loaded, Sean used the

mouse to position the helicopter in the center of the screen and then rolled the zoom wheel. The chopper grew larger and larger. In less than a second, the resolution corrected as the image software pulled more and more detail from the server in the basement. Finally the chopper and a man filled the screen.

"That's definitely a military chopper and the guy next to it is in a military uniform. Zoom in a little on him." Harry squinted at the screen. "Holy jeez, that's an admiral of the navy. What in the hell is he doing out there? Can you send this to Ken Washington? I'll bet dollars to doughnuts that's Kuchecki." Harry turned to Sean. "I gotta hit the men's room. Where is it? And is there a Coke machine close by? I just realized that we're going to be at this a while. I'm parched."

"Sure," Sean replied, "I'll show you."

"Where is the IT security guy who was supposed to log us in to Mandy's computer? We could be done with that by now."

"We'll stop by IT on the way back and remind them."

HARRY AND SEAN WALKED FROM THE PANTRY NEXT to the rest room back to Sean's office. When they got to the door, Harry noticed that the deadbolt was extended. This prevented the door from closing completely, much in the same way hotel housekeepers set the door when cleaning a room.

He gripped Sean's arm with his left hand to stop him, then put his right forefinger to his lips to signal quiet. Harry peered through the narrow crack between the door and the frame to see Sean's cubicle at the back wall. Two uniformed security officers were standing side-by-side. One stared down at Sean's desk while the other looked across the cubicle tops.

Harry jerked his head back, turned down the hall toward the front lobby and motioned to Sean to follow him. The pair made their way toward the lobby, then stopped at the final turn before the hallway opened into the large space filled with display cases of imaging memorabilia from Iraq, Afghanistan and Bosnia as well as a mockup of an optical satellite.

Harry bent low and peered around the corner. An extra guard was stationed at the entry desk. Out front, he saw two SUVs with "Security" on the doors in the newer font that most city police departments used. These, however, were from NGA Security Division, specially trained former SpecOps who, for the most part, were tasked with protecting assets classified at levels higher than Top Secret. Only the Secret Service Presidential Protective Detail had more latitude in the use of deadly force to accomplish their mission. And even that was sometimes hotly debated at local bars.

He pulled back and shooed Sean back down the hallway. "Where is the loading dock?"

"It's downstairs in the Acquisition and Logistics Department."

"Take me there."

The two men quietly entered a stairwell and walked rapidly downstairs. At the bottom, they scanned the empty hallway, then moved quickly toward Acquisition and Logistics at the rear of the building. Sean led the way to the dock where they stopped in front of a large roll-up door and an adjoining small door. Both crossed to the small door and Harry watched as Sean swiped his access card to exit.

As soon as the proximity card neared the reader, a klaxon blatted repeatedly inside the dock. The bolt locks on the roll-up door engaged. Sean hit the crash bar on the smaller door. It opened but the hydraulic closer started to push back. Sean strained against the door but the closer was stronger and forced him backward into the dock. The door lock clicked.

"They've gone into lock-down. We're stuck inside. What's going on?"

Harry looked around frantically as he answered Sean. "Somebody doesn't want us to find out what's going on." He spotted their last chance to escape and hurried a few feet to his right to pull the fire alarm. The locks at the large end of the crash bar clicked loudly. Sean hit the bar and pushed hard. The door popped open and Harry ran through with Sean close behind him.

They bolted toward the parking lot. As they rounded the building, they saw a security SUV pull into the driveway.

"Head for the back fence," Sean said and pointed to his left.

Harry turned and ran. About halfway to the fence, his weight took its toll. He wheezed hard as he choked out, "Sean, I've got to slow down."

"Ok, but we're only about a hundred yards away. I'm going to run ahead and pry the fence up so we can slide under."

"There are probably tamper sensors."

"Yeah, but we've already set off the alarm so what the hell."

Harry slowed to a walk as Sean sprinted ahead. He looked back, expecting to see Security right behind, but so far, nothing. *I'm making so much racket breathing, he thought, I'm surprised the guard at the desk can't hear me.*

He took a deep breath and half stumbled the last few yards to the fence. Sean, already on the other side, held the bottom of the chain link fabric as high as he could. Harry struggled to sit down on the ground, then rolled under the fence. His shirt caught but he squirmed and wriggled until he heard a slight rip in the fabric. He was out.

Both men moved away as quickly as Harry's battered physique would allow. Once they were hidden in the woods, Harry had to stop. "I can't ...go much... farther right... now. Let's take... a moment."

Sean stopped and turned to the older man who was bent over with his hands on his knees. His back moved up and down like a bizarre merry-go-round creature as he tried to catch his breath.

"So what happened back there?" Sean asked.

"Seems someone wants to stop us for some reason. The way they stared at your desk, my gut says this concerns the images we were working on."

"But how did you get the door open when they went to lock-down?"

"The fire alarm has a built-in safety feature that releases the doors in case of fire, a code requirement to let people out. My neighbor works for the county fire marshal and he continually bores me with the details of his work." He looked up. "Thank goodness."

Harry reached into his pocket and extracted his cell phone. "I must have forgotten to put this in the locker when I came back. Since it was off, the cell phone sensor didn't sound."

He dialed a number. "Ken, Harry. We're outside of NGA and in a bit of trouble. Did you get the image Sean sent you a bit ago?"

"Yes," came the reply. "What is the image though?

"No time to explain right now. Forward it to Peyton ASAP." He could hear the click of the keyboard as Ken typed.

"Done."

"Ok, now go to my office and get the files we've

been working on and bring them to your office. I'll hold. I want to know they're safe."

He heard the receiver hit the desk and waited. Only seconds passed before he heard Ken's voice again, "There are two security guards in the hall outside your office with a cart loaded with all your files. What's going on?"

Shit! Harry thought, as he pressed the end button.

Chapter 24

Near Zabol Training Camp
Eastern Iran

PEYTON SCRAMBLED ACROSS THE SAND AND positioned himself behind a stand of three scruffy little trees. Flown first by jet to Bagram Air Base thirty-five miles north of Kabul, he then boarded a waiting MH-53 Pave Low helicopter and was soon at a US forward base near Farah in western Afghanistan. He then climbed into the back seat of a desert tan RAH-66 Comanche for a lightning-fast incursion into Iran.

Deposited just over the Iranian border six miles from a Revolutionary Guard Corps training camp, he listened for the sound of the helicopter fading into the distance. When the Pentagon killed the Comanche program in 2004, intelligence agencies quickly scooped up the handful of prototypes from the Boeing/Sikorsky development team. These stealth machines were fast, quiet and had the radar cross section of a seagull. Even though the chopper was only a few seconds away, Peyton now heard only the rush of wind that blew through the clumps of trees scattered across the high plateau.

He stayed low and moved slowly to the edge of the escarpment. Lying down, he pulled his field glasses from his pack and scanned the low flat area beneath him. Apparently a lake at one time, the terrain was now filled with dry fine sand that would readily show footprints if he tried to cross it. Crossing, however, was not on today's agenda.

The neat rows and columns of tents at the training

camp were barely visible through the haze. The high, curved ridge that protected the camp from the area's famous "Winds of 120 Days" also gave Peyton a bird's eye view of the camp, as long as he kept his silhouette low.

He backed away from the edge on hands and toes until he was safely below the sight line on the ridge top. Turning to his left, he began the long walk in the 107-degree heat to his final vantage point. An hour ago NGA had located the truck suspected of carrying the stolen weapon as it crossed the border from Afghanistan into Iran. In a few hours, the nuclear device should be here. *Just about the time I get into position*, he thought. *I hope NGA got it right.*

He walked slowly in the heat and thought about Rachel. Wondered how she was making out in Kazakhstan. She had been distant on the drive to the airport. He'd repeatedly tried to figure out what might be wrong but only got stilted responses. It was like that frustrating *"if you don't know, I'm not going to tell you"* bullshit that happens between younger people in relationships. He remembered heading toward the shower when the phone rang. He'd talked to Ace for a few minutes and then everything was different.

Wait a minute...could this be about Ace? Does she think there's something going on with Ace? For that matter, what does *she think? Come to think of it, Ace was acting a little funny, too.*

The wump-a-wump of a helicopter rotor brought him back to the present. It grew louder as another chopper approached. He was actually thankful that, for now at least, he only had bad guys to worry about instead of trying to figure out women. He crawled to a spot directly above the camp and watched soldiers go about a universal military routine: train, sweep, paint.

Stuck in the rinse/repeat cycle, you poor slobs, he thought. As the helicopter passed over, he tucked in tightly under the sparse brush. If he were seen in his Arab peasant disguise out in the open, more likely than not, no one would notice, but why push it?

The wind from the rotor downwash sent up a cloud of dust that obscured the chopper and several of the administrative buildings next to the helipad. Peyton used the opportunity to crawl to the edge of the ridge and look down. He smiled to himself while the whine of the engine started its slow unwinding and the pitch of the turbines decreased octave by octave. Something was definitely going on here. A Major and two aides trotted from the administration building toward the helicopter. This must be important, or at least expected, since they were dressed in freshly pressed uniforms and wore their "fruit salad" ribbon bars above their left shirt pockets.

He watched as they walked up to the helicopter. The Major reached out to the door, hesitated, and then reached again. Before he could make contact, the door opened and the three snapped to attention. A figure got out and the Major snapped off a salute that wasn't returned. *Bingo!* Peyton thought as he zoomed the glasses in on the visitor dressed in the white uniform of the Iranian Navy. *Kuchecki!*

After they disappeared into the administration building, Peyton lay still and watched more camp routine. The back of his neck began to hurt from lying flat and looking forward so he put the glasses down and stretched. When he looked back toward the camp, he noticed a dust cloud in the distance. The cloud got larger and he zoomed the glasses to twenty power. He saw a vehicle at the front of the cloud but the heat waves distorted the air. Unable to identify the type, make, or model, he rolled onto his back to relax his body and clear his mind while he waited. Anticipation and assumption could cloud his response. When he rolled back to prone position, the image was less distorted. Through the glasses, he could see a truck that grew larger as it approached. The driver pulled up near the buildings and several soldiers gestured and spoke as they walked over. But they were too far away for Peyton to hear them.

The passenger door of the truck opened and an old Arab stepped out. A soldier jerked open the driver's door and hauled out a kid who appeared to be a young teen. Old enough to drive evidently, the boy moved back and forth until he freed himself from the soldier's grasp. The older man spoke and waggled a crooked finger at both of them.

The door to the administration building opened and all but the old man and the boy snapped to attention. The old Arab walked toward the building with the boy close behind. Kuchecki stepped from the shadows and hurried over to the man. The two embraced and kissed each cheek, the traditional Arab greeting of close friends. *Must be Ali,* Peyton thought.

The two men walked to the back of the truck and Ali pulled at a couple of hay bales. Kuchecki signaled to two soldiers who immediately jumped up onto the back of the truck and heaved bales over the side. When they jumped down, Peyton zoomed the field glasses and peered into the hole left by the missing hay. A crate imprinted with what appeared to be Cyrillic lettering was nestled in the hay. *Holy shit!*

Without taking his eyes off the truck, he reached over and pulled the encrypted PDA from his backpack, put the glasses down, and began typing: *In position alpha seven above Zabol training camp. Package has arrived. All the guests are at the party.*

He glanced at the scene below and was about to look down at the 'send' button when he heard it. A pebble moved close behind him. He slowly positioned his hand at his side to push himself up and felt the hot steel of the rifle barrel at the back of his neck. He reached for the PDA but a boot kicked it over the edge of the ridge. The device careened faster and faster down the slope. The battery cover, then the battery, then smaller pieces sprayed from the device.

He heard the bolt slide back in the carrier and then slam quickly forward as the IRGC soldier chambered a round. "Get up!" he said in Arabic. The soldier barely opened his teeth when he spoke and his voice sounded like the growl a Rottweiler makes just before a barking fit. Peyton still played the part of an Arab peasant. "Salam Aliekom." The soldier looked out of the side of his eyes while he rooted around in Peyton's pack and examined some of the items. Peyton knew that it would be difficult to maintain his cover now but he grinned at the soldier and said, "I'm surveying the border for my farm."

The soldier's eyes narrowed and his lips pursed as he pulled Peyton's Jericho automatic from the pack. He walked over and spun Peyton around so that he faced the edge of the ridge. Using the butt of his rifle, the soldier pushed him down a small path toward the camp.

PEYTON LAY ON A BLANKET IN A TENT AT THE EDGE of the camp. His hands were secured behind his back with zip ties and his ankles were bound together. The open sides of the tent, raised to let the heat out, gave him a view of the other tents around him. The heat approached unbearable. Nearby a guard sat cross-legged on the floor with his head tilted forward, chin on chest. At first Peyton thought the man's body language to be a sign of belligerence. When the man looked at Stone from the tops of his eyes, the malice was electric. Peyton then realized that this guy was more pissed about having to sit inside a hot tent than anything else.

Just outside, someone cleared his throat. A soldier entered, set a chair near the tent's center pole, and stood back. Within minutes a portly man in a white Navy uniform entered and looked at Stone. "So you've had a look at my camp," Kuchecki said.

Stone rolled up into a kneeling position and looked at the floor.

"Why would you do this?"

Stone continued to look at the floor and said quietly, "I was simply surveying the edge of my farm."

Kuchecki sat in the chair, almost at eye level with Stone. "You have some very sophisticated surveying equipment." His tone reminded Peyton of a school principal who had once baited him into a confession that he had thrown a spitball.

"It belongs to my employer, Zabol Farms."

"So then it is not your farm as you said but the property of Zabol farms. You lied to me."

Nice try, asshole. "I think of it as mine because I live there, but the farm does not belong to me directly."

"There is one other matter." Kuchecki stood up and took a step toward Peyton. "You had an Israeli-manufactured pistol in your possession." Kuchecki moved forward again, hit Stone square in the face, and knocked him onto his back.

The pain shot across both shoulders as the back of his head hit the floor. His feet were pinned under him because he had been in a kneeling position. He tried to roll over but Kuchecki's boot caught him in the stomach. The kick pushed the air out of his lungs and blood shot from his nose onto Kuchecki's pant leg.

"Stand him up." Kuchecki's thunderous voice boomed an order, not a request. "Look at me."

Peyton's eyes remained averted.

"Where did you get this weapon?" The admiral waved the Jericho under Peyton's nose.

"From my employer."

Kuchecki reached out and grabbed at Peyton's throat but Stone snapped his head back quickly. The admiral clutched a handful of false beard and stage make-up stained the cuff of his sleeve. He looked down in confusion, as he tried to make sense of what had just happened. His head rose, fell and then came up slowly for a closer look as realization began to set in. He reached out and grabbed Stone by the neck and pulled him closer.

Peyton kept his eyes averted but Kuchecki grabbed his face in one beefy hand and pulled him even closer. Kuchecki looked, searched, studied, turned Peyton's face from side to side. Then he snatched off more false beard. The admiral glared at Stone and suddenly snapped back as if a snake had bitten him. "YOU!!" He screamed loudly enough to be heard several hundred yards away. Two guards hurried over.

"First you come into my base in Bushehr and now you are here. This time I don't care who sent you or why. In three days none of this will matter at all. And this time you won't escape." To the guard, he barked, "Free his feet and bring him with me."

PEYTON SAT ON THE EDGE OF WHAT PASSED FOR A porch on the front of the administration building, the crate that arrived on Ali's truck at his feet. Kuchecki snapped his fingers and pointed at the wooden box. Two soldiers quickly pried off the top to reveal a shiny sphere inside. The weapon, Stone thought. He looked down at the core of the nuclear device, a ball of plutonium known as "the pit" in nuclear weaponry jargon. This energy source was ready to be inserted inside the explosive trigger. Much had been written that anyone could build a nuclear bomb with information from the Internet, but, without the pit, nothing nuclear would happen.

The two soldiers stood back as Kuchecki walked over to the crate and looked inside. His manner seemed almost reverent. Peyton was sure the admiral saw the object as a gift from Allah. Kuchecki leaned over, touched the device and smiled. He slid his fingers over the smooth surface of the metal with the tenderness one might use in foreplay. The admiral then moved some of the packing straw to the side and revealed another identical globe.

Holy shit, Peyton thought, *he has two of them.*

Kuchecki stood and turned toward Peyton. "Now you've seen the terror that I'm ready to unleash. I can't sit idly by and watch the destruction of all that is holy to me through this abomination of a treaty. Such a union will dilute the Muslim faith. This sellout to the West has to be stopped and I am the one chosen by Allah Himself to stop it."

The soldiers shifted from one foot to the other. Stone simply looked at Kuchecki.

"One of these is for Tel Aviv and one for Haifa. I will spare Jerusalem because of the holy mosque there. Once these angels from Allah have delivered their message, my supporters will rise up to govern Iran. We will take our country back from the traitors in Tehran. We will control our destiny once again."

Peyton watched Kuchecki deliver his messianic declaration and then asked, "Do you think the United States will sit back and let you get away with this?"

Kuchecki laughed. "Do you really believe that your

country has the stomach for nuclear war? They don't know the number of devices in our possession. America will be careful and hesitant, then your leaders will debate and shake impotent fists with manufactured rage. But your country won't sign the treaty. Everyone will look for a scapegoat: the President. That's when the second part of the plan unfolds."

Kuchecki motioned to several soldiers nearby. "Take this crate and put it in my helicopter. Tell the pilots we leave in twenty minutes." He then looked at the two remaining soldiers. "Take him back to the tent. Let him think about this for a time." The Admiral leaned in, his face less than an inch from Stone's, his sour breath reminiscent of boiled cabbage. His eyes never moved from Stone's face as he spoke quietly to the guard. "When the sun comes up in the morning, shoot him."

PEYTON DRIFTED IN AND OUT OF A FITFUL SLEEP ON the ground. He hurt all over even though the blows had come only to his face and stomach. The violence had set off a chain reaction throughout his body and he could feel each muscle cry out for relief. He dreamed that Kuchecki continued to ask him questions. During the somnolent interrogation, the big man pulled back and slugged Peyton in the stomach. Stone let out an "oof" and collapsed on the ground.

With this, he woke with a start, momentarily unsure whether the encounter was a dream or real. He sensed a presence in the darkness. *The guard, of course*, he thought. His head had started to clear when he heard someone say in clear English, "Shhhh, we must go." Then he felt a hand on his shoulder.

In the dim light he could see a shadow of a man with his finger to his lips to signal quiet. As the man helped him to his feet, Peyton saw the vague outline of the guard prone on the floor and realized that the man's collapse was the "oof" that he had heard in his dream. Still foggy, he thought, *How odd the way dreams and reality merge*. Then, *Please let this rescue be real*.

Peyton summoned all of his strength to stand, then reached deeper still and found the strength to move. The man, dressed in dark clothing, all but invisible on this moonless night, clipped the restraining ties. He then untucked his shirt, wrapped Peyton's fingers around the black shirttail and held them there for a few seconds to signal Peyton to hold on. Then he moved swiftly but silently across the open ground toward the low hills about a half-mile away. Peyton did his best not to trip or make a sound but, in his current state, he was a little clumsy. Twice they stopped after Peyton scuffed his feet on some rocks but no response came from the camp either time. The pair remained bent over, as low to the ground as possible, while they moved quickly across the sandy ground. They didn't slow down until they had passed around the end of the hill. Peyton wanted desperately to ask, *Who are you?* But he didn't know where or if guards were posted. As long as they were headed away from the camp, he was content to follow silently.

They continued to scurry silently along the backside of the hill in complete darkness. The only artificial light in the area was a sodium vapor streetlight outside the administration building on the opposite side of the hill. The two men continued onto the firing range and walked quickly over to the small storage shed. Peyton was out of breath. He tried to ask where they were going but couldn't get any words out. Recognizing the American's distress, his attempts to speak, the man said softly, "Talk later. We must be silent. Stay here." The voice had a familiar tone but Peyton couldn't place it.

The man quickly opened the door to the storage shed. Peyton stood still, visually tracking the man's movements as he went inside. He noticed that the magnetic intrusion sensor on the door had a small magnet taped to it to keep the alarm from sounding. This guy had been here before, probably on his way in, and he knew what he was doing. Could he be with the Agency? Peyton pondered, then thought, Very possible.

Peyton was finally beginning to catch his breath when the man returned and handed him two rifles. He went back in and retrieved a metal box of ammunition, grabbed Peyton's shoulder, and nudged him onward.

They moved as quickly as possible along the firing range and stayed close to the hills until they came to a small copse of trees. The man headed into the trees and Peyton did his best to follow. They had only gone a short way when Peyton lost contact but he heard the man quietly set the ammunition box on the ground. A hand grabbed his wrist and pulled him deeper into the trees until they came out the other side. There was a dull glint and Peyton tried his best to make out what sat in front of him. He stared for a full minute in the dark until he recognized a vehicle of some sort. *A car, perhaps? No, a four-wheel drive vehicle.* The man took the rifles and disappeared around the back of the SUV. When he returned, he put Peyton's hand on the door handle and whispered urgently, "I am Xu. We must go." Peyton's old friend quickly walked around the front of the car and climbed behind the wheel.

Peyton stood dumbfounded, completely unable to move.

Chapter 25

Second Naval District HQ
Bushehr, Iran

ADMIRAL KUCHECKI CAREFULLY IMITATED THE swirling loops of Adazi's signature. *The arrogance of the man was astounding,* he thought. Even his signature was an affront to any devout Muslim with its ornate flourishes, a clear violation of the Prophet's admonitions against vanity. This time Kuchecki had perfected his forgery. Now it was time to put the signature where it counted. He carefully copied the embellishments once more as he signed an official Navy attack order that authorized the release of nuclear weapons through the "every means possible" clause.

The final stroke of the pen complete, Kuchecki held the document up to the light to inspect the authenticity. *Perfect,* he thought, unaware of his own pride. Now he had only to make a copy since he would not ordinarily have the original. He would put the copy in his safe. He hadn't decided yet whether he should put the original in a file or destroy it. Either way, the coming attack would be connected to the sitting government and his actions justified to the world community.

He pulled his prayer rug from its cover and spread it on the floor facing the Kabaa. His prayer to Allah for guidance in his steps toward the final reckoning was interrupted when the intercom on his desk buzzed. He considered whether he was ready to see anyone or if he wanted to spend a little more time in prayer and reflection but decided that the moment had passed. He quickly got up, placed the attack order in a manila file folder and locked it in his desk drawer as the intercom continued to buzz. He opened the next desk drawer down, confirmed that the pistol was there, then pressed the button. "Yes?"

The tinny reply came through the speaker. "Captain Sadiq to see you, Sir."

"Good. Send him in." Kuchecki quickly gave his desk a visual inspection to make sure that no damning evidence remained. "Clean desk, clean mind" came to mind, drilled into him years ago in officer training. *What a load of crap.*

Sayed Sadiq opened the door, marched smartly to Kuchecki's desk, and saluted. Kuchecki smiled slightly as he looked at him but Sadiq stood ramrod straight, his eyes glued to a spot on the wall behind Kuchecki and just above his head.

"Sayed." Kuchecki rose and extended his hand. "Good to see you. It seems as if years have passed though it has only been a short time since we reorganized the office here." Kuchecki's designation of "reorganization" was at best euphemistic. Every deck hand knew that Adazi had taken advantage of the new structure in Tehran and pushed Kuchecki aside to gain a promotion. Two distinct camps formed: those who would have done the same thing in similar circumstances and those who considered the betrayal of a fellow shipmate to be a breach of honor. No middle ground existed in this matter. Kuchecki counted on Sadiq to be part of the latter camp.

"Please, sit. Would you like mint tea?" Kuchecki pointed at a couch along the far wall and pressed the intercom button.

"Some fruit juice would be good." Sadiq stepped toward the couch but did not sit.

"Two fruit juices and two teas," Kuchecki said into

the intercom, then motioned to the sofa again. Sadiq sat down on the couch and faced the Captain. A relaxed smile on his face, Kuchecki spoke. "Tell me how you've progressed in outfitting your boat."

Sadiq shifted in his seat slightly. He was always careful when he formulated an answer for the brass. Since admirals had time only for a specific agenda, the answer to the first question often set the direction for any conversation that would ensue. Sadiq had never been called in to chat about his daily activities. He and the Admiral had worked together on a number of projects and Sadiq was loyal, but they could hardly be called friends in the formal sense of the word. He fidgeted a little more and then cleared his throat to cover his hesitation.

"Well, after taking over command, I have been outfitting the Nuh with the new Chinese Club-S1A missile upgrades. Of course, you know that since you were the one who was kind enough to give me that assignment."

"A well deserved command and an easy decision for me."

"Thank you, Sir," Sadiq replied. The compliment felt good but the question of why he had been called here loomed over him. He was starting to relax a little, though, as the conversation took on a casual tone.

"Not at all," Kuchecki replied with a dismissive wave of his hand. "How is the assignment going, by the way?"

"Very well, actually. I have hand picked my crew from previous commands and added as well some of the best men fresh from training. We've had many sea training missions in the Gulf. I've worked with some of these men in various assignments for over ten years and I trust them to do their jobs. The crew is a well-oiled machine."

"An Admiral always likes to hear that, especially when he has the charge to appoint competent men to their positions. You have done well and I'm proud that you serve our country."

"Again, thank you, Admiral." The stream of flattery was both out of character and disarming. Sadiq was still unsure of his superior's intentions. "The Nuh is out of dry dock now," he continued, "as we've completed an upgrade to the new Club-S1A missile system. This will allow greater range and a larger payload. We have also been upgraded to the new super quiet and ultra-fast Pump-Jet ducted propeller systems. She has just completed her initial sea trial. The eleven-bladed screw can push her through the water at over thirty-five knots and is so efficient that the range is greatly extended. She is one fine boat, Sir." Sadiq beamed.

"And the stealth trials with the freighter? How have those proceeded?"

Said shifted his weight so that he faced the admiral. "Complete, sir. It was a challenge to stay directly under the ship in shallow water but, with some practice, we were able to do it. I must ask," he stopped short of questioning this strange maneuver and said instead, "how this will be applied in a tactical situation."

The door opened and the ever present tea boy arrived with a tray that held two tall tumblers of fruit juice, two cups of mint tea and a small teapot. He placed the tray on the table in front of the couch and quickly left as the two men picked up their drinks.

When the door closed, Kuchecki looked at Sadiq for a few seconds as he carefully measured both the man and his own words. He then quickly put his teacup on the tray and sat back with his right elbow on the back of the couch, brought his left hand across and interlaced his fingers.

"Sadiq," he began, "I have a very important task for you, one that is highly secret. I need to know that I can trust you to carry out this assignment which, seemingly, flies in the face of reason and common sense."

"Admiral, I am an officer of the IRIN and you are my superior. Of course, I will do as you ask without question."

"And I appreciate that, of course, but I need to know that you have a personal stake in this. Are you married?"

"Uh, no, Sir. I was married but my wife passed away a year ago from cancer."

Kuchecki sat back. "I'm so sorry to hear of her death," he said, disturbed that he was unaware of this. He leaned forward again. "What if I told you that I could make you a wealthy man? You could leave the Navy at the end of your mission and be a part of a new order in the Muslim world."

Sadiq was taken aback, "I don't know, Sir."

"Well, obviously we are in a very delicate situation. I must be able to trust that you will be agreeable to a task but I can't share details until you are agreeable. You can't agree until I tell you the task. Around and around we go." Kuchecki shrugged and smiled at Sadiq. "So we must approach this a different way. You are a good Muslim, yes?" Kuchecki tilted his head to the side and looked deeply into Sadiq's eyes as he waited for the answer.

Sadiq suddenly felt as if the temperature in the room had gone up a few degrees. Perhaps the air conditioning had stopped. "Of course."

"What if I told you that you could play a major role in bringing Islam to the rest of the world? What if I told you that Allah, may His blessings be upon us, took your wife to be with Him in order to prepare the way for you to be a key player in the return of the Madhi. To do this, you would have to leave Iran for a short time, launch what some would call an unthinkable attack on another country. But, if you do this, Allah, through me, would ensure that you live very comfortably. In fact, you would be in a highly-placed government position, not in the current regime but in a new Muslim government. Would that appeal to you?"

Sadiq sat back abruptly. His eyes opened just a bit and quickly relaxed, "You're saying that I am chosen to prepare the way for the twelfth Imam, the Madhi? How is this possible?"

"As it says in the Holy Qur'an, 'And Allah knows best what they gather, so announce to them a painful torment. Save those who believe and do righteous good deeds, for them is a reward that will never come to an end.' That reward, my friend, is Paradise. You and I have been chosen by Allah to bring the world forward to the final days. You, as the captain of the Nuh, also known as Noah, who said to his people, 'Oh my people! Worship Allah! You have no other God but Him. I fear for you the torment of a great day.' That day is coming and you and I have been chosen to bring it, to bring for ourselves Paradise." Kuchecki appeared to enter a semi-trancelike state as he continued to mumble a prayer under his breath.

"How do I do this," Sadiq asked quietly, "and what of your role in this?"

Irritation crept in to Kuchecki's mind but he kept it in check. "I have the details already drawn out but I need your commitment first. Once you are in, only Allah can release you and betrayal will bring his wrath."

"This is a mysterious puzzle," Sadiq said as he sat

back on the couch with his juice. "I suppose that I will do as I am ordered."

"Suppose is not good enough. I need to know with certainty that I can count on you."

Sadiq sat very still for a moment and then slowly leaned forward. He placed his glass on the table carefully as though he might shatter the tabletop. "Of course you can count on me. If what you say is Allah's will, then I have no choice but to obey."

"So here's what you must do…"

Kuchecki quickly outlined the plan while Sadiq listened with ever-widening eyes. "Do you mean that I am to launch a nuclear missile at Israel? They will pound us with nuclear missiles. It will be the end of Iran!"

"No they won't. They will at first reel from the shock of the attack. Then they will have to get their government and military in order. The United States will already know what has happened and I will contact their government and announce that I have taken control in Tehran from the traitors who did this thing. The United States will put a leash on Israel."

"But how does this start the global jihad?"

"The world will be in disarray for several days trying to make sense of the events. Remember the confusion after the attacks on the US World Trade Center?"

Sadiq nodded slowly.

"While they are trying to recover and plan the next step, our brothers in Iraq, Pakistan, Malaysia, and Africa will rise up around the globe and move forward. We have to put a unified and thoughtful government in place, an Islamic government. In order to bring true peace and enlightenment to the world, we have to conquer all of our enemies. Only then can we address the poverty and inequality in the world."

When Kuchecki sat back, he exuded the confidence that had procured his former command position in the first place. The captain obviously believed him, just as Kuchecki expected he would. But Sadiq noticed the wild look in his superior's eyes as he spoke about the jihad. Was the admiral unhinged or brilliant?

Sadiq looked hard at Kuchecki, "You are right, certainly, but surely the world will fight back"

Kuchecki stood, raised his hand above his head and pointed to the sky. His dark eyes blazed at Sadiq as he roared, "The Holy Qur'an says clearly, 'Jihad is ordained for you though you dislike it, and it may be that you dislike something that is good for you and that you like a thing that is bad for you. Allah knows but you don't know'." His eyes opened wide as he finished his quote, "Allah himself, his blessings upon us, has ordained this mission. He has told me that the plan is necessary. He has told me that he has chosen me. There is no way we can fail."

The admiral took a deep breath and let it out slowly. He felt the tension release from his chest and smiled broadly at Sadiq. "We owe it to our brothers who have little, who scratch a living from the soil most days but not every day. We owe them a better life. Not a life dictated by the infidels in the west but a good and healthy life, healthy in body and soul. We've waited for thousands of years. The only way that has worked in the past is to vanquish our enemies and establish the Caliphate. Wherever that happened, peace followed. We must return to this path now on a global scale."

Sadiq sank back against the seat cowed, intimidated and convinced. He looked at the floor. "I hope I am worthy to be at your command."

Kuchecki shook Sadiq's hand and both men smiled.

He leaned forward and touched his index finger to his head to indicate an additional thought. "By the way," he said, "now that you are on the inside, you know exactly what will happen if this information leaks out before its time. We will both be executed. Don't think that you can have second thoughts and live. Neither of us can do that. As of this moment, we are in this completely and we are in it together. Success will bring us to Paradise in the end of our days. Betrayal will bring immediate descent into the fires of hell."

The message was not lost on Sadiq. *Keep your mouth shut or suffer greatly for it.* "Yes, we are in this together," Sadiq replied. But this time he didn't smile.

Chapter 26

Western Afghanistan

PEYTON STRETCHED HIS LEGS ON THE ROADSIDE, hurriedly climbed into the Rover, then he and Xu sped off down the highway. Dawn lit the sky in front of them. The few high clouds in the distance over the mountains were edged in purple and pink. Peyton shook his head and asked, "Do you know what I've been through over the past week?"

Xu looked at him with a playful smile. "Well, you were captured by terrorists, beaten, taken to Iran, and now you have escaped."

"Not that, you asshole." Peyton smacked Xu's shoulder with the back of his hand. "I thought you were dead. Did you ever consider the grief? Or the fact that the search for your killer is what got me into all of this other crap in the first place?"

"Oh, that," Xu said with a dismissive wave of his hand. "As we said in Vietnam, 'Xin Loi,' sorry about that." He then burst out laughing.

Peyton tried hard to remain serious, as anger bubbled below the surface, but the joy that his friend was alive was immense. He bounced between relief, irritation, and pure rage, a perfect storm of emotions. Finally, relief won out and a huge smile spread across his face as he addressed his friend. "Look, you ungrateful prick, next time I'll just sweep your ashes under the rug and you won't get a second thought from me. Now what the hell is this all about?"

Xu took a deep breath, "Well, several weeks ago, I got a call from the Chinese Ministry of State Security –

the MSS. They had uncovered a plot through some informants about an attempt to steal a nuclear weapon of some kind from our stockpiles. The Chinese Government took precautions and tracked down the would be thief at the nuclear storage facility. They transferred him to a post in Beijing to prevent the theft of the weapon and to monitor what he did and who he talked to. They also wanted to see how the events would play out in order to make a case against others."

"They found out that someone named Fang who calls himself an 'arms facilitator' was involved." Xu rolled his eyes. "Fang is a dangerous guy, trained in the Zhao Lin arts. He has contacts all over the world and can make just about anything happen, from surplus machine guns to a nuclear weapon. A few days ago, he arranged for a nuke to be bought from a Russian government employee, an amateur, who was then killed after he stole the device and delivered it to Fang."

"But how did you end up involved and what about your murder at the Embassy Hotel? I saw your body at the morgue." Peyton struggled to make sense of recent events.

"Oh, yeah, that," Xu chuckled. "Well, remember, my friend, that, although I am married to a US citizen, I have a lot of family in China. You are aware that I couldn't get cleared for a green badge at Langley because the family connection was a security risk. And I've maintained my contacts at the MSS...one reason I've had success acquiring security work in China." Peyton stared at Xu, his mouth open. Xu glanced at him, looked quickly back at the road, then turned toward Peyton again. He shrugged, with a half smile, and gestured with his right palm. "Hey, what can I say?"

"Do you mean you're an agent of the Chinese Government?"

Xu shrugged, "I can't comment on that. Are you an agent of the US Government?"

Peyton stared out the windshield, gave a humorless laugh, and said, "Aw, man, shut up."

Xu smiled. They were friends with a rich history who could forgive almost anything. Still, he wondered if this would completely go away.

Peyton's response reflected the divide. "Shit, man! I can't believe it."

"I can say that I'm not exactly an agent. I have loyalties to both countries but when they conflict, I back away."

"And now I'm supposed to believe you. We've been friends for years. You saved my life. I trusted you." Peyton was angered by the revelation that Xu had withheld from him the fact that he worked for Chinese Intelligence. The bullshit was getting deeper and deeper.

Xu shot back. "Have you forgotten that I pulled you out of the hands of the Iranian Qods Corps just hours ago? By the way, what were you doing there? Perhaps there's something you can't comment on. If so, then I don't really know why you're so angry."

"All right, fair enough. Let's not go there." Peyton took a deep breath. "But what about Joni? Your wife and kids think you're dead. How could you do that? That, I *don't* understand."

Xu's shoulders slumped and he looked down for a moment. Peyton thought Xu was about to speak but he looked back at the road. Finally, he answered. "Something had to be done. I had no choice." He paused, troubled. "Believe me, it sucks that I put them through such anguish. But subterfuge was necessary given the situation we're up against."

"Wait a minute." Peyton leaned forward in the seat and stared at Xu. "I saw your body in the morgue. If that wasn't you, who was it? I'm completely lost here."

"As I looked into Fang's activities, I found some files in his office that pointed to his connection with Ali and also with the Russian supplier. This confirmed what the MSS had learned from some SIGINT of a conversation between Fang and Kuchecki. When I left Fang's office, I looked up and saw the camera move with me as I walked out of the suite. I knew I would be made but needed to stay on the case. As long as Fang thought I was alive and a threat to his operation, I couldn't. So I contacted our ops folks and arranged for a condemned prisoner to be heavily sedated and placed in my bed at the hotel. I knew how ruthless Fang was likely to be. That's when I called you to explain all of this ahead of time."

"The voice mail..." Peyton finally understood.

Xu said nothing. Let Peyton continue processing the information.

"So he killed a condemned prisoner? Doesn't that push the law a bit?"

"US law maybe, but in China the government has certain latitudes that the US doesn't."

"Wow," Peyton sat back in the seat, stunned. "I thought you were dead. I'm here because I thought you were dead. He looked at Xu and finished, "and now I find out you're not."

"You're here because I'm not. Anyway, don't sound too disappointed." Xu looked at Peyton with mock sadness. "I'll go one day."

Peyton's face soured. "That's not what I meant and you know it. An investigation into your supposed death led me here. I was also attacked in Shanghai the same day your murder was staged by some big Asian guy who turned out to be Fang."

Peyton looked down as he processed this latest info.

"So, what's next? How do we get out of here and get word out to the US? They need to know what we know."

"Right," Xu pointed at Peyton, "but, first, you have a loose end to tie up. The Arab that you saw in the camp yesterday is the go-between with Fang and the Iranians. He's a terrorist named Ali al- Muzzafar, one of the richest men in the world until the US cracked his financial model and froze most of his assets. Billions from what I hear. He has sworn revenge and this plot is just a first step. We need him neutralized."

"Neutralized? Do you mean..."

"Just like Southeast Asia, Peyton," Xu was serious now. "Neutralized completely. With extreme prejudice."

"And how do you propose to do that?"

"Simple, I propose that you do it."

"Oh, really?" Peyton raised one eyebrow cynically while he grappled with possible solutions. The sun was now a large orange ball that glared mercilessly. Peyton squinted and leaned forward. Both men lowered their sun visors simultaneously.

"Ali and the boy will most likely leave the camp this morning. They'll travel this way to return to his place in the hills. Just up the road from here, this valley becomes narrow and winds for about three miles. Ali doesn't drive so the boy will be at the wheel." Xu glanced at Peyton before he continued. "This stretch of road is slow-going, no more than thirty miles per hour. From the top of the bluff, you can get a clear shot as they round a curve and head up the hill. The quarter mile long, straight section of road leads directly toward you. I can spot for you so you can line up the shot."

"And what do I use to take this shot?" Peyton, still assimilating the sudden, shocking turn of events, stared intently at Xu.

Xu, uncomfortable at first with his friend's stare, looked at Peyton. "Look, I know I've thrown a lot at you quickly. But check out the back seat. You'll find a case and inside is a Remington M24 rifle with .300 Winchester Magnum match-grade ammunition and a 10 x 40 Leupold Ultra M3 scope, a gift of the US Army to the government of China. It's been zeroed at seven hundred yards and the supersonic ammunition will punch through the windshield of the truck while maintaining a fair degree of accuracy. You'll likely have to take two or three quick shots, however. Nothing is certain."

"Well, you certainly know the way to my heart. The M24 and I are good friends, but I don't like the way this is setting up," Peyton said. "A bullet that passes through glass does unpredictable things. If it starts to precess in flight, a slam into the windshield at an odd angle can send it anywhere. On top of that, this is a cold, clean barrel and I don't really know what compensation is necessary. And with a boy in the cab…"

Xu jumped in. "I agree that the boy should be spared but if he gets in the way and gets himself hurt or killed, you have to remember that he is a terrorist in training. The odds are highly unlikely that he'll ever be reformed, so we have to choose the path of least guilt on this one. Besides, the truck will be coming straight at you so the accuracy won't be off that much. I got you match-quality ammo so at that distance the bullet should still be straight and true. Ideally, you'll punch his ticket on the first shot. Worst case scenario, the first shot takes out the windshield and the follow-up shot nails the bastard before he even knows what happened."

"I hear you, but there's still the kid. I'd feel better

if we could get them out of the truck."

"Not likely. I could go down there and pretend to be broken down on the side of the road but, A, they may not stop; B, they may stop in such a way that you can't get the shot; C, you won't have a spotter; and D, I'll be stuck dealing with the boy once Ali goes down. Besides they'll be driving straight into the sun. You'll have all the advantage."

Peyton frowned and smacked the dashboard with his fist, then sat quietly for a minute. "Ok, we'll do it your way. Let's get positioned. How do you plan to hide the Rover?"

"There's a spot just off the road where we can park. We'll climb up to the top of the bluff."

Twenty minutes later they pulled into a small group of trees and began the trek up the incline. The sun at this point was behind the peak so they made their way easily through the shadows with little chance of exposure. Detection assumed that people were up and about and close enough to see them. They were far from a town at this early hour. The road was largely deserted, with only the occasional passerby headed to work.

When they reached the top, they made their way quickly to the edge of the bluff that overlooked the road. Just as Xu had described, they looked straight down a quarter mile stretch of highway that disappeared at the far end around curve. The road was uphill as it came toward them, which ensured that the old truck's speed would be minimal. Peyton walked to several spots on the edge of the bluff as he looked for the best place to get the most direct, head-on position down the roadway. After a thorough evaluation, he put the rifle case down and turned to Xu. "Looks like our spot." Xu watched as his friend stared down the valley and visualized the path of the bullet.

Peyton opened the case and lifted the rifle from the foam insert cushion. Months had passed since he had been to the range and practiced, but the rifle felt as natural in his hands as a kitchen knife in the hands of a master chef. Xu spread a blanket that he had brought from the car and Peyton extended the bipod on the rifle and set it on the grey wool cover. He attached the scope, lay down behind the weapon and sighted down the road. "I'd sure feel better about this with a couple of practice shots so that I can feel the characteristics of this barrel," Peyton said.

"Let me get the binoculars and look for other people. Maybe you can squeeze off a couple." Xu scurried over to the edge of the bluff where he could see in both directions, up and down the road.

Peyton inserted five rounds so that he could take down the target without reloading. Every ounce made a difference in performance and he liked the consistency of doing the same thing in the same way every time. The barrel of the M24 was free floating and only touched the rest of the rifle at the receiver. Neither the pressure of the shooter's hands on the stock nor the weight of the sling or the bipod affected the barrel. Even so, every unknown that he could take out of the equation made for a better shot.

Peyton looked through the scope and found a paint mark on the roadway. That would be his sighting range point. He moved his sight slightly to the right and found a power pole, which he figured to be about forty feet tall. Then he lined up the pole with the dots in the "Mil-dot" scope and confirmed that the range was almost dead-on his estimate of five hundred yards. After this, he put the rifle down, reached over and pulled out the ballistics tables that came with the ammunition. At five hundred yards, he should expect a bullet drop of thirty-five inches. However, the rifle was zeroed at seven hundred yards so that should reduce his correction to the difference of two hundred yards.

Xu set up the twenty-power spotter scope next to Peyton and peered through it, studying the ripples that the warm air made. "Wind's fore and aft, no windage correction. Good wind at our backs up here but it's slower down on the road. Shouldn't be an issue unless the direction changes."

Peyton looked through the scope, lined it up, and studied the sight picture. Xu stood up, looked in both directions through the binoculars, then took a quick look over his shoulder before he tapped Peyton's shoulder, a "go" sign. Peyton put the crosshairs on his aiming spot and let his muscles settle. He instinctively followed the BRASS method – breathe, relax, aim, slack, squeeze. His vision narrowed to the center of the scope reticule and he felt a familiar calm, floating sensation as he got into the zone. He took a breath, let half of it out, checked his aiming point, took up the slack in the trigger and then gently squeezed until he felt the stock kick back into his shoulder. The rifle kicked up and to the left just slightly as the bullet spun down the barrel and exited the muzzle at just over nineteen hundred miles per hour. Peyton brought the scope back over the target just as piece of painted macadam the size of a quarter flew off into space. Sweet, Peyton thought and he listened to the sound of the rifle crack roll off the canyon walls, decreasing in pitch with each reflection.

"I'm ready," Peyton said to Xu. "That's a right nice weapon."

"I thought you might like it," Xu replied. "I spent a lot of time getting it ready for you."

A wry look on his face, Peyton looked at Xu and said, "Gee, thanks, buddy. The least you could do, under the circumstances, wouldn't you agree?" The two old friends smiled as they settled into a familiar routine.

Peyton closed his eyes and thought about the last few years with his partner. They had accomplished much in their business as they put together systems that protected airports around the globe, the Super Bowl, and the new World Trade Center. They had worked to make the world a safer place. To be thrown together under these circumstances, to stop a threat of this scale, seemed surreal, but here they were. Yesterday, Peyton thought, I believed Xu was dead and now we're back in the thick of things as if nothing had happened. Essentially nothing had happened except that, once again, Xu had saved his life.

Peyton lay on the ground and looked down the road, alternately through the scope and then eyes-only. The sun was well above the horizon now. The air shimmered as the heat increased by the minute. Through the scope, the world was completely out of focus. Peyton thought quickly about the thinning air as it heated up and considered adjusting the bullet drop for the different flight characteristics. But he really didn't have enough detailed information to make more than an educated guess, so he might as well go with his instincts. Be the bullet, he thought, instantly realizing that boredom and hunger were playing silly games with his brain. He quickly regained his sniper focus.

An hour later he sensed Xu stiffen. He glanced over and saw him adjust the spotter scope. "Here they come," Xu said. "One thousand yards."

Peyton saw an old truck round the curve and start slowly up the hill.

Xu spoke softly. "The boy is driving and the target is in the passenger seat. Left side of the windshield as you see it."

Peyton studied the truck through the scope. He figured at this speed he had about thirty seconds before the truck got to the paint strip that he used as his range point. He found his aim point just above the Arab's head.

"I'll give you a count," Xu said. "Seven hundred fifty yards."

He waited for Xu to estimate the time to the paint strip. He heard the whispered count, "Seven, six, five, four, three..." Xu's quiet voice allowed him to concentrate and the sequence went on automatic. Peyton squeezed. The rifle kicked slightly upward just as it had before. He chambered another round, using the forward motion of his hand on the bolt to gently push the crosshairs back to his aiming point as he squeezed off another round. As the second bullet left the barrel, the windshield of the truck shattered and a red spot appeared on the Arab's chest just below the sternum, followed by a second red spot near his neck as the second bullet hit. Just as quickly as before, Peyton chambered another round, adjusted his aim slightly and squeezed again. This time, he saw the Arab turn and look at the boy as if to ask what was going on. A second later his turban flew backwards and his face disappeared in a red spray.

The boy looked over at his uncle and his face contorted in a lightning fast sequence of surprise, understanding, shock and horror as he realized what had just happened. The truck swerved as the boy reacted. The thirteen-year-old desperately wanted to reach out to his uncle across the seat but realized that he had to control the moving truck. He pulled over to the shoulder of the now-silent roadway. Through the scope, Peyton saw the boy's face contort. The gravity of the situation penetrated the boy's consciousness. Then, his mouth opened and he visibly pushed the rage-filled air from his body. Peyton quickly took his eye from the scope and carefully laid the rifle down on the blanket. The boy's screams of rage and grief reached him. This was the worst of all successful scenarios. To take out a soldier in battle was one thing. But kill targets with family present, no matter how murderous the bad guys were, was always gut-wrenching.

Peyton quickly disassembled the scope from the rifle and placed everything in the cushioned container, while Xu packed the spotter scope. *One down,* he thought. *How many more before this is over?*

They climbed down to the roadway before they finally spoke. "Ok," Peyton said. "We need to get to Bushehr."

Chapter 27

Second Naval District HQ
Bushehr, Iran

MOHAMMED REZA PERSPIRED SLIGHTLY AS HE entered the Headquarters building and announced to the security person at the reception desk that a member of the Majlis was here to discuss the Navy's training budget with Admiral Kuchecki. The armpits of his pale blue cotton shirt were dark and he could feel a droplet of sweat run down the middle of his back. Not an unlikely occurrence at one hundred and ten degrees, he knew, however, that he was accustomed to the heat.

The man standing next to him wore a dishdasha, the long white robe traditionally worn by Middle Eastern men, his head covered by a black checked shemagh held in place with the familiar rope-like loops of an igal. Reza knew only that this bearded and mustached man was named Jamal and was from the Finance Ministry. He looked perfectly comfortable, with not even a drop of sweat evident on what little skin was exposed.

He had flown the two hundred forty miles from Tehran by helicopter rather than by plane, to the helipad just north of the Second Naval District headquarters building. The western half of the base was laid out in a semicircle. From the air, the facility looked like a large horseshoe with the headquarters building in the center of the shoe. After his five hundred foot walk to the entrance of the building in the searing heat, he had expected someone to meet him since he was a Majlis member but perhaps he was too junior for that.

The young sailor, a member of the Naval Security

detachment, directed Reza down the hall to the second door on the left. When he entered, he found himself in the Admiral's outer office occupied by three orderlies. *Surprisingly plain for an admiral,* he thought. Kuchecki had indeed been demoted in both stature and position, if not in rank. The look and feel of the office underscored how far he had fallen. Reza felt a twinge of sympathy but then remembered why he was here and quickly steeled himself against such emotions. Ordered to get the budget information from the Admiral and, in the process, shape the conversation in accordance with a script provided by the Guardian Council, he needed to accomplish this quickly, then leave.

"I'm Mohammed Reza from the Majlis Military Budget Committee and this is Jamal from the Finance Ministry," he told the orderly closest to the door. "We're here for the budget meeting with Admiral Kuchecki."

The orderly jumped to his feet, cut his eyes quickly toward the second orderly who hurried from the room. "The Admiral is expecting you. Please." He made a sweeping gesture with his hand toward the door at the back of the room. Reza followed him and was ushered into the office. The space, small for an Admiral, seemed especially cramped for a man of Kuchecki's size. The Admiral, who looked uncomfortable in the space, mustered his poise, stood, and came around the desk to greet Reza.

"Good to see you again, Mohammed," Kuchecki said as he grabbed both of Reza's shoulders and gave him the customary kiss on each cheek. "Please, sit down so we can talk." Reza introduced Jamal as an auditor from the Finance Ministry. The second orderly scurried in with a tray containing clear glass cups filled with mint tea and a plate of shortbread cookies, He placed the tray on the table and stood erect for a moment until Kuchecki nodded slightly, then walked quickly from the room.

Reza sat on the couch and picked up a cup of tea. As he sipped, he gathered his thoughts for a moment, then spoke. "I have reviewed your training budget and, while generally acceptable, I want to go over a couple of items with you."

"And you flew here personally to review this with me?" Kuchecki asked. "I am honored, but I wonder why this budget is different than any others. Why would one as busy as you take a personal interest in my budget?"

Reza shifted in his chair before he answered the Admiral. "This budget comes at a time when many changes are occurring in our government. My job is to maintain consistency with the current policy. I find this is best done in person.

"I see." Kuchecki's mannerism indicated a different view of the situation but he did not press farther.

Reza stared at the tea as he carefully placed the cup back on the table. "Let's look first the line item for fast patrol boat training in the gulf. Is that related to the strategy for attacking our neighbors across the Gulf or for defending against aggressors in the event they attack our shores?"

"The latter, of course," Kuchecki replied. "Our large fleet of patrol boats is essential to the defense of our sovereignty. The strategy is that of the hyena who attacks the lion. The US is strong like the lion but they put all of their firepower in a few big ships. We are small like the hyena but we have many fast boats and can nip at the lion until it becomes tired then move in for the kill." Kuchecki's demeanor was like that of a grandfather explaining to a boy the complexities of an operation using animal metaphors, a ploy that irritated Reza immensely.

He held up his hand to stop the Admiral. "You talk of US firepower. Why would this be a threat given our new position with them?"

Kuchecki's broad smile revealed all of this teeth. He spread his arms and said, "Forgive me. Old habits. Of course I meant attacks by any enemies."

"Ah, well, a very worthy item," Reza said. He looked at Jamal who nodded in agreement. "I will personally see that this is approved by the committee. Any strategy to keep us safe is a correct strategy in my book."

"We are of a similar mind, you and I." Kuchecki leaned forward slightly and expounded. "I am gratified to know that there are still some in the Majlis who feel the urgency to be prepared for any move. I'm not yet convinced that the United States, along with its lapdog, Israel, will honor this treaty but I hope they do. Israel is truly a danger only with American support. The U.S. is the primary threat. Take the American infidels out of the equation and you've removed the teeth from the lion. Without teeth, the lion can't last very long against even a small band of hyenas."

"True enough, but with the new treaty, the United States is not such a threat."

With this, Kuchecki sat straight in his chair. His voice took on a hushed quality, a forced sincerity. "Not such a threat? The treaty makes them an even greater menace. Without so much as a small resistance, we have abandoned our holy path to the Sunnah and turned our backs on our destiny. Believe me, I don't want people to suffer or be hurt. I'm not a terrorist. But the only way to political peace is to ensure spiritual peace. Spiritual peace will come only when everyone in the world embraces the true word, the Holy Qur'an. The United States and Israel are both opposed to this yet now we align ourselves with them? Allah, peace be upon him, will not stand for such weakness."

"How," Reza interjected, "can we pull the teeth of a lion as big and as powerful as the United States? Your goals and observations are valid but are they truly possible?"

Kuchecki, the grandfather, leaned closer. "Perhaps not". He looked into Reza's eyes and added, "On the other hand, perhaps yes, if handled with the right approach."

Reza's stomach pitched with these last words. "And what approach would that be?"

"The right approach would not only pull the lion's teeth but remove its head in the process. America has great military might. The speed with which they crushed Afghanistan and Iraq, twice, proves their organization and ability to strike hard and fast. That organization, however, is a weakness based on two assumptions: that they have the element of surprise and communication from bottom to top and back again. Such an organization requires time to plan and obtain approval, plans which must be massaged again and again. America's first incursion into Iraq required months to mobilize; the second, nearly a year. This flaw can be exploited."

The Admiral continued. "Their other strength is the US economy. Although it fluctuates with the rest of the world, it is strong enough to invest in war and still provide necessities both at home and abroad." He paused for effect. This strength, however, can be a weakness as well, one that can be exploited."

"I'm not sure that I follow you. I don't understand." Reza's face didn't mirror his disquietude as he asked, "If they are so strong, how can they be weak at the same time?"

"Because Allah says they are weak. Because the

Qur'an says they are weak. Because they are weak." Kuchecki put his elbows on his thighs, interlaced the fingers of both hands and leaned forward, a sudden energy evident in his demeanor. "We agree that American strength lies in military might and the nation's economy. Yes?" He watched Reza who nodded once. "If we destroy or even severely damage both simultaneously, we would bring the Great Satan to its knees. They would implode and no longer be able to retaliate against an outside aggressor."

Reza sat back as he struggled to maintain his outward composure. His face was a mask but he shook inside. His breath came in short shallow gasps which he fought to conceal and control. "How exactly do you propose to demolish or cripple a country so powerful? And how do purport to destroy an economy, something that cannot be seen or touched?" He knew, in advance, the answer that would follow.

Kuchecki's smile was almost a sneer. "And you are part of the Majlis that supposedly runs our country?" He gave a quick and muffled snort. "The amount of money one has is but a single element of an economy. Saudi Arabia, Iran, and the other Gulf states have as much or more money than the US but the American economy still rules the financial world. Why do you think this is so?"

Reza stared at Kuchecki, uncertain whether an answer was expected or if the question was rhetorical. Resolution to this dilemma came quickly as Kuchecki plowed ahead. Kuchecki the Admiral spoke professorially as he assumed his role of Director of Training, "You see, much of the Saudi's money is either on deposit by the royal family or spent by them overseas. Their coffers are filled with billions in oil money. Yet, at the same time, they have a labor force of only six million, with a quarter to a third of them unemployed. In order for an economy to be healthy, for jobs to be created, for people to live well and be happy, money must change hands. The oil worker gets money from ARAMCO. The grocer gets money from the oil worker. The automobile dealer gets money from the grocer. The homeowner sells his home to the automobile dealer. The computer salesman gets money from the homeowner. And ARAMCO gets money from the computer salesman. As this cycle continues and expands, the economy strengthens. When people stop spending, the economy gets into trouble."

"Before you and I were born, the world was mired in a great depression. People starved. Banks closed and there were no jobs. In fact, however, no more or no less money existed in the world six months into the depression than on the day before the slide began. When people lost confidence and stuffed money in mattresses, cash stopped changing hands. At this point, the depression started to gain momentum. Such a scenario creates a vicious cycle."

"So back to my original point. The way to destroy an economy is to instill fear so that people lose confidence in the future and hoard their money. When that behavior takes hold, the economy will cool. America will slip into a depression and will not be able to indulge in its decadent ways any more."

"And how does one instill this level of fear in a country of three hundred million people?" Reza struggled to steady his voice as his abdomen quaked from fear and stress. He now believed that he was in the presence of a crazy man. Even more disturbing, Kuchecki was brilliant, an attribute that made him an even greater threat.

The Admiral smiled knowingly and said, "Such a feat is not easy but can be achieved."

Reza pressed. "And how can this be accomplished?"

"The ideal scenario would be a surprise nuclear attack to destroy Israel and destabilize the Middle East in a single lightning-quick stroke. Such an event would set off the perfect storm of events."

Reza feigned admiration in an effort to hide his shock and horror and to minimize personal endangerment. Was this the tirade of a demented man or had the Admiral broken in the face of his humiliation? He had no way of knowing Kuchecki's state of mind.

"By the perfect storm," Kuchecki continued, "I mean that the attack will cause oil prices to skyrocket. Iran and the rest of the Arab world would benefit greatly from this. Of course, the American response would be to horde, to protect their precious money. They won't invest, buy a car, much less a major appliance. The economy will slow to a crawl."

"At the same time, the element of surprise will confuse the Americans. Against whom should they retaliate? The attack against them must appear to be government-sanctioned. Once the chaos starts, right-thinking and like-minded people will rise up. Iran's rightful government will come back into power with Islam properly at the forefront.

"You speak as if you have a plan for something like this?" Reza commented.

"Better than a plan, steps are already in place."

"What do you mean?" Reza shifted in his chair, unable to get comfortable.

Kuchecki got up, walked to his office door, and turned the lock so that no one could walk in on the conversation. The hairs on Mohammed Reza's neck stood up when the Admiral removed a key ring from his pocket, found the deadbolt key and secured the second lock as well. Reza watched as the Admiral calmly returned the keys to his pocket, walked back over to the desk, and sat down. His forearms on the desk, he clasped his hands in front of him and interlaced his fingers like a teacher reviewing the answers to a classroom quiz.

"I have come into possession of a nuclear weapon – two, in fact. They are now on their way to the Mediterranean aboard one of my vessels, a submarine manned by a dedicated crew, one dedicated to the glory of Allah. These missiles will be launched as soon as the vessel is in place," Kuchecki said this matter-of-factly as if he were discussing a trip to the market.

"Good Lord," Reza exclaimed and drew in his breath. "How did you ever get authorization for a mission of this gravity? I wasn't even aware that we had such weapons. I certainly would know of the budget appropriations."

Kuchecki's face was impassive at first, but then a smile slowly spread up from his lips to his eyes, fiery with passion. "I don't need authorization," he bellowed. Aware that he needed to speak quietly so others in the next room wouldn't hear, he lowered his voice. "I was the supreme commander of the Iranian Navy before Adazi stole my position. He stole my office. He stole my title. He may have killed my sister and brother-in-law. But he did not steal my intellect nor did he steal my abilities. And he cannot possibly usurp the destiny that Allah has prepared for me." His eyes flared again and Reza fully grasped the admiral's unhinged mental state.

"But your sister was killed by terrorists who sought to assassinate the British diplomats."

"No matter. For twenty-seven years I worked my way up to my position, supported all the time by the blessings of Allah and guided by His wisdom. Along the way I made many friends, did many favors, and built a navy that is ready and willing to do whatever is required. They have followed my orders and will continue to do so. I have followed the strict and true path that Allah set down for me. I also built my reputation and my contacts in the international community." Kuchecki's voice became louder again and more stringent. "When I called Fang and proposed to purchase a weapon from China, he immediately came to my aid. He had his sources and contacts and was more than happy to help, not for the money alone but because I asked him. Me, the rightful commander of the Iranian Navy, the chosen one, chosen by Allah, sent by Allah." With each phrase, he pounded his fist against his desktop. "That imposter Adazi could never achieve this because, you see, I am the Madhi!!"

A sudden vicious pounding on the office door was followed by angry shouts to open up immediately. Kuchecki looked at the door, then at Reza, as understanding slowly dawned on him. He reached into a desk drawer and retrieved his side arm, a Glock nine millimeter automatic, pointed the gun at Reza, he shrieked, "What have you done?" A snarl on his face, his eyes cold and dark, he raised the Glock until Reza looked straight into the black hole at the center of the weapon's muzzle.

Reza swallowed hard and watched Kuchecki's finger tense on the trigger. At that instant, all conscious thought ceased and Reza fell sideways off the chair. The explosion in the chamber of the pistol pushed the bullet down the barrel at nearly the speed of sound. When the hot gasses erupted from the barrel, Reza felt the spray of fire and bits of powder. The bullet screamed past his cheek before imbedding into the wall opposite the desk.

"You can't stop me! You can't hurt me! You can't kill me! I am the Madhi!" Kuchecki's crazed voice screamed out for all to hear. His arm came around and he pointed the gun at Jamal. Jamal dove forward toward Kuchecki, until only the edge of the desk stood between himself and the Admiral. Reaching inside his *dishdasha*, he pulled a Jericho automatic from his waistband and fired three shots upward through the desk. He heard the thump of Kuchecki's body against the splintered desktop and crash of the gun as it hit the floor.

Jamal crawled over to the corner of the desk and looked slowly over the desktop before he stood. He pushed Kuchecki back into his chair. "Where is the ship with the weapons on it?"

Kuchecki's eyes rolled to the side. His white uniform front was now red with the blood from three chest wounds. He stared blankly for several seconds, then a smile crept across his face. "It's too late."

Jamal removed his headscarf and pulled the fake beard from his face. Kuchecki's eyes widened with recognition as Peyton Stone's face came into focus. "You again! But you're dead. I gave the execution order."

"Yeah, well, your orders don't seem to have the effect that they once did. Now where is the ship?"

"You can kill my earthly body but you can't stop me. I am the Madhi. I have returned." He grimaced as he coughed, then spoke again with less volume. "I will return." He grew silent, then a whisper came through his lips. "I cannot be stopped." His body went limp and slid off the chair onto the floor where he lay with lifeless eyes that stared up at his too-small desk in this lowly, plain room.

The office door crashed inward and two men with automatic weapons ran into the office and stepped sideways. The pair knelt, their weapons trained on Kuchecki's desk.

The IRGC Colonel walked to the open door and looked in at the blood on the opposite wall and at the Majlis member who lay on the floor. He walked quickly to Reza and bent down, "Are you hit?" he asked.

Reza shook his head, still unable to gain control of his breath and speak. He stared wide-eyed at the colonel in disbelief. After a dozen quick breaths, he calmed himself and said, "This has been the most horrific experience of my life. I could have died."

"Yes, but you didn't," the Colonel replied and stepped quickly over to Kuchecki's body, a lump on the floor. "He's dead. What happened here?"

The colonel looked up at Peyton, "Who are you? What's going on?"

Peyton began to speak but Reza jumped in, "He is Jamal from the Finance Ministry. He and I were meeting with Admiral Kuchecki when the Admiral just suddenly went insane before our eyes. He started screaming and shot at me. If it hadn't been for Jamal I would be dead."

The Colonel turned to Peyton who shrugged and said. "That's pretty much what happened."

"Jamal and I will return to Teheran immediately and I will launch a formal investigation of this. You can clean up here and then wait for further instructions." Reza said. With that, PHILOSOPHER grabbed Peyton's arm and they left for the heliport.

Chapter 28

Entrance to the Suez Canal
El Suweis, Egypt

ABBAS STOOD NEXT TO THE LION STATUE AT THE edge of the old park. His mind wandered aimlessly as he savored his Marlboro. *Only the Americans can produce these rich tobaccos.* What do the Turks know about tobacco? He looked out into the Gulf of Suez and took a step to the side, then turned and leaned on the carved lion captured in mid-pounce. Funny, he mused, if the lion were real he would jump right into the canal. He imagined that the lion was real and he told it to go jump in the canal – as sometimes people told him when he asked for money or a small favor – and the great beast did. His own name, Abbas, meant "description of the lion" in Arabic. His small stature notwithstanding - one hundred eighty pounds, barely five feet seven inches in his boots - he thought of himself as a lion.

He finished his cigarette and looked at the stub of filter and tobacco. *How could a country so morally bankrupt produce such a fine cigarette? Perhaps,* he thought, *self-indulgence gives rise to perfection. Or are those crazies in the park right? Am I decadent for buying American cigarettes?* The internal struggle quickly dissipated. The cigarettes were good, he enjoyed them, and that was that.

The sun slipped under the sand across the canal. Abbas decided to return to his apartment and make dinner. He flicked the cigarette butt into the water and stood for another minute to watch yet another container ship enter the canal on the northward journey. Container

343

ships, tankers, military ships of many nations traversed the Suez Canal which connected the Red Sea and the Mediterranean. Abbas had often seen the huge American aircraft carriers pass through the waterway. Many of his friends bemoaned the fact that American war machinery, the infidel's military might, crossed through Egyptian territory to wreak havoc on fellow Muslims. Abbas considered this but also thought about Muslim brothers who not only slaughtered Americans and Israelis but focused their cruelty most often on other Muslims. In truth, the mayhem didn't make sense to him. But, as was his habit, if physically removed from a situation, he chose not to dwell on heavy thoughts.

Suez and the adjoining Sinai had long been the stage for turmoil between East and West. A French engineer, Ferdinand De Lesseps, conceived the one hundred mile long shipping canal in the 1800s and acquired the desert land from his friend, Said Pasha, then Viceroy of Egypt. De Lesseps' vision was to shorten the trade routes between London and Bombay by eliminating the five thousand mile voyage around Africa. The canal opened on November 17, 1869, with a new city at the northern end of the canal named Port Said in honor of Said Pasha. Currently, approximately eighty ships traversed the canal each day in alternating northbound and southbound convoys that transported roughly four million tons of cargo each year. The vessels traveled halfway to a divided channel and waited for the oncoming convoy to pass, then proceeded. The design allowed ships to sail in both directions most of the time.

The container ship that Abbas now watched had the letters COSCO painted on the side, along with what he imagined were Chinese characters displayed in various places along the hull. He had no idea that COSCO stood for China Ocean Shipping Company nor did he particularly care. The ships moved through the canal twenty-four hours a day at a standard three kilometers separation, which meant that every twenty minutes or so another ship would arrive. Abbas never tired of watching these behemoths move effortlessly through the water.

In his peripheral vision, he sensed movement in the water. He turned and saw a disturbance, a wake of some sort to the side and near the back, all but lost in the shadow of the ship. He strained to see more in the failing light but the wake had dissipated. *Maybe a dolphin or fish are swimming in the ship's wake*, he thought. Shrugging, he turned toward the park for the six-block walk to his apartment building.

"DOWN PERISCOPE," SAYED SADIQ SAID AND THE silver tube descended silently into the floor of the control room. The *Nuh* was about to enter the Suez Canal on its way to its mission launch point. This was a tricky part of the journey. They could be easily observed at several points along the canal and had neither authorization nor political backing to be here. Sadiq waited until dark to pilot his submarine alongside and slightly underneath the COSCO container ship, *Cho Hai*, as it entered the canal. This was a test of his own skills as captain and his crew's precision in piloting the nearly two-hundred-fifty-foot long submarine in close formation with the container vessel.

The *Cho Hai*, over twice as long as the submarine, was, at five hundred fifty feet, small by container ship standards. By comparison, the Emma Maersk, who flew the flag of Denmark, measured thirteen hundred feet with a gross tonnage in excess of one hundred fifty tons. *Cho Hai* had just unloaded four thousand TEU, Twenty-foot Equivalent Units, the standard measure for container capacity, in Dubai. This amounted to roughly the equivalent of eighteen hundred semi-trailers. Most of her cargo was fresh produce for the Sultan Grocery chain, the Middle Eastern subsidiary of Safeway. Nearly empty, she was now headed back to the port of Civitavecchia near Rome to pick up olives, wine and new Ferraris bound for London.

Sadiq chose this vessel to shadow for a number of reasons. First, she was entering the canal just after sundown so he had a good chance of remaining invisible to her crew. Second, while large enough to overshadow the sub in shallower water, the *Cho Hai's* beam measured only one hundred-fifty-five feet. This allowed him to fit his thirty-three foot diameter boat with a little room to spare in the two-hundred-ten foot wide channel. Finally, almost empty, she rode high in the water, with a draft of only eighteen feet. This gave him additional room to maneuver in the sixty-six foot deep water and allowed the sub to move directly under her if necessary. Fortunately, the Suez was constructed on flat land so there were no locks to traverse, just a steady run up to the Mediterranean.

Circumnavigating the Saudi peninsula beneath the *Cho Hai* was daring but brilliant. The *Nuh* was completely hidden from satellites and the watchful eyes of the American Navy ships that patrolled the Arabian Gulf, especially those that passed through the Straits of Hormuz. Even so, he was surprised by the two hour wait to get through the Straits. When he was able to nudge the periscope just above the water line, he saw the large American aircraft carrier that made its way north. Unaware that any exercises were going on, he immediately retracted the scope and allowed water to slowly run into the ballast tanks. The sub settled a little deeper while the American carrier passed.

"No drills for the next six hours until we get through the canal," Sadiq said to the Executive Officer. The XO looked relieved. "I want all crew members to stay on their toes as we pass through here, no unnecessary activity or noise. When we get to the Bitter Lake, we'll pull out into the wider channel and run fast along the bottom to save time. We'll make another passing run through the basin at *Isma'iliya* and then again up the channel at *Abu Kalifah*. The south bound convoy will be waiting for their time to move so we should be able to make good speed up the channel."

The XO nodded, walked behind the control panel operator, and proceeded down the gangway to pass the instructions to the crew. The walk gave him time to ponder the mission away from the captain. To launch missiles against friends of the United States would surely be suicide. Surely, the rumors that the weapons had nuclear warheads were false, but then again, perhaps not. In the final analysis, the means didn't matter. Attacking U.S. interests had never ended well...ever.

This mission was a great opportunity to practice a silent run. The biggest threat of detection on a submarine is noise. Although no known listening devices existed in the canal, the Nuh was aware that the Israelis had built a large net of passive sonar devices in the waters near their country. The system was designed to listen twenty-four hours a day to detect possible underwater terrorist activity. Submarine sounds came from a number of sources: small bubbles and water that flowed around the outer hull as the boat moved through the water, for example. The *Nuh's* whale-like teardrop shape, coupled with a special coating of anechoic rubber, however, minimized that noise.

A second source of noise was the normal sounds of

onboard activity. Machinery, footsteps on the metal decks, conversations, and tools that banged against pipes and other surfaces during normal working activities could also be heard by the sonar listening devices. The inside pressure hull of the *Nuh* was isolated from the outer hull by rubber pads to minimize the noise inside the tube where the crew lived and worked from being transmitted outside the boat. Every piece of machinery, every shaft, every connection point was mounted on sound isolators.

Most significantly, the sound of the propulsion system was not only audible but each propeller type had a characteristic sound pattern. A trained sonar operator could tell the class of the boat by its signature. The really good sonar men could tell one boat from another: the *Nuh* from the *Tareq* and the *Tareq* from the *Yunes* by the sounds they made as they sliced through the water. This would be harder now, at least in the case of the *Nuh*. During the last upgrade, the *Nuh* had its six-bladed propeller removed. The entire aft end of the boat was replaced and outfitted with a new ducted propeller system – more a turbine than a standard propeller – called a pump-jet. This design increased speed by 50% while the smaller turbine blades decreased noise significantly. The new propulsion system, coupled with the nuclear-tipped land attack cruise missiles, made this boat not only the most powerful Kilo-class submarine but the most powerful Arab weapon on the planet.

Chapter 29

Intra Coastal Oil Regional HQ
Westville, NJ

DENNIS CARLSON SAT IN THE CONFERENCE ROOM while he waited for his guest to arrive. ICO's Eastern Regional Manager, Jim Wolcott, sat at the table with him and looked over financial projection reports.

"This is not good," Wolcott said. "No matter how you cut it, controls on oil prices will kill us. Our whole business model is based on the assumption that instability in the oil-producing regions will drive up prices. We can't even service the debt we built up during expansion, much less make a profit, if this treaty goes ahead."

"I know. I've been kicking some things around and thought we were in good shape to put this treaty thing behind us. I'm not sure what my guy, McKinley, has for us today. He insisted on coming here for a face to face meeting." Carlson sat hunched to one side in his chair with his right elbow on the table. The first two fingers on his right hand rubbed his temple idly, a habit when he was deep in thought.

"I'm not up to speed on this." Wolcott's tone mirrored his surprise and his head jerked slightly upward in anticipation of Carlson's detailed plans.

"Right. And I'm not sure you need to be. We'll see what McKinley has to say."

Wolcott's shoulders slumped slightly as he tried to hide his disappointment. "McKinley?"

"Admiral Daniel McKinley, U.S. Navy retired and Director of National Intelligence. I helped him get the job a few years ago and plan to support his run for President in the next election. The appointment moved him into the national spotlight. He insisted on a personal conference and took the train rather than an official jet. I don't know what this is about."

Wolcott's brow furrowed slightly. "Can you give me some background on…?"

He was cut off when the phone in the conference room buzzed and a female voice said, "Dan McKinley to see Mr. Carlson."

"Bring him in." Carlson replied and got up from the table. As Wolcott straightened his tie, he noticed that Carlson didn't bother.

McKinley entered and shook hands with Carlson. The DNI's light blue shirttail was out on one side, his suit coat rumpled as if he had worn it throughout the two-and-a-half-hour train ride from Washington's Union Station to the Thirty-Fourth Street Station in Philadelphia. His eyes were red and he obviously hadn't shaved since yesterday. A taxi receipt hung precariously from his shirt pocket.

Carlson introduced the DNI to Wolcott. "Sit down, Dan. You look overworked."

McKinley rubbed his right eye with his forefinger. Opening both eyes wide to counteract the rubbing, he took a deep breath, shook his head once and looked at the tabletop. "We've got a problem," he said.

Carlson leaned forward and raised his chin slightly, so that he looked straight into McKinley's eyes. In a brusque voice, he asked, "What's going on?"

McKinley looked up from the tabletop, glanced at Wolcott and sat back.

"Give us a minute, Jim." Carlson said.

When the office door closed and they were alone, McKinley tapped his fingertips on the table lightly, twice. "Kuchecki is dead."

"What?" Carlson sat up straight as his eyes ignited. "How?"

"Some guy in the Majli was on to him. Turns out the guy worked with us and brought in our asset to meet with Kuchecki to find out what he was up to. Words ensued. It turned ugly and Kuchecki pulled a gun from his desk."

"So if he had the gun, what happened to him?"

"Our asset was armed, how I don't know. But he took out Kuchecki."

Carlson slumped back in his chair, put his elbow on the table, and leaned his head to the side as he considered the possibilities. "Well, shit. What does that do to the overall plan?"

"How the hell should I know? There's a sub loose somewhere with a nuke and no way that I know of to control it now. This was supposed to be a threat of attack. Once the Iranian government was discredited and the treaty put aside, the sub would back down. Now I don't know what will happen.

"I thought I had our asset under control after that broad from SCEPTRE inserted herself into the middle of things. She found evidence in Pakistan that led right back to us. I tried my damnedest to keep a lid on it. I ordered the agency heads to run everything through me. Even kept an eye on some of our CIA guys and shut down the NRO feeds they were tracking. Tried to arrest them but the bastards got away. This has turned into one real cluster."

"Well," Carlson leaned forward, both elbows on the table, fingers interlocked, "stopping the treaty would have been good but a shooting war will drive the prices through the roof. This could be even better."

"So what are we going to do?" McKinley asked. He

looked like a boy who had just hit a baseball through a window and was trying to explain his way out of it. "If it gets out that we knew about this, we might as well go ahead and ship our personal effects to Leavenworth."

Carlson sat up and slapped his palm down on the table, his decision made. "We're going to do absolutely nothing. Let's stay the course, move forward and get to the end of this. If all hell breaks loose in the Middle East, then we'll work to discredit the president. We'll say she fell for the treaty and let the US be pushed into a box while the Iranians plotted nuclear war against Israel. You'll be the guy who can save us and that will be the driver behind your campaign."

Carlson smiled. "This is our saving strategy, Dan. We're going to…"

The phone on the table buzzed. "Mr. Carlson," the woman's voice said, "It's a Mr. Walid from the Teheran office. He wants to speak with you personally. He says it's urgent and can't wait."

Carlson' eyebrows went up. "Put him through." He pressed the speaker button.

"Mr. Carlson," Walid was breathless. His voice sounded half an octave too high. "It's terrible. I can't believe it."

Carlson and McKinley leaned toward the phone. "Easy, Walid, one step at a time. What's terrible?"

"It's Admiral Kuchecki. He's dead. Murdered in his own office."

"We heard. Calm down. Where are you?"

"In the office. Reza is with me now. He was there when it happened. The assassin was a US Intelligence agent. We've been betrayed."

Carlson stiffened. "Are you on speakerphone?"

"Yes. Mr. Reza is with me."

"Pick up."

In the Intra Coastal board room there were clicks and a bump as Walid lifted the receiver. "Yessir?" The voice was timid.

"Be careful what you say. Reza could take your words to mean nothing or he could see right through to what's really going on here."

McKinley leaned directly over the speakerphone. He put one hand on either side of the phone. The table creaked. "Walid, this is Dan McKinley. Did Reza get anything from the conversation with Kuchecki that might have led him to understand what's really going on here?"

"Do you mean about the weapon from China?"

Carlson snatched the handset from the cradle. "Walid, get Reza out of the office and call back on the secure line."

He tossed the receiver into the cradle. "That was damned stupid, Dan. Stupid of Walid to call on an unsecured line, stupid of him to mention the weapon in front of Reza, and especially stupid of you to give your name. Have you forgotten you're the damn DNI?"

McKinley sat back down and glared across the table, unable to think of a response.

Sixty miles to the south, two analysts at Ft. Meade stared at each other, their open mouths slowly turning up into smiles of amazement. "Do you believe this?"

"Walid from our watch list is talking with the DNI?"

"Must be an operation?"

"Yeah, could be. But to identify himself on an open call with Walid and discuss a Chinese weapon?"

"Maybe we should call the boss."

"Ya think?"

The analyst reached for the phone. "You send the

transcript, private and encrypted, and I'll call upstairs."

"I'm on it."

Chapter 30

White House
Washington, DC

UPLIGHTS EXPERTLY CONCEALED IN THE LANDSCAPE by the US Park Service shone up on the White House. In the pre-dawn darkness, President Harkins was in the Oval office, pouring her own coffee at four a.m. She could call a kitchen steward any time of the day or night, two of them if she wanted. On the rare occasion, though, when stress was high but her schedule not filled with back-to-back meetings, she liked to make her own coffee. For these brief, illusory moments, she was Maggie Harkins, regular citizen, back home on Upland Road in the Broadmoor neighborhood of Colorado Springs who hoped that problems were in her control, that they could be solved in a day, and that life would go on.

She returned to reality, poured a second cup and handed it to Mike Kopanski who sat on the couch in front of her desk. The President then took her seat at the other end of the couch. The DCI had gotten a call a couple of hours ago from the Operations Center regarding the NSA's intercept of a conversation between the DNI, an oil company executive, and an Iranian operative. He immediately called the White House.

Kopanski took the cup, added two spoons of sugar to the strong black brew, took a sip, then added another spoonful. Harkins watched him, bemused. When he looked up and saw her expression, she gave a little laugh. "We need a little starter to get going this early, don't we?" Then, all business, her tone changed as she asked, "So what do we know?"

"We first need to consider how all of this ties together." Kopanski took a deep breath and reeled off a summary of the intercept. "McKinley was in a meeting with the CEO of Intra-Coastal Oil when the CEO received a call from a guy named Walid who said that Admiral Kuchecki was dead."

"And why would the CEO, or anyone at Intra-Coastal for that matter, be interested in this?

"That's an excellent question. Walid is in ICO's Tehran office. We know that ICO has moved funds from an offshore account to a Swiss account. These funds were then transferred to a Cayman account owned by Ali-al-Muzzafar before being deposited into a Martinique account owned by an arms dealer named Fang."

"So ICO is buying arms on the black market?"

"I don't think so. At least, I can't figure out why they would. Yet the money seems to travel from ICO to Fang through this Swiss account. On the other hand, the timing could be coincidental."

"You mean the money moved from ICO to Switzerland and, purely coincidentally, different money moved from Switzerland to Fang. Seems a bit of a stretch."

"I agree. The Agency doesn't believe in coincidences."

The president took a sip of coffee.

"Another thing in the mix," Kopanski continued, "is that one of our agents, Randy Perkins, worked for ICO as a cover. His office was set up with ICO's cooperation. Walid was not ours. He's a regular ICO employee."

"I didn't think we mixed our people with private citizens." Harkins tilted her head and looked hard at

Kopanski as small ridges formed between her eyebrows.

"We don't officially. Often, though, it's how we get things done." Kopanski's left elbow rested on the arm of the couch. As he continued, he put his left hand out palm up. "This time we had no choice. The Iranians scoured the background of the corporation. Had we used a dummy company, we would have been caught."

The President sat for a moment, then turned and set the china cup and saucer on the end table. "So how does all of this tie back to McKinley?"

"Another excellent question." Kopanski shifted his weight to the right, leaned forward and set his cup and saucer on the low table in front of him. "McKinley appears to be doing some studies to pave the way for a run at the White House at the end of your term."

Harkins expelled a burst of air. Kopanski was quite certain that a quiet expletive had been muffled by the loud sigh.

He looked at her with a wry smile. "Yeah, I know, but a lot of wing nuts out there worship anyone in uniform, whether or not they ever accomplished anything noteworthy. You know I'm a patriot, but some misguided people wrap themselves in the flag and the crazies come out of the woodwork to salute it. Look at George W."

"Ok, let's not go there. It's old news. How does that tie in to what we're talking about?"

"Intel indicates that ICO is funding the studies. We'll confirm that with the Election Commission to see if it's an official position."

Harkins looked at Kopanski for several seconds. Sitting back, she ran her tongue across the inside of her lower lip. "Well, now isn't that interesting? Has he established a campaign war chest yet?"

"We're looking into that with the Commission now.

I wouldn't be surprised but it may be too early to require reporting."

The President reached to her side for her cup and took a long slow sip of the dark liquid. "So, we still haven't nailed the connection between Walid and McKinley, other than both have a connection to ICO. How do they relate to each other?"

"That I don't know. The intercept was clear but the conversation was short." Kopanski reached for a sheet of paper on the coffee table and re-read the notes. "Walid reported that Kuchecki had been killed and somehow an American intelligence agent was involved. McKinley identified himself when Walid was talking about the Chinese weapon. Carlson told Walid to call back on a secure line and broke the connection."

"I think we have to be very careful but at the same time we can't just sit back and let events unfold." The President leaned forward. "I know that policy is my responsibility, but I really need to know what you think, Mike, because I respect your ability to look at the big picture. I don't mean to put you on the spot but pretend for a minute you were me. What would you do?"

Kopanski felt a warm flush at the compliment but tried not to show it. He took a deep breath, placed the palms of his hands together and rested his chin on his thumbs with the tips of his fingers on his lips. He stared at a spot on the couch while he collected his thoughts. Then he let out his breath in a rush. "Madam President, I appreciate your confidence in me and I hope you'll understand that I'm a little uncomfortable." She smiled kindly, her only response. "But since you asked, I think that there is at least the threat of a nuclear strike in the near future. I like to parse problems into manageable chunks. I think, then, that we need to decide what to do about it from three angles: how to stop it, what to do at home while we try, and what to do afterwards if we can't. So here's is a first pass scenario." He paused briefly, then continued. "With Kuchecki dead, the plot seems to be stopped. Now we need to clean up the loose ends. Our guy Stone definitely ID'd the weapons so we have to find them. That's a huge missing link. We need to figure out the connection with McKinley. It may be completely official and I, or we, are out of the loop. That is, we could assume that it's an operation that the DNI is running. The scary thing is what if it's not."

The President nodded slightly. "It does sound fishy. For now, it is imperative to keep this under wraps until we get it resolved. If this leaks, futures traders will panic, oil prices will rise, and people could get concerned about their own personal safety. At any rate, the treaty will be in jeopardy, commerce will slow down drastically and businesses will start to lose money. The stock market will react and we're right back where we were a couple of years ago."

Kopanski sighed again. "Let's just hope that we can deal with this quickly. You have to sign the treaty. If even a whiff of this gets to the 'right to know' crowd, we won't be able to put the genie back in the bottle."

"I agree. Give this the highest classification possible. Pull together everyone who knows about this and threaten them with whatever you need to contain this."

"I will. But the flip side is that, should the worst happen, the inevitable second guessing about what you knew, when you knew it, and what you did about it, will erupt."

"Welcome to my world, Mike." The President stood to signal the end of the meeting. "There's never an easy answer."

Kopanski nodded in agreement and walked out into

the reception area where the President's Chief of Staff conferred with Harkins's administrative assistant who had yet to put her purse away and get a cup of coffee. "It's about time the day shift showed up," Kopanski grinned as he passed them.

"Who said we ever left?" Frank Adams quipped, smiling.

Kopanski waved over his shoulder as he walked out into the filtered morning sun and waited under the porte-cochere for his car to take him back to Langley.

Chapter 31

Aboard the Nuh

"HOW DARE YOU QUESTION THE AUTHORITY OF MY orders!" Sayed Sadiq screamed at the Nuh's Executive Officer, then pulled back and punched him full in the face. The XO landed on his back on the deck of the control room.

"No, please!! You misunderstand me." The man wailed as he rubbed his cheek. "I only asked you a question of clarification. I would never question your authority," he lied.

As the Nuh had passed into the Mediterranean, over the Nile Fan, she had gone deep, near her one thousand foot test depth, below the thermocline, below that layer where the temperature of the water changes so rapidly that it acts as a boundary between the surface layer and the deep layer. The characteristics of sound traveling above or below the thermocline are different. Sound waves don't easily pass between the layers in either direction. In this zone, the Nuh and its crew were invisible from sonar carried on surface ships and from the sonar buoys dropped from anti-submarine warfare, or ASW, aircraft.

The boat was rife with rumors so the Captain decided to put these to bed by laying out the plan. Sadiq gathered the officers in the wardroom and briefed them about the mission. All heard the orders and sat silently. After the meeting broke up, the XO asked Sayed if he thought that attacking Israel with nuclear weapons was a good idea. Sayed viewed the question as a challenge to his authority, an intolerable affront.

The XO was slightly larger than Sadiq. In a bar fight, the outcome might have been different, but this battle was between XO and Captain and rank trumped. Sadiq glared down at the Executive Officer who still lay on the deck. "Do you have more questions?" the Captain shouted.

"No, Sir." The XO said simply.

"Mr. Hashami, put this man in chains and confine him to his quarters until I say otherwise."

"Aye, Captain." The largest man on the ship, Torpedo Mate First Class Hashami, helped his superior officer to his feet and escorted him down the gangway to his quarters.

"Are there any more questions or opinions?" The Captain faced the stunned crew, mute and perfectly still.

"No? I thought not. Now get back to your duties. We have an appointment with destiny." Sadiq checked the gauges as the submarine leveled off at 980 feet and turned up the revolutions on the newly improved propeller system gearbox. When the boat's speed reached 38 knots, Sadiq sat down in the Captain's chair. "Any cavitations from the propeller at this speed?" he asked the sonar man.

"No, sir. All quiet."

"Hold her steady then," he said as he leaned back, closed his eyes and slowly rubbed the ache from his knuckles.

In the Oval Office, as President Harkins stood at the window and stared out at the Rose Garden, the door opened behind her. A Secret Service agent walked in and held the door for the DNI, as he always did. He didn't quietly close the door and wait outside the Oval Office as usual but entered as another agent quietly followed. The two men agents flanked the door with their hands clasped in front of them.

Dan McKinley looked at each in turn and his face paled slightly. He hesitated for a beat, then continued to the spot in front of the president's desk.

Harkins turned slowly, her mouth a thin line. She glanced at McKinley, then slowly picked up a sheet of paper from her desk which she handed to him. "Care to explain this, Dan?"

McKinley took the paper and read the brief but concise paragraphs. He unsuccessfully tried to keep a poker face. His mouth opened, then closed. "It seems to be a transcript of some kind from an illegal wiretap."

"Illegal wiretap?"

"Yes, it appears to be a conversation involving US citizens that was recorded by the NSA. Under Executive Order 12333, that's illegal."

"That would be true except that a former president made it legal if the calls originate outside of the US. The Congress approved that action with the Foreign Intelligence Surveillance Amendments Act. I never really agreed with that in principle but it seems to have paid off in this case."

McKinley stared at her and awaited the next move.

"The question I have is this: what is your relationship to Intra-Coastal Oil? I'd be interested in hearing why you were there."

McKinley shifted his weight from his right to left foot, then back again. He maintained eye contact with Harkins and began slowly. "I am a friend of their CEO, Dennis Carlson. My visit was of a personal nature."

"None of my business. Is that your answer?"

"With all respect, yes, ma'am." A bead of perspiration rolled down his right temple. Harkins noticed and he quickly wiped it away. Perspiration mottled his light blue shirt with dark blue splotches.

"Well, Dan, I think it is my business. You were talking with Walid al-Sharadi, an ICO employee who is also a known Iranian operative. That's why we were specifically monitoring him. There's evidence that he was involved in the murder of Randall Perkins, a CIA employee in Iran who was shot on the rooftop of the office where Walid worked."

"I knew nothing of that," McKinley replied. Another bead of perspiration rolled down his cheek. He let it go.

"Maybe you did, maybe not, but that's not the point. Our intercept operators heard and recorded you personally identify yourself to an Iranian agent, one whom we have reason to believe is involved in some action in the Middle East that you are charged with investigating. He seemed pretty familiar when he mentioned a Chinese weapon that you are supposed to be finding. Does any of this sound odd to you?" The volume of her question rose as she leaned across her desk, fists planted firmly on the polished wood surface.

McKinley stared at Harkins. "Well, of course it's not odd. As you said, I'm investigating. We keep tabs on foreign operatives and sometimes we pretend to be friendly. It's what we do." He looked at his watch. "I have appointments that I must keep. Are we going to be much longer?"

"No, Dan. We're done."

McKinley turned to leave but the two Secret Service agents each took a step toward each other and blocked the door. He blinked as one of the agents spun him around and each took an arm, held them tight together and applied the handcuffs. McKinley shouted, "This is a fucking outrage." If he said more than that, the President didn't hear it through the quickly closed door.

Harkins picked up her desk phone and pressed a

button. "Send Mike in," she said to her assistant.

Mike Kopanski entered the office.

Harkins stood. "You heard?" she asked and motioned to the couch.

"Yes, ma'am."

She walked around the desk and stood at the end of the couch. Kopanski walked to the couch but decided not to sit.

"Mike, the details will have to remain 'need to know' because, if and when this threat is neutralized, and if we find that McKinley has something to do with it, his arrest would stir up a hornet's nest and the American people would be terrified if all of the facts were made public. That's the last thing we need. But I want the case built against McKinley as DNI and I want it airtight. Bury him." She looked at Mike with the subtlest of smiles and added, "Well, not literally. But one can dream."

"You got it." He nodded, proud to serve at the pleasure of this President.

"But first, we still have a nuclear weapon loose out there somewhere. We have two days until the United States has an historic opportunity to sign a treaty with Iran and take a huge step toward ending the madness over there. Time is of the essence."

"Yes, ma'am. I'm on it." He turned and left.

Harkins watched the door close and took a deep breath. She held it for a second, then felt the tension release inside her chest. She let the breath out loudly, walked around her desk, sat down, and looked at the next item on her daybook.

HARRY KNOCKED ON THE DOOR OF THE TOWNHOUSE in Burke, Virginia, hoping he had the right address. He had only been here once before but he typically had no problem with directions. *Come on, come on, you've got to be here.* He heard sounds from inside the house and the door slowly opened. An eye peeked out past the security chain. The door closed and he could hear the chain rattle before the door opened wide.

"Harry!" Dana stood next to a black mailbox mounted by her front door. Harry noticed a name on the box for the first time and smiled. The box should have been labeled with the name "Radke" but the gold adhesive "d" had fallen off.

Harry said, "Miss Rake, may I come in?" Dana was puzzled until Harry pointed at the box.

"Oh, dear." Her eyes scanned the floor for the errant letter, then looked up. "Forgive me, Harry. Of course, come in." She moved as far to the side as she could to let Harry squeeze past and asked, "What brings you here?"

"I need a place to work for a day or two. My office is being watched and I imagine my house is, too."

"Why? What have you done?"

"Nothing!" Harry said, his voice a bit too forcefully.

Dana stepped back and blinked.

"Sorry. I'm investigating a money trail connected with events in the Middle East."

"The KKH thing that you and Ken talked to me about." She said, her interest evident.

"Right, but ever since we started getting close to answers, weird things have been happening." Dana tried not to smile at Harry's syntax. She secretly considered his mangled language both a part of his charm and a refreshing departure from stilted beltway double-talk. He continued. "The missing message that I talked to you about was one of them. Computers started acting funny. I was chased down by security at NGA for a login violation that didn't involve me. My office was raided and files taken. Luckily, Ken had given me the FIO files so they didn't get them."

Dana almost clapped her hands in excitement but hesitated. She dropped her arms to her side instead and flexed her hands. "And now you need my help?"

"You could say that." *Geez*, he thought, *did you hear anything I just said?*

"Then, yes! I will." This time she clapped.

Harry sighed. "I haven't been able to locate Ken Washington ever since he connected the dots on some funds transfers. We can't be overt about looking for him either. But mostly I need a place to lay low and look over some financial documents."

"And you want to stay here?" Her enthusiasm subsided as she realized she wasn't going to have a direct role in Harry's work. He simply wanted to use her house.

"Just for a little while. I have to follow the threads and get this nailed down."

"Well, ok." Her tone cooled. "But I thought you wanted me to help. You know, with the investigation."

Harry eyed her sideways. "Well, what do you know about financial transactions in off-shore accounts?"

Dana looked at the ceiling, pretended to be deep in thought, then spoke. "Let's see. I worked in Metrobank's IT department where I ran their on-line overseas transactions web applications. I learned how the bank serviced its international customers. Does that qualify me to sit at the right hand of the great Harry Morrison?"

She crossed her arms and stepped back on her right foot with her head held high and looked slightly down at Harry.

Harry glanced at the floor and replied, "Ok, point

taken. I'm stressed about all that's going on, but that's not your problem." He waited a moment and said, "Let's sit somewhere and go over these. Do you have a kitchen table?"

"As a matter of fact, I do. It would be, let's see now…in the kitchen. Now, come on back and let's see what you have here."

Harry tried and failed to suppress his irritation and followed Dana to the kitchen. Both sat down at the round table. He took the stack of papers from his leather briefcase and spread them across the white cloth.

"So far," he began, "I've traced several million dollars from Intra-Coastal Oil to a couple of accounts. One is Swiss and the other is in Prague." He pointed to the transactions.

Dana sat straight. "Well, this is a coincidence. The Swift code is First Fairfax Bank. I have a friend who can help us run a trace if you can get an authorization. As good a friend as she is, the bank has a strict policy on sharing information with anyone except the account holder. She will need a Treasury authorization or a subpoena."

"There's no time. Can you get in? You worked for a bank IT department."

"Well, maybe, but I doubt it. The network is really secure." She paused and then said, "But I can try a couple of things."

"Do it."

"Ok, but this is beyond illegal. I don't want to go to jail."

"Right. Neither do I. But if we find what I think we will, we're not the ones going to jail."

Dana logged into her computer and then surfed through a number of bank web pages. She found the one she wanted and entered some characters. "Ok, I'm in. I can't believe some of my old tricks still work. It's lapses like this that..."

Harry cut her off. "Who is the account holder?"

"The account is registered to a Czech with a name I can't begin to pronounce.

Harry looked over her shoulder.

"Let me get the photo registration and signature cards pulled up. Those may help." She clicked a few more times and entered some letters.

Harry thought he heard a noise outside. He crossed into the unlit living room, parted the drapes and looked out.

From the kitchen, Dana called out. "Oh my God, Harry, look at this!"

Harry dropped the curtain, walked quickly to the kitchen and stood behind Dana's chair. They both looked in amazement at the laptop display which showed an account access photo card with a long Czech name below the picture. Admiral Daniel McKinley's face stared back at them from the screen.

Chapter 32

Burke, VA

HARRY AND DANA SAT AT THE KITCHEN TABLE BENT over the financial printouts. Their heads almost touched but neither was aware, each completely focused on the numbers.

Harry sat up. "Now, here's something strange that I noticed. This is where I called Ken and he didn't answer."

"What did you find?"

"Well, when I look at all of the transactions among these suspect accounts they don't balance. The goes-inta's and the goes-outa's don't match."

"And?"

"And that means that money is missing. We've seen that ICO is making campaign contributions to McKinley but that's all on the up and up. Then there's the secret account that McKinley has in Prague, the account for Fang, the account for Ali, and the Swiss account, which we all agree, is most likely Kuchecki's. But, even with all of these, there's still some money missing. I'll bet when we find the source for all of this, we'll find some interesting things going on."

Dana sat back and furrowed her brow. "Wait a minute. Look at this."

Harry leaned across the table on his forearms and elbows. He put his knee on the seat of his chair so he had enough room for his belly to rest on the table. "What is it?"

"I see an account in Iran under ICO for the local office but a million a year goes straight through without stopping. Transfer in, transfer out, same day."

"Sounds like a payoff, which is highly illegal all by itself under the Foreign Corrupt Practices Act, but we got other things to look at without getting into the Justice Department's sandbox."

"Well, that's just it. In the last three months there have been eight transactions worth over twenty million dollars, all to the same account. They don't show up easily because the routing numbers are the same, except for these three digits." She pointed to a grouping of numbers. "Someone went to a lot of trouble," Dana continued, "even matching account numbers. The routing, though, is to a branch of the National Bank of Iran." Most of the money comes out of Ali's account but some comes out of ICO."

"Who owns the receiving account?"

"That's the tricky part, but let me see what I can do." She composed an email to her friend at a New York bank and sent it. Then she got up and poured another cup of coffee.

MOHAMED REZA SAT AT THE OFFICE MANAGER'S desk in the Intra-Coastal Oil offices above the clothing store in Tehran. Walid was the last loose end who could endanger the plan. The CIA agent Stone believed he had derailed the attack when he killed Kuchecki. He was probably tracking Fang now. No matter, in forty-eight hours, all would be over and the country would be his. Kuchecki's plan was sound. After all Reza had spoon-fed it to him one conversation at a time.

Walid walked into the office. "Mr. Reza. I wasn't expecting anyone. What brings a Majli member to these humble surroundings?"

"Enough of this pleasantry. You have seen me here many times with that devil Perkins. He thinks he made me wealthy with tips on oil prices but those investments never did anything. He was only using me to get information about our Government to feed back to those infidels in the United States."

"Yes, I know. But he was taken out. A deserved end to traitorous behavior."

"And you know of Kuchecki's death?"

"Yes, I heard of it right after it happened."

"And how did you hear about it?" Reza squinted his left eye unconsciously.

The cold edge of nervousness crept across Walid's chest. "My good friends at the Navy Base told me. I always keep an ear to the ground."

"And who did you tell?"

"Mohamed, what's this about? Why all of these questions? Do you suddenly not trust me?"

Reza pounded the desk. "My distrust of you is not sudden." His voice filled the tiny room and pushed against the walls.

Walid sat hard into the wooden chair in front of the desk. "I don't understand. I have done nothing to betray your trust."

"That is exactly the problem. You think you have done nothing while you discuss this operation with friends at the Navy Base, make calls on non-secure telephones and only God Himself knows what else you have done to compromise my position."

Walid clasped his hands together almost pleading, praying, "All that I've done, I've done for you; for the cause. I have risked my life, just as you and others have, to support this plan. I have worked hard to remove the weak and impious and to open the way for the Sunnah."

"That's what Kuchecki thought he was doing as well but the man was mentally unstable. He had to be eliminated before his incredible ego gave away everything. I tested that pig Perkins to see what he knew but he didn't know anything. Too bad for him that I still had to take him out. And now you wish to derail our hard won position. You wish to see the treaty signed and the infidel take over our country?"

"No, of course not."

"Well, at least we see eye to eye on that. Kuchecki did accomplish something. Before he died, he ordered a submarine loaded with two nuclear tipped missiles dispatched to the Mediterranean. It will be in range of Tel Aviv and Haifa by tomorrow dawn. The dawn will have three suns tomorrow. Two will rise for us."

"It will be the beginning of the *Sunnah*." Walid tried too hard to smile, his expression a grimace instead.

"It will be the beginning of my rise to power and the consolidation of the Muslim world under my leadership. All of the oil-producing states will unite as we throw off the yoke of the Crusader.

Walid blinked, "How can I be of service to you in this, Mohamed? Simply name it."

Mohamed raised his hand from behind the desk and brought Kuchecki's silenced Glock level with Walid's head. "You may be quiet."

Walid's eyes grew big. "Of course I will. You may count on it."

"I know that." Mohamed said and pulled the trigger.

FIVE HUNDRED YARDS AWAY ON THE VALENJAK Overlook, Peyton Stone listened to the amplified voices as he recorded them onto a digital chip. Bingo, Asshole. He packed up the parabolic microphone and recorder and hurried down the stairs while he fished his cell phone out of his pocket. He dialed Harry.

"Harry, Peyton." he said when he heard the familiar

growl on the other end. "I just heard Reza admit to the entire thing. He was talking to Walid and then I heard what sounded like a silenced shot. I think he took out Walid."

"Did you record the conversation?"

"Yep, I got the whole thing but Reza's on the move. I'm going to stay with him. I'll upload the recording when I get a minute. You should be able to get it through diplomatic channels to the Iranians."

"Why don't you just send it and let them take care of it?" Harry already knew the answer.

"I don't have time. He may go to ground, implement the overthrow, and then we'll lose him for good. I'm going to stay with him. I'll call you with updates." He hit the end button before Harry could protest.

REZA STEPPED OUT INTO THE LATE MORNING AIR ON Sasan Street below the ICO office. The day was already warm, heading for scorching heat, but it wasn't quite there yet. He needed to stretch and relax a little before he met with his new handpicked ruling council. He looked down the street at what he could see of Tehran from this vantage point. Tomorrow this would all be different. He would be on his way to power. He would have taken the first step as Saddam had, as Lenin had, even as Hitler had before he became drunk with his power and surrounded himself with dangerous men.

Reza would not let that happen. His was to be a pious Islamic state but one that would survive, one that he would rule. He had carefully chosen loyal and devout followers who would see to the cultural preservation of the Islamic State. Not the self-serving Khomeini Style or that idiot Ahmadinejad, or even the well-meaning but too secular government now in power. *For the next twenty-four to forty-eight hours, that is.* The thought brought a smile to his face.

His government would improve everyday Islamic life through the unlimited resources that would result from the drastic reduction of all oil production in the Islamic world which currently supplied 70% of the total global yield. This he would see to personally. If the plan brought riches to him for the glory of Allah, then so be it. The Saudis, Kuwaitis, and that traitorous Prince of the Emirates would now bow to him.

As he turned down Twenty Fifth Street, he saw a car pull into the vacant lot at the other end of the block. The occupant, not the car, drew his attention. The door opened and a familiar person stepped into the sunlight. Peyton Stone. *Now what does he want? I thought he'd returned to wherever he came from after he killed Kuchecki for me.*

PEYTON HAD STORED HIS GEAR IN THE TRUNK OF THE car and driven down the short hill two blocks to the sand lot. He bumped his wheels over the curb and parked, then saw Reza turn the corner and head in his direction. *What now? Just confront him. You have the recording.* Walking to the edge of the lot, he waved at Reza. Reza hesitated, then returned the greeting.

Stone walked down the street to where Reza was standing. "Fine day for a walk, eh, Mohamed?

Reza stared for a minute, tilted his head to the side and held it for a second. His eyes blinked in the bright sunlight. He straightened up and said, "I thought you left."

Peyton flashed a big smile, what Ace called his "used car salesman grin". "Now I couldn't leave the CIA's most valuable Iranian asset alone, could I?"

Reza's body twitched as if an insect had stung him.

"What do you mean? How dare you address me like that!"

"Now come on, Mohamed," Peyton drew out his words. "You are our best guy, right? I think Walid would agree. Let's go ask him."

Reza jerked again, looked quickly left and right, then spun and ran in the opposite direction. He reached into his pocket and pulled out his cell phone. Stone chased after him and saw him hit a speed dial button. He spoke quickly into the phone as he disappeared around the corner. Seconds later Peyton rounded the same corner and heard an engine start. A black Mercedes sedan left the curb on the opposite side of the street and raced toward Reza. Peyton pulled out his Jericho and put four quick shots into the radiator. He aimed more carefully at the driver as Reza dove through the door into the back seat. The car pulled away from the curb and Stone's next shot hit the passenger in the front seat instead of the driver.

Peyton ran back to his car. The tires spun in the sand before he bounced hard across the curb and raced down to street to the corner. The Mercedes sedan was already five blocks away. Steam was billowing across its top.

He sped up and gained on the car. As he passed Thirteenth Street, a shadow passed the passenger side window. A black SUV clipped the right rear bumper and drifted sideways into the street behind him. Peyton felt the rear end move left. He downshifted, pressed the gas pedal to the floor and steered right to straighten the car's direction before the sedan slid out of control.

The car in front started to slow and move erratically as the engine strained against the expanding pistons inside it. Steam from the holes in the radiator boiled out from underneath. Peyton looked in the rear view mirror as the SUV got a running start in an effort to bump him from behind. He watched intently and nailed the timing. A second before the SUV made contact, he slammed the brakes and pulled up on the hand brake. The SUV brakes squealed as it slammed into the back end of his car. He watched the airbags explode. The impact, which released the powder packed with the bags to keep them dry, filled the car with a cloud of white that coated the driver's face. He let go of the wheel to cover his face when the bag hit him and the SUV's front bumper caromed off a parked car. The big machine spun around and the back end reached out into the oncoming lane and grabbed a Volvo wagon. Both cars danced down the middle of the street before coming to a stop on a soccer field. Stone checked the mirror once but saw no one get out of either car. Not an issue. Focus on what's in front of you.

The Mercedes turned right on Eleventh and made another right at Velenjak, then headed north again. Stone turned behind them and began to close the gap again. But the back of his car had suffered a lot of damage when the SUV plowed into it. He could hear metal scraping tires and could feel a shimmy in the back end. The smell of gasoline also wafted up into the interior. Ruptured gas tank.

Reza's car slowed significantly and finally pulled over to the curb at Twenty-first Street. Peyton drew up next to it and scraped the side of his car along the driver's side of the Mercedes as he stopped to block the driver's door. The driver raised a pistol and fired as Peyton dove out onto the street. He felt a searing in his right shoulder as though someone had poured molten lead on him. Blood spattered from his shoulder and he almost passed out when he hit the street. His face against the asphalt, he watched gasoline pour out of his ruptured tank. The fuel streamed onto the pavement and ran down the crown of the street, then puddled under the Mercedes. At that moment, gas dropped onto the hot exhaust pipe and the resulting conflagration engulfed both Stone's rental and the black limousine.

Peyton rolled quickly away. He stayed low and used his left arm to crawl to the middle of the street where cars had stopped to avoid the fireball. Just as Reza piled out of the back, Peyton jumped up and ran toward Sasan Street. He saw the desperate Mercedes' driver try to climb over his dead passenger so he made a wide berth around the burning cars and headed after Reza.

He ran as fast as he could and finally spotted Reza turning the corner at the end of the block. By the time Peyton got to the next street, Reza was nowhere to be found. Peyton slowed and trotted sideways looking into building lobbies, alleys, passageways. Nothing. Shit! He stared into the alley in the middle of the next block. Something wasn't right. He couldn't put his finger on it but something was out of place. The pile of crates? The dumpster? He took two steps into the alley when the dumpster hurtled toward him and knocked him backwards into the street. He looked up at the underside of a bumper directly over his head. He quickly rolled as the horrified driver braked and came to a stop. His shoulder was on fire but he managed to jump up. Reza was headed for the building that housed the ICO office. Peyton took off after him.

He wrenched open the front door, ran up the stairs and into the office. Just inside he tripped over Walid's body and went down hard. Instinct made him reach out to break his fall. His shoulder erupted in pain and blood. He cried out in agony as Reza walked from behind the doorframe and kicked the bloody wound.

Stone nearly passed out. His head swam and the

room looked as if he were viewing it from under water. A wave of nausea swept over him. Reza kicked out again but this time Stone managed to roll to his left to avoid contact. When Reza took a step forward for another kick, Stone rolled back so that he was now inside the arc of the kick. He summoned every ounce of strength he could muster and got to his knees, punched forward with his left hand, and caught Reza squarely in the crotch. Reza howled and doubled over. Peyton half rolled, half crawled out from under him and got to his feet.

As Reza looked up at Peyton, contempt boiled over. "You can't do this! You can't stop the inevitable! The sub is already off the coast of Israel. It's too late. Join us. You can't turn down riches and salvation."

"Watch me, you arrogant prick," Peyton replied, as he struggled to get the Jericho out of his waistband with his left hand.

Reza spun and ran from the room toward the back of the office.

Stone followed and found the spiral staircase up to the roof. Got you now.

He headed slowly up the stairs while he tried to get the Jericho comfortable in his left hand. He had shot pretty well from the left in the past, but the Jericho had finger indentations on the grip to give better stability for a right-handed shooter. They pressed into the palm of his left hand and produced the opposite effect. He'd just have to deal with it.

At the top of the stairs, he knew there were a number of things that could happen, none of them good. Reza might wait, ready to deliver a kick to the head or to his shoulder. Or he could have a gun and take a well-aimed shot. Peyton was not in a good position.

He eased up the stairs until he could see the wall

and open door at the top, then he raised his gun and fired two shots out the door. Seven gone, five left. He continued up. As he reached the landing at the top, he fired two more shots out the door. Three left.

He had lost a lot of blood. His head felt woozy and he had trouble focusing. His fingers felt cold even in the heat of the day. He crouched down and looked around the doorframe. No one there. Where is he? He suddenly realized his mistake and fell backward onto the landing just as the door slammed shut. Seconds had made the difference between a crushed skull and a glancing blow.

He stood up and took a deep breath. Then, reaching deep inside himself, he pushed on the door. Reza held it shut. Stone fired once into the door. Two left. He used his left shoulder to push against the door as hard as he could. Unexpectedly, it flew open and he careened onto the roof. He saw Reza duck behind the stair structure and he raised his gun and fired. Miss. One left. He took careful aim and fired again just before Reza disappeared. *Miss*.

Peyton pressed the clip release and let the empty clip fall to the roof. Reza stepped out from behind the structure. "Looks like you're done here, CIA. Your gun is empty. Tomorrow will be a new day and a new nation will emerge. We will not only embark on a new Islamic state here but we'll use your own gluttony for oil to crush you. You tried hard to stop me and you should be proud of your efforts but you're finished. Your country is finished. Through me, Allah will reign supreme."

Stone's knees were weak and he wobbled slightly. The nausea rolled across him again and his head felt light. He took a deep breath and held it for a beat to force oxygen into his blood stream. Then he raised the pistol and saw amusement in Reza's smile. Amusement at what seemed a last attempt to save himself. Peyton fired the last bullet in the chamber through Reza's forehead.

Reza fell to the rooftop on top of Randall Perkins' dried blood. Stone stared as a viscous red stream poured from the fanatic's head. He reached into his pocket for his cell phone, uploaded the recorded conversation and limped toward the stairs. There he propped against the door jamb for a moment and recalled how he made it a habit to chamber a round and replace it in the clip. He looked back at Reza's lifeless body and said, "Now it's empty."

Chapter 33

Southern Pennsylvania

THE MH-60 HELICOPTER KNOWN AS MARINE ONE flew up the valley from the east, turned left and landed softly on the helipad. The President and the Chairman of the Joint Chiefs, General Meyers, descended the steps of the chopper and walked rapidly to the Installation Commander's black Honda CRV. A security vehicle in front and a fire truck and ambulance in tow, the commander drove quickly to the vehicle entry gate, into Tunnel Number One that took them to the center of the solid granite mountain. If all went well, the President would fly the six-and-a-quarter miles to Camp David to receive the Iranian President and sign the historic treaty. If things didn't go well, a thousand feet of rock between the outside world and the President with a skeleton staff would be a minimal safeguard.

The small caravan moved as fast as possible along the narrow road following the curve in the tunnel, engineered to ensure that no blast wave path could penetrate straight into the complex. They turned right at an intersection and followed the tunnel another quarter of a mile to the core of the mountain.

The President, the installation commander, Colonel Johnson, and his boss, the JCS Chairman, stood on the narrow sidewalk in the tunnel as the big white pedestrian blast door slowly opened three feet. Ducking quickly around the door and into the airlock, they walked past the guard desk and waited at the white line on the floor as the blast door closed behind them and the vault lock mechanism secured the door. The trio waited

382

impatiently while the next blast door slowly opened three feet, enough for them to squeeze through the space and out of the airlock. The process took time because the three foot thick steel blast doors were interlocked so that at least one was closed and locked at all times. The doors were engineered as a protection against intruders, should any manage to pass through multiple levels of security outside. But, more importantly, in the event of a nuclear attack, the design prevented any blast effects from reaching the interior, even while people were entering the facility.

Once inside the inner chamber, the party crossed the tunnel that led to the storage area and entered what, from the outside, looked like a building. This structure's facade, however, was not a glass curtain wall but rough hewn granite carved out of the middle of the mountain. The party passed through the revolving door, down the hall and up to the second floor, then arrived at the Alternate National Military Command Center – the ANMCC, or "A-Nimmick". This room had direct connection to all US military assets in the world. People from the Army, Navy, Air Force, CIA, White House, DNI and a number of other essential agencies who are required to manage a crisis manned the dozen desks arrayed in front of the display screens.

"What do we have?" General Meyers asked the Battle Captain, another name for the ANMCC floor supervisor, a Major Ramirez.

"We have ASW aircraft in the area looking for the target where Stone's message said it should be. We also have a Predator unmanned aerial vehicle out of Doha Air Base and countless Israeli assets looking. A UUV was just launched from a Sea Stallion helicopter in the area where we first spotted something that looked like a hostile target." The Major looked at the President and added somewhat nervously, "an unmanned underwater vehicle, Ma'am." Her expression serious, she nodded graciously, as he continued. "This asset is controlled out of Navy SPAWAR System Center in San Diego through a Command and Control link aboard the Predator. Some whiz kid who invented the thing is operating the UUV. The UUV is new technology that was brought to the Med for sea trials so, given the circumstances, we're going with it as is. Outfitted with plastique and detonators by the explosive ordinance techs at Zaragosa, Spain, it can place some significant explosives if we can find this sub. Of course, our ASW aircraft are armed with torpedoes and the Predator has a mini-gun on board. This came up so fast that deploying the exact desired aggregation of resources wasn't possible."

"We also have three carrier battle groups and three Virginia Class submarines in the Arabian Gulf in case this is really an attack by Iran. These have nuclear capability aboard and a whole pile of firepower. We have a boomer in the Med, a nuclear powered submarine with sixteen Trident missiles carrying fourteen MIRVS." This time he didn't look at the President as he added, "Multiple Independent Re-entry Vehicle Systems, each of which has more firepower than the bomb we dropped on Nagasaki. It's headed to a position in the west end to be available in the event we need it. In the time we have, I assure you, we're doing all we can."

"What can we see from here?" President Harkins asked.

"We have a feed from the Predator," Major Ramirez said, "but the video from the UUV is a different format. We can't see it, but it is being relayed along with on-board telemetry to San Diego and to the Navy Seal base near Kuwait."

"Ok," the President replied. "Put what you can on

the screens."

Ramirez pushed several buttons on his console and four plasma screens mounted to the wall flickered to life. As Ramirez sat back it suddenly hit him that this was not just another official visitor going through a demo presentation, this was his Commander-in-Chief. He was actually taking personal direction from the President of the United States. Holy crap, he thought, how cool is this?

"Madam, President," Lisa Cunningham's face came up on a video monitor across the room, "I have an urgent message for you."

"Hello, Secretary Cunningham, where are you?

"I'm at Mount Weather," she replied, referring to an underground FEMA site in northern Virginia, "Once this passes, I can be at Camp David within thirty minutes." Her tone urgent, she said, "We just received a communiqué from Moscow. The Russians are saying that if we attack Iran without hard evidence, they will be forced to attack our interests in the 'Stans' immediately." Lisa was referring to a number of former Soviet states where the US had built bases to support actions in the Middle East: Turkmenistan, Kazakhstan, Uzbekistan and Tajikistan.

"How do they know that this is going on?"

"I'm not clear on that but it must have been a leak from the Iranians," Lisa speculated.

The President sounded tired and frustrated, "Well, send a response that says we're cooperating with the Iranians and they with us. Emphasize that we're doing everything we can to head this off diplomatically. But, for God's sake, Lisa, we can't have this get out in the press. Every third-world country eager to flex its military muscle will join in the fray. These aren't war games we're playing. The world is one foolish step away from nuclear holocaust because of a handful of greedy, power-hungry fanatics. Use every asset, go through all possible channels, call in favors, do whatever is required, but handle this. I don't need to know the details. Just do it. Now."

"Yes, Ma'am, I'm on it." As the picture flicked off and the screen went dark, the room was silent. No one present had heard President Harkins in full-command mode before. Now, no one doubted her abilities after hearing the call.

BRYAN STONE LOOKED AT THE DISPLAY AND SAW the gray shape that loomed in the dim light hovering at roughly 125 feet. "Gotcha!" he whispered to himself as he matched the shape and the sensor readings to confirm that he had indeed found a 240-foot long Kilo class submarine within striking distance of the Israeli coast.

As he maneuvered the UUV closer, fondly named *Hokie* after his Virginia Tech alma mater, he could make out the details of the sub. A large number 902 painted on the dorsal sail, along with the rest of the markings, confirmed that this was the renegade IRIN submarine, *Nuh*. Now the question was whether he could get the *Hokie* close enough to find out what was going on inside.

The small electric motors in the UUV would be virtually transparent to the sub's listening devices. At only 12 feet long, its size and shape would resemble a large fish should the sub decide to check it out with sonar. As added countermeasures, *Hokie* was equipped with a small sound system chip that played dolphin clicks very softly to cover any inadvertent noise from the electric motor.

The *Nuh* was moving east at about 10 knots when it suddenly came to a stop. Bryan brought up the video

386

feed from the Predator drone that was circling over 5,000 feet above the UUV. Now for the big test. Could both the *Hokie's* signal and the Predator signal be fed to a Navy Seal explosives specialist in Kuwait so that he could control the placement of the two blocks of plastique explosives that *Hokie* carried onto the sub once Bryan got the UUV into position? Could the explosives expert then set the timers so that Bryan had enough time to get *Hokie* safely away before the explosives were detonated?

At the same time, the Air Force pilot needed to control the mini-gun on the Predator in case the sub tried to surface and make a run for it before the explosives could be placed. And, of course, all of this had to be coordinated between Bryan, who piloted Hokie, and the pilot of the Predator, who was in a top secret building on Doha Air Base in the deserts of Qatar.

Bryan had hoped to conduct several experiments to ascertain that the interface program he had written actually worked before putting the system to the ultimate test. But here he was, without the luxury of confirmation. Over the last nine months he had analyzed the various control and communications signals used by the Navy, the Army, and the Air Force to operate their autonomous robotic systems. He had developed a protocol that could encapsulate most, if not all, of these signals and transport them over the military's private Internet, FORCEnet. He had some successes as well as a few glitches but today everything had to work perfectly the first time. This was not a test that could be studied and then tried again.

Bryan could barely make out the shape of the sub in the overhead shot from the Predator. *Hokie* was invisible from the surface at this depth. "The Predator seems to be in a good position. The sub has stopped, so

let's hold here while I take a closer look under water."
Bryan said to the Air Force pilot.

"Predator One, roger that, *Hokie*," came the reply
from over eleven thousand miles away. The Predator
had two functions at the moment. Not only was did it
stand guard against any activity on the surface but it was
also served as a radio relay between the UUV and Doha,
because this configuration had less delay than going up
on a satellite link. This relay was also a surer link since
water conditions frequently blocked the satellite signal.
Not a problem for data relay, but in real-time
coordinated operations, reliable communication was
critical.

Once the signal reached the radio receiver at Doha,
it hopped onto the fiber optic lines that were part of the
global FORCEnet backbone. At this point anyone with
the proper authentication could access the information.
Under ordinary circumstances, the Joint Chiefs would
view these activities in the National Military Command
Center at the Pentagon and the President's staff would
watch in the Presidential Emergency Operations Center
under the East Wing of the White House. But today the
leadership had been split up and whisked away to "Site
R" deep under the mountain in southern Pennsylvania
and a similar site under Mount Weather in northern
Virginia as a precaution.

Back in San Diego, Bryan used radio signals to
steer the UUV a dozen feet past the front of the *Nuh*, far
enough to clear the bow, then turned his boat around to
run straight at the front of the sub. On the video
monitor, he could see the modified nose on the sub that
allowed two larger torpedo tubes to be installed. The
bulge in the front of the sub indicated a capability to
carry the longer and more powerful 3M-16TE cruise
missiles. This sub could, indeed, be carrying nuclear

weapons destined for almost anywhere in the eastern Mediterranean.

He lined up *Hokie* on the nose of the sub and cut the power to let the smaller vessel drift in for a closer look at the *Nuh*. When the UUV was about eight feet away, Bryan noticed a very small burst of bubbles coming from a valve above the port side torpedo tube. Then the outer door of the tube began to open slowly.

THE AIR IN THE CONTROL ROOM FELT INCREASINGLY close. No, thick was a better description, or perhaps heavy: heavy with the smell of perspiration as the six men monitored the heartbeat of the sub. They had passed through the Suez Canal undetected. As the goal drew nearer and tensions rose, the already small spaces seemed more cramped and the atmosphere took on an oppressive quality. On top of that, the faint yellow lights had been dimmed even more to save electricity. They'd stayed submerged since leaving Bushehr, hidden first under a Chinese freighter and then under the cover of darkness. It was impossible to surface and run the generators or even communicate with the outside world until they accomplished what they had come here to do. Detection now would lead not only to failure, but to another, more personal consequence. Whether they were sunk by the Israelis or captured and returned to Iran, the indisputable outcome of failure to complete the assignment was death for every member of the crew. Kuchecki had made that crystal clear.

But they were sure that they would not fail. *Today is the day that I secure my place in Heaven,* thought Sayed Mahmud Sadiq. He sat at the captain's station of the Islamic Republic of Iran's Navy submarine *Nuh* and checked the control panel carefully. The panel showed all green lights on the system indicators and the electrical and mechanical system monitors showed nominal performance.

"Up on the bow planes. Make your depth 100 meters," Sadiq called out almost nonchalantly. The response was immediate. Three sets of "Up bow planes, 100 meters, aye," echoed from the Executive Officer, Officer of the Deck and the helmsman. A slight hissing sound could be heard as compressed air pushed a small amount of seawater out of the ballast tanks and the boat rose. The push of the propeller and the change in the ratio of air to water inside the tanks combined to make the sub more buoyant. The hull creaked and popped twice as the pressure changed outside.

"Come about to heading zero-nine-zero for five minutes and then left to zero-four-five." The same set of repeated commands came back, just as they always did. The crew of fifty-two highly trained men performed faultlessly. In the two years he had been with them, they had become a single entity, efficient and practiced. Today they would need the same coordination and teamwork they had displayed when they guided the Nuh undetected through the Suez Canal only a day ago.

"We are thirty-six nautical miles from our final coordinates. Estimate two hours to be in position," the navigator called out.

Sadiq thought for a moment. "Send the missile launch team to their stations. Have them recheck everything. We get only one chance today for the ultimate glory of Allah."

The XO picked up the intercom and relayed the command to the crew quarters then waited while the launch team commander repeated it, a signal that the team members were up and on their way.

The Nuh, an Improved Kilo Class 877EKM purchased by Iran from Russia, known there as Project

636 Varshavyanka, had recently been upgraded with the Club-S1A missile system. Like its predecessor, the Club-S, the Club-S1A upgrade included two Novator Land Attack Cruise Missiles. Unlike the old 3M-14TE missile, the new 3M-16 had extended range and the ability to carry a small nuclear warhead. Today the Nuh carried only two missiles, the pride of Sadiq's crew. Left behind were the normal armament of eighteen torpedoes, twenty-four mines and any other weight that could be sacrificed for speed. Today wasn't a test of the new missile system. Today was not a drill. Today was a test of Sadiq's crew's ability to launch a real attack and change history.

SADIQ LOOKED UP FROM HIS CHARTS AS HE HEARD the call he had been waiting for. "Ten minutes to launch point. Missiles are hot. War heads are active." The XO whispered almost reverently. "Should we radio home base for final release?"

"Our orders are clear." Sadiq tried to keep the irritation out of his voice. "Our mission is to reach the launch point and fire the missiles. That is what we will do and we do not need to double check to see whether the Navy brass is in a position to contradict Allah's will."

"Aye, Sir. The missiles are ready." The XO didn't want to provoke Sadiq even though he was hesitant to launch this attack. He had already made the mistake of questioning the assignment which resulted in confinement to quarters for eight hours, handcuffed...proof that the captain could run the boat quite well without him. With the punishment, though, he also saw arrogance. A "just because I can" attitude emanated from the captain and did not bolster his confidence.

The captain's thoughts drifted a hundred miles away at that moment. He had never been to Israel but had seen many pictures of it, particularly on television news reports. It was the heart of the beast and he often imagined it as a rubble-strewn ruin, much as the Israelis had turned the homes of his Palestinian brothers to ruin. He had grown up in the years that followed the last days of the Shah and had learned to hate the Americans and their Jewish allies. His parents, his teachers, his schoolbooks, all told of the evils of Western and particularly Zionist Israeli thought and culture. The hatred seemed equally split between the two enemies: the United States for their presence in Saudi Arabia – guardian of Mecca and Medina, the two holiest shrines in Islam – and Israel, occupiers of the Palestine, home to the gold-domed Al-Aqsa Mosque, the third most holy site in Islam.

Sadiq looked at the CCTV monitor and saw the two torpedo tubes that held the instruments of Israel's destruction. The missiles inside them had been checked, adjusted and checked again so that failure would be impossible. His crews had run drills every day since leaving Second District Headquarters in Bushehr, Iran. These nuclear-tipped missiles, soon to be on their way down the throat of the evil one, would signal the start of the global jihad. The institution of the ummah would follow, a properly conservative global Islamic nation that spanned every region on earth. At least, that's what the Admiral had told him. For his part, Sadiq expected to receive the highest honors his Government could bestow. More importantly, though, he knew he would receive the highest honor that Allah, in his infinite wisdom, could dream for him.

"In position. One hundred eighty miles from Tel Aviv." the helmsman said.

"In position," the XO repeated.

"Sonar, what do you hear?" Sadiq asked.

"Sonar, no targets," came the reply.

Perfect, thought Sadiq. *No one knows we are here.*

"Open the outer doors," Sadiq called out and listened as the XO and the missile team commander repeated the order. There was a brief rumbling sensation as the metal doors opened on their hydraulic cylinders. Sadiq could feel the butterflies come to life in his stomach.

"SOMETHING'S HAPPENING!" BRYAN YELLED INTO the headset. He immediately flushed at his reaction but this was all new to him. Playing Submariner on a video game looked the same but felt different, much different.

"Move to the right and get yourself just behind the opening," came a crisp command from the Seal. "Predator One, weapons ready. This is going to happen fast."

The President's voice came over the net, "For the record, you are weapons free. Do what you must."

"Predator One, thank you Ma'am. Heads up guys!"

"*Hokie*, this is Navy Alpha, get the explosive package in the extender arm and get ready to place it. Get as close as you can to the door but stay behind it. Predator One, stand by. If we don't get the charge placed before they launch, you'll need to be on your toes."

"Predator One, Roger."

"Navy Alpha, *Hokie*, I have the package and the arm is extending. I'm having a little trouble with the balance as the arm comes forward. I'm using a lot of battery on the stabilizer motor. We're going to have to do this now if we want to have enough battery to get *Hokie* back home." The possibility that the object of his nine months of hard work might not make it back had never dawned on Bryan. *Hokie* might be a machine but, after all his hard work, the tiny sub was part of his everyday life, his child. It would be tough not to bring it back home.

"MISSILES READY, TARGETING DATA CONFIRMED," the XO called out.

This is for you and all of your Zionist ways, thought Sadiq. "Fire one!" he yelled at the XO.

"Missiles fire one," repeated the startled XO.

"Missiles fire one, Aye!" said the fire control officer. With that, he flipped open the plastic safety cover and pressed the flashing red button. He heard a thump and a whoosh as the pressure of the ram kicked the missile out of the torpedo tube.

When the green light illuminated on the fire control officer's panel, he called out, "Missile one away! Ready on two."

Allahu Akbar, thought Sadiq. *This is truly a great day.*

A BURST OF WATER PRESSURE SHOT FROM THE OPEN torpedo tube and a missile slid past *Hokie's* cameras. "Holy shit!" yelled Bryan.

"Predator, live missile coming at you." The Seal's delivery sounded cool, measured, and belied the intense pucker factor on his end of the com link.

"I see it," the Predator pilot answered just as the booster fired and put the missile in a vertical assent.

Back at the sub, *Hokie* rocked backwards as the pressure wave spread from the front of the tube. The explosives package, still attached in the extender arm, was sucked into the tube by the inrush of water that sought to equalize the pressure differences. As the package and the extender arm entered the tube, the outer door clamped shut and trapped *Hokie* on the front of the sub.

"Navy Alpha, *Hokie* is stuck!" cried Bryan. As he tried to maneuver the trapped UUV, he noticed the other torpedo tube slowly open.

"Don't move it, *Hokie*," the Seal replied as he pressed the remote detonator button. "We have only one choice now and let's hope that the door didn't cut the detonator signal cable."

"No!" screamed Bryan when he saw orange fire form around the torpedo tube door as the explosion of the package built pressure in the torpedo tube. Then the screen went blue.

SAYED SADIQ SILENTLY CONGRATULATED HIMSELF on the first launch. "Open number two outer doors."

Another triple reply was issued from the various officers and crew. "Number two, aye."

At the moment that the number two door should have been open and the "Fire Two" command given, the air in the sub became unbearably heavy and a bright light flashed in the front of the boat. The detonation of *Hokie's* explosive package in the empty number one torpedo tube burst through the tube walls and ruptured the number two tube, bending it and lodging the remaining nuclear tipped missile securely inside. The fire control officer was thrown forward by the blast and hit the missile-firing button, which caused the water ram to fire and flood the forward compartment through the ruptured tube wall. Fire from the initial explosion tore through the skin of the missile and ignited the solid propellant. The resulting detonation caused the water in the forward compartment to vaporize and behave like a giant steam ram that sheared off the front of the submarine. The remains turned end over end all the way to the bottom of the Mediterranean.

"PREDATOR ONE HAS THE MISSILE JUST BREAKING the surface," the UAV pilot called out as he switched to the gun sight camera on the GAU-17/A Gatlin Gun. This particular gun was mounted as part of the Predator's gun pod and could fire as many as 2,000 rounds of NATO standard 7.62mm rounds per minute.

The pilot pressed a button on his control panel and the Predator went into autopilot mode. The gun sight followed the pilot's eyes through the head-up display in his visor. The pilot could see the missile climb ever faster as the booster now fired full force. He looked at the nose of the missile and squeezed the trigger on his flight control stick. The tracer stream reached out to the missile and connected briefly. The missile quivered and kept climbing.

"I've got to knock it down before it goes supersonic or we'll never get it," the pilot said, more to himself than anyone else. His volume increased as he commanded, "Come on. Be there!"

The tongue of tracer flame reached out again and barely touched the missile that again quivered and continued to rise. After ten seconds the sound of the spinning gun barrels was all that the pilot could hear as the last round that the Predator carried flew toward the missile.

"I tagged it a couple of times, at least I'm pretty sure I did," the pilot spoke too quickly and too loudly as adrenalin still coursed through his veins, "but the son of a bitch is still going. Shit guys, I tried."

At that instant, the Predator was knocked sideways by the blast wave from the explosion of the submarine. The pilot adjusted the camera to look down and saw the roiling sea as water blown into the air by the blast rained back down to the surface. Well, it looks like we got the sub anyway, he thought.

"So what do we do now?" the pilot asked, "Even if I could catch up to the missile, I have no ammo left."

"I guess we pray," a woman's plaintive voice replied over the net.

The JCS Chairman stepped in. "I'm sorry, Madam President, we did the best we could."

"How long before it hits?"

"It's hard to say, Ma'am, but certainly no more than ten to fifteen minutes."

"God help us. All we can do is wait."

"Yes, Ma'am. I'm afraid so," General Meyers said. Try as might, he just couldn't think of anything else to say.

The Predator pilot's voice crackled over the speaker. "Debris is on the surface now. I'm going to circle around and take a look." All eyes focused on the flotsam from the submarine which offered a brief escape from the imminent and fateful attack on Tel Aviv.

"I'm going to pan out so we can get an idea of the size of the debris field," the pilot said. As everyone continued to stare at the screen, the picture seemed to move back.

"What was that? It looked like a splash ahead and to the left." Bryan pointed to his screen although no one could actually see him.

"This is Predator. I think I saw it, too. I'll head over that way and take a look."

The camera moved quickly across the water and then zoomed on a spot of dissipating foam. "I don't see anything." His voice waned, then rose again. "Wait a minute. There's something but it's sinking. Something hit the water but I can't tell what it is. It could be debris from the sub explosion."

Bryan jumped in. "Let me do a screen grab off my Predator feed here and see if I can enhance it." He, like all present, hoped for a reprieve, a miracle. The silence that followed seemed interminable. Suddenly Bryan shouted, "I see a fin! It's the back part of the missile!!"

"Are you sure?" asked the President and the General in unison.

"Well, pretty sure, Ma'am, er, Sir." *Pretty sure? Ma'am, er, Sir? Geez, how lame can I be? A President and a general insulted in one fell swoop. So much for my career.* He took a breath and quickly re-grouped. "The image is pixilated and fuzzy, but I don't know what else it could be. You must have punctured the second stage, Predator. When the first stage burned out and the second stage fired, the weakened structure couldn't hold together."

A new voice came through the speakers. "Navy Alpha, this is the *USS Virginia*. We confirm that the missile target we were tracking on radar suddenly disappeared about two minutes ago."

With this verification that disaster had been averted, loud cheers erupted in Pennsylvania, San Diego and Doha.

Epilogue

Eastern Virginia
December

PEYTON SAT IN A WORN, LEATHER CHAIR FACING A large multi-paned window, his feet propped on a over-sized ottoman. He watched the large flakes of snow fall silently in the night. The only sounds were the fire's crackle and the muffled snores of his grown sons that echoed from nearby bedrooms. On a table in front of the window, a flame burned in an old hurricane lamp. Stephanie always lit a candle after the boys were tucked in bed. He thought of how she would curl up next to him on the sofa, a peaceful close to their hectic days. Tears streamed down his face while he watched the flame dance with the draft and call up their late nights together. How he longed to cup his hand beneath her chin once again and raise her face to his. Her scent, her eyes - especially her eyes - her soft smile...all emerged from the darkness of the lost years. He could taste the kisses and feel his hand on her waist when they finally rose and walked down the hall to their bedroom.

Eighteen months had passed since Harry had rescued him from the Fairfax County lockup, since Xu had seriously confronted him and help get him dried out. Every moment since had been consumed with discovering the truth behind Stephanie's death. Driven by vengeance, inconsolable, Peyton had finally been reunited with his sons, though. Months of phone calls, stolen weekends, and emails had begun the dialog of healing and forgiveness. They were a family again and he would make sure that, wherever their jobs took them, they would all remain in touch. Whenever possible, they would return to this cabin in the deep woods that his grandfather had built. The last ten days had been filled with hikes, chess, debates, and time around the table, eating, talking, laughing. Healing the relationship with his sons did not so much dissipate the anger that roiled inside as give him focus and a reason to move forward without self-destruction.

He recalled the small, very private ceremony in the Oval Office when his son, Bryan, stood in awe in front of the assembled group. The President had called together the Vice President, the Chairman of the Joint Chiefs, the Director of the CIA, and the Secretaries of Defense and State to present Bryan with the Medal of Freedom. McKinley's absence was barely noticed as he awaited trial for conspiracy and treason.

"Our nation is grateful to you for what you did to stop a devastating terrorist attack," she said " We are all proud of your service to your country. Although few will know what happened here, the entire country owes you a debt of gratitude." The president shook Bryan's hand and placed the red, white and blue ribbon with the medal on it around his neck.

"Thank you, Ma'am," was all he could manage to say. Each of the dignitaries shook his hand in turn and the White House photographer took pictures with each while Peyton beamed …and wished that Stephanie could have been with them.

Peyton had needed time to decompress after all that had happened. One day at his desk, after another fruitless day, he recalled standing in front of the statues in the entrance of the Three Monkey's Pub in Tel Aviv one afternoon: See No Evil, Hear No Evil, and Speak No Evil. If only the world lived up to the names, he had thought. After all, he had seen and heard more than his share of evil and said nothing. He had resolved to make significant changes in his life, to leave the heroics to younger, eager men and women. In the intervening months, he had tried to reach Rachel multiple times to no avail. Perhaps this was for the best. His life couldn't move forward without closure. But the hope of resolution was nothing more than a distant dream. Memories of the night with Rachel remained ever-present but he knew that she deserved a whole, healthy man by her side. Perhaps, he thought, someday, staring into the fire. He wondered where she was tonight, what she was doing, who she was with.

Earlier, when he noticed his sons' yawns as they lay in front of the fire, filled to the brim with toasted marshmallows and hot cocoa, he'd said, "Get up before you fall asleep on the floor. You're too big for me to drag, much less carry, to bed." He added that he wanted to finish a book before going to sleep. Bryan walked over and messed his dad's hair as he said goodnight. Ron picked up the pillows piled in front of the fireplace, and carried them to the large sofa. Stalling, waiting for his brother to leave the room, he approached the chair by the window and looked at his father who tensed a bit. After a brief pause, Ron said, "Thanks for all this." Peyton breathed a sigh of relief as he watched his son shuffle toward the hallway. Ron stopped and turned toward his dad, then, with a lop-sided smile, added, "Love you."

A lump in rose in Peyton's throat. "I know. Love you, too, bud."

Now, at midnight, he re-lived the evening, committed every moment to memory. In the semi-darkness, he took an envelope from his pocket and looked at it. Peyton had poured his heart into the letter written in the early morning hours to his wife. All day, he had waited for this moment alone with her. A single tear fell on the folded page as he rose from the chair. He crossed the heart pine floor and stoked the fire, then leaned down and tucked the letter into the glowing embers. He lowered himself onto a small bench in front of the large stone hearth and watched the corners curl and darken. When the paper was caught up in the flames, he lingered as small fiery bits swept up the chimney, up into the night sky. "Merry Christmas, my darling."

He rose slowly from the bench and returned to his place by the window. The fire slowly died. Lit only by the glowing embers and one small lamp, the room grew darker. Peyton looked up at the black, star-filled sky once more, picked up the hurricane lamp, and began a solitary journey toward a small loft bedroom. The room with the large brass bed at the end of the hall held too many memories. Tonight he would climb to the space he loved as a boy and fall asleep with dreams of what had once been his life. Tomorrow the three men would pack up and return to their homes and jobs. He and Xu had not really talked much since the crisis. Xu had issues of his own evidently. But they would eventually talk about things other than business. He could turn to no one else.

Before he climbed the circular stairs, he stopped at each of the two bedrooms where his sons lay sprawled underneath ancient quilts. He thought of how Stephanie had looked when she first held each of the boys. He'd been overwhelmed by love and gratitude for his wife and for each of the new lives she had brought into the world, grateful they were well. Fast-forwarding, he recalled two toddlers who ran everywhere, constantly into anything and everything. Years of baseball, soccer, and homework morphed into the teen years when music blared from their rooms. Their locked doors bore signs that read, "No Admittance Under ANY Circumstances." Where, he wondered, had the time gone? He watched them sleep, now young men with lives of their own. After he had pulled himself up the curved, iron steps, he turned the covers back, crawled into the narrow bed, and shifted his tall frame until he found a comfortable position. He thought one more time about Stephanie, then extinguished the lamp and looked up at the skylight toward the heavens and spoke. "I will find whoever did this, I promise. Good night, my love."

EARLIER THAT EVENING, HARRY MORRISON LEFT HIS home dressed in a tuxedo now dangerously out-distanced by his mid-section. As he drove into the city, he wondered if all of this was a dream or, worse yet, a prank. Three days earlier, he had grudgingly answered the telephone. The voice on the other end said simply, "This is the White House operator. Please hold for President Harkins." Yeah, right, Harry thought, and I'm the King of Siam. At first, he thought Peyton was up to his old tricks but something was brewing with his friend. No, this is probably Ken's doing.

"Hello, Mr. Morrison." Harry dropped his book as he recognized the President's voice. "I heard through channels that you are an opera buff. Is this correct?"

"Er, uh, yes, ma'am. I am."

"And I understand that you are quite content to attend alone. I received an invitation for a special performance but have a previous engagement. I'd like to pass this along to you, a small thank-you for your outstanding service during the Iranian crisis and for uncovering the money connection between ICO and Mohammed Reza. The Attorney General is prosecuting a conspiracy case against ICO and the former DNI. You can pick up the ticket at the "will call" window, along with an invitation to cocktails and a reception prior to the performance. I hope you enjoy the evening."

"Thank you, Madame President," he stammered. "I assure you that I will. But," he hesitated, "excuse me for asking, how do you know about my love of opera?"

"That, sir, I am not at liberty to divulge. Let's just say that a friend couldn't think of a better way to wish you a Merry Christmas." With that, she said good-bye.

AFTER ARRIVING AT THE KENNEDY CENTER, HARRY stuffed himself with hors d'oeurves in the company of Washington's power players. Only after he sat down in one of the best seats in the house did he believe that this was no dream. A stud popped off his shirt and he shifted his girth to retrieve it from the floor. When he sat up, he glimpsed her in profile. She sat in the second row, directly in front of him. On each ear, a pale blue briolette-cut topaz drop dangled below a single baroque pearl and glistened in the reflected stage light. For the rest of the evening, she might as have well have been chatting away because he could not take his eyes off her. Once, when she brushed a tear from the corner of her eye, the elegant movement of her hand was hypnotic.

Finally, the opera ended. Harry joined the standing ovation and turned to leave. As he looked down to check his studs, he realized she was passing and strained to glimpse her face but she had turned to help an elderly woman struggling to rise from her seat. Wearing a long deep blue-green and black burn-out velvet opera coat over a black silk ankle length gown, she took his breath away. Against what was now a familiar neck, loose wisps of dark hair at the nape curled over long strands of creamy baroque pearls that hung away from her body as she stooped slightly. A couple blocked Harry's exit when they suddenly bent over to look for a dropped program. He stood on tiptoes and caught sight of her elegant black pleated taffeta pumps with a curved heel and a shapely calf that peaked through the slit in the back of her skirt. Rooted to the carpet, Harry helplessly stood by and watched her slip through the queue out of sight.

As he drove home, he thought of nothing but her. He had never noticed what anyone wore but he could describe every detail of her appearance, albeit not with the correct terminology. That didn't matter because he knew that she would return again and again in his dreams. He sighed as he looked in the rear view mirror and thought, Women like her never notice me, but the dreams sure will be nice. And he smiled.

Sitting at the last traffic light before he reached home, he thought of all that had happened this year. Still worried about Peyton's mood, he hoped that the Stones had a good holiday reunion. Harry would make a point to call his friend next week. He and Ken had shared a good laugh when the crisis was over as each described their quick exits and hideaways. Harry chuckled and started to hum an aria when suddenly a name came from nowhere. That's how the President found out, he thought. Dana. She was the only one who knew. After the Treaty signing, President Harkins had made a point of contacting all involved in the crisis resolution, to thank each personally for their contribution. Dana, a humbled Harry thought, I owe you one.

A WORLD AWAY IN THE MIDDLE OF NOWHERE AT THE border between China and Afghanistan, Saddam al-Talibani, an Egyptian Brotherhood operative tried to comprehend the events that had unfolded since early summer. Saddam had met a fourteen-year-old boy at the home of a friend in Pakistan. He had had been given a key and some GPS coordinates and had then been driven across the Northern Areas through Pakistani-controlled Kashmir. After a series of hair-raising four-wheel drive dashes in the dark, he was brought across Kilik Pass, given an envelope and deposited next to a small river where a herd of sheep grazed.

He was instructed to look like a shepherd so that he wouldn't attract any attention and follow the map to the preprogrammed coordinates. When he arrived, he was to follow the instructions written in the letter. Six fellow Brotherhood lieutenants would accompany him and pose as extended family. When all seven had completed their assignments, their wives and children would no longer be in danger from reprisals.

The group had made slow but steady progress first east down the valley, then north up the larger valley where two rivers intersected, on to the farming region just over a hundred miles away. At eight thousand feet, the air was dry and thin, as well as cold, and it was not easy to move very fast.

Earlier in the day, they had reunited with the boy, turned west and entered a steep-sided valley that twisted and turned while rising up five hundred feet. On one side of the valley wall, a cave was hidden in a cleft in the rocks. Inside the cave they could see a wooden structure. The seven men left the sheep to graze on the sparse short grass, returned to the cave and entered the hut.

They went, as instructed, to the back room where they dug down five feet at the back left corner of the room until they heard the clunk of their shovels hitting concrete. They pushed the dirt aside with their hands, uncovered a bolted trap door and quickly used the key they had been given to unlock it. The open door revealed another room below the hut.

Saddam retrieved a flashlight from his pack, turned

it on and headed down the ladder that was fastened to the wall of the lower room. Along one wall of the room were shelves with packing boxes stacked on them and on the opposite wall were wooden crates stacked four high.

Using screwdrivers, the group quickly opened one of the crates, full of automatic weapons and ammunition. Assuming that the rest contained the same thing, they walked over and opened one of the storage boxes.

All eyes widened as the men took in the sight before them. Inside the storage boxes were stacks of U.S. one hundred dollar bill packets. They picked up several stacks from one of the boxes, counted the number of packets in a stack, and then quickly counted the boxes. "There must be close to ten million dollars here," Saddam had said to no one in particular. With that, the entire group turned to the southwest toward Mecca, dropped to the floor, and gave thanks.

Outside, alone, the teen-aged boy stood erect at the entrance to the cave as he had often done when visiting his uncle. This time the boyish features were gone. He had a defiant gleam in his eye. All that he heard was the bleating of sheep and a barely audible sound coming from inside the cave, "*Allahu Akbar*," over and over again.

###

NOTES FROM THE AUTHOR:

This is a work of fiction. Any resemblance to real people or events is purely coincidental.

The places in this book are real and are described as they were when I was there. Some details of these places may have changed over time. One exception: the house with the slanted floor where Peyton wakes up is actually in Damascus not Bushehr.

The NGA mission is as I described it. These people do amazing things with information. The fusion of IMINT, HUMINT and COMINT to develop MASINT truly is "Magic and Sorcery." They present it exactly where it is needed in near real time. New Campus East is a real place, one of several, where they do this work.

The National Action Center is a real place but is called something else and may be in a different location than the one described in the book. It has capabilities far beyond those described in the book. Sorry, if I told you, they'd kill us both.

The ANMCC is a real place – somewhere.

The Unmanned Underwater Vehicle Program is a real program within the US Navy and has some weird and wild vehicles that do amazing and very essential things. These vehicles are piloted remotely and some even accomplish complex missions without any human input at all. These latter robot versions are called Autonomous Unmanned Vehicles or AUVs.

ABOUT THE AUTHOR

William Sewell can't confirm or deny much of anything but is a Vietnam veteran and served in the US Air Force. After leaving Government service he was a contractor with the Department of State, Department of Defense and spent over a decade working with the US Intelligence Community. He has consulted on security matters with the governments of Kuwait, Australia, India, Oman, Abu Dhabi, Hong Kong, China, Canada and with the European Council of Mayors. He currently lives with his wife in Southern California.

CPSIA information can be obtained
at www.ICGtesting.com
Printed in the USA
LVHW112156080519
617192LV00001B/184/P